HAVOC

Rebecca Wait

riverrun

First published in Great Britain in 2025 by

riverrun

An imprint of

Quercus Editions Limited
Carmelite House
50 Victoria Embankment
London EC4Y 0DZ

An Hachette UK company

The authorised representative in the EEA is Hachette Ireland,
8 Castlecourt Centre, Dublin 15, D15 XTP3, Ireland (email: info@hbgi.ie)

A CIP catalogue record for this book is available
from the British Library

Hardback ISBN 978 1 52943 445 3
Trade Paperback ISBN 978 1 52943 446 0
eBook ISBN 978 1 52943 447 7

1

Typeset in Monotype Fournier by CC Book Production
Printed and bound in Great Britain by Clays Ltd, Elcograf S.p.A.

Papers used by riverrun are from well-managed forests and other responsible sources.

HAVOC

Also by Rebecca Wait

For my parents

Part 1

Fax from neurologist Dr James Halliwell to Dr George Fisher
Thursday, 1st November 1984, 1 p.m.

Police still at the school, though so far they haven't actually managed to arrest anyone, to their obvious disappointment (there are moments when I think they'd quite like to arrest me, if only to get me out from under their feet). Men from Environmental Health still here too. Remaining girls terrified of catching 'it', whatever it is. Teachers & parents panicking. And here I am in the middle of it all, making as little progress as the rest of them.

Can you come, George? & how soon can you get here?

I

September 1984

S HE HAD NEVER BEEN a particularly punctual person, but even
to Ida, being late by a week seemed to be stretching the bounds of
good manners. She had phoned the school to explain, but it was a bad
line and, although the woman on the other end had sounded friendly in
between all the crackling and static, Ida doubted that her explanation
about the storm and the ferries had been absorbed.

All in all, it had been a difficult journey. Though Ida eventually made
the crossing, in the absence of any ferries, on her neighbour's alarmingly
rusty fishing boat, her train from Oban had been delayed by heavy rain.
Then at the hostel in Glasgow there was the man who said he wanted
to show her a card trick but had in fact tried to show her something
quite different, until the woman from Dumfries had chased him out of
the room yelling, 'Ya think you've got something there to write home
about, do ya?'

And even now, as her train finally pulled into the station, all the way
down in the south of England, Ida came a cropper. When she leaned
out of the window to open the carriage door, the handle stuck so that
she nearly remained trapped on the train as it departed. During those
panicked moments as she wrenched at the handle, she might almost have
been willing to admit that her mother and sister were right, that she was

making a terrible mistake (this, at least, was her mother's view; Charlotte had suggested the mistake was on the part of the school).

Then, at the last moment, a man seemed to appear out of nowhere, leaping forward and yanking the door open. Ida tumbled out of the train, turning just in time to snatch out her holdall and rucksack as the train moved away, the door still gaping open. It was late afternoon, and the small rural station seemed to be entirely deserted except for Ida and her rescuer.

Ida looked at him. Middle-aged, dressed shabbily in cords and a green anorak. She wondered if this could be the teacher they said would come to meet her. She had expected a woman.

He looked back at her.

'I'm a new pupil at St Anne's,' Ida volunteered.

'Are you, love? You look a bit old to be a new pupil.'

'I'm joining the Sixth Form. I'm sixteen,' she added, sounding more defensive than she'd intended.

'Ah, is that right? Good for you.'

There was a silence. It had dawned on Ida that this man had no affiliation with the school at all, was in fact just an unsuspecting passer-by who must think she loved to share information about herself with strangers. She gave him a polite smile, and then took her luggage over to the single bench on the platform. The man stayed where he was, scribbling something in a small notebook he carried. After a while, he wandered towards the exit and disappeared from view. Ida sat on the bench with her rucksack on her knees. Her plan was to wait a while to see if anyone did show up to collect her. In the meantime, she'd try to come up with a contingency plan. Her whole life sometimes felt like one long contingency plan.

'Are you sure you want to leave the Western Isles?' the headmistress,

Miss Christie, had asked her during their original phone call, the one where she'd offered Ida the scholarship. 'You'll be fairly safe there, at least.'

'Safe from what?' Ida had said.

'The bomb. Things seem to be hotting up again at the moment. Or cooling down, perhaps I should say. You know the doomsday clock is set at three minutes to midnight?'

Ida had no idea what the doomsday clock was, and didn't dare ask. She couldn't quite tell if Miss Christie was being serious. There didn't seem to be any humour in her voice, but it was difficult to work these things out on the phone.

'I'm sure,' she said.

'There's a programme on the radio this evening that you should listen to,' Miss Christie said. 'Radio 4, seven p.m. It's about Britain's nuclear preparations. You ought to hear it before you make a final decision.'

Ida had taped the programme so she could listen to it back on her Walkman. She was worried there would be some kind of test on it. The information had been alarming, but it hadn't changed her mind. She was already faced with the ongoing fallout from what her mother had done; she simply didn't have the capacity to worry about what the Soviets might do.

Now, sitting on the bench at the train station, she tried for a while to enjoy the peace. At least here nobody knew who she was, nobody had heard even the faintest rumour of her mother's disgrace. No one would insult Ida, or cast aspersions (a figure of speech she had recently discovered from her friend Mrs Kelly at the Oban public library), or piss in her bag (unfortunately not a figure of speech), or, worst of all, look at her with that cold expression that Ida initially interpreted as disappointment and later realized was contempt. Because of course they all believed she'd been in on it. They believed it with such conviction that some days Ida even believed it herself.

When she looked at her watch, twenty minutes had passed, and still no one had come to collect her. Ida didn't feel especially surprised to find herself abandoned again.

'All right?' The man in the green anorak had reappeared. 'Thought I'd come and see if you were still here. I mentioned meeting you to the wife, and she told me to pop back to see if you'd gone.'

'Do you know if there's a bus I can get to St Anne's?' Ida said. 'Or a taxi?' She knew she didn't have enough money left for a taxi, but perhaps someone at the school could lend her the money when she arrived.

The question seemed to amuse him. 'A bus or a taxi? Not round here, love. But listen, I can't leave you sitting here on your own. The wife was quite insistent about that. I'll drive you there. The wife suggested it. And she said to mention her a few times, so you don't think I'm an oddball.'

'It's very kind of you,' Ida said. She hoped he wouldn't offer to show her a card trick on the way.

'It's no trouble,' he said, reaching for her holdall. 'The wife's idea, as I said. "But make sure you mention you have a wife," she told me, "so she knows you're not just wanting to murder her."'

Ida felt she would have been more reassured without any mention of murder.

'Though I suppose,' the man added as they left the platform, 'a woman can't always be counted on.'

'No, I suppose not,' Ida said.

'Just look at Myra Hindley.'

He led her to an elderly-looking red car parked on the grass verge of the narrow road outside the station.

As they set off: 'There's also the fact that you haven't seen my wife.'

'That's true,' Ida said.

'She is real, though.'

'I'm sure she is,' Ida said. She left her seat belt off so she could open the door and roll out at short notice.

It was a scenic drive, along roads squeezed between hedgerows, and then up higher on to the cliffs so the sea stretched out below them on one side, fields on the other.

'St Anne's, eh?' the man said after a while. 'Interesting place.'

'Aye, it sounds like it,' Ida said.

'You see the girls in the village every now and then. At the end of term and so on.' He swung the car round a particularly tight bend. 'They all seem absolutely crackers. If you don't mind me saying.'

This worried Ida. 'Do they?'

'It's not healthy, if you ask me. Locking all those young girls up together, up there on a cliff, away from everything.'

'But that's what all boarding schools are like, isn't it?' Ida said anxiously.

'There's boarding schools,' the man said, 'and there's boarding schools.'

Ida couldn't think how to reply, and they lapsed into silence again.

'I hope you brought plenty of warm clothes,' the man said eventually. 'Gets chilly round here, especially when the wind's coming in off the sea.'

'I'm from Scotland,' Ida said. 'I only have warm clothes.'

'That's good, love. I dare say you'll be fine. Well, here we are,' he added, as they passed by a high stone wall and turned through the gate pillars on to a wide gravel driveway. He brought the car to a stop. There, loomingly, was the Victorian frontage of Ida's new school.

The location could hardly be less hospitable, set high on a cliff, whipped by cold winds coming off the English Channel. But Ida wasn't sure the school buildings would have been appealing in any setting. Before her was a large manor house that looked as if it had been caught in the act of falling down, and was now doing its best to hold itself together until you looked away again. The roof of the main house seemed to have lost a fair few tiles, and the buttresses that propped it up were all cracked or missing chunks. Pointed rooftop windows were set at intervals, with a turret at either end of the building. A couple of the windows were cracked, and one of them was actually broken.

'A sight for sore eyes, isn't it?' the man said.

'It looked different in the prospectus,' Ida said faintly.

'There was a photo, was there?'

'It was a painting,' Ida admitted.

The man gave a shout of laughter. 'A painting? That was canny of them.'

The watercolour on the front of the prospectus had shown a pretty country manor house bathed in golden, late-afternoon light. That building had been in immaculate condition, windows uncracked, stonework complete and roof tiles in place. At the time, it hadn't occurred to Ida to wonder why they'd opted for a painting instead of a photograph; she'd assumed it was all in keeping with the general sophistication of the place.

'Used to be a convent, didn't it?' the man said.

'I didn't know that.' Ida's prior research was coming to seem more inadequate by the second.

'There was some kind of scandal with the nuns, so it had to close. I can't remember the full story. Somebody died, I think. There was a fire. There's always a fire, isn't there? Anyway, the details escape me.'

Ida reached for the door handle. 'Thanks ever so much for the lift,' she said. She was aware, now she no longer feared for her life, of how kind he had been.

'That's all right, love. And good luck to you!' he added, somewhat disconcertingly.

He drove off with a final cheery wave, and Ida was left standing alone in the drizzle with her rucksack and her holdall.

She smelled the salt in the air and briefly felt at home, and then, conversely, very homesick – though for what she couldn't say. Certainly not for the island, certainly not for her mother.

She only allowed herself to hesitate for a few moments longer before climbing the steps with her bags and ringing the doorbell.

2

IDA HAD NEVER MET her father (so far as she was aware), but her mother always insisted she wasn't missing much. Charlotte's father, on the other hand, was worth talking about, even after they'd fled back to Glasgow to escape him.

'Say what you like about him,' their mother said. 'He had *presence*.'

He was English, but he'd met Ida's mother while he was working in Glasgow. Apparently, they'd met on a bus – he wasn't Charlotte's father then, he was still just Peter – and Ida's mother had neglected to mention for quite some time that she already had a child, so perhaps Peter could be forgiven for feeling ambushed by Ida when she was finally produced.

Peter had a nasal voice and sucked air in through his teeth every time he finished speaking, as if for emphasis. He had strong views on many things, but especially on women's lib, the Welsh, and the growing population of urban foxes. 'The thing is, they don't know what's good for them.' (Teeth suck.) 'They force themselves in where they aren't wanted.' (Teeth suck.) He had a tendency to move rapidly between subjects within the same conversation, so his listener would sometimes be surprised to discover that the Welsh had been going through his bins at night, or that a pair of women's libbers had been mating loudly outside his window.

His other passion was sending faxes. By the time Ida and Charlotte and their mother were living with him, he had a fax machine of his own – an old model salvaged from his workplace. He set it up in the front room on a small table, which slightly resembled a shrine, and forbade anyone else from touching it. He sent faxes to *The Times* whenever he spotted in their pages a stray comma or a split infinitive, and he sent faxes to his local MP with updates and complaints about his most recent fox sightings. He also had his own meteorological equipment and began each day by using his barometer to measure the air pressure and checking his rain gauge, which recorded overnight precipitation, faxing his latest findings to the Met Office. He was undeterred by the lack of any faxes in response. (His boss had, in fact, neglected to mention that the reason they were getting rid of the machine in the first place was that it was malfunctioning, and was able to send but not to receive faxes. Otherwise it's possible that Peter would have received several *cease and desist* faxes.)

CHARLOTTE, FOUR YEARS YOUNGER than Ida, must have got her presence from her father, just as Ida got whatever its opposite was – absence, presumably – from her own, nondescript father. Whoever he was.

Peter, a man of action (albeit chiefly through the medium of faxes), was annoyed by Ida's wishy-washiness.

'Why is she so quiet?' he would ask Ida's mother. 'It's strange.'

'It's not strange,' Ida's mother said. 'It's just the way she is.'

'Why does she look so miserable? Is she not grateful to be in *my* house, eating *my* food?'

He made it sound as if Ida were helping herself directly from his plate.

'She is grateful,' Ida's mother said. 'Leave her be. She's shy.'

This was the first time Ida learned that she was shy, but it came as a relief to discover it. After that, whenever she found herself being awkward or strange, she would remember that she was shy, and that explained it.

For the first few years of her life, she hadn't needed to be shy because she had her grandparents. Her mother always said that Ida couldn't remember living with them, but Ida was nearly four when she and her mother left, just before Charlotte was born, and she did remember. Her mother hadn't been around much by the end of that period, because by then she'd met Peter, so it was mostly Ida's grandparents who looked after her. Ida had her own bedroom at her grandparents' house, a little room at the back that looked out over their overgrown garden. She spent hours in the garden with her grandparents. She remembered picking strawberries round the side of the house with her grandad, and learning the names her granny taught her: hawthorn, dog rose, blackthorn, laburnum. Even many years later, when she had almost forgotten what her grandparents looked like, Ida would find herself chanting the names of their trees and hedges to herself like a prayer.

She had to leave the house on the edge of Glasgow with its wild garden after Peter got his new job. She went with her mother and Peter all the way to Preston, which was nearly 200 miles away, across the border in England, where they lived in a small house that had thin walls and felt cold and damp all the time. Not long afterwards, Ida's mother went into hospital and Ida had to stay in the new house with Peter for two days. He gave her cheese sandwiches for every meal, without any butter on the bread, and didn't tell her when she was supposed to go to bed, so Ida had to work it out on her own. Then Ida's mother came home with the new baby.

It was around this time that Ida began to be hungry all the time, even when she'd just eaten. She could be on the point of being sick because she'd eaten so much, and she'd still want to eat more. She was so ravenous that she ate anything she could find between meals, any food in the lower cupboards she could reach, or on the bottom shelves of the fridge, or left out on the side. Still, though, she felt hollow.

'There's something wrong with that kid,' Peter said. 'Take her to the doctor's, get her dewormed. I'm not paying extra for her.' He sucked the air in through his teeth to underline this last point.

Fortunately he wasn't around much while Charlotte was little. Charlotte was an angry, dissatisfied baby, just as she would later be an angry, dissatisfied child (and when she hit puberty, God help them all). Nothing could soothe her. She screamed and screamed, and slept for no more than half an hour at a time. Ida's mother paced around the house, her hair wild and her clothes stained, holding Charlotte and going, 'Shhh, shhh, shhh, *please* shhh.' And then sometimes she'd just sit on the sofa with the screaming baby, rocking and crying herself.

Peter would often stay late at work during this time, and when he was at home, he would be shut away in the front room mounting his fax campaigns. And since Ida's mother was always dealing with Charlotte, or trying to clean the house up because otherwise Peter would be angry, Ida was free to eat whatever she could forage. She would only get in trouble later, when her mother discovered the food was gone. Then her mother would hit the roof. Peter gave her housekeeping money, but there wasn't enough to be replacing food all the time.

'But why are you doing this?' Ida's mother said, when she caught Ida red-handed one day, cramming a slice of dry bread into her mouth. 'I gave you lunch, didn't I? What am I doing *wrong*?' And at this last part, her voice rose to a shout, and Ida, cheeks bulging with the bread, burst into tears. And because her mouth was so full, it was difficult to cry properly, and she started coughing, and then gagging, and out came the nasty half-swallowed mess and Ida continued to sob. Her mother started crying too, and put her arms round Ida.

'It's all right,' she said. 'Never mind, hen. I'm very tired. It's all right. Hush, you'll wake the baby. Come and lie down with me.'

Ida stopped crying. Her mother smelled of herself – a fetid, milky, unwashed scent that Ida breathed in deeply.

And they went into the bedroom her mother shared with Peter, and lay down together in the bed, even though it was the middle of the day. They went to sleep holding on to each other, until the baby cried out a while later and her mother jerked awake and stumbled from the bed.

IDA DISCOVERED WHEN SHE was older that her grandparents had said she could stay behind and live with them instead of going to Preston with her mother and Peter. Ida learned this from her mother.

'They wanted me to leave you with them. They really thought I'd just abandon you. That's what they think of me. But I wasn't being parted from my own child. I would never leave you.'

Ida felt the anguish of her own disloyalty in her immediate knowledge that she would rather have been left.

They hadn't visited Glasgow much after the move. Peter said it was too far, and that anyway, Ida's grandparents didn't like him, so they could fuck off. Ida's mother wasn't allowed to use the car without Peter because she wasn't a good driver, and she didn't show much interest in seeing her parents anyway.

'I could never do anything right in their eyes,' she told Ida once. 'I was never good enough. They were disgusted after I got pregnant with you. *Disgusted*.'

But her grandparents had never found Ida disgusting. Ida knew this, in the way you knew these things. She used to fantasize about running away back to them, back to her old bedroom with the robin on the wall. Her grandparents sent her and Charlotte presents and cards for their birthdays and at Christmas, and they always wrote *God bless* at the end of the cards, before they added their love, which comforted Ida. Sometimes they rang Ida up to speak to her on the phone, and they said 'God bless' at the end of the calls too, and told Ida to be a good girl, and Ida said she would be. She liked the way they said it, as if they already knew she would be good.

Ida's grandfather died when she was eleven, and then her grandmother when she was thirteen, so that was that. Still, it was the money that came to her mother after this that allowed her to leave Peter. They'd been living in Manchester by then, in a larger house, but with the money from the will their mother took them back to Glasgow. They went on the train in the night, with only one bag each, and after that they lived for a few weeks in a hostel, and then in a rented flat. But when Peter discovered their whereabouts and started sending vengeful faxes to the office where Ida's mother worked as a receptionist, they moved again. He wouldn't rest until he'd killed her, Ida's mother said, so they were going somewhere he'd never find them.

This turned out to be a small, windswept island forty miles off the mainland.

Charlotte, ten now, was appalled. 'It's in the middle of nowhere!'

Ida said, 'It might not be so bad.'

'It's all right for you,' Charlotte said. 'You don't have any friends. You won't notice the difference.'

It might have been all right, anyway. The island was beautiful, and Peter did not find them – or if he did, he couldn't be bothered to get the ferry all that way just to murder them. There was a good while on the island, before things started to go wrong, when Ida thought life wasn't too bad. She was temperamentally suited to living on a remote island. Her shyness didn't seem like such a problem here, as there weren't many people to be shy around, and those there were didn't seem to mind if she was sometimes awkward. Nobody seemed to expect much from each other in the way of social graces, but they were kind, and later, very kind. And then, finally, not kind at all.

AFTER IT ALL CAME out, what her mother had done, no one would speak to them anymore, except occasionally to express their disgust. Most of the islanders simply avoided them. It gave Ida the bewildering sense that she was fading away, little by little, until one day she might disappear altogether. When she ran into someone in the shop now, they wouldn't meet her eye, even nice old Mrs Paterson, who'd used to drop a cake round for Ida and Charlotte from time to time. Ida wished she could avoid the shop, but since her mother would no longer leave the house – would often not even leave her bedroom – it was Ida who had to get the messages. She was nearly sixteen by that point, which was old enough, her mother said, to take some responsibility.

'Why should I have to do everything?' she said. 'Look what it's done to me. Worn me down. Worn me out.'

Ida said nothing.

'Stop standing there silently,' her mother said, her voice suddenly rising. 'Fucking *say* something.'

Ida said, 'I hope you feel better soon.'

LIKE MANY OF THE kids from the smaller islands, Ida – and Charlotte, once she finished at the tiny primary school on the island – attended high school on the mainland and lodged in the school hostel during the week. Ida might have hoped this would provide some relief, but the school community was a patchwork of the island communities and of course word travelled fast, especially as there wasn't much else to talk about.

'It's sick, what you and your mam did,' a girl said to Ida as she was walking into school on her first day back. The girl said it very seriously, without evident malice, which made Ida feel worse than if it had been intended to hurt her. Then, in the corridor, a gang of younger boys shoved into her so she dropped her backpack, and another one kicked it across the floor before they all scattered, whooping.

Ida hoped that after the first couple of days the hostility might subside, but instead everything got worse. Since as far as the other kids were concerned Ida had been in on it, they felt that everything that happened to her she had coming. One day, going back to collect her bag after lunch, Ida found it soaking wet. The smell of urine was overpowering, and she retched as she carried the bag to the toilets to wash it in the sink. Her books within the bag were damp too, and though she did her best to wipe them down before drying them out, her history and maths textbooks always carried a faint, queasy smell of stale pee after that.

Charlotte fared better. Most kids were too scared to say anything to her face in case she decked them (though she was only in S1, she was big for her age, and more than willing to use her teeth). And Charlotte wasn't the type to care what people said when they weren't right in front of her, so whisper campaigns were wasted on her. Still, she didn't escape completely. Ida heard on the grapevine that one day some boys in Charlotte's form group had tied fishing line to one of her chair legs. When Charlotte returned to her classroom and went to sit down, the boy holding the end of the fishing line tugged it, jerking the chair out from under her so that she toppled backwards on to the floor, to the loud amusement of the boys. Charlotte had got up off the floor and picked up the chair. Then she went for the culprits, wielding her chair like a Viking warrior. It was partly her self-control that made people afraid of her. If she had been shouting or crying, the boys would only have laughed more. As it was, Charlotte attacked with cool, vicious resolve. The boys tried to get away from her, to put desks and other students between them, shielding their heads with their arms, until a male teacher finally came in, wrestled the chair off Charlotte, and sent her to the head teacher. It was a miracle no one was seriously hurt. Ida didn't find out what happened next, except that, somewhat surprisingly, Charlotte wasn't suspended.

More cowardly than Charlotte, Ida took to hiding in the toilets during lunchtimes, though this carried the risk of running into some of her persecutors in an enclosed space where there was no hope of a teacher coming to her aid. Sometimes she would slip out of school and spend her lunchtimes walking round town in the drizzle. The afternoons and evenings were more of a problem, since she was in a shared dormitory at the hostel. Usually she would go to the public library straight after school and stay there until it closed, then go for one of her long walks, only returning to the hostel in time for the evening register. Charlotte avoided her in the evenings, as if their contamination would increase exponentially with greater proximity. Ida ate her supper as quickly as possible, and then read in the corner of the dorm until lights out, ignoring any comments that came her way, her air of determined withdrawal repelling even the nicer girls, who might have wanted to help her.

During this time, the library was the only place Ida felt happy – or at least not quite so unhappy. The librarian was an energetic, middle-aged woman called Mrs Kelly. She was kind to Ida, in her brisk way, and took to recommending books she thought Ida might enjoy. This is how Ida came to be working her way through all the novels of Agatha Christie.

'It's not high art,' Mrs Kelly told Ida as she handed her a rather battered copy of *Death on the Nile* one day. 'But it's very good escapism.'

And noting the serious look Mrs Kelly gave her, Ida realized that news of her family's disgrace had spread even as far as Oban public library.

In the space of a few weeks, she had finished all the Agatha Christies in the library's catalogue. Mrs Kelly ordered in more for her, without Ida even needing to ask. And it was while reading *Cat Among the Pigeons*, a bizarre mystery set in a girls' boarding school, involving stolen jewels and an enigmatic sheikh, that Ida had her idea.

She boarded during the week already, of course, like the other island kids. But what if she could board further away, where no one knew her – and for a whole term at a time? What boarding schools might be like in real life did not concern her; anywhere would be preferable to here. Worse than the constant fear of ambush from her peers was her awareness of what everyone now believed about her – that she was wicked, that she was as bad as her mother. And worst of all was the knowledge that her mother had lied: not just to everyone else, but to Ida. And she had made Ida guilty alongside her. Ida was old enough to know that you would not do that to your own child unless you did not love them, had never loved them at all.

AFTER SOME CAREFUL THOUGHT, she used the library's copy of the Yellow Pages to look up the correspondence address of the Independent Schools Joint Council. Then, feeling very bold, she wrote a letter requesting a list of all girls' boarding schools in the UK that offered full scholarships at Sixth Form.

The list she received in response was not extensive, but Ida felt encouraged by the progress she'd made already. She drafted a letter to each of the schools, requesting details of their scholarship applications, labouring over every sentence; she had little idea of how to write a formal letter, and she didn't want to make a bad impression. She took her stack of letters across to the mainland to post, feeling hopeful for the first time in ages.

After a couple of weeks, the replies began to arrive. Ida had already taken precautions to ensure Charlotte or her mother didn't get to her letters before her. She'd asked Mrs Anderson, the island's post mistress, to hold on to anything addressed to her, so she could pick them up at the weekend from the post office. Ida had been anxious about making this request. Mrs Anderson had never been especially friendly; even when they first came to the island, she had been terse when cashing the giro cheques for Ida's mother. And now she had a reason to hate them.

But Mrs Anderson had only given Ida a long look and said, 'Something you don't want your mam to know?' Then, when Ida didn't answer, she had shrugged and said, 'Aye, I'll try to remember.'

And, to Ida's surprise, she had. Whenever Ida stopped by, Mrs Anderson would hand the letters over without a word, usually without bothering to look at her. Ida wasn't sure why Mrs Anderson would help her at all, unless she saw it as a way of slighting Ida's mother.

But the responses from the schools were disheartening: as well as requiring evidence of academic prowess beyond Ida's reach (she had forgotten to factor in that she was at best an average student), most required an in-person interview, and in some cases also provided the date on which she would be required to sit their scholarship exam. Ida had hoped it might simply be a case of sending off some of her best schoolwork, and perhaps writing an effusive essay on why she wanted to attend the school. She knew that even if by some miracle she managed to do well enough in an exam, there was no way she would impress at interview. For one thing, there was her shyness, and, for another, there was her unappealing appearance. She was small and pale, and her posture was bad. Her mother, clearly in a charitable mood that day, had once described Ida's hair as 'dirty blonde', but Charlotte said, more accurately, that it was the colour of a dead rat's fur and had a similar texture. (How was the fur of a dead rat any different from that of a living rat? Ida wondered, though did not ask.)

Besides, even if she weren't going to repel an interviewer, there was also the logistical issue: it would be too difficult to travel all the way from the island to undertake interviews and exams. Ida felt absurd not to have realized any of this in advance.

'What's that?' Charlotte said, entering Ida's room without knocking while Ida was disconsolately reading one of these letters.

Ida said quickly, 'It's a letter from my French pen pal. From France.' She was impressed with her own improvisational skills.

'Oh yeah?' Charlotte said. 'What's her name, then?'

Ida managed, after only the briefest of hesitations: 'Marie-Claire.'

'What are her hobbies?' Charlotte said.

'Cinema,' Ida said. 'Ice skating. *Jouer au foot.*'

'Parents' names?'

'Ah . . . Louis and . . . Marie-Antoinette.'

Charlotte paused for a moment, giving Ida a quizzical look. 'Surname?' she said.

'Um . . .' Ida's mind went blank. 'Croissant,' she said.

Charlotte frowned. 'Your pen pal is called Marie-Claire *Croissant*?' she said. 'Daughter of Louis and Marie-Antoinette Croissant?'

'Yes,' Ida said.

'Hmm,' Charlotte said, and left the room.

Ida breathed out slowly. She put the letter away, resolving to take the whole lot with her to the beach later, to burn. She knew Charlotte would have no qualms about ransacking her room in search of information.

*

ONE SATURDAY ALMOST A fortnight after Ida had given up on the boarding-school plan, she was trudging past the post office when Mrs Anderson stuck her head out of the door and said, 'Ida, another one for you.' She disappeared for a moment, and then returned to hand Ida a slim package.

Not wanting to risk Charlotte's suspicious eyes at home, Ida headed off the road and across the moorland. She scrambled up a rocky outcrop, sat down amid the heather and opened her package, watched only by a couple of wild goats.

It contained a letter and the prospectus for a school called St Anne's. Ida stared at the image on the front of the prospectus: a watercolour reproduction of a handsome Victorian manor house with sweeping lawns.

The accompanying letter was very brief. It ran:

Dear Miss Campbell,

Thank you for your enquiry. We are able to offer a full schol-arship to the right candidate, with a start date of 1st September 1984. Please write a letter in response telling me about yourself, and I will consider your application.

It was signed *Miss Elizabeth Christie, Headmistress*. There was a slightly puzzling *P.S.* added below the signature: *It would be helpful if you could read* Z for Zachariah *by Robert C. O'Brien, if you have not done so already.*

The letter made no mention of academic references, nor of an exam or interview, though Ida hardly dared get her hopes up. These impassable obstacles would surely materialize in due course.

The prospectus, which was rather slim, described the school's loca-tion on the south coast of England as 'peaceful and picturesque', which sounded very nice to Ida. She scanned the rest of the pages, learning that the school was founded in 1901 by a philanthropist called Reginald Carey, who had intended it as a 'shelter from worldliness' for young ladies, whatever that meant. The school's values and aims were expressed in similar terms to those in the other prospectuses Ida had seen, words like 'diligence', 'integrity' and 'team spirit' recurring. The only thing that perplexed Ida was the passing but frequent reference to something called 'Roedean'. Embedded in the preamble on the first page about the school's founder was the observation in parentheses: 'which makes this school older than Roedean', and throughout the subsequent pages St Anne's was described in turn as 'more affordable than Roedean', 'better value than Roedean' and 'in possession of better sea views than Roedean'. Ida wondered if it was some kind of fancy southern expression she'd never come across before, just as when they were living in Lancashire she'd been regularly mystified by allusions to 'soft Mick'. She'd managed to live in Preston for almost a decade without ever discovering who soft Mick was, or why he seemed to have so much of everything. Roedean, she concluded, might be a sort of reverse soft Mick. Soft Mick's pauper cousin.

SHE TOOK HER TIME drafting her letter in response to Miss Christie. She described in detail the beauty of the island, while also expressing — trying not to sound suspiciously eager — a desire to see a different part of the world and to expand her horizons. With the help of Mrs Kelly at Oban public library, she also procured a copy of *Z for Zachariah*, which turned out to be a terrifying novel about a girl surviving alone in the aftermath of a nuclear war. Ida read it in a single afternoon, utterly gripped, and included her thoughts on the book in her reply to Miss Christie: *I have read* Z *for Zachariah, and I thought it was very good but*

also very frightening. Ann was very brave and resourceful, and had integrity.
I didn't trust Loomis from the start, but I can see why Ann was keen for a
bit of company and the opportunity to work with somebody else. (She added
this last part because she thought it would make her sound like she had
team spirit; but actually she imagined it would be quite nice to be the sole
survivor of a nuclear attack and not to have to endure human company
ever again.) *I am glad he got his comeuppance,* she added, then crossed out
this line in case it made her sound vengeful. She wrote instead, *Things*
would probably have gone better if Loomis had been a girl.

When she was finally happy with her draft, she copied out a neat
version, posted it, and held her breath for two weeks until the reply came.

'YOU'VE DONE *WHAT*?' her mother said.

'Why would anyone give *you* a scholarship?' Charlotte said.

'Why are you doing this to me?' her mother said.

'You know they'll all be lesbians,' Charlotte said.

Their mother began to cry.

'Though I dare say you'll be safe,' Charlotte added, looking Ida up
and down.

Their mother said, 'Hen, you haven't thought this through. You can't
be serious.'

Ida was serious. 'I have to get away,' she said again. She'd dreaded
this moment of revelation so much that now it was upon her she had
a strange feeling of detachment, as if the conversation were unfolding
without her influence: the cold paralysis of a nightmare.

Charlotte said, 'They'll probably send you straight back once they
get to know you.'

Ida was somewhat concerned about this herself.

'I need a change,' she said, repeating the statement she'd begun with.

Her mother said, 'Have you always hated me?'

And Ida looked at her and realized that no, she had not always hated her mother, but in fact she did hate her now, and probably had for some time.

And although her mother wept, she did not try to stop Ida from going. It was perhaps the first victory of Ida's life.

So there it was: she was away to England to escape, to get an education, to reinvent herself; or at the very least to replace her current situation with a different, more bearable kind of misery.

3

IDA HAD TO WAIT outside the school's front door for some minutes before anyone answered. She was just starting to wonder if she should ring the bell again when the wooden door was heaved open and a square-faced young woman appeared, wearing slacks and a double-breasted blazer in a very bright blue. Her hair was teased up into voluminous waves of the kind that always made Ida conscious of the dispiriting flatness of her own (dead rat) hair.

The young woman seemed perplexed to see Ida and simply stared at her for a few moments.

Ida introduced herself.

The woman said, 'Who?'

'I'm a new Sixth Form student,' Ida said.

The woman was still looking blank. 'Term started last week,' she said. 'And we don't have any new students.' Then, in an apparent flash of inspiration: 'Have you confused us with Roedean? That's further along the coast. Don't worry, you can call them and they'll send someone to get you. This happens from time to time.'

Ida reassured her that she hadn't arrived by accident.

'You *intended* to come?'

'I did.' Awkwardly, Ida added, 'I got the Sixth Form scholarship.'

'You're the scholarship girl?' The woman looked astonished at this. 'Oh, but we weren't expecting you to actually *come*.' When Ida didn't immediately reply to this (she didn't know what to say), the woman went on, 'You said you'd changed your mind.'

'No, I didn't,' Ida said.

'You didn't change your mind, or you didn't *say* you'd changed your mind?'

'Both,' Ida said. 'Neither.' She was flustered. 'I got delayed. But I did ring up to say I was still coming.'

'You spoke to someone?'

'Yes. Um . . .' She realized now that she hadn't caught the name of the woman on the phone. 'She sounded Irish?'

'Oh goodness, but she isn't allowed to use the telephone. We usually manage to intercept her before she gets to it, but she can be quite determined.' There was a pause, then the blue-blazered woman said cautiously, 'I'm going to have to consult on this. You'd better come in.' She ushered Ida through into a reception area: wood-panelled walls, a black-and-white tiled floor like a chessboard, cracked in places as though there had been a recent earthquake. The centrepiece of the room was a grand staircase in dark wood, which turned twice in its ascent to the landing above.

'Have a seat,' the young woman said, gesturing at a pair of sagging green armchairs that had been placed side by side against the wall, with the appearance of a pair of malefactors sent there in disgrace. Then she disappeared through a wooden door.

Ida sat down and waited. The reception area was quiet and echoey, and the door had not fully closed behind the woman, so although the conversation behind it was taking place in hushed tones, Ida was able to hear most of it.

'The scholarship girl? She's *come*?' a new voice, also female but deeper, was saying. Ida thought it sounded like Miss Christie, but couldn't be certain.

28

'Yes,' the original woman replied. 'She's here.'

'I was told she rang up to say she'd changed her mind.'

'Apparently she rang up to say she *hadn't* changed her mind.'

'Why would she ring up to say she hadn't changed her mind?'

'I've no idea.'

'Maura Doyle must not be allowed to answer the telephone.'

'I know. I'm sorry, Miss Christie. I was in the toilet at the time.'

'*Lavatory*, please, Miss Morton,' the deeper voice, which it seemed did belong to Miss Christie, said.

'Sorry. But what shall I tell her? There was the leak in 1B, so we've nowhere to put her.'

'There's the Adler girl,' Miss Christie said.

'Surely we can't do that—'

'Situations evolve, Miss Morton. It behoves us to remain limber.'

Just as Ida thought she might actually burst into flames of mortification, the young woman in the blazer re-emerged through the wooden door, accompanied by a second woman in a tweed suit, who Ida assumed was Miss Christie. She was older, grey-haired, very upright in her bearing.

'There seems to have been a bit of a miscommunication,' Miss Christie said to Ida, not unkindly. 'Wires have been crossed.'

'I'm sorry I'm so late,' Ida began. 'The ferries weren't running—'

'It's quite all right. I'm Miss Christie. It's a pleasure to meet you in person.'

Her gracious tone, combined with her regal bearing, made Ida want to curtsey. The stress of the day must be getting to her, she thought.

Miss Christie turned to the woman in the blue blazer. 'Miss Morton, please go and fetch the key for the annexe, and collect Sophie Merritt from outside my office. She's waiting there for a chit. Write her up for silliness in Home Economics and bring her here.'

The younger woman headed up the staircase, leaving Ida alone with Miss Christie.

'Here you are, then,' Miss Christie said.

'Here I am,' Ida agreed. And, seeking again to exonerate herself for her lateness, she added, 'There was a storm last week, and they always cancel the ferries when the sea's rough. I got stranded.'

'Marooned,' Miss Christie said.

'Yes, exactly.'

'I imagine you'll be wanting to let your parents know you've arrived safely.'

'Oh,' Ida said. 'Yes, I suppose I will.'

'Would you like to use the telephone on the desk?'

There seemed no way to avoid this. Ida went over to the desk and, self-conscious under Miss Christie's gaze, dialled her home number. She waited nervously as it rang. And rang.

Ida felt tremendous relief when she realized the phone wasn't going to be answered. But as she began to move the receiver away from her ear, there was a small click and she heard her mother's voice say, 'Hello?'

Ida contemplated simply putting the phone down, but couldn't quite bring herself to do it. Instead she said, 'Hi, Mam. It's me.'

'Ida.' Her mother's voice was flat.

Conscious of Miss Christie's presence, Ida said with forced heartiness, 'Just letting you know I've arrived safely.'

A pause. Then her mother said, 'Good.'

'Everything all right at home?' Ida said, when her mother didn't speak again.

'Not really. You know what it's like here. But you left me anyway.'

Ida didn't know what to say to this. It was excruciating conducting her side of the conversation within earshot of Miss Christie. She said, 'Is Charlotte all right?'

'Charlotte is Charlotte.'

Another silence. Ida said, 'Well, I'd better go. Got to unpack and so on.'

'All right,' her mother said. 'You do that.'

'I'll write soon,' Ida said. Then, when her mother didn't reply, she said as brightly as she could, 'Yes, love you too!' and put the phone down.

'Well, that's that,' Miss Christie said. 'Good.'

Miss Morton was coming back down the stairs. This time she was accompanied by a girl about Ida's age, with a lot of very wild brown curls. This girl was wearing school uniform: a pleated grey skirt that stopped just below her knees and a white shirt with a maroon V-neck jumper over the top. Ida became conscious for the first time of her own jeans and sweatshirt, neither of which was in the first flush of youth, and wished she'd put on something smarter for her arrival at school.

'You have the key?' Miss Christie said as Miss Morton rejoined them, followed by the pupil.

'Yes,' Miss Morton said. She handed a key on a wooden key ring to Ida. 'And this is Sophie Merritt, who will show you where to go. You've made it just in time for supper,' she added, delivering this last comment rather suspiciously, as though Ida's sudden arrival had been driven by greed alone.

'This is Ida,' Miss Christie said to the pupil. 'And Sophie, your hair should be *up*.'

'Sorry, Miss Christie!' Hurriedly, the girl pulled a scrunchie off her wrist and bundled her hair up into a ponytail. 'It was up earlier,' she explained as she completed this process. 'But although it's not very heavy in itself, it seems to experience the pull of gravity very powerfully, so it sort of makes its way down throughout the day.'

'Hairspray,' Miss Christie said. 'Or else cut it off.'

Sophie blanched at this idea. 'I don't think short hair would become me, Miss Christie. But perhaps we could compromise and I could wear my swimming cap to lessons. May I?'

'You may not.'

Her hair temporarily subdued by the scrunchie, Sophie gave Ida a smile that revealed large, crooked teeth, and then grabbed Ida's holdall and rucksack off her with such alacrity that Ida felt as if she were being mugged.

'It's OK,' she said to Sophie. 'I can carry them.'

'Oh my *goodness*!' Sophie said in astonishment, dropping the holdall. 'You're *Scottish*!'

'I am,' Ida said.

'I've never met a Scotswoman before,' Sophie said. 'Or a Scotsman. Or a Scotschild. Is Ida a Scottish name? Is it short for anything?'

'No,' Ida said, retrieving the holdall. 'Just Ida.'

'I've never met an Ida before, either,' Sophie said. 'What an exciting day.'

'Off you go, girls,' Miss Christie said pointedly.

'Right, yes, we'd better get our skates on,' Sophie said. And she set off at speed, still holding on to Ida's rucksack, which she'd refused to relinquish. 'The reason I'm rushing,' she added over her shoulder as she led Ida out through a side door, 'is that we don't have much time before supper. You need to get there early on a Thursday, because it's chips day, but inexplicably they only ever cook enough chips for about half of us. So the queue becomes quite lawless.' She seemed to do everything at speed; she spoke so quickly that Ida had the impression of a cassette tape on fast-forward.

They passed down a narrow stone alley, out into a small courtyard, and into another alley. 'But be careful,' Sophie went on, 'because one thing they never run out of is rhubarb crumble, and you can get caught out that way. It's basically cement. Barbara Bridges in Fifth Form has special bags she'll sell you for 10p. You line your pockets with them and then transfer the crumble, bit by bit. Oh, and watch out for the chicken as well. There was a mass poisoning last term and April Stephens went round saying it was the Soviets, but we're almost certain it was the chicken.'

They emerged from the second alley, and a large stone courtyard opened out before them.

'This is Yard,' Sophie announced, bouncing along with Ida's rucksack on her shoulders.

Ida looked across the stone courtyard. Over the far wall, she could see a laburnum tree, no longer flowering, its branches drooping instead with browning seed pods. She experienced a pang as it took her back to her grandparents' garden, a strange homesickness for a home she hadn't seen in many years and could barely even picture.

'I should warn you,' Sophie said as they crossed the courtyard, 'the layout here is dead confusing. The main house looks regular from the outside, but then there are all these extra parts sort of scattered about, and it ends up being a bit of a maze.'

'I suppose you must get used to it,' Ida said, still thinking of her grandparents.

'Oh, not at all!' Sophie said. 'Mary Hughes, who's been at the school for five years, got lost on her way to Geography last term. We still haven't found her. Apparently the house and outbuildings were the grand project of some rich aristocrat in the eighteenth century, only then he got committed to an asylum before it was all finished, because it turned out he thought he was Julius Caesar. Do you like history?'

'Yes,' Ida said. 'I'm doing it as one of my A-levels.'

'Well, good, because there's lots of history here. Wait till you hear what the nuns used to get up to.'

'What did they get up to?' Ida said.

'Oh, we're not allowed to talk about it.'

They had crossed Yard now and turned into another stone passageway, emerging into another, smaller courtyard. Ida was still hoping for more information about the nuns, but Sophie instead began a running commentary on the different buildings.

'So that's Burnham's, one of the houses, and that one over there with the red door is Swift's, but before it was Swift's it was Wolsey, which was the Home Ec building, but that's now off Yard. And down that passageway is College, which is for scholars only, but only scholars elected during Lower School, not Sixth Form scholars like you, because we never have any of those.'

'But Miss Christie told me they offer a Sixth Form scholarship every year,' Ida said.

'Well, apparently it's a condition of the endowment that the school offers one Sixth Form scholarship each year. It's meant to go to either an orphan or a young lady at risk of falling into moral disrepute. Which are you?'

Ida said, 'Well, I'm not an orphan. Though I don't have a dad.'

'Oh, don't you? *Bad* luck. Did they only give you half the scholarship, then?'

'No, I think they gave me all of it,' Ida said.

'Right, well, that's good,' Sophie said. Now they passed through another side door into a building, where Sophie led Ida down a long, linoleum-tiled corridor that had a stale, damp smell. 'Maybe the thing about orphans and fallen women is more advisory than compulsory, then,' she continued. 'The Sixth Form scholars never seem to end up coming, so we don't usually get to find out. I've been here since First Year, and you're the first one I've met.'

'Why don't they come?' Ida said, more dismayed by the second.

'Oh, well, I'm not sure. I think sometimes they get a better offer, and sometimes they learn a bit more about St Anne's and decide their old school isn't so bad after all.'

'Do *you* like it here?' Ida said, as they exited the corridor through another side door and found themselves outside again.

Sophie looked amazed at the question.

'Do I like it here?' she repeated.

'Yes.'

'I don't know. I've never really thought about it. I'm just here, aren't I? If I weren't here, I'd just be somewhere else.'

Hard to argue with this.

Finally, they came to a stop at a green door set within a relatively unassuming red-brick building.

'Well, this is Wroth's,' Sophie said. 'I'm in Burnham's, but Wroth's is all right, as houses go.' She pushed open the door, revealing a corridor with a worn carpet and a series of blue doors. 'What's your room number? It'll say on your key ring.'

Ida got it out of her pocket and looked at it. 'Seven,' she said.

Sophie shook her head. 'No, you must have read it upside down. Does it say four?'

'I don't think so,' Ida said. She held out the key for Sophie to inspect.

'It does say seven,' Sophie conceded, frowning. 'But I can't believe they'd do that. Especially to a half-orphan.'

Ida stared at her.

'Come on,' Sophie said. 'You'd better follow me.'

She led Ida to a door at the end of the corridor and up a staircase. At the top of the stairs was a door, and beyond that, another door, this time with a number seven on it.

'They put her out of the way up here,' Sophie whispered. 'In the annexe.'

'Who?' Ida whispered back.

'Louise Adler,' Sophie hissed, raising her eyebrows significantly, as if the name alone were explanation enough. Tentatively, she raised her hand and gave a small knock at the door.

They waited. Ida discovered after a moment that she was holding her breath.

When no answer came, Sophie said, with visible relief, 'I don't think she's in. Try your key.'

Ida put her key in the lock and pushed the door open. The room before her was small, with two single beds against opposite walls, a chest of drawers at the foot of each bed and a small sink in the corner. It showed signs of occupation: crumpled clothes spread across one bed, a pot of face cream on one of the bedside tables, books stacked on the windowsill. There was a book face-up on the pillow of the bed with clothes on, too, and Ida was struck by the disturbing cover illustration: a human head, the space where the mouth should be sealed over with pale, wrinkled skin and one ear deformed to resemble the conical end of a trumpet. Tiny, squatting limbs protruded grotesquely from where its body should be. Ida read the title: *I Have No Mouth, and I Must Scream*.

'If you just drop your things off now,' Sophie said, 'we can go straight to supper. You can unpack afterwards. Do you need the loo? It's downstairs. We can stop on the way.' Then, when Ida hesitated – she was still staring at the unsettling book cover – Sophie said, 'The thing is, if we hurry, we can avoid seeing Louise Adler at all, and that's probably safest.'

'But surely I'll have to see her eventually,' Ida said. 'Since I'm sharing a room with her.'

'Yes, I suppose you will,' Sophie said. 'Though I won't.' There was a pause, then she added encouragingly, 'Maybe you can find some ways around it. You could pretend to be asleep every time she comes in, and get up really early in the mornings, so you've left before she wakes up. You could probably go weeks without having to introduce yourself.'

'What's wrong with her?' Ida said, following Sophie as she hastily made her way back down the stairs.

'Oh, well, there's quite a long story there . . .' Sophie began. 'But, look, we'd better hurry or we'll miss our chips.'

Fax from Dr James Halliwell to Dr George Fisher
Thursday, 1st November 1984, 10 p.m.

Chances of a psychopathic poisoner on the loose at a minor girls' boarding school seem fairly slim, don't they? Police absolutely determined to discover one, but, as you used to tell me, one can't just light upon the most abstruse scenario in order to make one's own job more interesting.

Tried to suggest this, tactfully, to detective sergeant, but he wasn't very receptive.

On the other hand, though no doubt police will be disappointed not to find their poisoner, from my point of view this case is shaping up to be very interesting indeed.

George, would it be too much to ask for you to answer the bloody phone?

4

THERE HAD BEEN A death in the holidays.

'A *natural* death,' Miss Christie told the assembled staff, which seemed to Eleanor an unnecessarily dramatic clarification.

They all knew already, of course, that poor Miss Hamilton, an elderly history teacher and the school's longest-serving member of staff, had passed away shortly before the start of the new term. It had been Miss Christie herself who had noticed Miss Hamilton's uncharacteristic absence from evensong, and she'd sent someone to look for her. Miss Hamilton had been discovered sitting motionless in the chair in her classroom. She had been in the midst of preparing for the upcoming term, and appeared at first only to be asleep.

'At least she died doing what she loved,' remarked Margaret Hobbes, the school's other history teacher. 'Planning a lesson on the Diet of Worms.'

Dear Miss Hamilton, Eleanor thought. When Eleanor had first started at the school almost twenty years ago, a newly qualified and somewhat reluctant young geography teacher, Miss Hamilton had been very kind to her. Back then, Eleanor had struggled to keep even a class of the meekest girls under control. There had not seemed to be much appetite among her students for a knowledge of soil erosion or continental drift.

'Just remember that you're all on the same side,' Miss Hamilton had told her. 'Even though it doesn't feel like it. Imagine that you are and you'll start to believe it, and they'll believe it too.'

It had been rather a modern way of approaching teaching, and it had made a difference. Or perhaps it was simply that Miss Hamilton seemed to take it for granted that Eleanor could learn to do this job, that she wouldn't have to resign in humiliation at the end of her first term.

Miss Hamilton's death had left them in a somewhat inconvenient position, Miss Christie told them. 'Though I dare say,' she added after a moment, 'that this was not Miss Hamilton's intention.' Term started in under a week, and now they had no history teacher for Miss Hamilton's classes. They would have to be covered by everyone else until a replacement could be found, though Miss Christie said she had already begun making enquiries.

Despite their sadness about Miss Hamilton, it was quite exciting to think of someone new coming to join them. Eleanor said as much that evening to Vera Clarke, the Classics teacher with whom she shared a double set.

'Oh, nonsense – it won't be exciting, it'll be dismal,' Vera said, sipping her Ovaltine morosely. 'Christie will have a nightmare trying to recruit at this stage, and even if she were by some miracle to find someone decent, there's no money to pay them properly, so no one decent will agree to come.'

'But our girls can be so delightful,' Eleanor said, feeling she must offer a dose of cheerfulness.

'They are not delightful,' Vera said. 'They are mostly halfwits. Our only hope will be someone extremely young, with a shiny new PGCE and no experience at all, who therefore doesn't know any better. No doubt she'll be bursting with enthusiasm and, above all, very cheap. She'll stay for a term or so, realize she's made a terrible mistake, and be off before we know it to work in a nice grammar school.'

'Oh, come now,' Eleanor said. 'That seems rather a pessimistic view.'

'People know a sinking ship when they see it,' Vera said.

'She might relish the challenge,' Eleanor suggested.

'Oh, I dare say the crew of the *Titanic* relished the challenge too, once they spotted the iceberg,' Vera said, with a rather hurtful amount of sarcasm.

Eleanor often had the feeling that she annoyed Vera. They had shared this double set for the past three years, ever since Pamela Harrison, Vera's previous room-mate, had surprised them all by leaving to get married. Eleanor had lived fairly contentedly in a single room before that, with a bathroom along the corridor which she shared with several other teachers, and the luxury of her own kettle and hotplate in her room. The larger double sets, each with their own sitting room and bathroom, and two bedrooms attached, were generally coveted, but there were only three of them and vacancies did not often come up since, on the whole, the kind of teachers who ended up working at St Anne's were not the kind to try to move on to better things, nor indeed to be welcomed with open arms by better things.

Not long after Pamela Harrison's imminent departure had been announced, Vera had marched up to Eleanor at breakfast.

'With Pam leaving, there will be a vacancy in my double set,' she said. 'It'll have to be filled, of course. There's no chance Christie will let me keep the rooms to myself.'

'No, I suppose not,' Eleanor said, still recovering from being accosted so abruptly over her porridge.

'I thought you might like to move in,' Vera said.

Eleanor had been amazed. She and Vera knew each other reasonably well, as was inevitable with any of the staff members at a small boarding school, but she had never thought of her as a friend (unless it was normal to be slightly frightened of your friends); they had never, as one of the girls might put it, 'clicked'. Vera was fifteen years older than Eleanor, and didn't much resemble a traditional Latin teacher (who Eleanor imagined would be bookish and quiet, rather like Eleanor herself). Instead, Vera had the weather-beaten appearance and brusque manner of a games mistress, the sort who had tormented Eleanor at her own school many years before. Still, Vera had been teaching Latin to underwhelmed schoolgirls for almost three decades, so perhaps it was understandable if she hadn't emerged from the experience with much residual grace. She was a big fan of Tacitus, gave her hearty approbation to Caesar and found Ovid frivolous. She retained a slightly surprising soft spot for Catullus, whom she seemed to view with indulgence in the manner of a favourite, incorrigible nephew.

'It might as well be you,' Vera went on. 'Otherwise Christie will just foist someone else on me. And goodness knows who I'd end up with then. One of the English department, no doubt. I can't be coming back after a long day to find someone weeping over Wordsworth. You're a quiet sort. You wouldn't bother me much at all.'

She looked so challengingly at Eleanor when she said this that Eleanor felt compelled to defend herself. 'No, I wouldn't bother you.'

'Good,' Vera said. 'So that's settled.'

And off she marched again, leaving Eleanor perplexed as to how this had all come about so quickly, and without any input from her. The next day, Miss Christie had informed her that she could move her things into the double set as soon as Pamela had gone. It seemed too late by then to demur, so sharing the double set with Vera Clarke became yet another one of those things that seemed to have befallen Eleanor rather than been chosen by her.

Now Eleanor said, in an effort to lighten the mood, 'Well, if the ship really is going down, I suppose we'd better make the best of it. Like the musicians on the deck of the *Titanic*,' she added playfully.

She thought Vera would appreciate her effort in extending the original metaphor, but Vera only looked at her narrowly and said, 'Eleanor, at times you show an unfortunate tendency towards *whimsy*.'

Eleanor, chastened, fell silent.

As it transpired, however, she had been right all along: the arrival of Miss Hamilton's replacement almost a week into term *was* exciting.

It was a man.

THE FIRST THING ELEANOR thought when she saw him (the thought coming to her entirely unbidden) was, He's going to cause trouble.

He wasn't especially good-looking, but he was young enough to create a stir among the girls – in his early to mid thirties, by the looks of it. It was difficult for Eleanor to put her finger on the source of her unease, since Matthew Langfield appeared so normal, so entirely unthreatening. Perhaps it was only that he was dressed so much like a teacher that it felt somehow off-putting, as if he'd procured a costume for the occasion, dressed himself as the platonic ideal of the male teacher: corduroy trousers, a shirt (slightly creased), a tweed jacket (patches on the elbows). He had sandy hair (rumpled) and he was clean-shaven.

Eleanor was able to observe these things because she found herself having supper with him on his very first evening. She had arrived early for the second sitting, just as the last girls were leaving – she was on prep duty at seven p.m. and so needed to finish her supper promptly. Most teachers had not yet arrived, and Eleanor sat alone at the end of one of the long oak tables, working her way through a rather dispiriting plate of fish pie and greens.

She had her eyes fixed on her plate and was lost in her thoughts, so it startled her when a tray suddenly descended into her eyeline, held by a large pair of hands edged by shirt cuffs. The hands placed the tray opposite Eleanor's, on the other side of the table.

Eleanor registered all this briefly before a man's voice said, with unexpected formality, 'Good evening.' And there he was.

It was not quite Eleanor's first sighting. She'd spotted him already, earlier in the day, crossing the main quad in the company of Miss Christie. He'd had a suitcase in his hand. There hadn't been the chance to notice much about him then, beyond the fact that he was tall, light-haired and, incontrovertibly, male. Now, Eleanor looked up to meet his blue eyes and, feeling rather ambushed, attempted to give him a welcoming smile while her mouth was still full of fish pie.

'I'm Matthew Langfield,' he said, sitting down. 'The new history teacher.'

Eleanor swallowed, gave her mouth a quick wipe with her napkin, and said, 'Eleanor Alston. I teach geography.'

'Ah, geography!' he said, with more enthusiasm that Eleanor felt was warranted. 'So you'll be able to help me if I get lost. The layout of the school seems rather confusing.' He gave her a smile.

A very slight accent. This interested Eleanor. There was a barely detectable curl to some of his words, some of the vowels just a little flattened or shortened. West Country? East Anglia? Whatever it was, it was subtle.

He had seated himself on the bench now, manoeuvring his long legs

44

with some difficulty under the table, and he and Eleanor faced each other. He suddenly seemed to her very close – the table was long but narrow, and their trays were almost touching. She wished another teacher would arrive to join them.

She said, 'I'm afraid the layout *is* confusing. You do get used to it, in time.' Then, trying to sound encouraging, 'But you'll be in Austen's for your lessons – that's where all the humanities are taught. So as long as you can find your way between Austen's, Galbraith and School, that will be sufficient – for now, at least. It gets more complicated when you have duties in other buildings.'

'School?' he said. 'Is that the name of the main building?'

She nodded. 'An unhelpful name, I know.'

'I suppose whoever was naming the buildings had got a bit tired by that point.'

'Oh, well, they weren't all named at the same time,' Eleanor said. Then she wondered why on earth she'd felt the need to explain this. Of course she'd known he was making a joke. She wondered if she had become incapable of interacting normally with men.

He smiled at her and picked up his cutlery. Eleanor noticed herself failing to warm to him, which surprised her. But his smile seemed to her to have a slightly blank, distancing quality, almost like the performance of a smile rather than the real thing. It was a strange thought, but once it had occurred to her she couldn't shake it.

He said, 'Lovely to have a hot meal. And fish pie, too. How delicious.'

Eleanor felt sorry for his impending disillusionment. She said, 'Did you have a long journey to get here?'

'Not too bad,' he said, taking his first mouthful. Eleanor watched as he pulled an involuntary face, then chewed determinedly, swallowed. 'I came down from London on the train this morning.'

'London,' she repeated. 'Were you teaching there?'

'That's right,' he said, taking another mouthful, more hesitantly this time. 'Do you know what kind of fish is in this?' he said.

'I'm not precisely sure,' Eleanor said. 'It could be dogfish or coley, perhaps. Maybe some mackerel and herring in there too.'

'It's got quite a strong flavour, hasn't it?' he said.

'Yes, I'm not sure what they do with it to make it taste like that. I tend to add a lot of salt and pepper, and pretend it's smoked.'

He picked up the salt shaker uncertainly. 'I suppose you have fish pie a lot,' he said, 'being by the sea.'

'Not very often,' Eleanor said, so as not to depress him. 'Was it another girls' school you taught in before?'

'Boys,' he said.

'Oh, really? Which school?'

He had his mouth full again, and paused to swallow before replying. 'Westminster.'

'Goodness,' Eleanor said. 'I suppose that must be very different to here.'

'I don't know yet,' he said. Another of those smiles. 'I'll report back in a week or so. Would you like some water?' He took two glasses from the small stack in the middle of the table and laid them out, then filled them from the water jug. 'How long have you worked here?'

'About twenty years.' She did not much like having to confess this to a stranger.

'Twenty years!' he said. 'You must know this place inside out. I'm sure you'll be able to show me the ropes.'

He was almost charming, Eleanor thought again, and yet she was not charmed. It was partly that he seemed to be trying to ingratiate himself with her, which she found disconcerting. And there was something in his manner that struck a wrong note. But it was unreasonable to take against him on such short acquaintance, especially as he might be feeling out of his depth and self-conscious. And it was not as though Eleanor herself were a model of ease.

She said, 'Of course, it's changed a lot since I started.' It hadn't really. When Eleanor thought about it, she felt the school had hardly altered at all since she arrived in the mid sixties; and who could say, perhaps it hadn't even changed much since Miss Hamilton's arrival in the thirties. Matthew Langfield was probably expecting a modern, energetic institution, educating the next generation of career women. He was about to discover he had entered some kind of time warp.

'I'm sure,' he said. 'Though I hope some of its old traditions remain. Continuity is good too. Westminster was very hot on tradition, of course.'

Eleanor didn't answer him immediately. She had grown suddenly concerned that she might count as one of the school's old traditions. Perhaps she, like the school, had not altered much over the course of many years. It sometimes seemed to her that she had got rather stuck. She would be forty next year; she was more than halfway through her life, and she had done so little with it.

It was a relief to look up and see Trudy Pearson and Linda Fox approaching with their trays, though relief was not the main feeling Eleanor usually associated with seeing the pair. Both were English teachers, and prone to declaiming lines of verse with little prior warning (especially Tennyson, whom they worshipped). Trudy was in her late twenties, with an ethereal look about her: colouring so fair her skin appeared close to translucent and her hair, eyebrows and eyelashes almost white. She had a collection of old-fashioned housecoats which she had embroidered beautifully herself with gold and silver thread, and liked to wear to supper, despite Miss Christie's obvious disapproval (she and Trudy had a difference of opinion about the distinction between evening wear and nightwear). Linda was a few years older, tall and thin, with large, rather bulging dark eyes. The thing Eleanor knew most particularly about Linda was that she had been born still inside the gestational sack, with a full head of hair and a full set of teeth. This was information Eleanor had never solicited, but Linda often retold the story, especially at mealtimes.

'Ah, have you met?' Eleanor said, as the two women sat down. 'This is Matthew Langfield, who's joining the history department. And this,' she said to Matthew, 'is Trudy Pearson and Linda Fox, who both teach English here.'

Linda and Trudy were visibly agog at this encounter with their new male colleague.

'We heard you'd arrived,' Trudy said. She had taken the seat opposite him, next to Eleanor, while Linda sat beside him, a little closer than might be deemed appropriate by most people. Both women, having settled into their seats, then stared expectantly at him, as if waiting for this new specimen to do something noteworthy.

'Matthew taught at Westminster previously,' Eleanor said, since she felt there ought to be conversation to accompany the staring.

'Westminster?' Trudy said. 'How on earth have you ended up here?'

'Bad luck,' Linda added. 'What a shame.'

'Oh, no,' Matthew Langfield said confusedly. 'Not a shame at all. I just wanted a change. It can be a bit stuffy, a school like that.'

'It must be odd for you, suddenly finding yourself alone amongst all these women,' Linda said, leaning even closer towards him, her large, plaintive eyes unblinking.

'And out here in the middle of nowhere, after the bustle of London,' Eleanor said briskly, in an attempt to deflect Linda's intensity. 'I hope you won't be bored. We live a quiet life here, I'm afraid.'

'Hardly!' Trudy said, seeming offended. 'Maybe some of the *older* teachers live a quiet life –' with a pointed look at Eleanor – 'but for me and Linda at least, our weekends are very lively.'

'Do you tend to go off site at weekends?' Matthew said.

'Yes,' Linda said. 'If we're not on duty. You have every other weekend off. Though lots of teachers end up staying on site anyway, and just reading, or marking.'

'*We* always go off site,' Trudy said. 'It would get very boring otherwise. We go to Brighton or Eastbourne, to the pubs. We always swap our duties around so our free weekends coincide. You can do the same, and then we can arrange a little trip to show you the sights. I have a car,' she added, with an attempt at modesty. 'Not everybody here does.'

'Eleanor used to,' Linda observed in her dreamy way. 'A natty red MG.'

Trudy said quickly, unwilling to allow Eleanor this level of glamour, 'Oh, but it was only a two-seater, so no good for lifts. And anyway, it wasn't hers, it was her fiancé's.'

Eleanor felt her face going red.

'*Trudy*,' Linda hissed, which made the situation worse. Trudy was looking ashamed.

'Oh, you're going to be married?' Matthew Langfield said, smiling at Eleanor. 'Congratulations.'

Eleanor was so dismayed by the turn the conversation had taken that she wasn't sure how to answer, so it fell to Trudy to say contritely into the silence, 'Unfortunately, she isn't anymore.'

It was difficult to say who was more embarrassed now, Eleanor or Matthew Langfield.

'Goodness, I'm sorry,' he said. His face had reddened as well. And of course he didn't know whether he was offering condolences on a bereavement or a jilting, which placed him in an even more uncomfortable position.

There was no way to smooth over the awkwardness, so Eleanor simply said, 'Thank you,' and then, with some desperation, tried to move the conversation on. 'Girls are admitted in the Sixth Form at Westminster now, aren't they?'

'Yes, that's right,' he said, recovering himself a little.

'That must have been a big change. Did that happen during your time there?'

'No,' he said, with what seemed to Eleanor a fractional hesitation. 'Just before.'

'And do they have a hard time?' Eleanor asked.

'They manage to hold their own,' he said. Another of those smiles.

'You'll be teaching in Miss Hamilton's classroom,' Trudy said, probably growing tired of Eleanor's laboured conversation.

'Yes, you'll be in Austen's, A8,' Linda said. 'Second floor.'

'Oh, right,' he said politely. 'Is that a nice room?'

'Yes, a lovely room,' Trudy said.

'Where Miss Hamilton breathed her last,' Linda added.

'Oh!' Matthew Langfield said, flustered again. 'I didn't realize.'

'Yes, she passed away in her chair,' Trudy said.

'The very same chair you'll be sitting in for your lessons,' Linda said.

'Goodness,' Matthew said.

'All in all, I think it was a good death,' Trudy said. 'It is a very comfortable chair.'

Matthew nodded, and Eleanor hoped the subject was now closed.

But Linda said, 'Of course, even those who had good deaths have been known to return.'

'To *walk*,' Trudy said.

'I'm sure Miss Hamilton is peacefully at rest,' Eleanor said. She was worried about where this was going; she knew from experience that it could be hard to divert Trudy and Linda once they'd got started.

'Well, if she does return, I dare say she'll mean you no harm,' Trudy was reassuring Matthew now.

'I certainly hope not,' he said, with an attempt at levity.

'Though I suppose,' Linda added thoughtfully after a moment, 'she could be forgiven for thinking you've usurped her place.'

'Matthew has very kindly stepped in at short notice to ensure our girls still have a teacher,' Eleanor said. 'I'd hardly call that "usurping" anyone's place.'

'Well, nor would I, of course,' Linda said. 'But the dead have their own logic, don't they?'

'The dead are simply dead,' Eleanor said. 'At rest,' she amended.

'Eleanor doesn't believe in ghosts,' Trudy explained to Matthew. 'But that doesn't mean they aren't real. I do hope you won't suddenly notice in the midst of your first lesson that Miss Hamilton has glided silently into the room.'

He blanched.

'And taken up her usual place in the teacher's chair,' Linda said.

'Like Banquo's ghost,' Trudy said.

'Thou canst not say I did it!' Linda said. 'Never shake thy gory locks at me!'

Really, Eleanor thought, Trudy and Linda could be as silly as some of the girls.

Fortunately, Vera Clarke arrived at that point. Eleanor was surprised, though very relieved, when she opted to join them; Vera did not usually have much tolerance for the English department. But Eleanor supposed she was as curious as everyone else about the new teacher.

'So you're here, then?' Vera said abruptly to Matthew, depositing her tray and herself heavily beside Eleanor.

'I am,' he said. And, holding out his hand: 'Matthew Langfield.'

Vera looked at the extended hand, but didn't take it. 'I suppose they've warned you about our girls?'

'I – no,' he said, and laughed.

'Oh, Vera, come on,' Eleanor said.

'Matthew used to teach at Westminster!' Trudy said breathlessly. 'Can you imagine?'

'Westminster, eh?' Vera said. 'Well, in that case, you appear to have made a very surprising career decision.'

'Oh, not at all,' Matthew said. 'I just felt like a change. And some sea air, of course. I've never liked cities much.'

'Did you grow up near the coast?' Eleanor said.

'Yes,' he said. 'But not this coast. Norfolk.'

'How lovely,' she said. 'Whereabouts?'

'Not too far from Norwich,' he said. 'Between there and the coast.'

'Anywhere near Great Yarmouth?' Trudy said. 'I went on holiday there once.'

'And it's in Dickens, too,' Linda added. *David Copperfield.*

'Quite near,' he said. It all seemed rather vague to Eleanor, but then she supposed that none of them knew Norfolk well, so further specificity would be wasted on them.

Vera said, having taken no interest in the conversation about Norfolk, 'Husband of a friend teaches at Westminster. Maths department. Name of Rodney Trowbridge. I dare say you knew him.'

'Oh, yes,' Matthew said, smiling at her. 'Rodney. Yes, of course. Nice chap.'

'If you say so,' Vera said. 'Personally, I've always found him a crashing bore.'

Matthew laughed at this. 'Well, I suppose he could be a bit tedious.' He laid his cutlery neatly on his plate, having finished his fish pie now (a heroic effort). 'I'm sorry to leave you, but I think I'd better get on. I'm supposed to be meeting Miss Christie after supper, and I don't want to be late on my first day. It was very nice to meet you all.'

'Will you be able to find her office all right?' Eleanor said.

'Yes, I'll be all right. Thank you.'

'Good luck,' Linda said. 'And don't cut through College Garden when the light's fading. You don't want to run into the Gresham Lady.'

'Oh dear,' he said. 'No, I wouldn't want that.' Briefly, he met Eleanor's eye and there seemed to be a flicker of something there – amusement, was it? She kept her own expression clear, unwilling to ally herself with him so early.

'She haunts the laburnum tree,' Linda said. 'Rumour has it she was poisoned with laburnum tea.'

'Beautiful flowers in summer, though,' Trudy said. 'So perhaps she just likes laburnum.'

'And watch out for Constance Stoker if you go near the cloisters,' Linda said. 'She walks at night too.'

'Another ghost?' Matthew said.

'No, she's one of the kitchen staff,' Trudy explained. 'But she doesn't like to be disturbed on her evening walks. She's an unpleasant woman. The fish pie probably tastes so bad because it's seasoned with her malice.'

'Thank you for the warning,' he said, and with a final smile and a nod of his head he walked away.

'Well, he appears to be moderately sane,' Vera remarked, when he was barely out of earshot. 'Which I suppose is the best we can hope for.'

'He seems in possession of an interesting soul,' Linda said, to Vera's obvious irritation.

Eleanor was silent, watching Matthew disappear out of the door. She thought, unaccountably, I don't trust that man.

5

NINE P.M. ON IDA'S first evening and there was still no sign of the famous Louise Adler.

Ida had unpacked her things into the chest of drawers, put on her pyjamas, brushed her teeth and washed her face at the small sink. Then she had located the ancient, freezing bathroom downstairs so she could pee. She met no one, which was a relief.

She had been sitting up in bed for ages now, purportedly reading the copy of *Cranford* Mrs Kelly had given her as a going-away present, but really staring fixedly at the door in readiness for the moment Louise would enter and Ida would have to make the right impression. This, Sophie had told her at supper, was crucial.

'You need to avoid getting off on the wrong foot,' she had said, sitting across from Ida in the dining hall and eating her chips very rapidly and methodically. 'Otherwise you might have a difficult time.'

'How do I get off on the right foot?' Ida said. The walls of the dining hall were hung with gilt-framed portraits of notable women from history, but they all seemed to be bad copies. Poor Mary Wollstonecraft, directly in Ida's eyeline, had ended up with a bulging forehead and slightly wild eyes. It unsettled Ida as she ate.

Sophie thought about her question for a bit. 'Well, don't look at her too much. But don't look like you're avoiding looking at her either. And definitely don't say anything about fire.'

'Why would I?' Ida said. Then, 'Wait. Fire?'

'Oh, that's quite a long story.'

The thing about Sophie's long stories, Ida was fast learning, was that you never got to hear them.

'You need to appear non-threatening,' Sophie said. 'Make yourself as small as possible when she first comes in.'

'Got it,' Ida said. She wondered if Sophie had been watching David Attenborough over the summer.

'But don't make yourself seem like a pushover either,' Sophie added.

So, Ida reminded herself, as she sat tensely in her bed: make the right impression. Non-threatening, but not weak either. And better try not to look too flammable.

The time passed slowly. By ten p.m., Ida had started to calm down and the tiredness from her long day of travel was creeping over her. She had assumed a teacher would appear at some point to check everyone was in their rooms and tell them it was lights out, but nobody came. Ida wondered if there was someone she ought to alert to the fact that Louise Adler seemed to be missing, but even if she'd known who to tell, this didn't seem like the way to make the right impression on Louise.

It occurred to Ida now that since it was so late already, she could simply go to sleep and avoid having to make any impression on Louise at all until the next day. This seemed to her an excellent idea, so she reached out and turned off the bedside light.

THEN SHE WAS AWAKE. She didn't have any sense of the time, but it felt like the depths of the night. Someone was moving nearby. Ida lay very still. She tried to keep her breathing slow and even so the other person wouldn't realize she had woken. There was the sound of a zip and the rustle of fabric as the person, who must surely be Louise, undressed; then a slight creak as she climbed into bed and the swish of the covers being pulled over her. Finally, there was silence; but it felt tense and expectant to Ida. She continued to lie still, but she was sure Louise would be able to tell that she was awake. Neither of them spoke. Eventually, Ida heard Louise's breathing change as she drifted into sleep, but she herself lay awake for a long time after that.

WHEN SHE WOKE, IT was light outside and the other bed was empty again. Ida panicked for a moment that she had overslept on her first morning, but the little screen on her Casio read 06:32. Ida felt uneasy to think of Louise looming over her while she was in a vulnerable state of unconsciousness. Still, she was relieved to have again dodged an encounter. Perhaps Sophie was right, and she really could avoid Louise indefinitely by keeping different hours.

She got her washbag and towel, and went downstairs to the bathroom, which she was pleased to find empty. Showering proved a disconcerting experience. The water was freezing, emerging from the shower head in inconsistent bursts, with a lot of creaking and gurgling from the pipes in between. Ida wasn't sure if she felt invigorated or shell-shocked as she dried herself.

When she got back to her room, Louise was still absent. Ida got dressed as quickly as she could. Miss Christie had found her at the end of supper the previous evening and delivered a carrier bag containing her school uniform: two white shirts, one grey skirt, one maroon jumper, a medley of grey socks and one green tie. Everything seemed to fit, more or less. There was no mirror in the room, so Ida couldn't see what she looked like in her new uniform, but she hoped she looked acceptable.

While she was brushing her teeth over the sink, she was startled by a sudden noise. It seemed to emanate from above her head. She paused and listened. After a brief silence, it came again: a heavy creak, as if someone, or something, were moving around above her head.

Ida looked up quickly. She saw now that there was a trapdoor in the ceiling, both the door itself and its small, curved handle painted white to blend in. She wondered if it had been there the previous evening, and decided that it probably had.

She waited, her heart beating fast, but no more sounds came. There was most likely nothing up there at all, she thought. The creaking would just be one of those things that very old buildings did. Their cottage on the island had sometimes seemed to have a life of its own, its windows rattling and beams creaking even when the weather was still. If you hadn't known any better, you'd have thought it was haunted. But this reflection led Ida immediately to the horrifying thought that perhaps this school *was* haunted. Those nuns from long ago . . . Hadn't the man who gave her the lift mentioned a death, and a fire?

She tried to gather herself. It was very unlikely that there was a ghostly nun in the ceiling. There might, at worst, be a trapped cat up there that needed to be freed (it had sounded too heavy for a cat, though). To prove to herself that she wasn't an idiot who was scared of ghosts, Ida put down her toothbrush and wiped her mouth, then climbed up on her bed to reach the handle on the trapdoor.

She had intended to open it only a cautious inch or two, but she lost her balance at the crucial moment and fell forwards, still clutching the handle, pulling the trapdoor all the way open.

There was a cry above her, a sudden blur of motion, and as Ida fell, another person tumbled out of the ceiling, landing on top of her on the floor.

It hurt a lot. A knee banged into Ida's head, and she lay dazed for a few moments. Then she felt herself being pushed away roughly as the other person disentangled herself, and a voice, surely too cross to belong to a long-dead nun, said, 'What in the living *fuck* do you think you're doing?'

She was tall. This was the first thing Ida noticed as the girl unfurled herself and got to her feet. Beyond that, Ida had a vague impression of brown hair and pale eyes that might have been green; she didn't meet them for long enough to be sure.

She got quickly to her feet as well, since she felt at a disadvantage being on the floor while the other girl stood over her glaring. She said, 'I thought you might be a burglar.'

'What was the next stage in your plan if I had been?' the girl said. 'Hand-to-hand combat?'

Ida explained that she hadn't thought that far ahead.

The girl said, 'You could have killed me.'

'I doubt I could have killed you,' Ida said, feeling this was unreasonably hyperbolic. 'At worst, maybe broken your leg,' she conceded.

'Oh, terrific,' the girl said. 'Well, that's put my mind at rest. Just my leg. I'd probably hardly miss it.'

'You must be Louise,' Ida said. 'I'm Ida Campbell.'

'I know who you are,' the girl said. She was straightening her clothes, which had been disarrayed by the fall. 'Don't get too comfortable. You won't be staying.'

'Won't I?' Ida said, wondering what Louise knew that she didn't.

'No. I don't want a room-mate. I had one before. I didn't like it. She left.' Louise went to the mirror over the sink, checked her reflection and tidied her hair. 'They know that, so I don't know why they've put you in here with me.'

'You'll hardly notice I'm here,' Ida offered.

'I'd say you've made your presence felt already.'

Suddenly annoyed by the injustice of it all, Ida said, 'None of this was my first choice either.'

Louise's eyes met hers in the mirror for a moment, and Ida thought she saw a flicker of curiosity there. Then it was gone. Louise turned towards her bed, reaching under the pillow to retrieve her book. 'Look, I've given you fair warning,' she said, sitting down. 'I'm not having a room-mate. So either you leave of your own accord and go back to wherever the fuck you came from, or I'm going to make your life so miserable that you have no choice but to go. Got it?'

There was a short silence.

'Got it,' Ida said.

This must be that wrong foot Sophie was talking about, she thought.

IDA WAS LATE TO breakfast, chiefly because she didn't want to follow too closely behind Louise. Entering the dining room alone didn't bother her. She generally didn't mind being friendless, so long as no one pissed in her bag (though, having met Louise, she thought she might now be facing graver danger than that).

She covertly scanned the queue and then the rows of girls along the benches for any sign of Louise, but couldn't see her, which felt like a small reprieve. The *Today* programme was playing from somewhere, John Timpson in the middle of interviewing some politician or other, and it took Ida a few moments to locate the source of the sound, which turned out to be speakers placed on the walls at either end of the room.

As she queued at the hatch with her tray, she heard her name being called repeatedly over the hubbub, and turned to see Sophie waving her over to where she sat with a couple of other girls at the end of one of the long tables.

Ida took her cereal and tea over, thinking that Sophie at least really did seem nice, especially compared to Louise.

'This is Ida,' Sophie said to her companions as Ida joined them. 'Ida, this is Angela, she's famously beautiful –' gesturing at the girl on her left, who was, Ida had to admit, startlingly pretty – 'though generally agreed not to be quite as attractive as Jane Morehouse,' Sophie added, 'who you'll see later, so you can make up your own mind. And this is Victoria, who sadly has a squint, but makes excellent scones –' gesturing at the girl on her right, who wore glasses with thick lenses.

Ida put her tray down and slid on to the bench. 'Thanks,' she said. 'Hello.'

'So have you met her yet?' the beautiful Angela said.

'Who?'

'Louise Adler.'

'Oh,' Ida said, deflated by the memory. 'Sort of.'

'What do you mean, sort of?'

'Well, it was all a bit rushed.' Ida didn't feel she could quite bear to go into it all just now. The *Today* programme had moved on to a segment on the Iran–Iraq War, which didn't seem to be going very well for anyone. Ida said, 'Is the radio always on at breakfast?'

'Miss Christie makes us listen to it every morning,' Sophie said, 'because it's improving. And also she thinks we need to know what the Soviets are getting up to, in case they're about to attack.'

'And the speakers are also used when we have our nuclear drills,' Victoria of the scones and the squint said.

'When you have your what?' Ida said.

Just then there was a disturbance across the room. A dark-haired girl was on her feet shouting – after a moment, Ida could make out the words, 'Fuck the Ayatollah! *Fuck* the Ayatollah!' – and her friends were gathered around her, attempting to placate her.

'Don't worry about her,' Sophie said, seeing Ida staring. 'She's Iranian. Her family were dead cosy with the Shah, so they had to flee after the revolution. She's nice most of the time, but she goes absolutely berserk if anyone mentions the Ayatollah. And I see her point, because he does sound like a killjoy.'

A teacher had appeared and was speaking to the girl in a soothing tone. The girl was, at length, persuaded to sit down again.

'They lost all their money when they fled Iran,' Sophie told Ida. 'That's why Farah goes here instead of a proper school like Roedean, or whatever fancy school she was at in Iran. Now she's stuck here, having to make scones over and over again while listening to Miss Crawley talk about her sciatica. Scones are all we ever make in Home Ec. So it's strange really that only Victoria is any good at them.'

'I wasn't good at them for the first few years,' Victoria said modestly. 'It was only last year that my scones really took off.'

'Mine are still more like rock cakes,' Angela said. 'And Sophie's always come out flat.'

'Miss Crawley accuses me every week of forgetting the baking powder, but in fact I hardly ever forget it,' Sophie said. 'It's just something about my presence that seems to deactivate it. Ida, what lesson do you have first thing?'

'History,' Ida said. 'With, um, M. L., it says on my timetable.'

There was an excited intake of breath from the other girls.

'M. L.!' Sophie said. 'Oh, lucky you. That's the replacement for Miss Hamilton.'

'There's a rumour,' Angela said, 'that M. L. is actually a *man*. A man was sighted last night, crossing Yard in the company of Miss Christie. Though he could have just been there to fix the leaking roof in Nightingale's.'

'M. L.,' Sophie said dreamily. 'Mark, Matthew, Martin.'

'Michael, Max,' Victoria said.

'Marvin,' Angela said, and they all giggled.

'You'll have to let us know if he's handsome,' Sophie said to Ida.

'Louise does History too,' Angela said. 'So you might see her again.'

Brilliant, Ida thought. 'It's in A8,' she said. 'How do I get there?'

The other three girls took up this challenge enthusiastically.

'Go straight through Yard, keeping Swift's to your left, and then head through College Alley and bear left up Spenser's,' Angela said.

'No, go through Gibbons Arch and then diagonally across Green, and then along the west side of the cloisters. That's much quicker,' Sophie said.

'It's east of Marlowe's and perpendicular to Greene, that's the easiest way to think of it,' Victoria said.

'It's not perpendicular to Green!' Angela protested.

'Not Green, *Greene*,' Victoria said.

'Oh, I see,' Angela said. 'But it would still be better to go via College Alley. If you sneak into College Garden and climb over the wall into Small Yard, it would be even quicker. You can use the tree to help you climb. The crab-apple tree, not the laburnum. Don't climb the laburnum, because you'll just end up back in Yard. Can you actually tell trees apart, though? Lots of people can't.'

'Yes,' Ida said. 'But I'm still not sure how to get to History.'

'I have French in Pallbrook's, which is near Austen's,' Sophie conceded. 'So I'll just take you.'

*

HALF AN HOUR LATER, Ida had been delivered safely to her classroom and had taken a seat discreetly near the back. The room was starting to fill up. The other girls stared openly at Ida, but nobody seemed keen to chat to her, which was fine by Ida.

She was staring down at her desk lid when she became aware of two girls standing over her. Arranging her face into a friendly, quizzical expression, she looked up.

One of the girls had a lot of frizzy hair and was scowling at her, while the other had a much lovelier face – symmetrical features and wide-apart eyes – but beneath her prettiness, she looked exhausted. Her complexion was pallid and she had dark circles under her eyes.

'You must be the Scottish scholarship half-orphan,' the scowling girl said. 'We heard you'd arrived. This is where we sit. You need to move.'

'It's OK,' the other girl added, more gently. 'You didn't know. It's just that these are the best seats. You're partly blocked from the teacher's view.'

'And Diane here is Head Girl, so she gets first choice of seats,' the scowling girl said.

Ida was leaning down to pick up her bag and beginning her apology when Louise suddenly appeared, stepping around the other girls and sliding into the empty seat next to Ida.

'Why, hello, April,' she said to the scowling girl. And to the pretty, tired girl: 'Greetings, Diane.' She smiled. 'We'll allow Ida to sit here today, shall we? She's new. We must all be very kind to her.'

Ida was amazed that Louise was standing up for her. 'It's OK,' she began. 'I don't mind moving—' She half rose.

'Sit down,' Louise said, steel in her voice.

Ida sat.

'What's this, then? Have you two teamed up?' the girl called April said.

'Yes, we're thick as thieves,' Louise said.

64

April folded her arms. 'You make a good pair. Like something from a story. Nessie and the Wandering Jew.'

'What does that make you two, then?' Louise said. 'Dracula and Renfield? Sweeney Todd and Mrs Lovett?'

'Very funny.'

'Hitler and Goebbels?'

'Stop it, both of you,' Diane said. To April, she added, 'And don't call Louise a Jew.'

'She is a Jew.'

'You're not saying it in a nice way. And there's nothing wrong with being a Jew.'

'Thank you, Diane,' Louise said. 'I was thinking of killing myself, but now I can see there's no need.'

Just then, there was a small commotion as their new teacher entered. Some members of the class appeared not to have heard the rumour about him being a man, and seemed completely unprepared for the possibility: there was an audible gasp from several girls when he came in.

With a final frown at Louise, April and Diane took the remaining two desks in the middle of the room.

'Thanks,' Ida said to Louise.

'I didn't do it to help you, I did it to annoy them,' Louise said.

'Hello,' the teacher said. Eighteen expectant faces stared back at him. He cleared his throat a couple of times. 'I'm Mr Langfield.'

Maleness aside, he wasn't a very striking person. He was pale and slightly damp-looking, as if he'd been put in the washing machine too many times and his colour had been leached out. Ida also thought he looked very nervous.

A girl near the back burst out, unable to contain herself any longer, 'But *miss*, you're a *man*!'

The class collapsed.

Over the laughter, Mr Langfield, increasingly red in the face, struggled to make himself heard. 'Yes, that's right,' he said. 'And you can call me sir or Mr Langfield. Could everyone calm down, please?'

They could not.

'We'll be looking at the Reformation this term,' Mr Langfield said, raising his voice and clearly deciding to press on regardless of the fact that most of the class were still giggling helplessly. 'We'll start with an outline of the life of Martin Luther.' He cleared his throat again. 'I'm waiting for you all to be quiet.'

He waited. The class continued to giggle.

Eventually, Diane sighed and said, 'All right, shut up, everyone,' and the noise gradually died down.

Mr Langfield looked at her gratefully. 'Right,' he said. 'OK. Well, let's make a start.'

What followed was a short lecture on Martin Luther, delivered rather stammeringly. Some of the girls were listening politely, albeit without much enthusiasm, while others stared around the room or doodled in their books or wrote each other notes.

Ida suddenly realized that Louise was speaking to her in an undertone.

'So what did you do,' Louise said, 'to end up here?'

'What do you mean?' Ida whispered back. 'I didn't do anything.'

'Do your parents hate you?'

'I don't think so,' Ida said, thinking of her mother.

'So why did they send you here?'

'I sent myself,' Ida said.

Louise looked at her with the first stirrings of interest. 'Why?'

'To get an education.'

'You won't get that here.'

'I might.'

'Nope. And anyway, you won't be staying long enough.'

'You can't make me leave,' Ida said, since it seemed best to face the threat head on. She tried to keep her voice steady, but she couldn't make herself look at Louise.

'I probably can,' Louise said. 'Though I might reconsider if you tell me why you came here in the first place.'

'I wanted a change,' Ida said.

'From what?' Louise was still studying her.

'Nothing,' Ida said, losing patience with the interrogation. 'Why did *you* get sent here?'

'Same reason as everyone else,' Louise said airily. 'To get rid of me in the cheapest way possible.'

'Orphanages are free,' Ida said, and was gratified when Louise's lips moved into what could almost have been a smile.

At the front of the room, Mr Langfield cleared his throat and said, 'So that was a whistle-stop tour through some of the key events in Luther's life, taking us as far as the Diet of Worms.' He paused. 'Does anyone have any questions so far?'

There was a moment's delay. Then almost every hand in the room shot into the air at once.

'Miss, I mean sir, have you ever taught at a school for young ladies before?' a girl asked.

He blinked a few times. 'That is not a relevant question.'

'Have you ever taught in a *school* before?'

'Of course I have,' he said.

'Were they cleverer or less clever than us?'

He shook his head helplessly.

The next few questions followed a similar pattern, and received a similar response.

'Sir, is your accommodation comfortable?'

'Did you grow up in a town or in the countryside?'

'Do you have any nice plans for Christmas this year?'

'Sir, I was trying to throw my pencil case to Martha so she could borrow my ruler, but I seem to have accidentally thrown it out of the window. May I climb out and get it?'

'No, of course not.'

'It's a flat roof, so probably quite safe.'

'I said no. Girls, *girls*!' he said, addressing the room. 'No more questions unless they're on the subject of *history*.'

The hands were lowered. Then they all shot back into the air.

'Did Martin Luther bring his own hammer and nails when he put his notice up on the church door? Did he have them already or would he have procured some specially for the occasion?'

'Barbara Bridges was trying to sell us all candy bracelets for 15p each last term. You had to have one to sit on the top table at lunch, else they told you to get lost. Would you say she was selling indulgences?'

'How did Pope Leo manage to send a bull to Luther? Was it in a crate, or in a wagon of some sort?'

'Was the Diet of Worms any good for slimming?'

Mr Langfield did his best with these questions, but after a few minutes he said, 'That's enough. We really must continue the lesson now. No more questions until the end.'

The remaining hands went reluctantly down.

He began to talk again, and the class dozed.

A sudden yelp from the middle of the room. It was April, sitting to Diane's left. 'What's happening?' she said. 'Something's happening to her!'

Everyone turned to look. As they watched, Diane's right arm jerked violently forward, the movement seeming to originate in her shoulder. It sent her exercise book and pencil case flying off the desk. Diane reached for her shoulder as if to hold it in place, but her arm lurched again. Her fist was clenched.

'Oh, stop it, Diane,' the girl in front of Diane said.

'I'm – not – doing – it,' Diane said indistinctly. Her right side jerked forcefully again. It looked as if her arm had taken on a life of its own and was trying to detach itself from her body and fly across the room.

'She's possessed!' one girl cried. 'It's Miss Hamilton's ghost!'

'It's one of the burned nuns!' another girl cried.

'The power of Christ compels you!' someone screamed from the back.

'Everybody calm down,' Mr Langfield said loudly. There was a panicked note in his voice, but he hurried over to Diane's desk and crouched down at her eye level. Her arm spasmed again, almost hitting him. 'Diane?' he said. 'Are you all right?'

She gasped and gave a brief nod. Abruptly, the movements stopped and she slumped forwards, clutching her right shoulder with her unaffected hand. 'Don't know what happened,' she said after a few moments, breathing heavily. She'd gone even paler than before.

'You'd better go to the nurse,' Mr Langfield said. 'Are you able to walk?'

Diane got shakily to her feet. 'Yes,' she said.

'I think it would be safer if you carried her in your arms, sir,' a girl suggested, sounding indecently eager.

'I can walk,' Diane said.

'You go with her,' Mr Langfield said to April.

They all watched as Diane shuffled out, accompanied by April, who was carrying both their backpacks.

Ida glanced sideways at Louise, who was wearing a thoughtful expression.

'Has that happened to her before?' Ida said.

'Not that I know of. Very strange.'

'Is she faking it?'

'Now why would she do that?'

'For attention?' Ida said.

Louise shrugged. 'Maybe. Who knows. Maybe someone poisoned her.'

Ida felt a chill go through her. 'That's not funny.'

'Maybe you'll be next.'

'Right, settle down everyone,' Mr Langfield said. He'd resumed his position at the front of the room, but he looked shaken. 'I'm sure Diane will be all right. Now we need to turn our attention back to Martin Luther.'

'Sir,' a girl said, raising her hand. 'Do you think he's in the room with us *right now*?'

'No,' Mr Langfield said.

'Do you think it was Miss Hamilton's ghost, then?'

'That's enough silliness,' he said, with more irritation than before. 'I will write some summary notes on the board. You will copy them down in silence.'

The rest of the lesson passed in this way. When the bell went fifteen minutes later and he dismissed them, the atmosphere was a little calmer. But as soon as the girls were out in the corridor, everyone was again talking about Diane's mysteriously jerking arm. By the end of break, the story was all around the school. Opinion was split on whether it was a ghostly possession, a prank, or if Diane had been poisoned by the Russians and/or the kitchen staff.

Sophie, Angela and Victoria were delighted Ida had been in the class and was therefore able to give them a first-hand account. Ida did her best to describe exactly what she'd seen, though she quickly tired of retelling the story. She left out the part where Louise had mentioned poison. She was almost certain Louise was just trying to scare her. But despite the others' excitement, the incident had made her uneasy. She recalled the expression of fear on Diane's face, and felt as though some wrongness had followed her here, all the way from the island, and infected this new place, just when she thought she'd escaped.

6

DIANE FULBROOK HAD SPENT the morning in the sick bay. Eleanor, as her form teacher, had been to see her during break and found her recovered, more or less. Diane was pale and seemed very tired, but the sudden flailing that had overtaken her during History hadn't been repeated since.

'I don't know what happened, miss,' Diane said, sitting up on one of the beds and drinking a carton of Five Alive which the nurse had provided in order to raise her blood sugar. 'It was like my arm had a life of its own.'

'Has anything like that happened to you before?' Eleanor said, perching on the edge of the bed. Up close, she could see the livid dark circles under Diane's eyes.

'No.' Diane thought for a moment. 'Well, I think I've had a bit of a twitch in my arm sometimes. Like when your muscle jumps. And sometimes my body jerks like when you're just about to fall asleep, only it happened when I wasn't in bed or about to sleep. But it wasn't as bad as today.'

'I'm sure it's nothing to worry about,' Eleanor said, though she felt less confident than she sounded. Diane hadn't been herself this term. Eleanor had thought she'd seemed distracted in form time, and once or twice she had noticed her snapping at her friends, which was unlike her.

She said now, 'Has anything been worrying you recently, Diane?'

The girl shook her head.

'You look tired.'

'I've had a bit of trouble sleeping lately,' Diane admitted.

'Do you know what's keeping you awake?' And when Diane shrugged, she pressed gently, 'Anything going on at home?'

'No.' Diane seemed to hesitate again. 'Well, my father's dead set on me doing a secretarial course when I finish school. But I don't want to.'

'What do you want to do?'

'Join the police,' Diane said, somewhat surprisingly.

'And your father isn't keen?'

'He doesn't think it's suitable.'

'Well, he may have a point,' Eleanor said. 'I doubt it's much fun.' Then, seeing Diane's face, she added, 'But you've got nearly two years before you leave school, so plenty of time to decide. And maybe to bring your father round.'

Diane gave a small smile. Eleanor left her and went to speak to Kirsty, the school nurse, in the other room.

'No temperature,' Kirsty said. 'And she's eating and drinking fine. I've given her a couple of paracetamols.'

'What happened to her arm, do you think?'

'No idea,' Kirsty said blithely, though Eleanor thought she might at least pretend to give the matter some serious consideration. 'Just one of those strange things. The human body's infinitely mysterious.'

This was undoubtedly true, but again Eleanor couldn't help but feel that a nurse, of all people, should be more inclined to delve deeper into some of its mysteries.

She said, 'Should she see a doctor?'

'Doubt it,' Kirsty said. 'Not if it doesn't happen again. She can stay

73

here for the rest of the morning and have a nice rest, and then go back to her lessons after lunch. She's probably just overexerted herself.'

Eleanor went away, not entirely satisfied.

THE REST OF THE day was frantic. Eleanor taught every period and did a lunch duty. Then she spent a long time after her final lesson with a girl in her Lower School class who wanted to discuss some friendship issues; apparently the 'exile room' was in action again, and this girl had been ambushed in it the previous day and exiled by her friends. It was very unkind behaviour, and Eleanor went to find the three ringleaders in the Lower School common room. Two of the girls cried and promised to apologize, though the third remained defiant.

'I don't *want* to be friends with Hazel,' she said. 'I find her voice grating.'

Hazel did have a slightly annoying voice, Eleanor caught herself thinking, before she quickly suppressed the thought. She said, 'No one can force you to be friends with anyone else. But not being close friends with someone doesn't mean you have to be cruel to them. Do you understand the difference?'

'Yes,' the girl said sullenly, though Eleanor was not sure she did.

'If I hear anything more about the exile room,' she told the three girls, 'or even the faintest *whisper* of unkindness towards Hazel, you will lose your South Haven privileges and you will be in detention with me every day until the end of term. Do you understand?'

They said they did. It was one of those punishments, Eleanor reflected as she went back to her classroom, where she'd left Hazel tearfully reading a book, that would end up as much a punishment for herself as for the miscreants.

She allowed Hazel to stay with her in her classroom until supper time, and then sent her off a little happier, having extracted the promise that she would try to spend more time with Karen Michaels, who was a nice, thoughtful girl who was a little hard of hearing. Eleanor hoped the friendship would blossom.

It was not until she finally returned to her room after supper that she had a spare moment to think about Diane again. Eleanor put the kettle on, and allowed herself to sit quietly for a few moments until it boiled, a feeling of intense weariness coming over her. Briefly, she closed her eyes.

Then the kettle boiled and she roused herself again. While her tea was brewing, she fetched the stack of exercise books from her Lower Sixth geography set and rifled through them. Once she'd found Diane's book, she took it over to her armchair with her cup of tea.

The contents of the book alarmed her. Diane was usually meticulous; in fact, she'd got a B the previous year in her geography O-level, something of a triumph at St Anne's. But her notes from the past week were sloppy – odd, even. Diane's handwriting was larger and more jagged than her usual elegant cursive. There was punctuation missing, and a couple of sentences actually trailed off unfinished. The overall impression was one of extreme carelessness, but Diane was not a careless student. Dismayed, Eleanor turned to the diagram of a glacial system on the final page. It was almost unrecognizable as Diane's work. The outline was messy, most of the labels were missing, and even those that were present were in the wrong place. It looked like the drawing of a much younger child, and not one who was particularly interested in glacial systems.

Eleanor tried to reassure herself. They were only a week into term and lots of girls struggled to adjust to school again after the long summer break. They all needed a bit of time to shake down. Besides, this standard of work was not unusual for a girl at St Anne's. Plenty of them produced similarly slapdash notes. But Diane had never been slapdash, Eleanor thought. She felt she needed to do more, even if it were only to speak to Diane again tomorrow to try to get to the bottom of her unhappiness.

She was still wondering how best to proceed when Vera came in, throwing herself into the other armchair with an audible huff.

'I've just covered prep duty,' Vera said, without further greeting. 'Linda was claiming illness again. Ever noticed how her illnesses always seem to coincide with her duty nights? I dare say she'll have you doing beds for her tomorrow. That bloody English department.'

'How annoying,' Eleanor said. She debated the matter for a few moments, and then decided to confide her worries in Vera. 'I'm concerned about Diane Fulbrook,' she began.

Vera had been staring moodily at the electric fire, but now she looked up. 'Oh yes? I heard there was a to-do this morning.'

'Yes, a strange thing. She doesn't look well. And her schoolwork's suffering.'

'Oh, she probably had some kind of heartbreak over the summer,' Vera said. 'And now she's pining away, writing tear-stained letters to her beau.'

'Diane's a sensible girl,' Eleanor said. 'This isn't like her.'

'Don't be ridiculous,' Vera said. 'None of them are sensible girls.'

'And she's in disagreement with her father about her future career,' Eleanor said. 'I don't know if that's part of it.'

'Well, that seems like a waste of everyone's time,' Vera said. 'Our girls don't have careers. At best, they have jobs.'

Eleanor wondered if she herself had a job or a career. Probably a job, she concluded gloomily.

'And mostly,' Vera added, 'they don't have either for very long. They just go off and find a tedious husband and have a succession of tedious children.'

'Diane's keen to join the police,' Eleanor said. 'She says her father doesn't approve.'

'The police? Christ. She'll have a horrible time.'

'Yes, I dare say she'd meet some very unsavoury characters.'

'And that's only her colleagues,' Vera said. 'Still, I suppose if it's what she's set her heart on . . . And she wouldn't be the most alarming recruit from amongst our girls. God help us if April Stephens ever gets her hands on a truncheon.'

'Well, whether it's the career thing or not, something's clearly bothering her,' Eleanor said. 'I think I'd better give her parents a ring over the weekend.'

'I doubt they'll be very helpful,' Vera said, 'based on past experience. I can see why her father isn't happy with the police idea. Not the kind of job he would deem suitable for a girl. No, I wouldn't bother ringing her parents.'

'Well, if Diane's unhappy, I think they ought to know,' Eleanor said.

'Girls her age are supposed to be unhappy. They positively enjoy it. I dare say it'll pass.'

Eleanor didn't feel convinced. But since Vera wasn't being very helpful and they seemed to have reached the end of the road with their discussion of Diane, she decided to change the subject. 'Mr Langfield seems to be settling in all right. Although it was unfortunate that the business with Diane happened in his very first lesson. I think he was rather shaken.'

'Oh, Mr Langfield,' Vera said dismissively. 'He won't be here long. A pity, really,' she added more thoughtfully. 'My interest in him is growing. But he's not cut out for teaching.'

'He taught at Westminster,' Eleanor reminded her. 'He must be fairly competent.'

'I don't know why you'd assume the teachers at Westminster are competent,' Vera said. 'Besides,' she went on, almost as an afterthought, 'he didn't teach at Westminster.'

'What do you mean?' Eleanor wondered if she'd mixed up Westminster and Winchester again, these endless male institutions that might as well exist on the moon for all the relevance they held for her or the girls of St Anne's.

'He claimed to know my friend's husband, Rodney Trowbridge, who teaches in the maths department there.'

'Yes?'

'There is no Rodney Trowbridge,' Vera said impatiently. 'I would have thought that was obvious.'

'Vera!' Eleanor said in dismay. 'It wasn't nice to set a trap for him.'

'Wasn't nice?' Vera said. 'What on earth has niceness got to do with the price of salt? His story was totally implausible. The idea that a teacher would voluntarily come from Westminster to work here! Absurd. I concluded that there were two possible explanations: first, that he had not left Westminster of his own volition, but had been sacked; or, second, that he had never been at Westminster at all. And, you see, the second explanation proved the correct one. Which leaves one question remaining: why lie? Christie would have accepted almost anyone to work here, regardless of qualifications or experience; he needn't have embellished his credentials. Unless, of course, he's hiding something truly unacceptable, something beyond the pale even for a school like ours. I must say, Eleanor, I had low expectations when I met him, but I find myself intrigued.'

'Goodness,' Eleanor said. 'Well, there may be an innocent explanation.'

'Oh, don't be such a wet blanket, Eleanor,' Vera said. 'There will be a decidedly guilty one.'

*

ELEANOR WENT TO BED that night troubled by thoughts of Diane, and by Vera's revelation about Matthew Langfield. She had never been a good sleeper, not since she was a child, but tonight she could feel it was going to be a bad one. Lying in bed, a terrible feeling of desolation came over her. She got these moods occasionally, in the late evening or during the night. It had been worse since her mother had died. And she had dreaded her mother's death, had worried about it far in advance of it actually happening, long before her mother had even been unwell. She knew that once her mother was gone she would be entirely alone, with no one to care for her, which was a pathetic thing for a woman of her age to worry about, but there it was.

But she had friends, of course. She had Margot, the closest of her remaining school friends, perhaps because unlike the others Margot had never married, and therefore she and Eleanor were in the same boat, as it were. She and Margot went on walking holidays together sometimes; they suited each other well for the most part, although Margot could be a little overbearing at times (Eleanor sometimes wondered if this was simply a tendency she herself brought out in other people).

There were also her friends from teacher-training college, whom she had mostly kept in touch with, and there were her colleagues here. All in all, she was far less alone than many people, and she had her health; she knew she must resist this descent into self-pity. But these moods that came over her at night were unbearable. She wondered if other people ever felt such desolation. She imagined asking Vera, *Do you ever cry about how alone we all are?* The idea briefly amused her, and she felt better, but then the terror came back. And for all she knew, Vera did. Life was a dreadful business.

At times like this, she thought she got the smallest glimmer of what her father must have experienced: a darkness so terrible that he could not endure it. Perhaps this was part of her inheritance from him, along with a few hundred pounds in Premium Bonds and his old wristwatch, which still worked, and which she wore every day. And yet, she had not been a POW like him. She had not been tortured and starved. There was so little to her life. So little *of* it. The despair she felt at moments like this seemed out of all proportion to the quietness with which she lived. There was no grand drama here, no great tragedy. Just an unmarried geography teacher at a fourth-rate girls' school on the English coast.

She had been the one to clear out Miss Hamilton's room after her death, volunteering immediately in the fear that otherwise Linda and Trudy would morbidly embrace the role, despite not having been especially friendly with Miss Hamilton. It had been a sad task, placing the old jumpers and tweed skirts into bags, trying not to notice how threadbare some of Miss Hamilton's clothes had been. Piling up her books and letters. There had been no family except for a niece in Canada, so everything had gone in the end to the Salvation Army, except for the letters, which Eleanor had vacillated over, unsure whether Miss Hamilton would prefer them kept or destroyed, and which she had finally packaged up carefully and sent in a parcel to the niece.

Eleanor wondered now who might be tasked with clearing out her own possessions, when it came to it. Perhaps she would still be at St Anne's, like Miss Hamilton had been, afraid to leave the familiarity of the school, or perhaps having nowhere else to go. This was a particularly dangerous track for her thoughts to have found. At night, it was the future which terrified her the most. It seemed possible that any day now the school's precarious financial position might tip over into outright insolvency. They could not put the fees up any further because, if parents were having to pay proper fees, they might as well send their daughters to a better school. St Anne's unique position in the market essentially consisted of being cheap, of being willing to take anyone, and of not bothering parents more than was absolutely necessary. It was not a school for the modern world. The only surprise really was that it had survived for so long. And without her job here, Eleanor thought, what would become of her? This was her only home.

When she looked back on her engagement to Anthony, it seemed to her now that her primary feeling had been relief rather than love. This did not reflect well on her. So perhaps she had deserved some of what happened afterwards (she would not accept she had deserved it all).

The thing to do, she thought, was to get up and put the light on. Everything was worse in the darkness. She put on her dressing gown and went through to the sitting room, where she put the standing lamp on, got her old copy of *Persuasion* from the shelf and sat in her armchair.

She was still reading there an hour later, somewhat calmer now, when Vera appeared in the doorway, presumably on one of her night-time visits to the lavatory.

'Having a dark night of the soul?' Vera said, noticing Eleanor in the armchair.

Yes, Eleanor imagined replying. But she did not think Vera would have invited her to share the double set had she suspected Eleanor was susceptible to dark nights of the soul. So instead she managed to say lightly, 'Just having a bit of trouble sleeping.'

Vera nodded. 'What a nuisance. That casserole was very rich, wasn't it? I always find rich food before bed disturbs my sleep too.'

No, Eleanor concluded, Vera probably did not ever lie awake gripped by existential dread.

*

BY THE NEXT MORNING, the worst of the storm had passed. Eleanor felt weary, pale and wrung-out, but also saner by the light of day. She must keep herself busy, she thought, as she washed her face and got dressed. She must think less about herself. This kind of anguish was little more than self-indulgence.

It was a Saturday, and Eleanor found Diane in the Sixth Form common room after breakfast, in the middle of a game of jacks with some of her friends. The girls were absorbed, and Eleanor stood by the door for a moment, watching them. It was Diane's turn, and although she bounced the ball neatly, her movements to collect the jacks were clumsy, her hand scrabbling at the pieces but not managing to close on them in time for her to catch the ball.

Seeing her turn was over, Eleanor called her name and beckoned her over.

'How are you feeling today, Diane?'

'I'm all right,' the girl said.

'Did you sleep any better?'

'Yes, a bit,' Diane said.

She did look a little better, Eleanor thought: not quite so exhausted as the previous day, a bit more colour in her face.

'Have you got any plans for today?'

'Just my prep,' Diane said. 'It's not my weekend for South Haven. April and I are going to write our diaries together later.'

All the girls kept diaries. There was little else to do throughout the interminable weekends. Eleanor sometimes felt they ought to offer the girls a few more activities, but Miss Christie seemed resistant (most activities cost money). The best the girls got was a trip to South Haven every three weeks, in alternating groups, supervised by whichever unlucky teachers were on town duty that weekend. Although South Haven was just a small, somewhat tired little market town ten miles inland from the school, these trips always caused an unreasonable amount of excitement. The girls invariably flocked to Woolworths, where the pick 'n' mix counter caused some of them to lose their heads entirely. (On one occasion, Gloria Mulkerrins in Lower Sixth actually had to be wrestled to the floor by Vera and then dragged out sobbing after a physical altercation with another girl over some foam bananas.)

'Will you come and see me tomorrow to let me know how you are?' Eleanor said to Diane. 'I'll be in my classroom after lunch.'

'All right, miss. Thanks,' Diane said, and went back to rejoin her friends.

ELEANOR SPENT THE REST of the morning catching up on her marking and planning. On Saturday afternoons, the school minibus set off again from the school driveway, this time transporting any teachers who were not on duty into South Haven, where they could do their shopping and have a cup of tea in Betty's without the risk of being accosted by any pupils.

Eleanor had decided that a trip to town would do her good, since, if left to her own devices, she might descend once more into morbid thoughts.

As she boarded the bus with Vera at two p.m., she saw Matthew Langfield striding across the gravel to join them, and her heart sank. She felt too fragile today to want to chat to a stranger (and especially this stranger, whom she now had several qualms about). He chose a seat across the aisle from hers, and Eleanor steeled herself for small talk.

But Miss Christie herself was driving this week, and she always took on the duty with the air of an intrepid ambulance driver during the Blitz. Matthew seemed too distracted by her driving to attempt conversation.

He clutched the back of the seat in front of him, white-knuckled, as they hurtled along the narrow country lanes, jolting over potholes, veering round bends and scraping against the spiky hedgerows.

They were deposited twenty minutes later, somewhat shaken and queasy, in the municipal car park on the edge of the town. It had started to rain. South Haven seemed to possess its own microclimate of permanent drizzle.

'Meet back here at five,' Miss Christie said. 'We'll be home in plenty of time for supper.'

'If we survive the journey,' Vera said to Eleanor, putting up the hood of her mackintosh against the rain. 'Now, what will you do? I'm going to Marks and Spencer.'

'There's nothing in particular I need,' Eleanor said. 'I think I'll go to King's —' this was the second-hand bookshop on the high street — 'and then for a cup of tea in Betty's.'

'I may see you in there later, then,' Vera said.

Matthew Langfield had appeared behind them, still looking somewhat rattled from the journey. 'Perhaps you could recommend the best places to visit here, for a newcomer?' he said to them, with one of his smiles that seemed even more false to Eleanor after Vera's revelation.

'I couldn't tell you,' Vera said briskly. 'I'm going to Marks to purchase some smalls.'

He blushed deeply at this, and Eleanor took pity on him. 'There's a very nice second-hand bookshop,' she said. 'I'm going there myself. Perhaps you'd like to come?' She had been looking forward to visiting King's alone.

He agreed with an almost touching eagerness. Vera bid them goodbye and marched off on her own, even though the three of them would be walking in the same direction. Eleanor and Matthew set off towards the high street at a slower pace.

'It's a lovely little place, isn't it?' Matthew said as they passed the clock tower and the old market hall. 'Very quaint.'

'Yes, it must seem quaint after London,' Eleanor said. She already regretted inviting him to accompany her, though it would have been hard not to without seeming rude. But perhaps she should have been rude? She owed him nothing, she thought. And was he lying to them all, anyway? Was he having some kind of joke at their expense?

'I never liked London,' he said unexpectedly. 'I never felt I fitted in there.'

She glanced at him, surprised. 'Too busy and hectic? A lot of people find that, I imagine.'

'Not too busy. Too . . . I don't know.' He smiled at her, almost apologetic now. 'It's hard to decide where to put yourself, isn't it? If you don't stay in the area you grew up, where are you supposed to go? How do you decide?'

Eleanor waited a moment, supposing this question to be rhetorical. But then he added, 'Where did *you* grow up? And what made you move here?'

'I grew up near Chichester,' Eleanor said. 'So I haven't travelled that far, really. I suppose that's part of why I came here. It was close to my parents.'

'Are your parents still alive?'

'No.' A pause, then she thought to ask, 'Are yours?'

'No. There's just me and my brother, back in Norfolk.'

She nodded. They'd arrived at King's now, and Eleanor reached out to push the door open, but he stepped forward to do it for her, and then leaned across to hold it open for her while allowing her to go ahead of him. The door opened inwards, which made all this an awkward manoeuvre, and Eleanor had to squeeze herself past him to get into the shop. She was irritated with his show of gallantry. The bell above the door rang as they entered and the elderly man behind the counter glanced up, stared at them with no sign either of recognition or welcome – though Eleanor must have visited the shop hundreds of times by now – and returned to the book he was reading.

'I'm going to have a look at the fiction,' Eleanor said. She assumed, with resignation, that he would follow her, but he made a show of going over to look at the history section.

Eleanor took her time browsing the paperbacks. She found a copy of *The Woodlanders*, one of the few Hardy novels she'd never read, an old edition of Hughes's *The Hawk in the Rain*, and *The President's Child* by Fay Weldon. Pleased with her finds, she took her books over to the counter to pay. As usual, the owner took her pound coin and studied it with an air of distaste. He said, 'You do know the note is still legal tender.'

'Yes,' Eleanor said.

'You don't have to give in to them, you know. It's what they expect, but you don't have to capitulate.'

But who were 'they'? Eleanor wondered. It had never become clear from any of these exchanges. She said, 'Well, I don't really mind the coin.'

'You let them take one thing without a fight, and who knows what they'll take next,' he said. 'First they came for the shillings and I did not speak out . . .'

Eleanor murmured polite agreement as she took her change.

'They'll be after our stamps next,' he called as she walked away. 'Next thing you know, they'll be coming for the Queen herself.'

Matthew caught her eye – he was waiting by the biography shelf near the door – and minutely rolled his eyes and grinned. As if they were co-conspirators, or even friends.

'Shall we go and get a cup of tea now?' he said.

Eleanor acquiesced. She did want a cup of tea, and it seemed that if she were to have one, it must be with him. But she noted again how thin the line seemed to be for her between politeness and passivity. Perhaps it wasn't so surprising that someone as forceful as Vera found her irritating.

There were only two tea rooms in town, and since anyone associated with the school had been banned from the Tea Cosy since 1979 (unfair, given that the particular incident had involved girls, not teachers), they always went to Betty's. Eleanor didn't mind. She found Betty's comforting. It had existed as long as Eleanor had been at St Anne's, and longer; Miss Hamilton had claimed it was around before the war. It was not clear if the tablecloths had ever been washed during that time.

They each ordered a pot of tea, and Eleanor ordered a rock cake, and Matthew a fruit scone.

'How have you found your first few lessons here?' Eleanor said as they waited for their drinks.

He smiled. 'The girls aren't quite what I expected.'

'What did you expect?'

'I suppose I thought they'd be more . . . biddable. Compared to boys, I mean.'

'Ah.'

'A stupid assumption,' he said. 'I can see that now.'

Their tea and cakes arrived. Two separate teapots, which Eleanor always appreciated. She was aware the tea needed to brew longer in the pot to reach the strength she liked, but she poured herself a cup anyway, grateful for the distraction, and Matthew did the same. For a few moments they busied themselves with the ritual of stirring, passing the little milk jug between them, and taking the first sip of weak tea.

'And of course there was that poor girl who was taken ill in my first lesson,' Matthew said.

'Diane,' Eleanor said, slicing her rock cake carefully in two. 'Yes, that was unfortunate.'

'It was hard to calm the others down after she'd left.' He had taken a bite of his scone, and a large crumb had attached itself to his chin, just below his lower lip. Eleanor tried not to notice it. 'How is she now?' he asked.

'She's fine. The nurse says she'll be fine.'

'Rather a strange thing.' He took another bite of the scone, dislodging the crumb below his lip, to Eleanor's relief. 'Was it some sort of fit, do you think?'

'It was just her arm,' Eleanor said. 'And it only lasted a few moments.' But she was worrying about Diane again, remembering her pale face, her exhaustion. She said, aiming to reassure herself as much as him, 'Sometimes our bodies do strange things.' It felt odd to say the word 'bodies' to him. How ridiculous, she thought.

They sipped their tea in silence for a few moments.

Matthew said, 'Does it ever feel lonely, living all the way out here, at a school on the edge of a cliff?'

'Cloistered away from society?' she said, amused.

'I didn't mean you're sheltered. Just that it's very remote, isn't it?'

'I don't think it would suit everyone,' Eleanor said. 'But I think some people like the peace.'

'*Is* it peaceful?'

'You must have noticed it is.'

'I don't mean the location exactly,' he said. 'I mean . . . do you feel peaceful? I sometimes think if you're not a person who finds it easy to be peaceful, then you might as well be anywhere – you still won't feel any different.'

Eleanor wasn't sure whether he was talking about himself or her. She said carefully, 'I don't suppose anyone feels peaceful all the time. Do you think they do?'

He took a sip of tea. 'I've always found it troubling how impossible it is to know what goes on in anyone else's head. You have no idea what life seems like to anyone but yourself.'

'We can do our best to put ourselves in other people's shoes,' Eleanor said, disliking how prim she sounded.

'Yes, but it's still *ourselves* we're putting in their shoes. It always comes back to ourselves. So even when you're empathizing with other people, aren't you really just imagining you're them, and then empathizing with yourself?'

Was he prone to conversations like this? Eleanor wondered. She hadn't had enough sleep for it. Vera had once told her that there was something about her that attracted other people's confidences. (The observation had been delivered disapprovingly.)

'Perhaps making the attempt is enough, even if it's only partially successful,' she said.

'Perhaps,' Matthew replied. He was silent for a moment, then said, 'Though can't empathy be used for ill as well as for good?'

'What do you mean?'

He was focused on his cup now, his fingers playing with the handle. 'Well, I suppose if we can predict how other people might feel and react, can't we exploit them more effectively?'

'So, we can't ever know each other, and even if we could, we'd misuse the knowledge for our own nefarious purposes,' Eleanor said, smiling. 'You have rather a gloomy view of humanity.'

He looked up. 'Do I? Yes, I suppose I do. But not of every individual within it, I hope.' He seemed embarrassed now. 'Sorry. I don't know why I'm talking like this. Can I pour you some more tea?' He reached rather too abruptly for the teapot, knocking over the milk jug in the process. 'Oh, damn! Sorry.' He was snatching napkins, doing his best to wipe up the spill. 'Has any gone on you?'

It had, just a few splashes on her skirt, but Eleanor said, 'None at all. Please don't worry.' She helped him mop up the milk, and since he'd caused enough of a disturbance to attract attention, the waitress brought them a fresh jug.

Matthew was quiet now, and appeared crestfallen. He poured Eleanor a fresh cup of tea, with exaggerated carefulness, and then another for himself from his own pot, but didn't speak. Eleanor was starting to feel sorry for him again.

She said, 'Might you ever go back to Norfolk?'

'To live?' he said. 'No. The area I'm from, it always felt very *small* to me. Very insular. Everyone knows everyone else's business.'

'Well,' Eleanor said, 'I can see you're going to enjoy being at St Anne's.'

He laughed. 'It's different, I suppose. Different from everyone knowing every small thing that's ever happened to you, or that you've ever done, from birth up to the present day. You can arrive as a blank slate at a new school, can't you? Even if everyone knows everything about you from that point on.'

Eleanor briefly considered how it might be if she went to a new school now, became a blank slate, started again. Nobody would know about Anthony, for a start. And perhaps she could be a more interesting person, if she could only go back and begin again.

As if reading her thoughts, Matthew said, 'Did you always want to be a geography teacher?'

Eleanor smiled ruefully. 'Not exactly.'

It had been her father who suggested she become a teacher; he wanted her to have a decent job to fall back on. A gentle man, he would have made an excellent teacher himself. He had taught her Greek when she was a teenager, to complement the Latin she was learning at her grammar school. He had been endlessly patient as he guided her through Herodotus, and then Homer, his old copy of Wilding propped between them. He'd returned to his job as a solicitor by then, but he still had terrible nightmares, which she heard through the wall, though it was never discussed. It had been Eleanor who found him, the day he died. It had taken her many years to realize this was probably not what he had intended.

'I might have preferred to teach Classics,' she said now, surprising herself. 'But there wasn't a job going, and I wasn't really good enough anyway.'

He was looking at her with interest. 'I didn't know you were a classicist.'

'Oh, well, I'm not. Not really.' Maddeningly, she found she was blushing. 'I went to teacher-training college instead of university, so I haven't taken any subject very far, not even geography.'

There was a rush of cool air as the door opened again, and they both looked up, almost guiltily, to see Vera.

'Hello,' she said. 'I can see you two are having quite the tête-à-tête.'

'Do join us,' Eleanor said hurriedly, annoyed by her own embarrassment.

Vera took the remaining chair at their table and signalled briskly to the waitress.

'Did you have any luck with your shopping?' Eleanor said.

'They didn't have my size in stock,' Vera said. 'Most irritating. I expected better from Marks.'

The waitress arrived.

'A pot of tea, please,' Vera said. 'And a slice of Battenberg cake.'

The waitress blinked. 'I'm sorry, we don't have any Battenberg.'

'Battenberg,' Vera said sternly, 'is my favourite.'

'I'm sorry,' the waitress said again.

'Well, why don't you have it?' Vera said. The waitress was only in her early twenties, and Vera was treating her with the same impatience she directed at pupils who hadn't done their Latin prep.

'It's the Tea Cosy that does Battenberg,' Eleanor said, trying to soothe the situation.

'Well, I can hardly go there for it, can I?' Vera said. She turned back to the waitress. 'You ought to provide Battenberg. It isn't a difficult cake. It hardly requires atomic secrets!'

'We have a nice Victoria sponge today,' the waitress offered tremulously.

'Your Victoria sponge tends towards dryness,' Vera said.

'We have coffee and walnut, carrot cake—'

'*Carrot cake?* Is anyone in their right mind honestly going to choose *carrot cake?*'

'I've had the Victoria sponge before,' Eleanor interposed. 'It's very nice.'

'Oh, fine,' Vera said magnanimously. 'Bring me a piece of the dry Victoria sponge.' When the waitress had walked away, but was undoubtedly still in earshot, she remarked, 'This place is going to the dogs.'

'What's the Tea Cosy?' Matthew said.

'It's the other tea room,' Vera said. 'Far superior to this one. But we're all banned. A few years ago, one of the First Years set another girl on fire in there.'

'Goodness!' Matthew said.

'Yes, she set her skirt alight with a candle,' Vera said. 'And that in turn set the tablecloth on fire, and you can *imagine* how the other girls responded to that. Screaming, a stampede, tables overturned. Thankfully, our school skirts are mostly polyester, so it burned very slowly. More of a smoulder, really. Someone threw a jug of water over the girl and that was that. But the tablecloth went up like a bonfire. And the wallpaper burned too, and it made quite a mess before they could get the fire out. The place was closed for weeks, and we were all banned after that. Such a shame. Their Battenberg cake,' Vera concluded, 'was excellent.'

'They might have forgiven the fire,' Eleanor felt compelled to say out of fairness, 'but there had been one or two other incidents. The girls had a racket going on for a while where they stole sugar sachets to add to their school food, and there were a couple of instances where girls ran off without paying their bill. Oh!' she added, as she remembered. 'And there was one girl, she's left now, who would pretend – quite convincingly, I have to say – to be Habsburg royalty and insist on being served ginger-bread and strudel. So I think it was more that the fire was the final straw.'

'Who was the girl who started the fire?' Matthew said.

'Louise Adler,' Eleanor said. 'She's in Lower Sixth now.'

'She's in my one of classes,' Matthew said, seeming dismayed.

'Well, keep an eye out for sudden conflagrations,' Vera said. 'Ah!' Her cake had arrived. She took a bite and shook her head. 'Dry as a desert.'

'She sounds rather frightening,' Matthew said.

'She is,' Vera said. 'But these things happen, especially in Lower School. Last year, a girl was locked in the music practice room by her supposed friends. She was in there for almost two days before she was found, which just goes to show how conscientious our girls are about their music practice. Fortunately, she was able to drink the water from the saucers under the pot plants to keep herself going. And she'd improved her scales immeasurably by the time she was released.'

Matthew was looking horrified, and Eleanor thought it would be best to move the conversation on. She said, 'Did you always want to teach history?'

'Oh,' he said. 'Yes, I suppose so. I was always very interested in the past. The Romans and so on.'

'I think the Romans are vastly overrated,' Vera said. 'Typical men, all swagger and no finesse. I'll grant you a few exceptions. Caesar, Tacitus. Virgil, at a push.'

Matthew was smiling. 'It must be taxing, having to spend so much time teaching the writings of men you dislike.'

'Oh, I don't dislike them. They can't help their limitations. Besides, one has to teach something.'

'Eleanor was telling me earlier –' a glance at her – 'she might have preferred to be a Classics teacher.'

'Oh, not really,' Eleanor said, further embarrassed to have this half-forgotten ambition aired in front of Vera. 'That was just a silly idea I used to have.'

'Don't be coy, Eleanor,' Vera said. 'I've seen you with your Demosthenes, late at night.'

She made it sound, Eleanor thought, almost scandalous.

'I wonder how many people do end up doing exactly what they want to do,' Matthew said.

'Not very many,' Vera said briskly. 'Which I dare say is for the best.'

7

'CRADLE!' THE GAMES MISTRESS bellowed, mystifyingly, over the sound of the wind. 'CRADLE!'

Ida had yet to discover what she was supposed to be cradling, or why. She was already finding PE to be a miserable experience. The lacrosse pitch was behind the school, exposed to the full force of the wind as it whipped in over the cliffs, spattering the girls with salt spray. Sometimes it even tossed up clumps of seaweed or the occasional surprised crab from the sea below, which it deposited like votive offerings at the edge of the field.

All over the pitch, girls were running back and forth carrying the ball in their nets, or else throwing balls disconsolately between them.

'Catch!' Louise said, hurling the ball at Ida, who didn't manage to catch it, but did manage to duck just in time to stop it hitting her directly in the face.

'Poor effort,' Louise said, and Ida scowled at her. She suspected she had been paired with Louise as a punishment; the games mistress had already berated Ida during the first drill for 'not playing properly'. (How could she play properly? She hadn't the first idea what the game was supposed to involve.)

The closest pair to them were Diane and April. Diane's arm jerked from time to time, making her ball fly off in unexpected directions. It might have been funny under different circumstances, but even Louise didn't seem inclined to laugh. Ida wasn't sure why Diane was out here doing PE at all. Perhaps she'd insisted. She seemed like the sort of person who was able to get her own way.

Whenever the games mistress turned her back, Louise diverted her attention away from Ida and used her powerful throwing arm to release the ball in April's direction instead. After a few attempts, she managed to hit April on the side of the head.

April gave an angry shout and put her hand to her head. It must have hurt a lot, Ida thought. April turned in the direction the ball had come from, and began to stride towards Ida and Louise, Diane following more slowly behind her.

'It was Ida,' Louise said smoothly as April reached them. 'Sadly, her aim isn't very good.'

Ida was too shocked to deny it immediately, but April hissed, 'It was *you*, Louise. You bitch.' She turned towards the games mistress. 'Miss Webberly! MISS WEBBERLY!'

'Grass,' Louise said.

Diane was regarding her wearily. 'Louise,' she said. 'Can't you just stop?'

'Alas, no,' Louise said.

The teacher was coming over.

'Louise threw a ball at me!' April said.

The teacher looked hard at both of them. 'Did you, Louise?'

'Certainly not,' Louise said.

The teacher stared at them a moment longer, and then seemed to give up on untangling the matter. She snapped, 'Get back to your drills, all of you,' and strode off again.

Is that it? Ida thought.

Diane was resting her stick on the ground, holding it loosely by the top of the net, but now her arm jerked suddenly and the stick fell to the ground.

Louise stepped forward to pick it up for her, though whether out of kindness or in order to cause further mischief Ida never found out, because April got there more quickly, snatching the stick up and saying, 'Just go *away*, Louise. Leave us alone.'

Ida looked at Diane, who didn't speak as she took the stick back from April.

'Did you know Louise is an actual psycho?' April said to Ida. 'You should stay away from her.'

I'd love to, Ida thought.

'Louise's last room-mate,' April went on, 'had to leave the school because Louise was so vile to her. Her parents took her away because they didn't want her getting murdered by a psycho.'

Ida looked at Louise, who shrugged. 'I didn't like her. She was extremely annoying.'

'Louise won't stop at anything,' April said. 'Not even at pushing someone out of a window and breaking their arm.' The horror must have shown on Ida's face, because April added, with satisfaction, 'It's true. Ask her.'

Ida turned towards Louise again.

'Yes, it's true,' Louise said.

'Louise should have been *expelled* after that,' April said.

'Also true,' Louise said.

'Only, Miss Christie won't expel Louise, because her grandfather left money to the school.'

'It's very unfortunate,' Louise agreed. 'I'd love to be expelled, but will they do it? They will not. It's like that Sartre play. No bloody exit.'

'What happened to the other girl?' Ida said. 'The one who fell out of the window?'

'I didn't fall, I was *pushed*,' April snapped. 'And my arm took ages to heal. It *hurt*.'

'You got out of lacrosse for a whole term,' Louise said. 'You should have thanked me.'

Ida looked at Diane, who seemed to be the only person in this exchange who wasn't insane. But Diane barely seemed to be listening. Her eyes were looking beyond them, out towards the sea.

'She also once set a girl on fire,' April said.

'To be fair, that one really was an accident,' Louise said.

'Girls!' The games mistress was coming over again. 'I told you, back to your drills, *now*.'

IDA TRAILED AFTER LOUISE as they headed back towards the changing rooms after the lesson.

'Why do you hate April so much?' she said eventually.

'I don't,' Louise said. 'She hates me. Always has.'

'Is it because you're Jewish?' Ida said, hoping for an opportunity to express sympathy and perhaps win Louise over. She'd caught up with Louise now, and fell into step beside her.

'Doubt it,' Louise said. 'She has anger issues.'

'Don't you have those too?'

This seemed to amuse Louise, but she didn't reply.

'Is it true about your grandfather giving money to the school?' Ida said, pushing her luck.

'Yes,' Louise said shortly. 'And it's been a bloody disaster for me.'

She quickened her pace, putting distance between them, and this time Ida didn't try to catch up.

8

WHEN SHE REFLECTED ON it all later, Eleanor thought that if he'd been more charming she might have remained wary of him. As it was, she had grown used to that strange almost-charm he had; the essential impression was of someone trying too hard to please, without really knowing how to do so. Although it seemed possible, even likely, that he had lied about his previous employment, Eleanor couldn't hold on to much anxiety about it when the man was so clearly harmless. It was none of her business anyway, and she assumed Miss Christie had been satisfied with his references.

Vera had been making sly comments ever since their trip to South Haven about how Matthew had 'taken a shine' to Eleanor, and Eleanor had to admit, reluctantly, that this appeared to be true. Though why this might be, she couldn't imagine. No one else had ever found her a very exciting person, not even her short-lived fiancé.

'You probably remind him of his mother or something,' Vera said, dismayingly.

'I can't be more than a few years older than him, surely!' Eleanor protested.

'It's not about age,' Vera said. 'Nobody would ever mistake me for somebody's mother.' She delivered this last comment with a certain satisfaction.

But what did it mean, Eleanor wondered, to be childless and yet to be deemed maternal? She would have liked to have had children of her own, but of course it hadn't worked out that way. She had thought briefly, during her time with Anthony, that it was not too late for her after all; she had even allowed herself to imagine, from time to time, what it might be like to hold her own baby in her arms. Well, she had been very foolish.

And perhaps it was less that she herself was motherly in some indiscernible way, and more that Matthew himself seemed rather in need of a mother sometimes – a little lost, a little bewildered, and continually trying to conceal it, ineffectively. And maybe he came to her because she was patient with this pretence, and also because she didn't flirt terrifyingly with him like Trudy and Linda from the English department did.

She was spending more time than she might have chosen with Matthew recently, because he had volunteered, or perhaps had been volunteered by Miss Christie, to be in charge of the annual play, put on each year for the open day, which was to take place the week after half term. Linda had been responsible for it up to this point, but had pulled out midway through rehearsals this year, on the basis that it was pushing her to the brink of a nervous breakdown. Miss Christie had asked Eleanor to provide Matthew with whatever assistance she could, and Eleanor had always found it difficult to say no to Miss Christie.

The play Linda had chosen seemed unnecessarily complicated to Eleanor. It began as a conventional murder mystery set in a country hotel in the 1930s, but towards the end of Act One, a meta-theatrical twist revealed all the characters to be actors putting on a murder-mystery play, and what the audience had been watching up until now was in fact just a rehearsal. The 'director' of this play was then murdered, and the whole murder mystery began again, with a new police detective arriving.

It felt too ambitious a play to suit their girls, especially with the new accents and mannerisms the girls were suddenly required to adopt when the twist was revealed and they became their 'actor' characters. Rehearsals so far had been as chaotic as she would have predicted, and most of the time it wasn't clear, even to Eleanor (who was holding a copy of the script in her hands), what was supposed to be going on.

Eleanor arrived a little late to the school hall for rehearsals this evening. The girls in the play's cast were milling around on the stage without much obvious purpose. Nanda Kapoor seemed to be having a fierce argument with Martha Taylor over whom the script in Nanda's hand belonged to.

'It's got all my annotations in it,' she could hear Martha protesting.

'But it's got *my* name on the front!' Nanda said.

'That's because you wrote your name on the front of *my* script,' Martha said. 'You could just go and write your name on that chair over there, but that still wouldn't make it your chair.'

Matthew, who was standing to one side with a harried expression on his face, looked up as Eleanor arrived. His face was transformed by his smile when he saw her.

'Miss Alston!' he said, hurrying over to greet her. 'Thank goodness,' he added, more quietly, as he drew closer. 'I'm beginning to feel theatre is not my forte.'

Eleanor had noticed he was starting to behave more naturally around her; he seemed to be growing less self-conscious, less careful of himself.

Matthew's eyes fixed on something over her shoulder.

Diane had appeared in the doorway of the hall. She said, 'Sorry I'm late, miss. Sir.'

'Late for what, Diane?' Eleanor said.

Diane was not in the play's cast. She stared around the hall and then looked at Eleanor. She seemed at a loss. 'Assembly?' she said uncertainly.

Eleanor felt a chill go through her. She couldn't immediately think how to reply, but Matthew was quicker off the mark.

'This is the play rehearsal, Diane,' he said gently.

Diane blinked at him. 'The play?'

One of the other girls giggled.

'Quiet,' Matthew said sharply, and the girl stopped giggling. Eleanor could still hear some of the others whispering, though.

Matthew said, 'It's OK. It's just a miscommunication. It was probably my fault. Shall we go into the corridor to untangle it, Diane?'

He was trying to save Diane's embarrassment, Eleanor realized, but it was impossible to conceal from the others the strangeness of her behaviour.

Diane looked round the hall again, then back at Matthew and Eleanor. The heat was visibly rushing to her face. 'Sorry,' she said, and turned blindly towards the door.

'I'll go,' Eleanor said, as Matthew looked at her anxiously.

In the corridor, the door to the hall safely closed behind her, she said, 'Diane! Diane, wait a moment.'

Diane turned and came back to her. Her face was flushed, and now Eleanor saw that she had tears in her eyes. 'I think I got mixed up,' she said. 'Sorry.'

'It doesn't matter at all,' Eleanor said. 'But are you feeling all right?'

'Yes. I fell asleep after supper and then woke up again, and I think that got me in a muddle. I thought it was the morning.'

There was something off about her speech, Eleanor thought suddenly. It was barely perceptible, and perhaps not something she'd notice if she didn't know Diane well. But it seemed to Eleanor that there was a little too much space between her words, a little hesitancy, like someone speaking a foreign language in which they were proficient but not fluent.

'How are you sleeping generally?' she said.

'Not very well. I'm very tired. That's all it is. I'm very tired.'

'It's all right,' Eleanor said, though she had the feeling things were not all right. 'Let's get you back to your room, and you can rest.'

She reached out to touch Diane's arm, but Diane snatched it away and hissed, suddenly furious, 'Get off me!'

The change in her demeanour shocked Eleanor. There was a sheen of sweat across Diane's face.

Instinctively seeking to placate her, Eleanor spread her hands and took a step back. 'It's all right,' she said. 'It's all right. Can I take you to the nurse?'

Diane shook her head. She was still looking at Eleanor with distrust. She said, 'I hate the nurse. And she hates me.'

Taken aback, Eleanor said, 'Diane, that isn't true. Shall we go back to your room? Perhaps I could find April to sit with you.'

'April annoys me,' Diane said. 'I wish she'd leave me alone.' Abruptly, she began to cry, and this time when Eleanor reached for her she did not resist.

IT TOOK ELEANOR A while to get Diane settled in her room, but once she was satisfied Diane was comfortably resting, she went straight to find Miss Christie in her office.

Miss Christie listened gravely as Eleanor outlined the incident, and then leaned back in her chair, frowning. 'She sounds overtired and overwrought,' she said.

'I think it's more than that,' Eleanor said.

'Where is she now?'

'Back in her room. I hope she'll be able to get some sleep.'

Miss Christie said, 'Let's keep her off lessons tomorrow and make sure she has a proper rest. It's an intense time, at that age.'

'I think I ought to speak to her parents again,' Eleanor said.

'As you wish,' Miss Christie said. 'If they want us to take her to the GP, we'll do so. You can use the phone in here.'

Eleanor had hoped to speak to Mrs Fulbrook, but apparently it was her night for bridge, so she found herself, with trepidation, trying to convey her concerns to Diane's father instead.

Mr Fulbrook did not seem especially concerned about his daughter, instead seeming irritated with Eleanor for disturbing his evening.

'Has her arm been playing up again?' he said briskly, once Eleanor had introduced herself.

'No, not since last week, so far as I'm aware,' Eleanor said.

'And you spoke to my wife then,' he said. 'A muscle twitch. Growing pains.'

'Yes, I did speak to Mrs Fulbrook.'

He said, with an air of forced patience which Eleanor thought must be equally annoying to his wife, 'So is there some new matter you wish to discuss?'

'I'm concerned that Diane hasn't been herself recently.'

'Not herself? Well, who else has she been?'

Eleanor closed her eyes briefly. She realized at once that she disliked this man, which was inconvenient, and not the sort of strong reaction she usually experienced with parents, whom she generally classed as either 'sympathetic' or 'unsympathetic'. She said, 'She isn't sleeping well and she seems very unhappy.'

'What's she got to be unhappy about?' he said. 'She has an easy life. Is anyone giving her any trouble?'

'No,' Eleanor said.

'Then she needs to think less about herself. Life can't be enjoyable all the time. The sooner Diane learns that, the better.'

Eleanor described her encounter with Diane at the play rehearsal.

'She got her timetable confused?' he said. 'Is that it?'

'It's not like Diane to get muddled,' Eleanor said. She could hear how unconvincing all this sounded. 'And then, for a moment, she seemed . . . quite angry with me.'

'Well, I'm sorry for that, Miss Alston,' he said. 'I'm sorry if she was rude to you. That's not on.'

'No, it isn't that,' Eleanor said. 'It's just that she doesn't seem herself,' she said again, uselessly.

Mr Fulbrook said, 'Girls have these funny turns, don't they? Teenage hormones and so on.'

The call finished on this unsatisfactory note.

ELEANOR WENT TO LOOK for Diane at breakfast the next morning, and was relieved to find her lucid and calm, though she still looked very tired. April was sitting next to her with a protective, proprietorial air about her.

'Sorry about last night, miss,' Diane said. 'I think I might have been sleepwalking.'

'It's OK,' Eleanor said. She'd seen sleepwalkers before, and she knew Diane had been awake. If Diane was no better the following week, she decided, she would take her to the GP herself – whatever Mr Fulbrook had to say about it. 'We're just a bit worried about you, Diane. I'd like you to stay off lessons today and get some proper rest.'

'Oh,' Diane said heavily. 'There's no need for that. I'm all right.' She sighed and then repeated, more softly this time, 'I'm sure I'm all right.'

9

THE PREVIOUS DAY HAD been Ida's seventeenth birthday. She'd kept this information to herself, not wanting the fuss Sophie and the others might make. But now, lying on her bed before breakfast reading *Jane Eyre*, it began to seem strange that such a significant occasion had passed totally unmarked. Without quite knowing why, she called up in the direction of the trapdoor, 'You know, it was my birthday yesterday.'

There was a shuffling, and then the hatch opened and Louise's face appeared in the gap.

'Really?' she said. She sounded more interested than Ida might have expected, and Ida was briefly touched, until Louise said, 'But you didn't receive any post.'

Ida had not known Louise was monitoring her post.

'No,' she said. 'I didn't.'

Louise looked at her a few moments longer. 'Interesting,' she said.

Her head disappeared again.

Ida thought the interaction was over and returned to her book, but after a few moments, Louise's voice said from above her, 'It was my birthday on Thursday. We're almost exactly the same age.'

Ida absorbed this. 'You didn't receive any post,' she hazarded, though in fact she had no idea.

'No, I didn't,' Louise said.

'Interesting,' Ida said.

＊

BEFORE GOING TO BREAKFAST, she did stop by the post room again, but as usual there was nothing in her pigeonhole. Perhaps, she thought hopefully, Louise was stealing and destroying her post. She was briefly comforted by the idea, but had to concede that it was far more likely that her mother was simply punishing her with silence.

All in all, her second day as a seventeen-year-old was not shaping up very promisingly. Once she'd navigated the breakfast queue, she managed to bump into April with her tray.

'Shit!' Ida said. 'Sorry.'

'Look what you've done!' April said, her voice sharp. Her tea had slopped all over her tray, soaking her toast. Diane hovered beside her, but she didn't intercede on Ida's behalf. She was looking away from them, her eyes slightly glazed.

'We can swap,' Ida said. 'I've got the same as you.' She proffered her own tray humbly.

April set her ruined tray down with a bang next to some startled Second Years, took Ida's, and stalked off without another word, Diane following slowly after her.

My days are numbered, Ida thought, taking April's tray, awash with tea, over to where Sophie, Angela and Victoria were sitting.

'What was that?' Angela said.

'Banged into April,' Ida said.

'Bad luck. Why don't you go and get some more toast? That's all wet.'

'Can't be bothered to queue again,' Ida said.

'Have some of mine.' Sophie handed over half of her own slice.

Ida was moved by this.

'Don't worry about April,' Angela said. 'She's not as bad as Louise.

She was much scarier in First Year, before she became friends with Diane. It's probably making her go off the rails again, Diane going all funny. Usually Diane keeps her in check.'

'Diane *has* gone funny, hasn't she?' Sophie said. 'She forgot to do the lunch rota yesterday. It was chaos, First Years running all over the place and grabbing extra flapjacks like it was the last days of Rome. I wouldn't have voted for her as Head Girl if I'd known she'd be such a washout.'

'Ida, we were talking about Mr Langfield before you arrived,' Victoria said, with the air of someone determinedly steering the conversation back on track. 'Do *you* think he's handsome?'

'He's all right, I suppose,' Ida said.

'Well, *I* think he's very sexy,' Victoria said, and Angela said, 'Oh God, don't say "sexy", Victoria.'

As usual, the *Today* programme was coming out of the speakers in the corners of the dining room. They were currently doing a segment on the miners' strike.

'I wouldn't fancy being a miner,' Sophie said. She'd finished her cornflakes and was now drinking the remaining milk very carefully, spoonful by spoonful, after Angela had banned her from drinking straight from the bowl. 'Being covered in coal dust all the time. You'd think they'd be pleased to stop.'

'Yes, but they need to do something, Soph,' Victoria said. 'Otherwise they won't have a job.' She thought for a moment, then added, 'I bet Mr Langfield would look sexy even if he was a bit grubby.'

'Oh, stop it,' Angela said.

The *Today* programme was interrupted suddenly by the sound of the school bell, making Ida jump. It came in three shrill bursts, fell silent, then sounded again: the same three sharp bursts.

A general groan went up from around the room. Everywhere, girls were getting to their feet, abandoning their breakfast trays.

Ida said, 'What's going on?'

Sophie, Angela and Victoria were already on their feet, and Ida copied them. Everyone around them was hurrying out of the dining room.

'That's awful timing,' Angela said. 'I've got a free period first thing. Why does it never happen during lacrosse?'

'Angela, hurry up,' Sophie said, as Angela leaned over the table to take a final swig of her tea. 'I'm already on a chit for severe burns and I'll be gated if I get another.' Seeing Ida's confusion, she said, 'We have to go down to the bunkers. It's the Wroth's basement for you, but we need to go to Burnham's.'

'Don't panic,' Victoria added kindly. 'It's just a drill.'

'Do all boarding schools do this?' Ida said as they left the dining room.

'I expect so,' Sophie said.

'My brother's at Brighton College,' Angela said, 'and they don't do any drills there.'

'Well, Brighton College is going to feel pretty silly when the bomb falls,' Sophie said.

'Why does your brother get to go to a proper school when you have to come here?' Victoria said.

'Dunno,' Angela said. 'Well, he's a boy.'

'When we first started these drills,' Victoria said to Ida as they went down the steps and out into Yard, 'Miss Christie wanted to use the actual four-minute-warning sirens we'll hear just before a real attack. She got hold of a recording and broadcasted it over the school sound system. But that caused a bit too much panic, as it turned out. So now she's compromised and is using the school bell instead.'

In Yard, Ida said goodbye to the others, who ran in the direction of Burnham House. She herself joined the stream of girls making their way back to Wroth's, where they filed down a flight of stairs leading to the basement. The bell was still sounding in short bursts from a speaker positioned on the wall.

The basement was already half full, girls huddled together in small groups in the centre, and others sitting around the edges of the room with their backs to the wall. There was a stack of wooden boards leaning up against the wall by the door, along with a pile of sandbags. The room was lit by a single, dim lightbulb.

Ida hovered in the entrance for a moment, trying to get her bearings. Abruptly, the bell stopped. The unexpected silence seemed to have a sound of its own. After a moment, a hum of conversation started up again, this time in more hushed tones.

Diane and April came in behind her.

'Sixth Formers get the wall places,' April said, stopping next to Ida. 'So you can sit anywhere against the wall. Try not to spill anyone else's sodding tea on your way.'

'Thanks,' Ida said.

'It's good to have something to lean your back against,' Diane added, 'in case we're down here a while.' She looked particularly in need of a wall spot herself. Ida was struck by how unwell she looked in the dim light, her face more sallow than before and her eyes sunken and shadowed like in a skull.

'Will we be down here a while?' Ida said.

'Just until the all-clear sounds.'

'How long will that be?'

'It varies,' April said. 'Stop asking questions. Diane's not feeling well and you're draining her precious strength.'

She and Diane walked away and sat down with their backs against the wall in the corner, Diane walking stiffly, as though the movements were uncomfortable for her. Ida was pretty sure she wasn't invited to join them, so after a moment she went to sit by herself against the far wall, opposite the door.

Pupils were still filing into the basement, and now a teacher Ida didn't recognize had arrived alongside them. She looked like she was in her fifties, and was wearing a long, pleated wool skirt and a thick cardigan the colour of porridge. Louise was with her, looking mutinous.

'Get comfortable, girls,' the teacher said. 'Two minutes until the door's sealed. Louise, find yourself a seat. There's a space there, next to the new girl.'

Louise grudgingly joined Ida against the wall. 'She caught me before I could get away,' she said, by way of explanation.

'Did she wrestle you down here?' Ida said.

'Well, no. But I quite like Miss Faircross,' Louise said, surprising Ida, who had assumed Louise didn't like anyone. 'She was nice to me in Lower School. I didn't want to hurt her feelings by running off.'

Across the room, the teacher consulted her watch again and pushed the door closed.

'That's it, then,' she said. 'Time's up.'

There was a sudden, urgent knocking on the other side, and a voice said, 'Please, Miss Faircross. I'm only a few seconds late!'

'You know the rules, Martha,' the teacher said.

'I know, but I was in the toilet.'

A giggle around the room at this.

'We say *lavatory* at St Anne's, Martha,' the teacher reminded her.

'Lavatory. I came as quickly as I could,' the voice insisted. '*Please,* Miss Faircross. I don't want to get any more radiation burns. I'm already on a chit.' She sounded tearful now.

'Oh, very well,' Miss Faircross said, heaving the door open again.

A girl scurried inside. She had bad skin and wore her hair in a ponytail so high that it seemed to be erupting out of the top of her head. 'Thank you, Miss Faircross.'

'You've put the others at risk, Martha.' Miss Faircross closed the door again, and then took out a large iron key from her pocket which she used, with a somewhat ceremonial air, to lock the door. 'Please be punctual next time.'

'Yes, Miss Faircross. Thank you.'

'It'll serve you right if you're in the lavatory when the real bomb hits,' April said sharply. 'It would be a fitting end.'

'That will do, April,' Miss Faircross said. 'Martha, you can help with the barricade. Come on, monitors, as quickly as you can.'

A group of girls in the middle of the room got up and, assisted by Martha, began dragging the wooden boards and sandbags across to the door. They laid the boards against the door and then placed the sandbags in front of the boards.

'Let me get your chair, Miss Faircross,' Martha said when this task was complete, and she hurried over to the corner, returning with a camping chair which she unfolded and set down next to Miss Faircross.

'Thank you, Martha,' Miss Faircross said, and lowered herself into the chair. 'Louise, now the door is secure, you may hand out the water canteens. The new girl will help you.'

Ida followed Louise, who had got up and gone over to a large wicker hamper. Louise opened the lid. Inside were rows of military canteens, standing upright. Ida wondered how often the water inside them was changed. Louise scooped up an armful and began handing them out to the girls sitting nearby.

'Hurry up,' she said to Ida.

Ida gathered up some canteens and joined Louise in passing them out.

Miss Faircross said, 'Now, girls, which hymn shall we have as the bomb falls?'

A chorus of voices started up from around the room.

'"The Day Thou Gavest, Lord, Is Ended"!'

'"He Comes to Judge the Earth"!'

'"Mine Eyes Have Seen the Glory"!'

The hamper was empty now. Louise and Ida returned to their positions by the wall. Ida unscrewed the lid of her own canteen and took a cautious sip. The water tasted metallic and unpleasant.

The lightbulb flickered a final time and then abruptly went out. A small commotion in the darkness, and then a torch came on, the weak beam illuminating the area around Miss Faircross.

'Martha, fetch the other torches from the supply box. As she hands them out, we will sing "Abide with Me".'

In the near darkness, huddled amongst the other girls, Ida became conscious of the cold of the concrete floor and wall seeping through her clothes. All around her, voices took up the mournful tune of 'Abide with Me' as Martha stumbled about handing out torches.

'Abide with me —'

'Gosh, sorry, was that your foot?'

'Fast falls the eventide —'

'Oh, goodness, I got you a second time, didn't I?'

'The darkness deepens —'

'I thought you were a rolled-up blanket, you see.'

'Lord, with me abide.'

'Here you go. Oh, do stop shining it in my face, Farah.'

When they'd finished the last verse, there was a brief moment's silence before someone shouted, 'Now the bomb hits!'

'Boom!' someone else shouted.

Around the room, other voices joined in.

'It's flattened London!'

'There goes Liverpool!'

'Farewell, Southampton!'

'Calm down, girls.' (Miss Faircross.)

'Fallout spreads!'

'Crops fail!'

'Society collapses!'

'The nuclear winter begins!'

While these bulletins were being delivered, the sound of sobbing started up from a few places.

'There's always one or two who make a drama out of it,' Louise said to Ida under her breath.

Miss Faircross went over to one of the crying girls, who was sitting near Ida. She said kindly, 'There, there, Susan. You know, it's very unlikely that it'll ever come to this. And if it does, at least we'll be well prepared.'

'But what about my parents?' the girl wept. 'They're in London.'

'Out of all our cities, London is the best prepared for an attack,' Miss Faircross said. 'You mustn't worry, Susan. Your parents will be safe.'

Susan's crying subsided a little.

'Will we be in here much longer?' Ida said to Louise.

'No idea,' Louise said. 'I usually skip the drills. I'd rather die in the initial blast than perish in slow agony from the effects of radiation.'

Susan clearly heard this; she burst out sobbing again.

'It's the only sensible position to take,' Louise said. 'Haven't you read *When the Wind Blows*?'

'No,' Ida admitted.

Louise rolled her eyes. 'Well, you should. The images of the after-effects of radiation sickness are very arresting. Vomiting, hair falling out, gums bleeding, your skin falling off.'

(Wailing from Susan.)

'Are you in the CND, then?' Ida said.

'Of course not. Do you think anyone cares about a few kids wearing badges? Either they'll drop the bomb or they won't. Nothing I do will make any difference.'

'Don't you get in trouble for skipping the drills?' Ida said. She was both irritated and impressed by Louise's offhand way of talking about serious things.

'No. My father never does anything if Miss Christie rings him up. And they won't kick me out, whatever I do.'

Wouldn't be so sure about that, Ida thought.

'Did you just think something sinister?' Louise said.

'No.'

'You sort of narrowed your eyes.'

'No, I didn't.'

'Look,' Louise said. 'You clearly have your own bizarre reasons for wanting to stay here.' She paused.

Ida didn't say anything.

'I'm not asking you to confide in me,' Louise said.

'Good.'

'It's only that, if you're still worried about me trying to make you leave, then you needn't be.'

'Really?' Ida said, caught off guard. 'Don't you hate me anymore?'

'No, I don't hate you. I never hated you.' Louise didn't give Ida very long to feel touched by this before adding, 'I am completely indifferent to you. You're like human wallpaper to me.'

'Thank you,' Ida said.

'So let's continue as we are. I'll leave you alone, and you leave me alone.'

Before Ida could reply, the sound of the bell came again, this time emitting a single long blast.

'All right, ladies, well done,' Miss Faircross said, raising her voice to be heard above the noise of the bell. 'There's the all-clear. You can go to your morning lessons as usual.'

The monitors were already up, three of them clearing away the sandbags and boards from the door while one held up a torch to illuminate their work.

'Hurry *up*,' someone said. 'I need to get to Home Ec before Nanda steals my raisins.'

'That was an exemplary drill, girls,' Miss Faircross said, as the door reappeared and the bell fell silent. 'You are all to be congratulated. Oh dear.' She patted herself down. 'I seem to have misplaced the key.'

A groan from around the room.

'Now don't worry, it will be around here somewhere,' Miss Faircross said.

'Did you put it in your inside cardigan pocket, Miss Faircross?' Martha suggested. 'That's where you found it last time.'

'Alas, no, Martha,' Miss Faircross said. 'It isn't there this time. I believe I put it in my outer pocket, but unfortunately the moths have been at my cardigan and there are some quite substantial holes.'

All around Ida, girls were getting on to their hands and knees, holding their torches and groping about on the floor.

'We can at least be confident it won't have gone far,' Miss Faircross said.

Martha came to join Ida and Louise, who were searching their section of the room.

'Don't worry,' Martha said to Ida. 'People will notice we're missing eventually, and Miss Christie will send someone along with the master key.'

'Has this happened before, then?' Ida said.

'Oh, yes. If we get really hungry, there are tins of spam in the supply boxes. They're quite old, but apparently it doesn't really go off, as such.'

Ida did not feel especially reassured by this.

'Miss Faircross,' a girl nearby said, while the search continued, 'what's the point in us sitting our exams when we're all going to die in the nuclear holocaust anyway?'

'Well, Gloria,' Miss Faircross said, raising her voice to be heard over the sound of Susan crying again, 'I don't think a nuclear holocaust is a foregone conclusion. And you'd feel rather silly if you emerged from school with no qualifications and then there *wasn't* a nuclear holocaust after all, wouldn't you?'

'I dare say I would, Miss Faircross.'

'But most of us end up with no qualifications anyway,' Martha pointed out.

'That,' said Miss Faircross, 'is a separate matter.'

A sudden noise. It was a strange, unsettling sound, part way between a low cry and a groan. They all turned in the direction of the noise, and several torch-beams at once fell on Diane, who had dropped to the floor. April crouched beside her. Diane's body was rigid. Then her arms and legs began to jerk, rapidly and rhythmically, repeatedly bending and relaxing at their joints. Saliva dribbled from her mouth as her eyes remained wide open and unseeing.

There was a tense, horrified silence, filled only with the scuff of Diane's shoes moving against the floor.

'What's wrong with her?' April said. 'Diane?' She tried to take hold of her friend's shoulder, but Diane's body jerked violently out of her grasp and her limbs continued to thrash.

Miss Faircross hurried over and joined April on the floor beside Diane. She laid her torch on the ground, took off her cardigan and bunched it up under Diane's head to keep it from hitting the concrete floor.

'Diane, can you hear me?' she said.

In the dim, patchy light, Ida could now see froth at the corners of Diane's mouth as she kept jerking in the same eerie way.

'We need the nurse,' Miss Faircross said, and her voice sounded higher than usual, a note of panic in it that frightened Ida. 'Girls, find the key *now*.'

'I've got it!' Louise said. She was fumbling to get it out of her pocket. 'I was going to give it back in a bit.'

'Oh my God!' April said, getting quickly to her feet and facing Louise. '*You* did this! It was you! You took the key so we were all trapped, and you did something to Diane.'

'Of course I didn't,' Louise said. 'I just took the key because I thought it would be funny. It was stupid.' She had gone quickly to the door and was struggling with the lock.

The jerking of Diane's limbs slowed and then stilled. Finally, her body went limp. Miss Faircross put her hand on her cheek and said, 'Diane? Can you hear me?'

Diane didn't respond. Her eyes had been open and glassy, but now they were closed. They could hear the sound of her breathing, which was slow and deep, rasping in and out like she had a chest infection. A large wet patch bloomed on the front of her skirt.

April rounded on Louise again. 'You handed out the canteens too,' she said. 'You gave one to Diane. You could easily have put something in her drink.' She opened her mouth to say something else, but suddenly clutched her stomach and groaned. The next moment, she vomited all over the floor. The girls standing nearby leapt back to avoid the spatter.

April groaned again and sunk into a crouch. 'My head,' she said. 'It hurts.'

Miss Faircross had her arm round Diane's shoulders and raised her gently up into a sitting position. She reached out to April, but couldn't help both girls at the same time. Diane's head lolled on to Miss Faircross's shoulder.

Louise finally managed to wrench the door open. Daylight flooded into the room, and they all squinted at the sudden brightness.

Diane's eyelids flickered open slowly and she blinked, seeming to be half asleep. A trickle of blood emerged from her mouth and made its way down her chin. April had her head in her hands and was moaning quietly. Despite the open door, the smell of vomit was overpowering and the stench was making some of the other girls retch.

'Martha,' Miss Faircross said. 'Run for the nurse. As fast as you can.'

Martha was out the door and away.

'Diane, can you hear me?' Miss Faircross was saying again. This time, Diane nodded weakly. 'Do you know where you are?' Miss Faircross said.

Diane made no response to this. She had closed her eyes.

'Louise has poisoned us,' April said. She was weeping softly. There was vomit down her front.

'I haven't poisoned anyone,' Louise said, though she looked shaken.

'You put something in the water canteens.'

Ida fought a difficult internal battle and then said, somewhat belatedly, 'I was with Louise the whole time. I'd have seen if she put something in the canteens.'

Louise looked at her, apparently surprised by this show of loyalty. Ida was surprised herself.

'You're probably in on it too,' April said to Ida. 'You always seemed like a freak.'

Ida felt the heat rushing to her face.

'You're all right, Diane,' Miss Faircross was saying. 'You can rest now. But try to stay awake. And April, you try to rest too. Do you think you're going to be sick again?'

April shook her head, still staring hard at Ida and Louise.

Someone had taken off their jumper and laid it over Diane's lap to cover her accident.

'April,' someone said, 'what's your arm doing?'

April looked at her blankly for a few moments, then glanced down at her left shoulder, which seemed to be twitching of its own accord.

'Oh God, it's spreading,' somebody else said.

And now there was another scream from across the room.

'What's happening to me?' Susan's arm had risen into the air and was jerking up and down. 'I can't make it stop,' she said.

'What have you *done*?' April said to Louise with a sob.

'Nothing,' Louise said, bewildered.

April's left arm had started to jerk now: up and down, up and down.

Ida felt a strange, sympathetic tingle in her own arm, but held it still by her side.

'What have you done to us?' April said again. Around the room, a few girls had begun to cry.

'One of you,' Miss Faircross said, 'go and find Miss Christie. *Now*.'

Dear George,

It's been a while, hasn't it? Hope you are well, etc. etc., and enjoying the sights of London. Expect you are outside Buckingham Palace with your Nikon at this very moment. Needless to say, department is falling apart without you running it. Perhaps you should just come back? Would be like Richard the Lionheart returning at the end of the Crusades.

To business, George. Came across an unusual case on ward rounds this morning while covering for Lehman: 17-yr-old girl with recent history of convulsions, both myoclonic & more recently generalized tonic-clonic. Initial onset of myoclonus around 4 weeks ago. EEG showed some unusual abnormalities. I thought you might like to come & have a look at it yourself.

Lehman dead set on epilepsy diagnosis, & has got her on anticonvulsants that are controlling the seizures well. But I talked to girl again (yes, I know, George, but I was there anyway & it was interesting), & then to nurses dealing with her. She's also experiencing persistent confusion & memory loss. Nurses told me there are times when she's lucid, but when I spoke to her she couldn't count back from 100, & couldn't hold a sentence in her head for 2 minutes. Besides sporadic jerking of her limbs, she's also experiencing intermittent muscle weakness & chronic insomnia. Bloods show mild lymphocytosis, but apparently she's had a cold recently, so that's not very helpful.

What do you think? I think she needs a lumbar puncture, but will they do one? They will not. ('She's not even your sodding patient!' – Lehman, in fit of pique.) Rhys is much less amenable head of dept than you were. I think he has control issues. Possibly something to do with his mother. Also, he is broadly responsible for appointing Lehman consultant (unforgivable).

On subject of Lehman – as I pointed out, if he doesn't want other neurologists seeing his patients, he shouldn't be such a raging drunk that he can't roll out of bed for ward rounds next morning. (This didn't placate him. Continues to claim he had flu.)

Could you please pay us a visit down here, catch up with an old friend (me, not Lehman) & persuade our esteemed colleagues to do a lumbar puncture – & maybe organize a CT while we're about it?

J

P.S. By the way, apparently there are a couple of other girls suffering myoclonic seizures at patient's boarding school.

Now you're interested, aren't you?

10

'WHAT A BLOODY MESS,' Vera said. 'If we don't already have a reputation for being a madhouse, we'll quickly acquire one now.'

All the staff were vigilant now to the slightest unnatural movement in any of the pupils. Eleanor panicked every time a girl put her hand up in lessons, not immediately sure if it was a voluntary or involuntary movement, even if she'd just asked the class a direct question.

'Is her leg jerking?' she said to Vera as they crossed Yard during break, pointing to Barbara Bridges.

'No, she's always had an odd gait,' Vera said. 'But I did wonder about Jennifer Millbank in my first lesson today. Her eyelid kept twitching while she was reading out her translation, but when I spoke to her at the end of the lesson it transpired that she'd stayed up late completing the prep and then drunk four cups of coffee at breakfast to compensate. Good grief, I sometimes wonder how these girls will function when we turf them out into the real world. Any more news on Diane?'

'The consultant's diagnosed epilepsy,' Eleanor said. 'Her parents are distraught, of course.' (Her mother was distraught; her father seemed to feel more personally inconvenienced.) 'They'll be keeping her in hospital while they get the seizures under control, but I hope she can come back after half term.'

'Epilepsy?' Vera said impatiently. 'And in April and Susan too, are we meant to assume? It doesn't seem very likely.'

'Well, I've got all this second-hand,' Eleanor said. 'Nobody really seems to know what's going on.'

'If it's epilepsy, why is it spreading to the others?' Vera said. 'Are we just supposed to wait until more girls start fitting? What are these doctors about?'

Both April and Susan had been examined at the hospital, but since they were apparently in good health – apart from their unpredictably flailing arms, which seemed to Eleanor quite a significant qualification – the hospital had decided not to admit them. Instead they were being monitored as outpatients. Although April had suffered no recurrence of the headache and vomiting that had affected her during the nuclear drill, her arm was still jerking, and her parents had decided to take her home for the time being. Meanwhile, Susan's parents had opted for her to remain at school. Eleanor felt that it might be better for everyone if Susan went home too, if only because her affliction was unsettling for the others. There were various theories circulating as to the source of the girls' jerking. One was that they were simply doing it for attention, another that they had been deliberately poisoned (by Louise Adler, by the Soviets, by the kitchen staff), another that it was a mystery illness, and another that it was a demonic possession. Eleanor felt that Miss Christie ought to quash these rumours before they got out of hand, but Miss Christie seemed reluctant to address the situation head on.

'I think it's best not to feed the drama,' she told Eleanor. 'Diane's receiving the appropriate treatment, April's safely at home, and Susan's fine. You can see she is. It's only that her arm jerks a bit from time to time. It's hardly incapacitating.'

Surely it was a bit incapacitating, Eleanor thought. Susan had been drinking a cup of tea at breakfast that morning and had suddenly hurled its entire contents over her shoulder, drenching Gloria Mulkerrins in scalding liquid. They were lucky that most of it had been absorbed by Gloria's school jumper so they didn't have another girl in hospital. It did cross Eleanor's mind that the timing was interesting, given that Susan just happened to jerk her arm at the exact moment Gloria was passing behind her. But then, Susan had also brought her arm down hard on the bathroom sink, causing some nasty bruising, and it seemed unlikely that had been deliberate.

Eleanor had been to visit Diane in hospital the previous day. It had been a bleak experience. Diane was in a room by herself, looking very small and very young in her hospital bed, her eyes huge in her pale face. She had smiled vaguely when Eleanor went to sit in the chair by the bed.

'How are you feeling?' Eleanor said.

'Oh, all right,' Diane said. 'A bit better.' Then she frowned at Eleanor. 'Is it time for my medicine?'

'I don't know,' Eleanor said, thrown by this. For a horrible moment, she wondered if Diane knew who she was. She said, as steadily as she could, 'It's Miss Alston, Diane. From school.'

Diane stared at her. She said, 'I'm very tired. They won't let me sleep.' She seemed to be lost in some awful fog.

Eleanor said, 'The doctors will look after you. You'll soon be well enough to come back to school.'

Diane had closed her eyes. She said, 'That's good.' Then she said again, 'They won't let me sleep.'

Eleanor reached out tentatively and touched her hand. 'Try to rest, if you can't sleep. Your mother will be here again later.'

'My mother?'

'Yes. She's gone to get some more of your things.'

'She needs to bring my new comb,' Diane said. 'My old comb is broken. Somebody broke it.'

'I'm sure she will,' Eleanor said.

She had left not long after that, feeling more anxious than ever.

Outside the door, she was almost knocked over by a dark-haired young man dressed in a white coat over suit trousers and a very rumpled shirt.

'Sorry!' he said. 'Sorry. Always rushing. Were you visiting Diane?'

Eleanor said that she was, that she was her form teacher. 'Are you her doctor?' she added.

'One of them,' he said – slightly evasively, it seemed to Eleanor. He stuck out his hand. 'James Halliwell. Consultant neurologist.'

He seemed rather young for a consultant, Eleanor thought. Then she wondered if she'd just reached an age when everyone seemed young to her. It was a depressing idea.

Dr Halliwell looked tired, as doctors often seemed to. He also needed to shave. But he gave her a brief, lovely smile as he said, 'It was good of you to come. How did she seem to you?'

'Not herself,' Eleanor said. 'I think she—' She broke off, hesitated, then went on, 'I wondered if she was perhaps confused about who I was. Is that common with epilepsy?'

Dr Halliwell frowned at this. His nose looked like it had been broken at some point, and not set properly. 'Ye-es,' he said after a moment. 'There can be psychiatric complications. Usually immediately before or after a seizure. It's less common when the seizures are controlled. Can I ask you, Mrs . . . ?'

'Alston. Miss.'

'Miss Alston. Do you know if Diane's had any illnesses recently? Or even over the past few years? Anything that stands out?'

Eleanor thought back as carefully as she could. 'Not that I can recall,' she said. 'I mean, plenty of colds, of course. We all get them in school, especially during winter. But her parents would be able to tell you if there was anything significant.'

'Yes, of course,' he said. 'Just trying to get as much information as possible. How noticeable did her deterioration seem to you over the past few weeks?'

'Quite noticeable,' Eleanor said miserably. 'But we thought maybe she was unhappy about something else, or not getting enough sleep—'

He nodded. 'Those other two girls who are suffering from jerking of the arms – are they friends of Diane? Spend time together, and so on?'

'One of the girls is her best friend,' Eleanor said. 'But the other one isn't close. Though they're all in the same house, so I suppose in terms of physical proximity they're fairly close.'

'And I understand the three of them were together when they developed symptoms?'

'The whole of their house was together,' Eleanor said. 'They were in the basement, doing a –' she was suddenly reluctant to say 'nuclear drill' to this stranger, so at the last moment she changed to – 'fire drill.'

He frowned. 'In the basement? That doesn't seem like very good fire safety.'

'I suppose not,' Eleanor said.

'What's the ventilation like in the basement?'

'Well, it's a bit stuffy.'

'Did the girls seem distressed beforehand, or appear in any way unwell prior to the onset of symptoms?'

'I'm afraid I don't know,' Eleanor said. 'I wasn't there. But I don't believe so, no. With the exception of Diane, of course.'

Dr Halliwell paused, thoughtful. 'And did they eat or drink anything immediately before the incident?'

'Well, they'd just had breakfast,' Eleanor said. 'And then they also had water from the canteens in the basement, I think.'

'Right.' He seemed about to ask something else, but then his eyes moved to a spot somewhere beyond Eleanor's shoulder. Glancing back at her, he said quickly, 'Well, thanks very much. I'd better get on.' Then he raised his hand and called to someone behind her, 'Ah, Lehman! There you are. I must say, that's a striking tie today.'

Eleanor turned. The other man, approaching rapidly, looked disgruntled. He was fairer and more heavyset than Dr Halliwell; perhaps a few years older, too. He wore a suit, without a white coat. His tie, she couldn't help noticing, was very ugly: wide and striped orange and gold.

'This is Diane's form teacher, Miss Alston,' Dr Halliwell said as the other man reached them. 'Miss Alston, this is Dr Lehman, another consultant neurologist. I'll leave you to it. Late for Outpatients.' He gave Eleanor a final smile, turned on his heel, and walked away.

Dr Lehman glowered after Dr Halliwell for a few moments, then nodded curtly at Eleanor. 'Visiting the patient?'

'Yes,' she said.

'She'll be right as rain now we've got her on the anticonvulsants,' he said. 'It's just a question of fine-tuning the dosage.' He scowled again, and said, 'What was he asking you?'

Eleanor hoped his bedside manner with his patients was a little gentler than this. She said, 'Oh, just some questions about Diane. Past illnesses and so on.'

'Hmmm,' Dr Lehman said, still sounding annoyed. 'Well, now she's on the appropriate medication, we'll have her back with you in no time.'

Eleanor thanked him. She hoped he was right. Waiting for her bus back to South Haven, where Miss Christie would collect her, she turned up the collar of her coat against the drizzle and tried to suppress a sudden, irrational terror that Diane would never be back with them again.

*

SHE WENT TO MEET Matthew in the hall that evening for the play rehearsal and found him unpacking the last of three boxes of props he'd brought down from the attic space above the stage. Props and costumes, he had said, were vital for this production, since they would be used to demarcate the original characters from the 'actors' revealed to be playing them. Matthew seemed concerned about the paucity of their resources. The first box had been the most promising, containing an ancient, moth-holed fur wrap, a string of costume pearls, a maid's costume and a tweed waistcoat, all of which Matthew said they could use. In the second box they had found a selection of hats, including a cowboy hat, a sombrero and what seemed to be the helmet of a Nazi stormtrooper, complete with the image of the imperial eagle and swastika on the side, and which Eleanor had the unsettling feeling was not a replica. It was not yet clear how they might deploy any of these.

Studying the contents of the third box, Matthew said, 'Not much good, I'm afraid. This one mostly seems to be old school uniforms. Oh, and – goodness – what's this?'

He held out a small box to Eleanor, who took it from him gingerly and inspected it. 'Rat poison. Looks very old.' She shook it. It sounded half full. 'Not a prop, I don't think. I suppose rats have been a problem in that attic space in the past. We'd better throw it away.' She set it carefully to one side.

The girls were due to arrive for rehearsal in ten minutes, so now Eleanor and Matthew got to work sorting through the props and setting up the chairs on stage. It was not the best performance space, Eleanor thought; it was small, with a low ceiling, so while it was effective for conveying a drawing room, where much of the play was set, it also felt rather cramped as soon as three or more actors were on stage. No doubt Roedean could offer a lot better.

'Do you have any nice plans for half term?' she asked him as they moved the chairs into position.

'Me?' he said. 'Oh. Not really.'

'I wondered if you might go back to Norfolk to see family.'

'No,' he said. 'There's no one for me to visit there.'

Eleanor was almost certain he'd previously mentioned a brother. But perhaps she had been mistaken. She didn't trust him, and yet conversely there was something so guileless about him that it made her worry for him.

'So what will you do?' she said, hoping he wasn't going to stay on site for the week. She'd done that herself before, and it had been more depressing than she'd expected.

He said, 'I'm going to visit a friend in London.'

Eleanor managed to resist asking if it was a colleague from Westminster. 'That will be nice,' she said. It occurred to her that it might be a girlfriend he was visiting, and for some reason the thought embarrassed her.

'What about you?'

'A few days in Snowdonia with an old school friend,' she said. 'We're going to climb Snowdon.' She and Margot would stay in a B & B in Llanberis and ascend Snowdon on the clearest day. In previous years, they had climbed Scafell Pike together, and Ben Nevis, and Helvellyn. Both were good walkers, sensible about weather conditions and appropriate clothing. On the whole, they suited each other well, and Eleanor anticipated an enjoyable few days.

'That sounds *wonderful*,' Matthew said. He sounded disproportionately enthusiastic about it, and for an insane moment Eleanor wondered if she ought to invite him. The thought of Margot's face if Eleanor had to confess to this almost made her laugh.

'I hope it will be,' she said. 'It'll do me good. It's funny,' she added.

'I've lived near the coast for most of my life, but it's always mountains I've loved. Mountains and hills.'

'You don't love the sea as well?'

'Not really. I don't know why. I know most people do.'

'You wouldn't like Norfolk, I can tell you that. Limited supply of mountains there.'

She returned his smile. 'I dare say I wouldn't.'

'Have you ever considered leaving here?' he said. 'You could settle in the Cairngorms, or the Lake District, or somewhere like that.'

'No,' she said, shaking her head, still smiling. But he was staring at her so earnestly, so kindly, that something made her add, 'I did think about it once.'

'Ah!'

Eleanor said, not looking at him now, 'My fiancé and I were planning to move to Switzerland. I know that sounds ridiculous.'

'Not ridiculous at all,' he said. His expression had become sombre. 'I'm sorry that didn't happen.' He hesitated, and then said delicately, 'Did he—?'

'Die?' Eleanor said, to help him. She tried to keep her voice bright and careless. 'Oh no, nothing like that. He left me.' She could not confess the full, humiliating story. She had Anthony to thank, no doubt, for her ability to note the difference between a good and a bad liar. And the fact that she thought the difference mattered.

For a few moments, Matthew didn't speak, and Eleanor was in an agony of embarrassment. She couldn't look at him. And why had she felt the need to tell him this at all? She certainly didn't want his pity. It was, she thought suddenly, only that he was a stranger, and she had found it an uncomfortable experience over the past few weeks to glimpse herself, for the first time in a long while, through a stranger's eyes. In this moment, she had wanted him to know that her life might not, in other circumstances, have been so small. That she had wanted things once.

Matthew said, 'His loss.'

His gallantry touched Eleanor – though in another mood, or from somebody else, it might have irritated her. Perhaps it was that Matthew sounded as if he really meant it. She said, 'Well, it was just one of those things. It was for the best, I think.'

'I'm sure he must regret it all terribly.'

'I don't know . . .' Perhaps he did. But Eleanor was certain her own regrets were greater.

'You've been so kind to me since I came here,' Matthew said. 'And you're very kind to the girls, too. I've noticed.' He paused. 'In the café in South Haven, you said I seemed rather gloomy about human nature. Do you remember? You were right, I think. But I hope you don't believe I'm unable to recognize goodness in people, too.'

Eleanor could feel herself turning red, and couldn't think how to reply. She was looking for a way to move the conversation back into more impersonal territory when Nanda Kapoor burst in.

Eleanor's relief turned to alarm as Nanda said, '*Miss*, sir, Susan's leg's started going, now! It's on the same side as her dodgy arm. Both left, I think. Or maybe right. But anyway, the other side of her body's fine, so that's good news. Except I wonder if it means she'll be walking in circles. She's not walking at all at the moment.'

Eleanor and Matthew had moved quickly apart at Nanda's entrance, as if they'd been caught doing something illicit.

Eleanor said, 'Where is she, Nanda?'

'She's crying in the toilets.'

Matthew stayed to begin the rehearsal as the other girls started to arrive, while Eleanor went in search of Susan.

The toilets were empty except for the cubicle at the end, which was locked. A sound of sniffing came from within.

'Susan?' Eleanor called. 'Are you in there? Are you all right?'

More sniffing, and then the door was unlocked. It revealed Susan sitting on the closed toilet lid, her left leg outstretched. Before Eleanor's eyes, the leg gave a violent jerk.

'Oh, Susan,' Eleanor said.

'I don't understand what's happening to me,' Susan said. 'Why won't it stop?' She put both hands on her leg in an attempt to still it, but it jerked again. 'I swear I'm not doing it myself.'

'I know you're not,' Eleanor said.

'Some of the other girls say I am.'

'Ignore them.'

'Miss,' Susan said in despair, 'do you think I've been poisoned?'

'No,' Eleanor said firmly. 'And nor do the doctors.' Miss Christie should have done something about these rumours, she thought.

Susan began to sob, and Eleanor crouched down and put her hand on her shoulder. 'Does your leg hurt?' she asked.

'No,' Susan said. 'It just won't stop moving. I can't control it.'

'And how do you feel in yourself?'

'All right. It's just my leg. I'm scared.'

'I know.' Eleanor wondered what the best course of action was. She thought Susan's parents ought to be called immediately, and that she should be taken to hospital again without delay. Surely the doctors could do something now.

'Let's get you to the nurse,' she said.

Susan had been staring down at her leg, but now she looked up and Eleanor noticed the blood on her face.

'Susan,' she said. 'Your nose.'

'What is it?' Susan said. Then a large drop of blood plashed on to the floor.

'Your nose is bleeding,' Eleanor said, seeing Susan's panic. 'Let me get some tissues.' She grabbed a handful of toilet roll and passed it to Susan.

'My head hurts,' Susan said suddenly. 'Behind my eyes. I feel—'

And the next moment, she pitched forward against Eleanor, who caught her just in time.

Dear George,

Update for you: interestingly, one of the other 2 girls with myoclonic seizures has now developed headaches & nosebleeds, & fainted at school. Haven't been able to examine her yet – Lehman got there first. But tests are clear, & for now she's been sent home to her parents. I hope she'll start to improve there.

Rhys still unwilling to intervene over lumbar puncture for 1st patient. 'She's not your patient,' he said. 'Stop antagonizing Lehman.'

Give it another day or two & Lehman will probably try applying leeches to the poor girl. In the meantime, she's in a bad way: barely sleeps unless we sedate her, & is confused much of the time. She experiences sudden bursts of rage, which mother & form teacher say are markedly out of character. We have a nurse keeping an eye on her at all times, because she has a tendency to get up & wander, & then becomes distressed when she's unable to find her way back to her room. But muscle spasms are getting worse, & balance is deteriorating, so she may not be able to walk at all for much longer.

J

IN THE EARLY HOURS of Friday morning, the day before the half-term break was to start, the IRA tried to kill Margaret Thatcher. She survived the bomb they set off at the Grand Hotel in Brighton, but only just; her bathroom, where she'd been minutes before, was destroyed. Famously insomnolent, Thatcher was still awake at 2.54 a.m., the time of the blast, working on her speech to close the party conference later that day. The IRA had hoped not only to assassinate Thatcher herself, but also her entire cabinet, who were all staying at the hotel. The explosion killed five people, none of them members of the cabinet.

St Anne's was still digesting this news on Saturday morning, details coming via Radio 4, which played as usual over the speakers at breakfast.

'I can't believe it happened so nearby,' Victoria said to Ida, Sophie and Angela as they ate their cereal. 'Just think! It could have been us instead of the hotel.'

'Brighton's twenty miles away,' Angela pointed out. 'And I doubt it was a last-minute toss-up for the IRA between the British government and the girls of St Anne's.'

'They bomb pubs, don't they?' Victoria said insistently. 'And they bomb shops and stations and restaurants. It's not just the government and soldiers they want to kill. They kill everyone.'

'They wouldn't bomb a school,' Angela said.

Victoria appeared to have been waiting for this, and now played her trump card. 'They bombed Harrow, didn't they? So they *do* bomb schools. *Actually.*'

'Nobody died at Harrow,' Angela said. 'They weren't trying to kill anyone.'

'Oh yes, the lovely old IRA, how thoughtful of them,' Victoria snapped. 'God, why don't you just *marry them?*'

She seemed to be becoming hysterical, and Angela wisely chose not to reply.

'Victoria, Harrow is Harrow,' Sophie said gently. 'It's part of the Establishment. There's no way they'd bother bombing us. Nobody would care.'

'It's exhausting,' Victoria said. 'One minute we're worrying about the Russians, the next minute we have to worry about the IRA. Everyone's constantly trying to bomb us.'

It had been the turn of Victoria's form group two evenings before to watch *Threads*, a film about the nuclear holocaust, which Miss Christie had taped off the television so she could screen it for each form group in turn. Victoria had been in a state of barely contained terror ever since.

'And *that's* if the mystery illness doesn't get us first,' she said now. 'I bet you wish you were safely back in Scotland,' she went on, turning to Ida. 'No one will poison you there, or try to bomb you. Though I suppose Argentina might try to invade you again.'

A short silence followed.

'Victoria,' Angela said gently, 'you do know the Falklands aren't in Scotland, don't you?'

'Of course I know that,' Victoria snapped. Then, 'They're off the north coast of Scotland.'

Ida met Angela's eyes, and then Sophie's. They seemed to make a silent collective agreement to let this one go.

'Are you sad not to be going home, Ida?' Sophie said, changing the subject. As soon as breakfast was over, they'd all be going back to their rooms to collect their bags. Most girls would then assemble on the main drive to be collected by their parents, but the school minibus would also be doing shuttle runs to the village station for girls going home by train. Ida, meanwhile, would remain at school alone, loosely supervised by the handful of staff remaining on site, but more or less left to her own devices.

'It can't be helped,' she said to Sophie, not wishing to reveal how little she really minded. 'And I'll be OK. I'll go for walks, and do lots of reading. Miss Christie says she'll drop me off in South Haven one day so I can look around the shops.'

'You're going to be in the car with Miss Christie *alone*?' Victoria said. 'That's so strange. I'd die. What will you talk about?'

'You need to make serious grown-up conversation with her,' Angela said. 'Ask her how she votes.'

'Ask her if she has a boyfriend,' Sophie said, and they all giggled.

'But what if she's – ' Victoria lowered her voice to a whisper – 'a *lesbian*?'

'Well, she probably won't confide that in Ida.'

'Anyway,' Angela said, 'I'll be back a day early, and so will everyone else doing the play. Though I might be too busy with rehearsals to see you much, Ida.'

This prompted groans from the others.

'We *know*, Angie,' Sophie said. 'We know you're in the play, we know you're coming back early for your extra rehearsals, we know you're *very busy* with it all.'

'Only trouble is,' Angela went on, ignoring her, 'now Susan's gone home early, it's not clear whether she'll be able to carry on. We might need to get someone else to play the vicar.'

'Hopefully she'll come back normal again after half term,' Sophie said.

'I hope so,' Angela said. 'It's getting a bit late for anyone else to learn her lines. She doesn't have as many as me, because it's not such an important part, but there are still quite a few.'

'What part is it that you're playing again?' Ida said, though she didn't usually join in the teasing.

'I'm playing Lady Wendlesley,' Angela said earnestly. 'I get murdered during the first bit, which turns out to be the play within the play, so then I'm alive again, but acting a different part, if you see what I mean. And I have a particularly important role later on, when all is revealed, only I won't spoil it for you.'

'It all sounds a bit confusing,' Sophie said.

'Oh, no,' Angela said. 'It'll be quite clear what's happening. It's all explained when Nanda, who's the first police detective, is suddenly revealed to be a director from Texas, not a police detective at all. Nanda stops the play halfway through Act One – which is actually revealed to be just a rehearsal – and tells us it won't do, and I get up, alive again. I take off my fur wrap to show I'm not Lady Wendlesley anymore, and Nanda takes off her policeman's hat to show she's the director now, not the detective. But then shortly afterwards *he* gets murdered too, but *actually* murdered, unlike me. Only not *actually* actually murdered, because obviously it's still a play. Nobody dies,' she reassured them.

'Except maybe the audience,' Victoria said. 'Of confusion.'

'It's *not* confusing,' Angela said. 'Then Henrietta, who was playing the hotel maid at the start, but is now a French chorus girl, says, "But 'oo will 'elp uz solve zis ter-*reeble* mystery?" and that's when the real police detective enters – I mean, not actually real; he's played by Mary Maxwell – and then the real murder mystery begins.'

Ida felt exhausted just from listening to this explanation.

'The trouble is,' Angela said, 'Henrietta's line is obviously very important, because it's Mary's cue to enter as the second police detective. But Henrietta keeps forgetting to say it, so the play just sort of . . . stops. Miss Alston has been getting very cross with her in the last couple of rehearsals.'

'Can't somebody else say it, if Henrietta forgets it?' Ida suggested.

'Why would somebody else be speaking in a French accent?' Angela said.

'Well, they could say it in their normal accent.'

Angela stared at her.

'Well, anyway, we're really looking forward to it,' Sophie said loyally.

HAVING SAID GOODBYE TO the others, Ida returned to her room, where she found Louise lying on her bed listening to her pocket radio, which she was holding next to her ear like a telephone. She switched it off when Ida came in.

'You heard the latest?' she said.

'About the bombing?' Ida sat down on her own bed. 'Yeah.'

Louise waved her radio. 'I've been catching up on the details. It's a bad business,' she added, sounding like an elder statesman.

'Because Thatcher survived?' Ida said, trying to anticipate Louise's typically provocative position.

Louise looked at her. 'No.' She seemed offended. 'You know, Ida, just so we're clear, I'm not actually a big fan of the IRA.'

'But you don't like Thatcher.'

'I'd prefer her to be voted out, not murdered.'

Ida felt quite pleased to have manoeuvred Louise into being the voice of reason and restraint. She lay down with her hands behind her head.

After a moment, she said, 'But hypothetically, what if killing Thatcher saved more lives in the long run, or at least increased other people's overall happiness? And if the IRA could do it without hurting anyone else. Would you agree with it then?'

'I don't know,' Louise said. 'It's too hypothetical. But I think it's probably better not to murder people if you can avoid it.'

'OK, what about Hitler?' Ida said triumphantly. 'Would you plant a bomb to kill Hitler?'

Louise looked at her with interest. 'Prepare yourself for a shock, Ida. Hitler's actually been dead for some time.'

'I mean if you could somehow go back in time and kill Hitler, before he could start invading everywhere.'

'That's a different question,' Louise said.

'How is it different? It's still the one-life-to-save-many argument.'

Louise frowned. 'OK. Do we know, in this hypothetical scenario, of Hitler's plans?'

'Yes.'

'Well, then,' Louise said. 'Yes, I'd bomb him.'

'Even if it killed other people too? Say – ten people? A hundred?'

'Yes.'

'But how is that different from killing Thatcher?'

'Thatcher's a democratically elected leader.'

'So was Hitler.'

'All right,' Louise said. 'But Thatcher, whatever some people claim, isn't actually planning to round people up and send them to the gas chambers. So far as we know. That's the difference. Show me the blueprints for her camps. Show me the transport plans. Show me the ovens. Then I'll consider killing her.'

Ida felt chilled. Now she wished she hadn't brought up Hitler. Now there was all this darkness in the room with them, and it didn't feel hypothetical. The camps, the ovens.

'What do you think, anyway?' Louise said, when Ida didn't speak again. 'You're not very forthcoming with your own opinions.'

'It's nice that you're interested.'

'You're doing it again. You're avoiding answering.'

This accusation made Ida thoughtful. She wasn't being consciously evasive, but perhaps it came naturally to her these days. 'All right, I agree that the IRA are bad,' she said. 'I don't think we should kill Thatcher. I think it would be all right to kill Hitler. Anything else you want to know?'

'Yes,' Louise said swiftly. 'Why don't you ever mention your family?'

Ida stilled. Then she said, 'There's not much to say. You don't talk about yours either.'

'You never ask. I think you don't ask,' Louise went on, 'because you don't want me to ask any questions in return.'

'What happened to leaving each other alone?' Ida said. 'I thought I was meant to be human wallpaper.'

'You started it. You started chatting to me about whether or not I'm a terrorist.'

Ida stayed quiet, thinking. Then she said, 'What do you want to know?'

'Is there something wrong with your family?'

'No.'

'Was there a big row?'

'No.'

Louise frowned.

'Maybe I don't say much,' Ida said, 'because none of it's interesting.' She studied Louise. Then she said, suddenly noticing the customary mess on Louise's side of the room, 'Why haven't you packed?'

Louise sat up on her bed and swung her feet on to the floor. 'Packed?' she said. 'Oh, you mean for half term. I'm not going.'

'Not going?' Ida stared at her stupidly. 'What do you mean?'

'I'm not going home,' Louise said. 'Looks like we're both staying here.'

It took Ida a few moments to process this. 'Why not? And why on *earth* would you not have mentioned this before now? You say *I'm* not forthcoming!'

'I only found out last night,' Louise said. 'My father called up Miss Christie. Asked if I could stay here, at least until Wednesday or Thursday. Then I might be able to go home for a couple of days. My brothers aren't on half term until the week after, and my father's away with work this week. He wants my mother to go with him for a few days. He's going to Zurich, and they want to take in the lakes afterwards.'

'How nice for them,' Ida said cautiously.

'Yes, it will be.'

There was a silence. Ida was trying to form a sufficiently neutral question about how Louise felt about all this, but before she could come up with anything, Louise said, 'So anyway, I thought we could do a walk along the coast tomorrow, if you fancy it. I asked Miss Christie already and she says that's fine, so long as we're back before dark. I've got Wagon Wheels and crisps to keep us going. And there's a pub along the coast where we can get a shandy.'

Ida felt she could get whiplash from Louise's mood changes.

THEY WALKED OUT ACROSS the cliffs the next morning. It was a beautiful day: bright and clear, the sea brilliant under a low autumn sun. The coastal path was narrow so they walked in single file, the sea far below to their right, beyond the grassy cliff-face, and fields stretching away to their left, demarcated from the path by a low stone wall and clumps of gorse.

Louise seemed unusually cheerful. 'Such a relief to be away from school, isn't it?' she said over her shoulder.

Ida agreed. The views were beautiful, and they were free – for the whole day, too. 'It was nice of Miss Christie to give us permission,' she said.

'Miss Christie? Oh, she—' Louise said. She didn't turn back to say this, so some of her words were lost to the wind.

'What?' Ida said.

'I said, she didn't technically give us permission,' Louise repeated.

'*What?*'

'I said, *she didn't technically give us—*'

'I heard you!' Ida said.

'Then why did you keep saying "what"?'

'Are you trying to get us in trouble?'

'Take a chill pill,' Louise said, infuriatingly. 'No one's going to be checking up on us. They won't even notice we're gone.'

This alarmed Ida. She realized suddenly that she was alone with Louise, high up on the cliffs, and nobody knew where they were. If Louise could push April out of a window and pass it off as an accident, then what was to stop her pushing Ida off a cliff and claiming she'd slipped? Ida felt her heart rate accelerate.

'Look,' Louise was saying, 'wouldn't you rather get out for a bit? It's not healthy being shut up in those weird old crumbling buildings all the time.'

'We are allowed to go on walks around the grounds,' Ida said, still trying to calm herself.

'Yes, I know that,' Louise said. 'You can be very literal-minded sometimes.'

They paused at a fork in the path where the cliff dropped away and a sandy bay stretched out far below them.

'Left or right?' Louise said. 'They come out in more or less the same place eventually.'

'Left,' Ida said, since that fork curved away from the cliff edge and therefore seemed safer.

They took the left fork, falling back into single file.

'Don't you ever feel like you're suffocating in that place?' Louise said.

'No.' The buildings were much too draughty for anyone to suffocate. 'Have you always hated school?' It was easier, Ida found, to speak to Louise's back.

'Yes,' Louise said.

'Even when you first arrived?'

'Perhaps not quite so much during the first year. But the disillusionment soon set in.'

The path widened out again. Louise slowed a little, and Ida fell into step beside her.

'Maybe if you tried being nicer to people . . .' Ida began.

Louise gave her a scornful look, and Ida worried again that she might be about to get pushed off a cliff.

'I'm a lot better than most people,' Louise said. 'At least I'm not a hypocrite. My grandmother once told me, "Never say anything about someone that you wouldn't say to their face." And I've stuck to that.'

'I think that advice is telling you not to be horrible behind people's backs,' Ida said. 'Not telling you to be horrible to their faces.'

Unexpectedly, Louise laughed. 'All right. Well, I'm not horrible to you, am I?'

'You are a bit.'

'Am I?' Louise seemed genuinely taken aback by this.

'Well, less so than when I first arrived,' Ida conceded.

'There you go, then.'

THEY REACHED THE PUB at lunchtime, both of them hot and out of breath. Ida went to sit at a small table in the corner while Louise, who looked the older of the two, went to the bar to get their drinks. The pub was empty except for a man and woman at a table in the middle, their heads close together, and a couple of men drinking pints at the bar.

Louise returned with their shandies. 'Delicious and cheap,' she said, setting them down.

Ida wasn't used to drinking much at all. She'd never been invited out to any of the pubs in Oban with the kids from school due to her mother making them social exiles.

Louise drank her shandy in fast gulps. Ida was thirsty from the walk, but tried to go more slowly.

Neither of them spoke. It was more difficult to think of things to say now they were facing each other across a pub table. Louise didn't seem bothered by the silence, but Ida began to feel awkward.

Eventually, she said, 'Who's your favourite teacher?'

Louise snorted. 'What kind of question is that?'

'Just making conversation,' Ida said.

'Well, I don't have one. The English department are all lunatics, the maths department are innumerate. Mr Langfield's a human dishcloth. Miss Clarke in Classics is OK, I suppose. At least she doesn't pretend to be nice.'

'Right up your street, then,' Ida said.

'Do you want me to ask you who your favourite is?'

'No, it's all right.'

There was another silence.

Louise finished the last swig of her drink. She said offhandedly, 'Why are you so determined to stay at this awful school?'

'Why are you so determined to leave it?' Ida countered.

'Because it's a living death.' When Ida didn't reply, Louise added, 'Has it ever occurred to you that someone could look at our lives and have no idea what decade it is? What century it is, even? Everything important happens elsewhere. None of us get a proper education, because they expect us just to go off and get married, as though we're still in Victorian times. But there are other schools out there, normal schools, where we could actually learn things. Why can't I be at one of them?'

The shandy seemed to have loosened Louise's tongue, Ida thought. She felt a bit woozy herself. 'Do your parents know how much you want to leave?' She had almost said, *Do they know how unhappy you are?* But even with the lager in her bloodstream, she couldn't quite say those words to Louise.

'Of course they do,' Louise said. 'Back in Lower School, I begged them to take me away. *Begged* them. But my father has decided views on women's education. As in, he views it as an irrelevance.'

'What about your mother?'

Louise looked away. 'My mother is . . . She hasn't had an easy life.'

Ida waited, but Louise didn't seem inclined to expand on this.

'Can't they just let you go to a local school?' she said. 'It would be free.'

'They want me at boarding school, out of the way. They travel a lot. And my mother needs . . . She struggles sometimes. I've tried suggesting other boarding schools, better ones, but my father won't have it. So my only hope is to get kicked out. Trouble is, my grandfather gave all this bloody money to the school, and even though that's all gone now, it appears to have made it impossible for me to get expelled. Miss Christie seems to feel honour-bound to keep me.' She sipped her drink moodily. 'I'd blow the whole place sky high if I could.'

'You don't mean that,' Ida said. 'You wouldn't even blow up Thatcher yesterday.'

'It's a figure of speech,' Louise said. 'You and your painfully literal mind.'

Ida was about to say something else, but just then she caught the words 'St Anne's' from the man at the table in the middle of the room. He wasn't speaking loudly, but now Ida was paying careful attention, she could make out a little of what he was saying.

'What's—?' Louise began to say, noticing Ida's attention had shifted, but Ida shook her head and moved her eyes in the direction of the couple, and for once Louise fell silent.

She heard 'twitching' and 'girls', and felt pretty confident she knew what the man was talking about. She glanced discreetly at him, but didn't recognize him; as far as she knew, he had nothing to do with the school. He looked around forty, and a bit seedy, with stubble on his face. Probably just the sort of man Louise would go for, Ida thought, if he were a bit younger. The woman he was with looked considerably younger. Ida strained to hear more.

The man seemed to be giving instructions to the woman: something, Ida thought, about 'ringing up'.

She could see Louise was listening too. Their eyes met, and Louise slightly raised an eyebrow, as if to say, *Interesting*.

'Parent?' Ida mouthed at Louise when the man and woman paused and were each taking a drink.

'Journalist,' Louise mouthed back. 'You idiot.'

Then she turned on her stool towards the couple at the table and raised her voice as she said, 'Did you say St Anne's? That's our school.'

'Louise!' Ida hissed.

Louise had his attention now. 'Is that right?' he said. 'You mean the school nearby, on the cliff?'

'The very same.'

He smiled. 'Can I get you girls another drink?' he said.

'Campari and orange, please,' Louise said promptly. She glanced at Ida. 'Make that two.'

While the man was at the bar, Ida said to Louise, 'What on earth are you doing?'

'Getting a free drink,' Louise said.

When the man returned with their drinks, he also pulled the stool over from his table and gestured for the woman to join them.

'This is Jenny,' he said, 'and I'm Anthony. Very nice to make your acquaintance.'

He was even seedier close up, Ida thought, though he was handsome in a slightly florid way. There were burst capillaries visible on his nose and cheeks, but his eyes were an arresting dark blue, and clear and sharp.

'Our pleasure,' Louise said, taking a sip of her Campari and orange and giving Ida a seraphic smile that she immediately distrusted.

'And what brings you young ladies out here on a day like this?'

'We just fancied a walk,' Louise said.

'You walked from your school, then? It's quite a way.'

'We're young and fit,' Louise said.

'And healthy, I can see. I hear that isn't the case for some of the other girls at your school.'

Louise nodded.

'Terrible business,' he said. 'How many girls are ill now?'

'About twenty,' Louise said.

'Twenty?' He seemed taken aback by this. 'So many?'

Ida was staring at Louise, but Louise refused to notice. 'Yes. We're dropping like flies.'

'When did the first symptoms start?'

'The second week of term. The first girl collapsed and she's in hospital now.'

'I heard. How's she doing?'

'You'd have to ask her doctors.'

'Of course. And what were the first symptoms?'

'Well,' Louise said, 'she began to bark like a dog.'

His eyes widened.

'Yes, I know, it was very startling,' Louise said. 'Especially when more and more girls started joining in.'

'They were . . . barking?'

'That's right.'

'I heard the girls developed twitches at first,' he said. 'Can you confirm that?'

'No, not twitching,' Louise said. 'Barking.'

'And so many of them?'

'Yes, it feels like we live in a huge kennel now. And we thought that was bad, but then they began bleeding from their eyes. Imagine! All those barking girls with bleeding eyes.'

'She's having you on, Anthony,' the woman said, rolling her eyes.

His expression changed. 'Oh, for fuck's sake. You silly kid.'

Louise grinned at him. 'It would make a good story, though. Apparently there was once a convent in France where all the nuns started miaowing like cats. I thought you could come up with something similar.'

'Do you have any information for me that might *actually* be useful?' he said in irritation.

'Not really,' Louise said, with evident regret.

'No one's twitching?'

'One or two girls are twitching, actually,' Louise said. 'I don't think there's much of a story for you there, but who knows?' She was thoughtful for a moment. 'We've got the open day next Saturday, so you could come along and have a look for yourself.'

The man nodded curtly. 'All right. Thanks. Come on, Jenny,' he said, gathering up his coat. 'We'll get a bite to eat elsewhere.' He called to the barman, 'Oi! These girls are underage. You're breaking the law by having them in here.'

Obviously still annoyed about the barking thing, Ida thought.

Louise quickly finished the rest of her drink. 'I suppose we'd better go, too,' she said to Ida, once the door had closed behind the man and woman. 'I don't think we'll get served again.' The barman was watching them with a stony expression. 'Drink up.'

Ida gulped down as much of her Campari as she could – it was too bitter for her – and then stood up to follow Louise out.

'You shouldn't have mentioned the open day,' she said as they set off back to school. 'What if he actually does turn up?'

'Well, good,' Louise said. 'Maybe he'll write a lurid story about the twitching girls and get the school closed down. Still, probably a bit much to hope for. I'll have to think of something else.'

'Something else?' Ida said in alarm, but Louise didn't answer. Her amusement seemed to have faded, and she remained in a glum silence for the rest of the walk back.

THAT EVENING, IDA RANG home. She did not look forward to these Sunday phone calls; her mother alternated between outright hostility and self-pity, and Ida always came off the phone feeling awful. It would be even worse today, because her mother would go on again about her choosing not to come home for half term (as though it would have been possible, even if Ida had wanted it!). Still, the phone call was a duty, and dutifully Ida called.

Unexpectedly, it was Charlotte who answered. The conversation seemed to go wrong almost immediately.

'I didn't think you'd be at home,' Ida said, surprised. 'Isn't your half term next week?'

'Fuck off,' Charlotte said. 'I'm taking a few days off. What are you going to do, dob me in?'

'No, of course not.' A pause, as Ida wondered how to get back on the right foot. 'How are you?' she tried, deeming this question suitably neutral.

But Charlotte didn't operate in neutral. 'What do you care?' she said.

'Of course I care——' Ida began.

'Running off to England? Very caring.'

'I'm sorry,' Ida said.

'So how is it, then?' Charlotte said. 'Have they realized you're a freak yet?'

'It's all right,' Ida said. She looked for something to offer Charlotte, and then brightened as she remembered what April had said to her in the basement. 'One girl did call me a freak, actually.'

'Oh yeah? Why?'

'A misunderstanding,' Ida said.

'What's her name?'

'April Stephens. She just took against me. I didn't do anything to her.'

'This April Stephens must dislike your personality,' Charlotte said, sounding slightly mollified. 'Or your appearance.'

'She isn't very nice,' Ida said. She reminds me a bit of you, she almost added. But then she felt guilty, because April was ill, and because Charlotte had been left on her own.

'Well,' Charlotte said after a moment, 'it's probably for the best you're not here, anyway.'

'Why? Is Mum OK?'

'Oh, yeah. In fact, she's doing much better. She's told them all it was your idea, you see. She found out what you'd been telling people and then had to go along with it to protect you. You know, to stop people thinking you're insane.'

Ida felt a plunge of horror. 'You're lying,' she said.

'No. And come to think of it, maybe that was the truth all along. I can hardly remember now how it started. Was it you?'

'You know it wasn't.'

'You've always been a liar.'

'Put Mum on the phone,' Ida said.

'Can't,' Charlotte said. 'She's on the mainland. Staying overnight, too.'

'Why?'

'Peter,' Charlotte said laconically.

'*Peter?*'

'They've made up.'

'How did he find her?'

'I think she found him.'

'I'm sorry, Charlotte.'

'No, you're not. You're just glad to be away.'

This was true.

'But you'll have to come back eventually,' Charlotte added. 'Or are you hoping to spend the Christmas holidays with one of your new rich friends?'

'They're not rich,' Ida said. She wondered if she could really do this;

could she go home with Louise to meet her distant father and troubled mother? Perhaps Sophie would be a better bet. 'I'll be back at Christmas,' she said. Maybe Angela or Victoria could have her.

'Looking forward to it,' Charlotte said unpleasantly.

WHEN IDA RETURNED TO her room, Louise looked up from her book and said, 'Everything OK?' The novel she was reading was *Crash* by J. G. Ballard, and its cover illustration was distracting: the mangled remains of a car, with a naked woman lying in the foreground, apparently unconscious and with her legs spread.

'Yes,' Ida said. She went and sat down on her bed. Since their return, she'd been brooding on what Louise had said. 'Were you joking earlier, about trying to get the school closed?'

'Why?'

'Just wondered.'

Louise returned to her book. 'No, I wasn't joking.'

'You won't try anything at the open day, will you?' Ida said anxiously.

Louise raised her eyes briefly from the page again. 'Be careful, Ida. You're giving me ideas.'

'If the open day goes badly, there might not be enough fee payers for next year,' Ida said.

This amused Louise. 'Have you been appointed the new bursar? I dare say they'll be glad of the help.'

'I'm just saying,' Ida said. 'Some of us do actually want to be here.'

She felt Louise's eyes on her again.

'Why?' Louise said. 'This is an awful school. You know it is. Why are you so desperate for it to stay open?'

'I just really enjoy the sea air,' Ida said.

'You're from the Hebrides.'

'It has a different quality here.'

'Jesus Christ,' Louise said, more to herself than to Ida. 'Why do you have to be so strange?'

Dear George,

Thank you for your call to Rhys. Whatever you said, it certainly annoyed him. But it seems he's now pressured Lehman into getting lumbar puncture done for original patient. Lehman furious, naturally.

LP showed normal pressure & raised IgG. This isn't epilepsy, but we knew that already. Unfortunately, can't enjoy Lehman's exasperation fully because we still don't know cause of the encephalopathy. Out of curiosity, asked girl's parents & headmistress if they were aware of any recent animal bites, or if there are any bats at school. (Lehman: 'It's not *rabies*, you bloody idiot.') Have tested for herpes & varicella. Could it be CJD? But that would be so unlikely in a patient this young.

After some further lengthy negotiations with Rhys & Lehman, we've agreed to start the girl on an antiviral. Trying acyclovir first, though she hasn't responded so far. ('I told you so.' – Lehman). She's already on clobazam for seizures & myoclonus. Mother stays by bedside the whole time, & father makes occasional visit. He has some minor government role; clearly thinks Lehman & I are imbeciles. (Admittedly, he is 50% correct).

Rhys now wringing his hands over CT scan, which he's still reluctant to sign off on. Says we can't justify exposing a young girl to so much radiation without good evidence it will change her clinical management.

Also, apparently Radiology already annoyed with us.

I was curious about this & asked what he'd done to upset them.

He glared at me. Said something about my memory being very poor when it came to facts that are inconvenient to me. Then something else about my 'X-ray spree' over the summer.

What do you suggest I do next, George? To be completely frank, I'm worried she'll die.

J

'AND APPARENTLY,' VICTORIA SAID, 'Susan was supposed to come back yesterday, but she collapsed and started *foaming at the mouth*.'

'Has anybody seen her?' Ida said. 'Who told you?'

'Gloria Mulkerrins.'

'Well, she's hardly very reliable,' Sophie said. 'Last year she said she'd seen a visitation of the Holy Virgin.'

'Definitely wasn't Susan that time, then,' Angela said with a snort.

They were at breakfast, their first morning back after half term. The weather had turned and suddenly there was a chill in the air, which the draughty school buildings offered little protection against. Victoria, who seemed to particularly feel the cold, was wearing three school jumpers on top of each other, and had already been reprimanded by Miss Christie for wearing her scarf and hat at breakfast.

'What will happen to Susan's part in the play?' Sophie said.

'Martha Taylor's going to do it instead,' Angela said, 'only she can't learn all the lines in time, so Mr Langfield's had this brilliant idea that she'll carry a Bible with her, since she'll be playing a vicar, and she'll have her lines stuck in it. Isn't that clever of him? And Miss Alston will sit by the stage with the prompt book, too. So hopefully it'll be all right.'

'April's back, though,' Victoria said. 'So if you'd prefer someone with a twitching arm to play the vicar, you could ask her.'

'We don't *specifically* want someone with a twitching arm,' Angela said.

'Oh, well. Her arm's definitely still going if you change your mind,' Victoria said. 'We heard she got better once she was away from school, but I saw her last night at supper, and her arm was jerking away like anything.'

'Louise Adler is doing the sound effects, too,' Angela said. 'That's the other thing we're all worried about, because she keeps doing them at the wrong time and it's very startling. We think it's deliberate.'

'Louise is doing the sound effects?' Ida said in surprise. Louise had never mentioned it.

'Oh yes,' Angela said. 'She was dead keen, so Mr Langfield said yes. But everyone else thinks it's a very bad idea.'

'Can't you just manage without her?' Sophie said. 'How many sound effects can you possibly need? It all takes place in a hotel.'

'Oh no, the sound effects are really important,' Angela said. 'For the *atmosphere*. Louise has got a "crash box" that Mr Langfield made her. That's a theatre term. It means a big wooden box full of broken crockery, which she has to shake when Henrietta sees my dead body and drops the tea tray. And she's got another box with lentils in it for the sound of the rain at the start of Act One, which is what keeps everyone inside the hotel. And she's got two bits of wood she's got to bash together for a gunshot. That's for when Nanda dies, not me. I get stabbed, so there's no sound effect there, except for my scream. Louise will be doing them from the attic space above the stage, and we all think she'll find a way to ruin things.'

'Maybe she'll pour pigs' blood all over you through the trapdoor, like in *Carrie*,' Victoria said excitedly.

Angela paled. 'You don't really think——?'

'Of course not, Angie,' Sophie said. 'Where would she get pigs' blood from anyway?'

'She could use red paint,' Victoria said.

'Oh, come on,' Sophie said. 'She won't do that.'

'Even if she just poured a load of water over you all,' Victoria said, 'that would be enough to ruin the play, wouldn't it? Unless you all pretended the hotel was meant to have a leaking roof.'

'God,' Angela said. 'Why did Mr Langfield let her get involved?'

Ida had been listening to this discussion with increasing anxiety. Although she thought pigs' blood was unlikely, it seemed to her that the play would be the perfect opportunity for Louise to try something disruptive at the open day. There wasn't exactly a dearth of evidence when it came to Louise's violence and impulsivity.

'You can do loads of scary stuff from the attic space,' Victoria said. 'Remember when Miss Fox took us to that production of *Macbeth* in Eastbourne? Where Banquo's body fell down from the ceiling on a rope and just *hung there* for the rest of the play? It was horrible.'

'Yes, we were very worried about the poor actor,' Sophie said.

'But then eventually we realized it was a dummy, not the actor himself,' Victoria reassured Ida. 'Because the actor appeared as a ghost in the feast scene.'

'And Miss Fox was really cross with us because we'd got so worried about the poor man, before we realized it was a dummy,' Sophie said. 'She said we were disrupting the play.'

'But she was already in a bad mood,' Victoria said. 'Because we'd got confused earlier on when Macbeth kept going on about seeing a dagger, only none of us could see it. So we were just asking where it was.'

'She said she was never taking us to the theatre ever again,' Sophie said.

'And she never has,' Victoria said. 'Gosh, I hope Louise doesn't hang a dummy from the ceiling.'

'Where would she get one from?' Angela said, though she looked worried.

'You're right,' Victoria said. 'It would be easier for her to use pigs' blood, wouldn't it?' and Angela looked more panicked still.

Of course, Ida thought, if Louise really wanted to make Miss Christie angry enough to expel her, ruining the open day would be a good bet. Or ensuring the open day went so badly that they wouldn't get enough new pupils for the following year, meaning the school would have to close. She said nothing to her friends, but resolved to complete her own discreet investigations.

WHEN LOUISE WENT TO have her shower the following morning, Ida completed a quick search of her things.

She found nothing of note in Louise's drawers – just clothes, a few toiletries and Louise's collection of alarming novels. Under Louise's bed, she found more books and a long-handled broom.

She turned her attention to the attic space. She managed to pull the trapdoor open by standing on her tiptoes on her bed to reach the handle, just as she had done on her first evening, and then she hauled herself up the flimsy rope ladder that came down from the opening.

Being up here in this cramped space felt like a far greater intrusion than going through Louise's drawers. Still, there wasn't much to see. There was a small blanket and a cushion – so presumably Louise liked to be comfortable while avoiding Ida – a torch and two more books (*The Shining* by Stephen King and, more surprisingly, *Anna Karenina*).

Then, as a final check before manoeuvring herself down through the trapdoor again, she switched on the torch and shone it around the small space. In one of the shadowed corners, something caught her eye. A carrier bag. Ida crawled over to it. Inside, she found another book, a small carton of baking soda, a bottle of vinegar and a packet of Epsom salts.

The book was a paperback with a black cover bearing the puzzling title of *The Anarchist Cookbook*. Ida opened it. It took a few moments to understand what she was seeing. Then she heard herself actually gasp aloud.

She seemed to be holding in her hands a manual for bomb-making. The words *Molotov cocktail* leapt out at her from the contents page, beneath the heading *Chapter Four: EXPLOSIVES AND BOOBY TRAPS*. Also listed in this section were *Homemade hand grenade*, *Time delay devices* and *How to make nitroglycerin*.

Ida flicked through the book in horrified fascination. Its instructions seemed detailed and clear, and were often accompanied by simple diagrams. The Epsom salts, baking soda and vinegar worried her, since many of the explosives in the book seemed to be made from household items.

Then she remembered that Louise would be back any moment, and might not be best pleased to discover Ida looking at her secret bomb manual. In a panic, she closed the book and stuffed it back into the bag, which she replaced where she had found it. She swept the torch round the attic space a final time to check for anything she'd missed, then turned it off and laid it back on the floor, before lowering herself carefully through the trapdoor.

When Louise returned to the room, wet-haired and wearing her dressing gown, Ida was sitting innocently on her bed, flicking through her history textbook. She had managed to close the trapdoor (with the help of the long-handled broom from under Louise's bed, which she assumed was its purpose), and was confident she'd left no signs that any kind of search had been conducted. Still, she felt Louise looking at her hard.

'What?' Ida said.

Louise frowned. 'Nothing.' She began to towel her hair vigorously. 'Are you ogling pictures of your boyfriend Martin Luther again? You know he was a nutter and an anti-Semite?'

'Just doing the prep reading,' Ida said.

'What was it?'

'Pages seventy-two to seventy-nine, on the Council of Trent.'

'How tedious.'

Louise began to get dressed, and Ida pretended to go back to her reading. Her thoughts were moving fast, although to little purpose. She knew she ought to make a plan, but she had no idea what this plan should be. How did people just come up with plans? Was the plan supposed to arrive in her head fully formed?

She should alert the authorities, she thought. Who were the authorities? The police? Miss Christie? But what then? Ida suspected that the possession of a dodgy book and some bath salts might not be enough to get Louise expelled, if actually pushing another girl out of a window hadn't done it. So reporting it now would probably only succeed in inflaming Louise against her, just when it seemed they'd reached an understanding. On the other hand, if Ida allowed Louise to go through with whatever it was she was planning, perhaps Louise really would get expelled. Then at least Ida would be safe from her, if Louise was still a threat. But conversely, if Louise's actions were severe enough to finally get her expelled, they might also be severe enough to get the school closed. It was quite the conundrum. Ida didn't feel equal to working through all the different eventualities. She suspected that Louise, with her quick mind, would be best placed to advise, but unfortunately she couldn't ask Louise what she thought.

The thing to do, Ida decided eventually, was to watch Louise very carefully from this point on. She wasn't sure if this was an actual plan, or simply a way of postponing having to make a plan.

'I think I'll skip breakfast today,' she said to Louise, who often skipped breakfast herself. 'Stay here instead.'

'Why?' Louise said.

'I don't feel well,' Ida said vaguely.

Louise looked at her. 'You're not going to start twitching, are you?'

'I don't think so.'

'Good,' Louise said. 'Because I think I'd find that very irritating in a confined space.'

13

J UST A FEW DAYS until the open day, and Eleanor watched the
preparations unfold with even more anxiety than usual.

Miss Christie had insisted that every classroom have fresh displays
on its walls, ideally placed in such a way as to obscure the places where
the paint was peeling off, and so Eleanor had used her lesson time to get
the girls to produce hand-drawn maps of Europe for this purpose. The
results so far had been dispiriting, sometimes inaccurate to the point of
fantasy (especially Mary Hughes's effort, in which Germany seemed to
be sharing a border with both Russia and Wales).

All over the school, similar display work was being extracted from
pupils, and classrooms were being cleaned and rearranged. The part-time
groundsman was mowing the lawns and trying to shore up any parts
of the buildings that were most obviously about to fall off. There was
a hole in the wall of Galbraith, which hadn't bothered anyone unduly
up until now, but Miss Christie had directed that it be covered with a
roll of wallpaper for the open day. Similarly, all the buckets that were
usually placed along the corridor in Nightingale's to catch drips would
be hidden in a cupboard for the day (they would simply have to hope
it did not rain). The broken window at the front of School had been
boarded up, and then the plywood had been painted and labelled as a
Lower School art project.

This year, the tension around the open day was even greater than usual. Diane was still in hospital, and by all accounts not showing any signs of improvement. Susan was at home, apparently no longer experiencing nosebleeds, but with her arm and leg still jerking. April had returned to school after half term, the twitching of her arm lessened, but not gone completely. More worryingly still, another girl, this one in Lower School, had now developed a jerking arm too. So that made four sick girls — one in hospital, one at home and two at school. What on earth was happening? Eleanor thought.

In the circumstances, she wondered if they ought to postpone, or even cancel, the open day. But Miss Christie was impatient when Eleanor raised this with her.

'Postpone it? On what grounds? Only a few girls are unwell, and they're all receiving appropriate treatment. We can't postpone so close to the day itself, not without looking like we're in complete disarray. No, the show must go on.'

Eleanor went away, still troubled.

ON WEDNESDAY EVENING, THE termly governors' meeting took place. It was always followed by drinks in the headmistress's drawing room (a grand name for the rather shabby living room attached to Miss Christie's office), and teachers were encouraged to attend this portion of the evening too. Mostly, they all tried to get out of it: although it was an opportunity for a free drink, the drink Miss Christie offered tended to be cooking sherry, and not very palatable. Besides this, there was the danger of getting caught up in conversation with the chair of governors, Nigel Land, who used to be a sea captain in the merchant navy. He knew a lot about ships, and felt that everybody else ought to as well.

The governors overall were an eclectic group. The role of governor at St Anne's was not greatly sought after. There was a retired vicar, who also did their Sunday chapel services; a local businessman who owned a string of laundrettes across the area and seemed to think very highly of his own business acumen (he also referred to the prime minister as 'Mrs T', speaking of her as if she were a close personal friend); a teacher in her thirties who taught at a comprehensive in Eastbourne and was, Eleanor privately thought, the only competent one among them; and finally a parent governor, the mother of Jane Morehouse in Sixth Form, who was just as beautiful as her daughter but didn't seem terribly interested in the governance of the school, and additionally proved so distracting to the chair of governors – not through any particular efforts of her own, but simply by virtue of existing – that she might have been regarded as more of a hindrance than a help.

Eleanor had hoped to avoid the drinks this evening – she was behind on her marking due to all the evenings spent assisting with the play rehearsals – but unluckily she ran into Miss Christie on her way to supper, who reminded her of the gathering.

'I'll expect to see you there, Eleanor,' she added crisply.

Eleanor wondered briefly what it might be like to be Vera, to reply, *Well, you can expect all you like, Miss Christie, but you may find yourself disappointed.* But of course she was not Vera, she was herself, and there was no escaping it.

'I'm looking forward to it,' she said.

In the dining hall, she found Matthew, who was sitting with Trudy and Linda at the end of a table.

'Governors' drinks this evening,' Eleanor said, as she slid on to the bench next to him. 'Matthew, you'll come with me, won't you?'

'I'm sorry,' he said, smiling. 'I have prep duty.'

'You don't,' Trudy said. 'Linda and I swapped last week to make sure we wouldn't have to go to the drinks. We've got Lower School and Upper School covered between us.'

'Those occasions are so ghastly,' Linda said. 'The chair of governors always talks to me about seafaring. It's dreadful.'

'He once spent forty-five minutes explaining to me the difference between a boat and a ship,' Trudy said. 'I thought I might die.'

'Last year, he invited me to attend the Tall Ships Exhibition in London with him,' Linda said.

'But he has a wife!' Trudy said.

'He said she was coming too. I don't know what kind of perverse arrangement he was imagining.' Linda shot a sympathetic glance at Eleanor, who pretended not to notice.

'He tells you the most awful facts,' Trudy said, turning to Matthew. 'He once told me that during the war, ninety-one per cent of Britain's butter was imported by the merchant navy. And now I can't forget it! Ninety-one per cent of butter. I don't *want* that fact in my head, but every day it's *ninety-one per cent of butter*. It's stuck there forever.'

'Well, I don't think we even had much butter during the war,' Linda said. 'So it doesn't seem like they were doing a very good job.'

'You'd better not say that to him.'

'So, Matthew, if you don't have prep duty, I suppose you'll have to come with me,' Eleanor said, trying again. She felt she needed an ally to get through it.

'Oh, well, I don't think I can,' he said. 'I mixed up prep duty with detention. I have to supervise a detention. A few girls in Lower School are behind on their work.'

Eleanor was struck again by his manner. When someone is such a poor liar, why bother lying at all? Besides, if they gave out detentions for girls who got behind with their work, St Anne's might yield some very different O-level results.

'All right,' she said. 'Of course.' How often had she given him the benefit of the doubt over the past weeks? She was irritated – with herself as much as with him.

WHEN SHE ARRIVED IN the headmistress's drawing room after supper, the room was already half full. Eleanor could see all the governors scattered across the room, and Miss Christie herself, who was in conversation with the chair, Nigel Land, and a few members of the teaching staff who'd been roped in. Nearest to her, Michael Parker, the governor who owned the laundrettes, was self-importantly telling his latest conversational victim – a mild-mannered teacher from the maths department – that he'd just had a significant capital injection by a third-party investor.

'As Mrs T says, hard work is always rewarded,' he said to the teacher, who was looking rather glazed. 'I hope you instil that in your girls here.'

They definitely did not, Eleanor thought. She eased her way through the clusters of people and was relieved when she spotted Carol Walters, the teacher from Eastbourne and the youngest of the governors. Carol was standing alone near the fireplace, nursing her drink and wearing a world-weary expression that was no doubt the result of the two-hour governors' meeting she'd just attended.

'Felt even longer than usual this time,' Carol said after they'd greeted each other. 'Michael got on to the subject of the ills of socialism, and nobody could divert him.' She took a sip of her drink, pulled a face, and said, 'Someone should tell Miss Christie that sherry doesn't necessarily improve with age.'

Eleanor smiled. 'At least you won't have to attend another for a while.'

She knew the role of governor at St Anne's must be a frustrating one for someone sensible like Carol. She had asked Carol once why she had chosen to do it, but Carol had simply shrugged: 'I was curious. People talked about the strange school on the cliff. I wondered what it was really like.' Eleanor hadn't dared ask for her conclusions.

'Yes, thank heavens,' Carol said now. 'Though there's still the open day to get through, of course. Goodness knows you need the new blood. I dare say you're all feeling the pressure this week.'

'We are,' Eleanor said. 'It's such a nightmare every year. I'm sure it'll be all right in the end, though. It usually is.'

Carol's expression was not encouraging. 'Let's hope so,' she said. She seemed to hesitate for a moment, and then said, 'But between you and me, Eleanor, it might be worth keeping your ear to the ground about other jobs.'

Eleanor tried not to show the dismay she felt. 'Surely it hasn't come to that?'

'Well, maybe not. You might limp on for another few years. Let's see how many you get for next September. But to be honest, the numbers aren't looking good. I've tried to impress that upon the other governors, but obviously they don't listen to me. Maybe if I presented it as a series of nautical metaphors, Nigel would pay more attention.' She paused thoughtfully. 'Something about a sinking ship would be the obvious one.'

Eleanor's panic increased. 'But the numbers have always been bad, haven't they? But we've always got through, just the same.'

'Eleanor, you must know a school like this won't exist for much longer. It can't. And why should it? It's an anachronism. I'm sorry to be blunt, but you don't offer much in the way of an education here, do you?'

Chastened, Eleanor said, 'We do our best.'

'I know *you* do,' Carol said gently. 'Have you ever thought you might be able to do more good in a different kind of school? Comprehensives are always looking for decent, committed teachers. And you'll find kids there who have a real appetite to learn.'

'Our girls here have an appetite to learn,' Eleanor said, unconvinced by her own claim even as she made it. Well, if they didn't have much of an appetite in that direction, it was the school's fault, not the girls'. And besides, there was no point in being defensive; she knew Carol was right. 'Thank you for warning me,' she said.

'I've always thought you're rather wasted here anyway,' Carol said.

'Oh no,' Eleanor said. 'I don't think I'd be much good in a different kind of school.'

Carol looked at her shrewdly. 'You won't know until you try.' She paused, then said, 'Anyway, tell me more about this mysterious illness that's going round.'

'How much do you know already?' Eleanor said.

'The jerking arms. And poor Diane Fulbrook in hospital. Fiona Morehouse has been telling us about it. She knows from her daughter, of course. I'm surprised Miss Christie hasn't informed the governors herself. Not a word about it at the meeting. Though perhaps she simply couldn't get a word in edgeways between Michael and Nigel addressing the twin perils of socialism and the high seas.'

Eleanor was surprised too. 'I suppose she didn't want to alarm you, when we know so little.'

'When you're a governor at a school like this,' Carol said, 'it's your job to be alarmed. Apparently there's a local journalist sniffing round now. He called Fiona at home – Lord knows how he got her number. They've all been seen by a doctor, presumably?'

'Yes. By the GP and at the hospital. But the doctors don't seem to know what's wrong.' She felt even more anxious at the mention of the journalist.

'And they're not getting worse?'

'I don't know,' Eleanor said. She thought of Susan, her nose bleeding. 'It doesn't seem to be spreading, or at least not very fast.'

'Could it be some sort of hysteria?' Carol said.

'I've wondered that myself,' Eleanor said. 'But I don't think so. It looks so real.' When Carol didn't speak, she said, 'I know we should do something. But the thing is, nobody seems to know what, not even the doctors.'

'So for now you just carry on,' Carol said.

'I think that's Miss Christie's view, yes.'

'Until what? Well, I suppose we'll see soon enough. You can't really blame Miss Christie, I suppose. She has enough on her plate. And I doubt the journalist will have enough to go on. It's hardly much of a story, is it? Not yet, anyway. Oh Lord, here he comes.'

Eleanor followed her gaze and saw that the chair was approaching.

'It's Miss Alston, isn't it?' he said. 'Hello again, Carol.'

'Hello, Nigel,' Carol said, her tone bleak.

'Did you have a productive meeting?' Eleanor said, since somebody needed to make conversation.

'Very productive,' he said heartily. 'Isn't that right, Carol?'

'Well, as much as usual,' she said.

'Not quite as disciplined as the meetings I used to have with my officers,' he said, chuckling, then adding meaningfully to Eleanor, 'when I was in the navy.'

'Were you in the navy?' Carol said.

'It was the merchant navy, of course, Miss Alston,' he said self-deprecatingly, turning back to Eleanor. 'We didn't fire any cannons.'

He chuckled again at this. 'We just humbly advanced Her Majesty's commercial interests on the high seas. Though of course,' he added, growing serious, 'the seas are no less perilous for the merchant navy than for the Royal Navy.'

'No, of course not,' Eleanor said.

Carol took a large swig of her sherry, and half suppressed the small shudder this caused her.

'Are you ready for the open day?' Nigel said to Eleanor. 'Quite a stressful time of year for us all, isn't it?'

'Yes, we're getting everything shipshape,' Eleanor said, without quite meaning to. Carol made a noise that sounded like a barely stifled snort, and Eleanor tried not to look at her.

'Excellent,' Nigel said. 'A busy time.'

'All hands on deck,' Carol said. The sherry seemed to have gone to her head.

'Quite,' he said approvingly. 'We need to get those numbers up for next year. I dare say Carol's been telling you her gloomy predictions, Miss Alston?'

'Realistic predictions,' Carol said.

'It does sound rather worrying,' Eleanor said, feeling her spirits plunge again.

'Oh, it'll be fine.' He waved his hand. 'Don't listen to Carol. We learn resilience in the navy, and it's an attitude that's equally useful on dry land.'

'I just feel that we may be . . . sailing too close to the wind,' Carol said. Abruptly, she downed the rest of her drink and said, 'Oh, I must just go and refresh my glass. Can I get either of you anything?' Before they could answer, she had melted away.

Eleanor was left alone with Nigel, staring at him in mild panic.

'I hear you're putting on a play for the open day,' he said, in a manner that was probably intended to be encouraging, but would have been better suited to addressing a child.

'Yes,' Eleanor said. Then, reluctant to claim the credit for herself, she added, 'Well, Matthew Langfield's in charge of it really. He's directing it.'

'That's the new teacher, isn't it? The governors weren't involved in his recruitment and interview, which is quite irregular. Still, Miss Christie did well to find someone at such short notice. How is he getting on?'

'Very well,' Eleanor said.

'But he's not about this evening, is he?' He craned his neck to check the room again. 'I would have liked to meet him.'

'No, I think he has a duty,' Eleanor said.

'What a pity. We're all very curious about him. His name came up at the meeting. Unusual to have recruited a man to work here, and especially a young one. What school was he at previously? I think Miss Christie mentioned one in Norfolk?'

'I'm not sure,' Eleanor said cautiously, wondering what Matthew had said, and whether he had managed to keep his story straight. Goodness, if he was a conman, he was a very chaotic one. 'London, perhaps?'

'Oh, I would have remembered if it was London. We don't get London teachers down here. Now is it true that some of your girls are *twitching*?'

BY THE TIME SHE left the governors' drinks, Eleanor felt exhausted and had the beginnings of a headache starting up behind her eyes. It had been an awful evening, and she wasn't sure which had unsettled her more, the prospect of the school closing, or the talk about their sick girls.

She felt an anger that was out of character for her when she ran into Matthew on the stairs to her room.

'I was just coming to find you,' he said. 'I was hoping you'd be back from the drinks by now. I thought perhaps we could have a cocoa together. I've had a couple of last-minute ideas for staging.'

'Maybe tomorrow,' Eleanor said.

'Are you sure? Vera's still working in the library, so we won't disturb her.'

Suddenly, looking at his eager face, she wanted desperately to be rid of him, to be alone in her room and to lie on her bed in silence and try to think where she might go if the school closed. She was afraid of moments like this, when she was unsettled, when the future seemed hopeless; the feeling was inextricably linked to her father's death, to her finding him, to that terrible darkness that had followed ever since. She briefly closed her eyes and tried to take a breath.

'Are you all right?' he said. 'You don't look well. Can I get you something? Water?'

'I'm fine. Just tired.'

'Those governors' drinks must have been gruelling, then?'

'Yes.' She tried to smile at him. 'You were right to give them a miss.'

'This detention . . .' he said vaguely, though there was no need for him to keep up the lie now, when they were alone.

'I imagine the governors' drinks at Westminster were a grander affair,' she said, something cruel spiking in her suddenly.

'Oh. Well, yes, they were,' he said. 'I didn't used to go very often.'

And in that moment, her head throbbing, Eleanor said, 'No, I dare say you didn't. Especially as you never worked at Westminster.'

From the way his face changed she knew it was true. She had still half expected to be wrong, or at least for him to attempt to deny it. But his shoulders slumped, and he looked at her with an expression of fear. 'How did you know?'

'You must know you're not very good at lying,' she said, more gently now.

They were both silent, watching each other.

He said, 'I didn't mean to lie. It just came out. It was all a stupid mistake.'

'A mistake?' She was disappointed, and surprised at her own disappointment. Perhaps a part of her had hoped that he would provide an explanation that didn't make her feel contempt for him.

'Shall we have that cocoa after all?' he said, with an attempt at a smile. 'I can explain it all to you.'

'I'm tired,' Eleanor said again. She felt very heavy and sad. When she tried to step past him to open her door, he reached out and touched her arm.

'Please, Eleanor. Let me explain a little.'

She paused and sighed. 'All right. Go on.' She leaned against the closed door and waited.

And then he didn't seem to know what to say, especially hovering awkwardly at the top of the stairs like this, when anyone might come along. 'Well,' he began at last, 'I don't have much teaching experience. Hardly any at all. Well, none, actually. And I needed a job. Miss Christie wrote to a friend of mine about the job here, someone she'd worked with years ago, only he wasn't interested. But I thought perhaps I could do it. I did study history at university, so I'm not completely unqualified. So I wrote to her and pretended I was more experienced than I was. I didn't really expect her to offer me the job. And then when I got here it was suddenly all very real, and I thought everyone would realize I was no good, so I wanted you all to think I'd worked at a good school before.'

'If you've never been a teacher until now, what else have you been doing?'

'Oh,' he said, evasive again, and with all his usual obviousness about it. 'This and that.' He paused, then said, 'I worked for a stationery company for a bit, back in Norfolk. And then for the council. But I never seemed to be able to make things go my way. You know, I'm thirty-four now, and I've never really done anything. Nothing good, at least. Nothing of note. And I thought that here perhaps I could . . . start again.'

Eleanor laughed, the sound startling both of them.

'This isn't the place to start again,' she said. 'And besides, it'll probably close soon enough.' To her horror, she found that tears had come into her eyes. There was one horrible, hot moment when she struggled to get herself under control, but she failed, and the next moment she began to cry. She hadn't cried in front of anyone else for years. It was mortifying, but she simply couldn't stop. Matthew hovered for a few moments, presumably as appalled as she was. Then his arms went round her, which was more awkward still, and they both stood in a stiff embrace in the stairwell until Eleanor sniffed, managed to pull herself together and said, 'Sorry. Sorry, I didn't expect to . . .' She moved away from him. 'I need to go to bed. My head hurts.'

'Let me get you something,' he said. 'Some water, some paracetamol.'

'No. Thank you.' She had gone up the last few stairs to her door, wiping her sleeve across her face. She put her key in the lock. And although he hadn't asked her, perhaps because he hadn't asked her, she said, 'I won't mention anything about Westminster to anyone.' Before he could reply she had got herself inside the room and closed the door.

14

IT WAS ONLY ON the morning of the open day itself, while passing through reception on her way back from breakfast, that Ida finally came up with her plan. She approached the desk where Miss Morton was sitting, flicking through the pages of a magazine.

'May I have the key to the music practice room, please?' Ida said.

'Why?' Miss Morton said suspiciously.

'I want to do my piano practice.'

'Open day starts in half an hour,' Miss Morton said. 'Don't you have a duty?'

'Not until eleven,' Ida said. 'I'm doing scones for the Home Ec demonstration. I thought I could get my piano practice done before then.'

'I didn't know you played the piano.'

'Oh, I do,' Ida said emphatically. 'Very much so.'

Miss Morton shrugged and reached into the drawer for the key. 'Never liked the sound of it much myself,' she said, handing it over. 'There's something very self-satisfied about pianists.'

With the key safely in her pocket, Ida returned to her room where Louise was lying on her bed reading.

'Nice breakfast?' she said when Ida entered.

'Lovely,' Ida said. 'Look, I just saw Mr Langfield, and he told me to tell you he's put the props in the music practice room. We have to go and pick them up from there. He said I should help you carry them.'

She waited anxiously for a few seconds for Louise to become suspicious, but Louise shrugged, snapped her book shut and said, 'OK.'

The music room was situated in a shabby annexe attached to the main school building, up two flights of stairs and down a long, barely used corridor adjacent to the library. Since a section of the library roof currently consisted only of a hastily erected tarpaulin, and the door looked as if it had been smashed in with an axe like in *The Shining*, the annexe was out of bounds for open-day tours. The girls were under strict instructions not to let any parents venture beyond the school hall and reception.

At the door of the music room, Ida got the key out of her pocket. Through the small window to their left, she could see the school driveway. The first cars were already pulling up and disgorging their visitors, the men in suits and the women in smart skirts or dresses, some of them even in hats, which would no doubt mortify their daughters.

'Miss Alston said all the props are in the carrier bags under the piano,' she said to Louise, as she opened the door. 'See if they're there, will you? I've got the key stuck.' She wiggled it ineffectually, trying to pull it out of the lock.

Louise stepped into the room and went to look under the piano.

'They're not here,' she said. But even as she was turning back towards Ida, the door was closing again.

Ida locked it from the outside.

'Er, Ida?' Louise's voice said through the door. 'You seem to have locked me in.'

'Yes,' Ida said.

'Well, the idea is, you get both people on the outside of the door before you lock it.'

'I know,' said Ida. 'Look, I'm sorry, but you're going to have to stay in there for a bit.'

There was a short pause. Then, 'Please explain.' Louise's voice was icily calm.

'It's for the sake of the school,' Ida said. 'I can't have you ruining the open day.'

'What? I'm not going to do anything to your great, holy open day.'

'Maybe not, but I'm not risking it.'

'Are you fucking *insane*?' Louise said.

'No,' Ida said. 'Probably not.'

'Has Miss Christie put you up to this?'

'No,' Ida said. 'Look,' she went on reasonably, 'you want the school to close, I want it to stay open, and we can't both get what we want.'

'Fucking hell, Ida. What do you think I'm going to do?'

'I don't know. I just want to be on the safe side. So you'll have to stay in there until after the open day's over. It's only a few hours. I'm really sorry.'

'I'm going to kill you.'

Ida was a bit worried about this. 'Sorry,' she said again.

'I don't accept your fucking apology.' Then Louise started banging on the door. 'Help! Help!' she shouted.

'No one will hear you,' Ida said. 'Not all the way up here. That's why I chose the music room.'

'That is very sinister, Ida.'

'I really am sorry,' Ida said again.

There was a long silence.

'Ida?' Louise said.

'What?'

'I'm thirsty.'

'I put a canteen of water in there for you.'

'Oh, how generous of you.'

Another silence.

'Ida?'

'Yes.'

'I need to pee.'

'I put a bucket in there for you, just in case.'

'*Fuck*, Ida.'

'Sorry.' She paused, considering. Then she said, 'You have a book about making bombs.'

On the other side of the door, Louise was silent again. Ida waited. At length, Louise said, her voice cool, 'When did you go through my stuff?'

'The other day. While you were in the shower.'

'Why?'

'To see what you were planning.'

'And what was I planning?'

'I don't know. You had vinegar and baking soda too. How do I know you weren't planning on setting off a bomb today?'

'A bomb?' Louise said. 'I'm not sure how long you spent looking at that book, but you can't make a bomb out of vinegar and baking soda.'

'What about Epsom salts?'

'I use them in my bath on Sundays.'

'OK, well, maybe not a bomb,' Ida said. 'But you can make a right mess with those things you have. For instance, if you were to throw them on stage during the play.'

'I wasn't going to do anything during the play,' Louise said.

'I think you were.'

'I *wasn't*.'

'You were.'

'God. Fine. I suppose we'll never know either way.' She was quiet for a bit, then said, 'My brother gave me the book. It was just a joke.

It's written by some silly kid. I doubt any of the recipes in there actually work, and you shouldn't have gone through my stuff, and you definitely shouldn't have locked me up in a tiny room like I'm fucking Anne Frank.'

'You shouldn't joke about stuff like that,' Ida said, because she didn't have an answer to the rest of it. 'About Anne Frank.'

'*I'm* allowed to,' Louise said. 'I've earned it.'

There was a pause. Ida was taken aback by the bitterness in Louise's voice. She said tentatively, 'Has it been . . . bad? Being Jewish here?'

'No,' Louise said. 'Unless you object to being called "Jew" every five seconds. Though to be fair, that is mainly just April.'

'What's her problem?' Ida said.

'Don't know. But if you have further questions, I'm sure she'll be happy to lend you her copy of *The Protocols of the Elders of Zion*.' There was another silence. Eventually, Louise said, 'April doesn't bother me. But we talked about Hitler before. Do you remember?' She paused, and when she spoke again, her voice had changed. 'I didn't tell you that my mother was born in Prague. She came to England as a child. A train and then a boat full of Jewish children.'

Ida waited, unsure where Louise was going with this.

Louise said carefully, 'The rest of her family stayed behind. My grandparents, and my aunt, and all their other relatives. I assume you can work out what happened to them.'

'Yes,' Ida said after a moment. She had the disorientating sense of a trapdoor opening up beneath their feet. And she didn't know how the conversation had suddenly lurched into this awful territory. 'Do other people know?' she said.

'About the Holocaust? Yes, I imagine so. I think it was quite a big deal.'

'I meant about your family.'

'I know. Yes, I told Diane back in First Year. We were friends back then, as it happens, but it didn't last. Anyway, she might not have believed me. Or perhaps she thought it was too long ago to matter, it's all just merged into the rest of the sludge of history.'

'It's not like other things,' Ida said, aware of how feeble she sounded.

'Of course it is,' Louise said. 'And so much is gone already. It was only by accident that my mother survived, that she came here, grew up, had children herself. It's only because of that accident that I know who my grandparents were, and my aunt. I know my grandparents died in the ghetto at Theresienstadt, and my aunt died in Auschwitz. I know their names. But there are all these other families that nobody knows about now, because every single member was killed. They might as well never have existed. Hats off to the Nazis, they did a thorough job. It really is just luck that there's anyone left to remember my mother's family.'

Ida closed her eyes.

'When I think about that,' Louise said, 'I feel like a ghost, with all those other ghosts around me.'

Ida said, 'Why are you telling me this?'

'Because,' Louise said, 'I thought you might let me out.'

Ida frowned. 'I can't do that.'

'Fuck's sake, Ida.'

Instead, Ida decided to offer up the only thing she had. She said, 'The reason I came here was to get away from my mother. And that's also the reason I need the school to stay open.'

'Really?' Louise said.

'My mother,' Ida said, 'did something awful. I haven't told anyone here. Not Sophie, not anyone.'

'Well, unless your mother is actually a Nazi, I doubt you can shock me,' Louise said.

'It's quite a long story.'

Louise said, 'I seem to have found myself with time on my hands.'

'OK,' Ida said. 'OK. Well, it started just after we moved to the island.' She settled down with her back against the door and began to talk.

When Ida finally finished her story, Louise didn't speak. Ida wondered at first if she was so shocked that she'd been rendered dumb, although this didn't seem much like Louise.

'Louise?' she said tentatively after a few moments. Then, more loudly, 'Louise? Are you OK?'

She knocked on the door a couple of times. She was almost certain this was some kind of trick.

Finally, when five minutes had passed with no response, Ida gave in and unlocked the door, cautiously pushing it open a few inches, bracing herself for some kind of attack. But the room was empty.

It took Ida a moment to digest this extraordinary fact. There was nowhere in the room to hide. Ida swept her eyes over every corner, but there was no Louise.

At last, she looked at the ceiling. One of the large ceiling tiles was missing. Ida stood beneath it and looked up. Louise, ever the climber, had hoisted herself up into the air vents and escaped.

15

OPEN DAY WAS IN full swing. Eleanor was in the reception area with Miss Christie, helping to welcome the parents and offer refreshments. There was a trestle table set up against the far wall, with tea and coffee urns and trays of biscuits. Several of the governors milled around nearby. Carol caught Eleanor's eye and gave her a smile and then a slight grimace. Nigel Land, the chair of governors, was in conversation with some parents near the entrance, where he seemed to be holding court.

Then, as Eleanor's eyes scanned the room again, she saw him. For a few moments her brain simply didn't know what to do with the information. He was coming in through the main door, dressed just as he always was, that same blue sports jacket, hands in his pockets, hair a mess, all of him achingly, painfully familiar. Before she was able to catch up with herself, he'd seen her as well, and then he was coming towards her, smiling in that rueful way of his.

'Hi, Eleanor,' he said when he reached her.

'Hello, Anthony.' But his daughters were surely much too young still for him to have come as a prospective parent. She could make no sense of his presence here. Was it possible that he had come to see her? Her heart was beating much too fast, and she wondered if any of the other teachers would recognize him. Thank goodness Linda and Trudy were safely tucked away in the English classroom, ready to shout emotional lines of Tennyson at any unsuspecting parents who came their way.

'It's nice to see you,' he said.

'You too,' Eleanor said mechanically, though of course he must know it wasn't nice for her at all.

'I know this must feel like an awful intrusion,' he said. 'But I wondered if we might have a drink together.'

'There's coffee in the urns,' Eleanor said.

'A proper drink.'

'I'm afraid I'm rather busy.'

'I meant later. Perhaps once the open day's over.'

'I have prep duty,' she said, channelling Matthew. Then she thought, For goodness' sake, Eleanor, toughen up. So she looked up at him and said, 'Anyway, it isn't a good idea.' And more firmly still, 'I don't want to.'

His face fell. 'I understand,' he said. 'Of course I do.' She thought he would turn to go then, but instead he said, 'It must be a stressful time. You have your hands full.'

She looked at him blankly.

He said, 'The girls. The sickness.'

And finally she realized. 'You're writing a story.'

'No,' he said. 'No, I wanted to see you.'

'Don't be silly.'

'And I might want to send my girls here.'

'How old are they now?'

'Six and three.'

'A little early, don't you think, for you to be thinking about secondary school?'

'Maeve likes to plan ahead.'

Extraordinary of him to mention his wife to her. He seemed to realize this too, because he flushed and made a small movement with his arm, as if he were about to take her hand. But he thought better of it and dropped his arm again.

'I know I was a rat to you,' he said. 'I know you can't forgive me. But you must also know that I loved you.'

How could he make this kind of declaration to her here, now, like this? But it was so like him. 'I need to get on,' Eleanor said, hearing the primness in her own voice, and seeing clearly all over again why he could never have wanted someone like her.

'Please,' he said. 'Stay a little while. Tell me what you've been up to. I've missed you.'

She could feel how red her own face was now. How could she extricate herself with any kind of dignity in front of all these people, without making a scene?

And then – amazing good fortune – Nigel Land was coming towards them, and Eleanor raised her hand to him, as if she were hailing a passing ship while drowning.

She said in a rush, 'Nigel, may I introduce Anthony Marshall? Anthony, this is Nigel Land, chair of the governors. Nigel, you'll be pleased to know that Anthony has an amateur interest in the merchant navy, and I'm sure he'd like to pick your brains. I must just go and speak to Miss Christie about the refreshments.'

And strengthened by the look of bewilderment and hurt on Anthony's face, she sailed magnificently away.

HER RENEWED COURAGE LASTED long enough for her to inform Miss Christie, discreetly, that a local journalist was present.

She was relieved by Miss Christie's sanguine reaction.

'Well, we can hardly have him removed,' she said. 'And I doubt there's much of interest for him here anyway.' She glanced doubtfully over to where Susan Heller was standing with her parents. It had been Miss Christie who had suggested that Susan's parents bring her in for the open day, with a view to her making a full return to school the following week; Miss Christie was clearly now having second thoughts. Eleanor hoped Susan would keep her twitches to herself for today. 'Still, I'll get Vera Clarke to keep an eye on him. He won't be a match for her.'

Then it was time for Eleanor to go to the hall to find Matthew and get ready for the play to begin. This at least allowed her to avoid any risk of a further meeting with Anthony, though it was only marginally less awkward to be in Matthew's company at the moment. Since their conversation after the governors' drinks, Matthew had seemed eager to talk to Eleanor alone, perhaps hoping to explain himself further, while Eleanor was equally keen to avoid talking about it. She felt she might die of embarrassment if he tried to address it again. As a result, all their interactions felt stilted now, full of unintentional significances and implications, as he edged towards personal conversation and she skirted around it. Things had become, she could see now, far too personal between them, and far too quickly; she needed time to retreat and then to establish with him the kind of friendly but limited relationship she had with most of her colleagues. Fortunately, they had both been busy over the past few days with the final rehearsals and other preparations for the open day, and Eleanor had mostly escaped being alone with him. Still, she often felt his eyes on her when they were together, his expression slightly sorrowful. It was irritating to her.

Now, twenty minutes before the curtain was due to rise, they had plenty of last-minute concerns to occupy them. For one thing, Louise Adler, blasted girl, had gone AWOL so now Farah Razavi would be stepping in at the last minute to do the sound effects instead. This worried Eleanor, since Farah was hardly more reliable than Louise. Eleanor had given her a copy of the script with the pages marked for particular sound effects, and had told her to sit to the front left of the stage, where Eleanor herself and Matthew would be sitting; at least that way she could be prompted if necessary.

Farah was delighted to be given charge of the crash box, the rain box, and the two bits of wood she'd use for the gunshot, and practised enthusiastically until Eleanor told her to stop.

At quarter to eleven, the parents and governors began to file into the hall to take up their places on the rows of chairs set up for the occasion. Now the play was about to begin, Matthew seemed even more nervous than the girls, so Eleanor thought it wise to leave him in his seat while she went backstage to check the cast was ready.

In the little room next to the stage, she issued various reminders to the cast, saying to Nanda, 'Remember to face the audience,' and to Henrietta, 'Don't forget your line this time: "But who will help us solve this terrible mystery?" Otherwise Mary will never be able to enter as the detective, and the play won't be able to go on.'

'Miss,' Angela said, '*please* may I—'

'For the last time, no,' Eleanor said, turning to her. 'You may not smoke a cigarette on stage.'

'I really think Lady Wendlesley would be a smoker.'

'Angela, I've said no.'

'How about an unlit one?'

'Angela, if I see you with a cigarette, I will confiscate it, even if it means coming on stage in the middle of the play.'

Angela looked mutinous, but said no more.

'You're all going to be excellent,' Eleanor said, more encouragingly, though she had her doubts. 'Good luck. Get in your positions on stage now; then in a moment the lights will go down in the hall, and after that I'll raise the curtain.'

She returned to where Matthew and Farah were sitting in front of the stage.

'Is that everyone in?' Matthew said. 'Should we begin?' His top lip shone with perspiration.

'I think so,' Eleanor said. She looked over at Miss Christie for confirmation, who gave her a nod. Eleanor went to turn off the main lights in the hall, leaving the stage lit and the audience in semi-darkness. There was a murmur of excited expectation and the shuffling sound of everyone settling more comfortably into their seats.

Then finally Eleanor pulled on the rope to raise the curtain, revealing the drawing room of a hotel (signified by a shabby sofa, a rug and a side table). Jean Thomas, in her tweed jacket as the squire, was leaning against the side table in a posture of unconvincing ease; Angela was sitting on the sofa, smoking an unlit pencil (Eleanor hadn't expected her to improvise); and Martha Taylor was pacing back and forth holding an open bible and wearing an expression of terror.

'Goodness,' said Angela after a few moments. 'This rain is just ghastly.'

Eleanor, who had returned to her own seat now, gave Farah a little nudge, and Farah snatched up her rain box in a panic and shook it. Unfortunately, she had picked up the crash box by mistake, and the ensuing noise of broken crockery made both the audience and the actors on stage jump. Farah, who seemed quite startled herself, quickly put the crash box down at her feet again and picked up the box of lentils instead, tipping it back and forth rapidly to make the sound of rain.

'I know,' Jean said. 'Dreadful, isn't it? How is a fellow supposed to get a shoot in during a deluge like this?'

At the word 'shoot', Farah, in a panic now, dropped the rain box and banged her two bits of wood together, once again making everyone jump.

'Enough!' Eleanor whispered, snatching them off her. 'I'll tell you when to do the sound effects.'

'I suppose we shall have to fritter the day away inside,' Angela said. 'How very dreary. There's an old acquaintance of mine in the hotel whom I'd rather have avoided.'

'Oh, really?' Jean said. 'Who? Pray, do tell.'

'Well,' began Angela confidingly.

At this moment, Henrietta, in the guise of the hotel maid, was supposed to enter, causing Angela to break off what she was saying, leaving the audience and other characters in the dark as to whom she was trying to avoid.

Unfortunately, Henrietta did not enter.

Everybody waited.

Angela, looking panicked, said, 'Well,' again, and then cleared her throat, raised her voice and practically shouted, '*Well!*'

Still no Henrietta.

Eleanor got up and moved quickly to the side of the stage, entering the little room where the actors were supposed to be waiting. She found the others in there, but no Henrietta.

'She nipped to the loo, miss,' Nanda said. 'She always needs the loo when she's nervous.'

On stage, she could hear Angela heroically improvising. 'We go back a long way,' she said. 'A very long way.' She paused, and when Henrietta still didn't appear, she went on, 'But I really want to avoid him now.' Then, after another pause, realizing she might have given away too much of the plot: 'Or *her*, it could be a her. I saw him – *or her* – on the stairs earlier and had to hide in a cupboard.'

Oh my God, Eleanor thought.

And finally, Henrietta reappeared, coming in through the second door of the little backstage room, readjusting her maid's apron hurriedly.

'You're supposed to be on stage *now*,' Eleanor said to her sternly.

'Oh *God*! Sorry!' Henrietta said. She turned tail and hurled herself up the steps and on to the stage, shouting, 'CAN I GET YOU ANY REFRESHMENTS?'

A brief pause, while everyone on stage recovered from the shock, and then Jean said, 'Some tea, if you please. Lady Wendlesley, you'll partake? How about you, Vicar?'

'Don't mind if I do,' said Martha.

Eleanor breathed out slowly. She returned to her seat beside Matthew, who looked ill with stress.

The next ten minutes proceeded without serious incident, bar the girls talking over each other at times and standing with their backs to the audience. However, things started to unravel again when they got to the murder of Lady Wendlesley.

At her cue – Jean's line, 'Does anyone fancy a game of cards?' – Eleanor went to the light switch at the side of the stage and plunged the stage into darkness.

'I say!' came Martha's voice. 'I believe there's been a power cut! Stay calm, everyone. I shall go in search of some candles.'

In the darkness, there was a long, drawn-out scream. Angela had been practising her scream for weeks, until Eleanor had issued a moratorium.

After the scream, there was a low thump, then someone said, 'Ow!' and another person said, 'Let go!' followed by what sounded like a short scuffle.

The original plan was that after hearing Angela's scream, Eleanor would count slowly to five before switching the lights back on, to give

Angela time to lay herself down on the floor and look dead. This would also give Jean, who was closest to the sideboard, time to produce the stage knife from where it was hidden in the drawer and lay it down beside Angela's body, before returning to her original position. The lights coming on would then be Martha's cue to say, 'Oh God! Somebody has murdered Lady Wendlesley!'

This time, Eleanor counted to ten in the hope that whichever girls had collided in the dark would have time to recover themselves. When she got to ten, the sound of scuffling had stopped, so, with some trepidation, she turned the lights back on.

This revealed an unfortunate tableau: Angela, very much still alive, standing upright behind the sofa and wearing an expression of panic as she struggled to free her dress from where its ribbon had become snagged on the buttons of Jean's tweed jacket. Martha looked very surprised to see Angela still alive. Jean was still holding the knife in one hand as she pulled at the buttons of her waistcoat with the other. Feeling the audience's eyes suddenly on her, she froze, then looked down at the knife as guiltily as if she had actually been caught committing a murder.

Angela tugged uselessly at her ribbon again.

'Oh God!' Martha said loudly. 'Somebody has murdered Lady Wendlesley!'

Angela paused in her struggle to give her an incredulous look.

Jean dropped the knife and used both hands to try to unwind the ribbon. 'I just found that knife,' she told the audience. 'It isn't even mine. You're not supposed to think I did it.'

Since there seemed nothing else for it, Eleanor quickly switched the lights off again. She waited ten more seconds, taking deep breaths, hoping this nightmare would somehow have resolved itself when she switched the lights on again.

Thankfully this time when the lights came on, Angela and Jean had managed to disentangle themselves. Eleanor saw that Jean had shed her jacket. Angela was now lying on her side on the floor in front of the sofa, one arm outstretched gracefully above her head, the knife lying beside her body, and the tweed jacket just visible beneath her, still attached to her dress.

'Oh God!' Martha said, evincing an impressive level of surprise, all things considered. 'Somebody has murdered Lady Wendlesley!'

Henrietta entered, bang on cue for once, holding her tea tray. Farah, poised and ready, shook her crash box enthusiastically and the sudden noise caused Henrietta to drop the tea tray, the sound effect pre-empting the action it was supposed to accompany, as though they'd inverted the speed of light and sound.

'Heaven preserve us!' Henrietta cried. 'A terrible murder!'

'Somebody summon the police,' Jean said. 'We must find the murderer. It wasn't me,' she added, rather defensively; this line was not in the script, but Eleanor guessed that she was still thrown off by having been seen with the knife.

There was a brief pause as the characters on stage reacted to the murder and discussed who might be responsible, before Nanda entered, dressed as the police detective, announcing, 'I heard there has been a terrible murder!' and informing them that nobody could leave this room.

Now it was time for Martha to walk to the front of the stage and deliver her speech about there being a murderer among them. Unfortunately, as she got to her line, 'Danger lurks in every corner,' she illustrated the point by stumbling over Angela's prone form in front of the sofa. She tried to right herself, stumbled again, and fell off the edge of the stage.

There was a gasp from the audience.

Eleanor and Matthew leapt to their feet at the same time and rushed over to Martha.

'I'm all right,' she told them, sitting up gingerly as Eleanor checked her for obvious injuries. 'Nothing broken.'

She did seem unhurt, if a little winded.

Angela sat up so she could peer over the side of the stage. 'Are you all right, Martha? I mean, Vicar?'

'I'm fine,' Martha called wheezily.

'Lady Wendlesley,' Jean said sternly to Angela, 'you are supposed to be *dead*.'

Angela lay back down.

'Are you able to carry on?' Matthew said to Martha.

'Oh, yes.'

She hoisted herself back on to the stage and resumed her place by the sofa, to a smattering of encouraging applause from the audience. There was an expectant pause. All the actors stared at each other, waiting to continue. But nobody spoke.

'Whose line is it?' Matthew muttered to Eleanor.

'Jean's, I think,' Eleanor said. They'd all lost their place after Martha's dramatic exit from the stage. Eleanor was sure that Jean was supposed to answer the vicar's speech with some words of reassurance, but she couldn't remember the specific line. She'd dropped the prompt book in her hurry to help Martha, and now rushed to pick it up again.

As the pause on stage extended, growing more agonizing by the second, Henrietta seemed to lose her head completely. Perhaps panicking that she had once again forgotten her crucial line, she blurted out, 'But 'oo will 'elp uz solve zis ter-*reeble* mystery?'

'Oh no,' Matthew said softly to Eleanor, who was still rifling through the prompt book, looking for her place. 'She's said it too early.'

This line was Mary Maxwell's cue. She charged on to the stage from the wings, dressed as the second police detective, and shouted, 'I am here to investigate this shocking crime!'

The crime she was supposed to be investigating – the second murder, after the play within a play was revealed – had not yet taken place, and all the actors were still in the guise of their original characters. It was difficult to say who was more confused, the actors or the audience. Now there were two police detectives on stage, and as far as the audience could tell, the hotel maid had suddenly adopted an inexplicable French accent.

There were a few frozen moments of dismay as the girls on stage realized they'd jumped several pages ahead in the script. Eleanor felt paralysed herself, and turned to Matthew, who was looking equally panicked. 'Should we intervene?' she whispered to him. He shrugged helplessly, half rising from his seat and then sitting again.

But before they could do anything, the actors seemed to make a collective decision to embrace the play's sudden acceleration. Nanda dropped to the ground dead; Angela got to her feet, resurrected, and threw off her fur wrap; Jean took off her flat cap, Martha removed her clerical collar, and Henrietta took off her maid's apron. Their accents and mannerisms changed as they continued from the point in the play where the twist had been revealed and the second murder investigation had begun.

Martha, now swigging from a hip flask, said, 'Gee, this sure is a turn out for the books. I ain't seen a drama like this since I left Hollywood.'

Henrietta said, 'I would *neverrrrr* 'ave left France if I 'ad known of the *dangerrrrr* in *Angleterre*.'

Jean said, 'To be sure, the fella had it coming, so he did, the eejit.'

Farah, clearly distressed that she'd been deprived of her opportunity to make the gunshot noise that was supposed to signal Nanda's death, now bashed her two bits of wood together furiously, making a sound more suggestive of machine-gun fire than a handgun, so that the actors' next few lines were lost beneath the clatter.

The audience was understandably perplexed, but the girls on stage managed to proceed for the next few minutes, despite their obvious, growing panic.

Eleanor might have missed the first warning sign if she hadn't been looking straight at Mary when it took place. Part way through the lines she was delivering, Mary's arm gave a sudden, violent jerk. Eleanor glanced sideways at Matthew. She saw from his frown that he'd noticed it too. But Mary carried on and the twitch did not happen again. They were only a few minutes away from the interval now, when they'd all be able to regroup.

Afterwards she would remember the moment it happened as strangely surreal, something slow and balletic about it that couldn't possibly have been the case. Martha, standing upstage and delivering a barbed little speech in her role as the alcoholic failed Hollywood actor, suddenly broke off and dropped to the floor – gently, elegantly, it seemed to Eleanor, like a neat folding rather than a collapse. Behind her, Angela stood frozen for a few seconds and then did the same. Eleanor thought the girls were performing some odd improvisation at first, more crossed wires about what was supposed to be taking place in the play at this point. Then she saw the stiffening of Martha's body, followed by the ugly, jerking motions. The audience was absolutely silent. There was a *sweep-sweep* sound as Martha's legs and feet moved against the wooden floor, and then a louder *thwack* as her head banged against the boards. Her face was turned towards the audience, and Eleanor could see her eyes were squeezed tightly closed. Then Angela started to convulse as well.

Eleanor was on her feet and rushing up the steps on to the stage. 'Give me those cushions,' she said to Mary, gesturing towards the sofa.

Mary, her face pinched and frightened, made to pass them, but her arm jerked violently as she reached out for them and she gave a whimper. The next moment she too had dropped to the ground. Eleanor thought she had fainted, but then with a terrible inevitability the jerking started up in Mary's body.

With three girls now convulsing on the stage, the audience finally seemed to have realized this wasn't simply a further foray into avant-garde theatre. Miss Christie was hurrying down the middle aisle to get to the stage, and somebody else said, 'For God's sake, call an ambulance.'

Eleanor, who had now got cushions under the heads of the three girls, looked around for Matthew, who seemed to have disappeared entirely. Nanda was crouching at her elbow saying, 'Shall I run for the nurse?' and Eleanor said, 'Yes,' not because she believed the nurse would do anything useful, but because she thought it might reassure the girls if she was there.

Miss Christie had reached her. She said, 'I've sent Trudy to call an ambulance from the phone in the hall.'

'My arm's going,' Jean Thomas said to no one in particular, and Eleanor glanced back at her and saw that it was jerking.

In the audience, Susan Heller was sobbing; her arm had also begun to spasm uncontrollably.

Now one of the fathers had made it on to the stage and was saying, 'I'm a medical professional.'

Thank God, Eleanor thought, but then she heard his wife say quietly, 'Darling, you're a dentist,' which was less reassuring.

Another of the prospective parents had joined them on the stage, saying, 'I'm a doctor,' but the first man, who seemed to know him, said resentfully, 'A *dermatologist*, Clive.'

'I have actually gone through medical school,' the doctor said. 'Unlike you.' He knelt beside Martha, and then rolled her on to her side, her head angled towards the ground. Eleanor helped him repeat this with the other two convulsing girls.

'Don't try to hold them still,' he told the dentist, who seemed determined to be involved.

'I'm *not*,' the dentist said. 'And all you're doing is rolling them over. Anyone could have learned that on a basic first-aid course.'

Most of the parents in the audience were on their feet now. There was an anxious hum, but everyone kept their voices low in deference to the efforts taking place on stage.

Now that the three girls having fits had been moved on to their sides, Eleanor turned her attention to Jean, whose arm was still jerking up and down. 'Are you in any pain?' she said, and Jean shook her head, but there were tears streaming down her face.

Nanda returned with the nurse, who said, 'Are there any doctors here?' and the doctor said, 'Yes,' and then the dentist said, 'Hardly. He spends his days looking at rashes.'

Where was the ambulance? Eleanor couldn't tell how much time had passed: it could have been just a few minutes, or it could have been more than ten.

A scuffle in the audience: another girl had gone to the floor. Eleanor could only see her feet moving as girls thronged around her. When one stepped aside, she saw that the fitting girl was April Stephens. As Eleanor watched, the games mistress made it over to her and crouched by her side.

Eleanor heard Miss Christie say to someone over her head, 'Ring back and tell them we need more ambulances.'

Nanda said, 'Miss, are they going to die?'

'Of course not,' Eleanor said. Where was Matthew? she thought again. She felt sick with fear. Three girls were having convulsions on the stage, and at least one in the audience. Then at last she saw Matthew, reappearing behind her, his face white.

'I was looking for the nurse,' he said.

'She's already here.'

Nanda said, 'Miss, I feel strange.'

'We need to get everyone else out of the hall,' Eleanor said to Matthew, reaching her hand out to Nanda in case she collapsed. 'Miss Christie, can we evacuate everyone?'

Carol and another of the governors were already trying to usher audience members towards the door, but many of them appeared reluctant to leave, so transfixed were they by the scene unfolding on the stage.

Miss Christie raised her voice and called, 'Could everyone make their way calmly to the main reception, please?' But nobody seemed to hear her.

The next moment, Farah had jumped up on stage beside Miss Christie, brandishing her two bits of wood, which she thwacked loudly together. This caused a momentary lull in the chaos, as people's heads turned in the direction of the noise, and Miss Christie was able to make herself heard. 'Head to the main reception, please,' she repeated. 'We need to give these girls some space.'

And then in the midst of all of this, there was a creaking and a snap from somewhere over their heads, the trapdoor above the stage burst open, and Louise Adler and Ida Campbell fell out of the ceiling.

Part 2

A s if she hadn't had enough bad luck already, Ida's mother said when she became ill. It started with fatigue, and then breathlessness, aches in her limbs. At supper, Ida watched her mother pick at her food, then push the plate away. She must have picked up a virus somewhere. They'd all had bad colds that winter. The cold months seemed to go on forever on the island. In March, Ida's mother went to the doctor: not the island's long-standing GP, who'd retired in the autumn and moved to Stirling to be near his daughter, but one of the locums who were filling in until a permanent replacement could be found. The doctor said she needed to rest. But within a few weeks, she had difficulty even climbing the stairs. She had a fever, she said. She sweated through the bedclothes at night, even though it was freezing in their cottage. She went back to the doctor, who sent her across to Oban for some tests.

It wasn't good news. Of course it wasn't.

'It's bad timing, isn't it?' Ida's mother said to their neighbours. 'After I've moved out here, away from all the hospitals.' She was using her brave voice, as Ida had come to think of it: resigned, almost amused. Now her mother had to catch the ferry across to the mainland for chemotherapy every week, which was no joke when you felt as weak and sick as she did. Seasickness plus cancer sickness plus chemo sickness equalled a lot of sickness.

But in other ways, getting ill on the island proved to be a blessing.

They'd been outsiders before, occupying that most distrusted position of 'incomers' (though at least they hadn't the temerity to be English). But once word spread about the cancer, the community embraced them. Ida was amazed at the kindness of their neighbours. Meals were dropped off at their door, lifts were arranged to take Ida's mother across on the ferry each week, and a rota even seemed to have been put in place to help with the housework. Ida couldn't imagine people on their street in Preston or Glasgow doing this much for them.

Despite how unwell she was, Ida sometimes thought her mother seemed happier with the cancer than without it. She had used to complain about how isolated they were, how unwelcoming people had been since they moved to the island. Now, though she was pale and weak, she seemed cheerful and full of purpose, welcoming neighbours into their house from where she lay on the sofa and saying things like, 'Ruth, you're too good to us,' and, 'Another casserole for my girls! That's so kind.'

'It's the least we can do,' people would say, even terse Mrs Anderson from the post office, who brought round home-made chicken soup, and then, after Ida's mother said she struggled with rich food because of her nausea, home-made chicken broth. Everyone was impressed by her mother's courage, Ida could see, and touched by how grateful she was to them all, and how little she complained. She didn't need to complain for them all to know how unwell she felt. She looked awful: pallid, with dark rings under her eyes. Once she started losing her hair, she shaved all the rest of it off and wore a woolly hat, even indoors, though she was lucky that her eyebrows remained. Sometimes when one of their neighbours had stopped by to drop off food or to clean their kitchen, Ida's mother would have to rush to the bathroom and they would hear her throwing up.

'Your poor mam,' nice Flora Murray from down the road said, shaking her head as she scrubbed the hob. Then, seeing Ida's face, she added, 'Don't worry, hen. The doctors know what they're doing. She'll be right as rain in no time.'

Ida talked to no one about her fears. She was fifteen now, old enough to know that plenty of people died from cancer. When she imagined her mother being dead, she couldn't bear it. The horror felt physical, as if her chest were being squeezed so she couldn't breathe. There were practical concerns, too. What would happen to Ida and Charlotte if their mother died? It was never discussed, and Ida couldn't ask her mother because this would mean putting into her head the awful prospect that she might die, which perhaps she wasn't aware of. Ida wondered if Charlotte would be returned to Peter, since he was her father. Though they'd have to find him first, and even then Charlotte would be resistant, and Peter probably would be too. And what of Ida herself? She thought it unlikely that Peter would take her in. So she would presumably go into care. Ida pictured this as similar to the school hostel in Oban, but with more hardened kids.

She was about to take her O-grades, so perhaps her mother would live long enough for Ida to be ready to leave school and get a job. Then she and Charlotte could take a flat together in Oban until Charlotte left school. Ida wasn't certain this would be allowed, but she thought it would probably be all right since she herself would be over sixteen by then. There was no one she could ask, and she spent many nights lying awake worrying about it. It seemed monstrous to be thinking of herself when her mother was so ill.

IT WAS JUST CHANCE that it all came to an end. One of those silly things that could easily not have happened at all, or could perhaps have happened much earlier.

Ida had to hear the story later from Charlotte, who'd heard it from the kids at school, because their mother never did tell them what happened. As a result, the girls got a somewhat truncated version.

The longer version was this: Cathy Campbell had been dropped off as usual for her chemotherapy appointment at the hospital. It had been Mairi Gibson taking her across on the ferry this time. Mairi had planned to drive on to visit her adult daughter in Balindore while Cathy had her treatment, returning in time to take Cathy home again. But having dropped Cathy off at the hospital that day, Mairi found that she didn't feel well herself. She suffered from occasional migraines, and thought she could feel one coming on now. She decided she'd better sit for a few minutes in her car before setting off again, to see if the headache got worse. She took some painkillers, closed her eyes and dozed in the driver's seat for a while.

So it was that she was still in the hospital car park when Cathy emerged from the hospital half an hour later. Mairi had just opened her eyes and was surprised to see Cathy reappearing so early, when she shouldn't have been finished for hours. Mairi got out of the car and waved at Cathy, who was startled to see her still there waiting, until Mairi explained about her headache. Her appointment had been cancelled at the last moment, Cathy told her. There had been a mix-up and they'd moved it to the following day, but no one had thought to ring her – could you credit it? Mairi took Cathy home, but the funny thing was, when she happened to mention it in passing to her neighbour Graham, how inconsiderate the hospital had been to mess around with appointments when the poor woman was so ill, Graham had something strange to say in response: that he'd seen Cathy down by the harbour in Oban the previous week eating a fish supper when she was supposed to be having her appointment.

'Maybe it was cancelled that week too,' Mairi said.

But once the house of cards had started to collapse, it came down quickly. Although Dr Thorne was gone and the locums filling in for him were not closely involved in the island community, the doctor's secretary was Aileen Warner, who had lived on the island her whole life. She knew all about poor Cathy Campbell and her blood cancer, and had always wondered why she hadn't seen Cathy at the surgery more often. As wider suspicions grew, Aileen did the obvious thing and got Cathy's file out of the cabinet in the doctor's office.

'The first part was true,' she told Flora Murray and Mairi Gibson later that day. 'She did see the doctor, and he did send her for tests. But they all came back clear. No treatment needed. No cancer.'

'Perhaps there are more records at the hospital,' Mairi said.

'That isn't how it works, Mairi. And where are all the letters from the hospital? They're always copied to the GP.'

'Could they have been misplaced?'

'Mairi, don't be silly.'

'It's just so hard to believe,' Mairi said. 'Such a strange thing to do.'

'It is an evil thing,' Aileen said.

Mairi and Flora were still not quite contented. The final step they took was a bold one. The following week, it was Flora's turn to take Cathy to her appointment. Twenty minutes after Cathy had gone in through the hospital doors, Flora rang the oncology department from the car park.

'Hello,' she said, her voice sounding false to her own ears. 'My sister's having her chemotherapy at the moment. I'm supposed to be collecting her at four, but I've been delayed. Please could you get a message to her? Her name's Cathy Campbell.'

And she found she was dismayed, but in fact not surprised, to be informed by the receptionist, after some rustling of papers and voices in the background, that they had no patient of that name.

Flora drove around for a while, then returned to the hospital car park an hour early to pick Cathy up. She drank tea from her thermos, tried to read her book, but kept glancing around her. At half past three, she spotted Cathy heading into the car park from the road. Flora watched as she walked briskly across the car park and disappeared into the main doors of the hospital.

Flora continued to wait.

At quarter past four, Cathy emerged again. This time her walk was slow and her shoulders slumped. With apparent difficulty she shuffled across the car park to Flora's car, giving her a wan smile as Flora got out to open the door for her.

'Thanks,' Cathy said, easing herself into the passenger seat.

'How are you feeling?' Flora said.

'Sick,' Cathy murmured. 'It's miserable, being hooked up to that drip while they feed poison into your body. I've been throwing up for the past forty minutes. They had to keep me under observation. Sorry I'm a bit late.'

This was, finally, enough for Flora and Mairi. They reported back to Aileen, and then Graham, and after that the news got around the island fast.

SO: DISGRACE. CATHY'S DECEPTION would be a topic of conversation on the island and beyond it for years to come. People always came back to the question of why. Because she was wicked, some people said. Or because she was mad. She'd been laughing at them all along.

It was also an insoluble puzzle to Ida, her mother's thinking throughout the time she'd been pretending to be ill. At one stage, she came up with the explanation that her mother had done it for them, for her daughters, to help them be accepted on the island. Ida was pleased when she first thought of this, but soon found that she couldn't always muster the energy it took to believe it. Later, she would wonder if her mother had believed that in some ways she really *was* ill, and therefore deserved the attention and care she was getting. Perhaps there were moments when she even felt convinced she really was going to the mainland for chemotherapy, rather than to sit on the harbour wall in Oban eating a fish supper. People's minds are infinitely slippery and strange, Ida had discovered. And the mind holds hidden compartments, so that you might know something to be true, while also putting it out of sight.

Of course, Ida had no way of finding out what her mother had really thought throughout this time, because it was not discussed. It was another strangeness that Ida would not fully appreciate until she was an adult: during the terrible aftermath, her mother never acknowledged what she had done, even to her own daughters. She simply came home one day looking like she'd been crying, and shut herself away in her room. When Ida knocked and asked if she wanted dinner, her mother said she wasn't hungry, she needed to rest. Ida was afraid her mother had finally realized she might die, and she felt desperate for her, and for herself. But over the next few days, she began to notice that the visits from their neighbours had ceased. There were no more food deliveries, no more lifts, no more cleaning and cooking rotas. If Ida bumped into anybody else around the island, they did not greet her and would not even meet her eye. That week, Ida's mother kept them home from school because she said she didn't want to be alone, but although they were at home together, she did not talk to them much. And when Ida and Charlotte returned to school the following week, it wasn't long before they learned what their mother had done. She must have known they would discover it as soon as they were back at school, but still she did not broach it with them, still she did not prepare them. And Ida and Charlotte did not discuss it much with each other, not after the awful first discovery. Perhaps some things were so awful they could barely be spoken.

THE DISGRACE DID NOT only belong to their mother. Of course it was natural for people to assume that they were all in on it. Or if not Charlotte, then certainly Ida. Ida was almost grown, and did not seem like a fool. Could you really live up close alongside your own mother in that little cottage and be oblivious to whether or not she had cancer? It was no small thing, after all. And Cathy had needed Ida to play her part too: updating the neighbours on how her mother was feeling that day (weak, sick, it had been another bad night), taking on the role of anxious, dutiful daughter, taking delivery of all the myriad kindnesses the islanders offered. Hoarding their good deeds, exploiting their benevolence, and all along laughing at their credulity.

Ida's resentment was focused, for a long time, on the fact that her mother had allowed her daughters to come under suspicion in this way. It seemed horrible to Ida that she had been unwittingly made a part of the fraud, but she didn't know what she might say to make people believe she was innocent, even if she could commit this act of disloyalty against her mother. It would be a long time before she realized that her mother's greatest betrayal hadn't been in implicating Ida and Charlotte in the deception, but in *not* letting them in on it. Instead she had allowed her daughters to believe that she was dying.

IN THE WEEKS AND months afterwards, Ida's mother took to staying inside the cottage. If she went for a walk, it would only be at dusk, or after dark, and even then only rarely. She said she hated the island and would not endure people's eyes on her, those busybodies, those mean, small-minded teuchters, so Ida had to endure their eyes instead, as the shopping now fell to her, and she had to leave the cottage to go to school. It was possible, and even likely, that her mother had no idea that Ida and Charlotte were also the subject of hostility. Like many people, she tended to believe what was convenient to her. And yet she made no move to get them off the island. It seemed to Ida that her mother had entirely given up. When Ida asked, attempting to sound casual, whether they'd be going back to Glasgow, her mother said, 'You're at school in Oban. I'm not disrupting your education again.'

'We could move to Oban, then,' Ida suggested. She thought even that would be better than nothing. 'It would be easier than living here. What with the ferry and everything,' she added hurriedly, since she seemed to have skirted close to the forbidden subject. 'And me and Charlotte being gone all week. It's lonely for you.'

'I've been lonely all my life,' her mother said, beginning to cry. 'What difference does it make now?' Then she went back to her bedroom and closed the door. When Ida went to check on her later, she was in bed with her head under the covers and wouldn't answer when Ida spoke to her.

Ida's only route off the island, she could see, would be one she created for herself.

Fax from Dr James Halliwell to Dr George Fisher
Sunday, 28th October 1984, 4 p.m.

Dear George,

You'll like this: there are now 7 girls from the same school in hospital with what appear to be generalized tonic-clonic seizures, including original girl. For the newly admitted girls, seizures came on suddenly and almost simultaneously, at school open day yest. morning. It was during a play apparently, & 3 of the affected girls were in play's cast. Further 3 in audience.

In addition, 9 other girls have subsequently developed myoclonus, in form of jerking limbs & facial tics. Rhys says they won't be admitted unless they progress to generalized seizures (this delay chiefly because we've got nowhere to put them). We're examining those ones as outpatients in first instance.

Environmental Health investigating the site, & apparently police are there too, which seems like overkill to me. Lots of excitement, though – everyone keen to keep it out of papers, though I'm willing to bet that ship has sailed. Rhys has given us stern words about discretion, not speaking to outsiders, etc. Assume you don't count.

Was accosted on the ward earlier by man I'd never seen before. For some reason, he seemed to be in high dudgeon.

Wanted to know why he wasn't notified about girls' illness earlier.

Difficult question to answer, since I had no idea who he was.

He said he was the medical officer for Environmental Health. Did you know we had an MOEH? I didn't. He seemed quite angry, so I hedged & said I thought local authority would have notified him.

This didn't impress him. He said *as he was sure I was aware* (optimistic of him), there was a mandated chain of command (??). Apparently it was my duty as consulting physician to notify him, as MOEH, in cases such as these, regardless of whether or not I believed LA had already done so.

I brightened at this & explained that actually Lehman was consulting physician. Pointed him in direction of Lehman's office & said I was sure Lehman would be happy to explain why the MOEH hadn't been notified. Off he went to Lehman.

Back to the interesting stuff: EEGs on the 6 new admissions inconclusive, though a couple did show epileptiform changes. Probably a fluke. Lehman had another run yest. evening at peddling his epilepsy diagnosis – though as I reminded him (very slowly, using words of one syllable), epilepsy not contagious & does not cluster. Anticonvulsants seem to be controlling the seizures in some of the girls. I'd be interested to know what you make of that. Bloods normal; mild lymphocytosis in a couple, but again, several of them have had colds recently.

Have considered convulsive syncope as differential diagnosis, but it seems very unlikely; too much thrashing about, along with lack of pallor. If anything, they all look quite flushed

from their exertions, except for the first girl, who is very
pale.

In meantime, I'm worried about her. Despite acyclovir, her
condition's deteriorated further. She's losing ability to speak:
words garbled & mixed up. With Rhys's approval, we've taken
her off acyclovir & started her on amantadine instead.

Something else you'll find interesting, George: in the
seizures I've personally observed, & in others I've questioned
nurses about, the girls' eyes remain closed throughout. The first
girl – her name is Diane – fits with her eyes open.

J

2

'WELL,' LOUISE SAID. 'THINGS have certainly taken a turn since you arrived at the school.'

'It's not my fault,' Ida said crossly.

She and Louise were on chapel duty for the next fortnight as punishment for their open-day stunt. They were to perform a range of repair tasks for an hour between prep and supper. It was only Monday, so they still had nearly two weeks of this tedium ahead of them.

Ida had tried to explain that falling out of the trapdoor on to the stage had been a complete accident, but Miss Christie had snapped, 'You shouldn't have *been* up there in the first place,' which Ida had to concede was a fair point, except that she herself had only been up there trying to stop Louise from doing something nefarious, so really she should be treated as a hero, not a malefactor. Unfortunately she didn't feel she could point this out to Miss Christie.

'You were lucky not to have been seriously injured,' Miss Christie had concluded. It was fortunate: they had the low ceiling to thank for this, and the fact that they had landed directly on the sofa.

'Well, I am a bit bruised,' Louise said, adding rapidly when she saw Miss Christie's expression, 'Though it's my own fault, of course, and nothing that a few days spent not falling out of ceilings won't cure.'

For a while now Ida and Louise had been working in silence, taping the damaged spines of hymn books back together. It was freezing in the chapel, and Ida's hands were clumsy with the cold.

Perhaps sensing the hostility in Ida's silence, Louise said, 'You know, you didn't actually have to follow me. Nobody forced you to.'

'Somebody had to stop you,' Ida said.

'Stop me from what? Assassinating the governors with a sniper rifle? Blitzkrieging the First Years? Setting off a nuclear explosion? Declaring war on Russia?'

Louise had maintained since their fall out that she hadn't been trying to accomplish anything beyond escaping her makeshift prison. This argument had been grumbling back and forth between them for days now.

'I was *telling* you about my *mother*,' Ida said again, feeling the betrayal afresh.

'Oh, I heard most of that while I was removing the ceiling tile,' Louise said. 'She pretended to have cancer, you didn't know she was pretending. I assume everyone found out the truth eventually?'

'You didn't even stay to hear the end!' Ida said. She had been baring her soul, and this was all the thanks she got.

Louise said, 'I felt I'd got the gist.'

Despite its inconvenience, their punishment felt half-hearted; Miss Christie had too much else on her plate to give much thought to it. Six girls were now in hospital with seizures, including Angela, Martha Taylor and Mary Maxwell. April had been admitted too, and Susan, whose parents had brought her to the open day, and another girl, this one in Lower School, who'd been in the audience. All of them had had fits during or immediately after the fiasco with the play.

Moreover, other girls still at school had developed jerking limbs. A girl called Deborah Willis had been a particularly alarming case; her legs seemed to have taken on a life of their own and she looked like she was constantly trying to perform an Irish jig. Her parents had taken her away the previous day, to everyone's relief.

But the sickness seemed to be spreading. The council had stopped short, so far, of actually closing the school and had advised instead that all the remaining girls must be quarantined, which only meant that nobody could go into South Haven. Environmental Health had been an intermittent presence at the school since Saturday afternoon, an unimposing group of men in suits ('Shouldn't they be in protective gear?' Sophie said. 'Shouldn't *we* be in protective gear?' Victoria said). The police had also been at the school on and off, which had caused great excitement among the girls; there was a particularly handsome police sergeant who was followed at a short distance wherever he went by giggling First Years, like an unwilling Pied Piper. Miss Christie reprimanded these girls fiercely whenever she spotted them, but this only meant that the first group, retreating sheepishly, was quickly replaced by another. The sergeant seemed to have decided his only option was to ignore them, and he walked around the school with his eyes fixed determinedly ahead, girls trailing in his wake like clouds of glory.

They had all been told not to talk to reporters if any turned up at the school, but since Miss Clarke had been put on duty guarding the main entrance like Cerberus at the gates of the underworld, it seemed unlikely any reporters would make it far enough to get a quote.

Ida couldn't enjoy the novelty of any of this very much. For one thing, they were all worried about Angela and the other Sixth Form girls. Victoria was convinced they were going to die, and although Sophie and Ida had tried to reassure her, Victoria's continual pronouncements of doom were getting them all down. For another thing, Ida was dreading the prospect of the school's closure, which seemed increasingly likely; she feared she would be on the train back to Scotland within days.

'Ida? Louise?' Sophie had appeared in the doorway of the chapel. 'The Environmental Health men are taking away all the water canteens from the basement of Wroth's.'

They stared at her.

'Why?' Louise said.

Sophie looked awkward. 'I think . . . er, I think some girls have said you put poison in them.'

'Oh, for crying out loud,' Louise said.

'And you have to go to Miss Christie's office now,' Sophie said, looking more awkward still. 'That's what they sent me to say. The police want to talk to you.'

'The *police*?' Louise said. 'You can't be serious.'

'I'm afraid I am. It's only because of the rumours. I think they have to speak to you, just in case. I don't think they're going to arrest you or anything.'

'Oh, well,' Louise said. 'That's a relief.'

'Though I think they want to search your room,' Sophie said. 'I heard them say they might.'

Louise rolled her eyes, but Ida thought she'd turned a little pale. *They won't look in the attic*, she wanted to reassure her. *They won't think of looking up there.* But who was she to say? Maybe they would.

'Miss Christie said to come and see her right now,' Sophie said again. 'They're all waiting for you. Though if you like,' she added bravely, 'I could say I couldn't find you. Buy you some time.'

'No, it's all right,' Louise said. 'I'll go now.' She glanced at Ida. 'See you later.' Then she strode out of the chapel.

Sophie and Ida were left alone.

'Do you think she's definitely going to Miss Christie's office?' Sophie said. 'Or do you think she'll make a break for it?'

'I think she'll go to Miss Christie,' Ida said. 'She might as well get it over with. She hasn't poisoned anyone.'

'Are you sure?' Sophie said.

'Of course I'm sure.'

'OK, well, that's good.' Sophie brightened. 'She might get interviewed by that really handsome policeman! Imagine how jealous everyone will be. Are you coming to supper?'

'Yeah,' Ida said. 'Just need to drop my bag in my room. I'll see you there.'

She made her way as quickly as she could back to Wroth's, and once she was in her room she immediately hoisted herself up into the attic space. She retrieved *The Anarchist Cookbook*, hesitated for a moment, and then grabbed the baking soda and vinegar too. She slithered back down the rope ladder holding them carefully against her chest, and closed the trapdoor behind her again.

Then, standing in the middle of the room with the incriminating objects in her hands, she wondered what the hell she was meant to do with them now. She hadn't thought any further ahead than getting the book out of the way in case the police really did come to search their room. She put the book, the vinegar and the baking soda up her jumper and hurried out, trying to think of a suitable hiding place.

Closing the door of her room behind her, she went down the stairs and on to the floor below. There was no one around: everyone was at supper. Ida searched for inspiration. There was nowhere to hide things in this building except the basement, which would be locked. The toilet cistern? she thought. But no, it would only be a matter of time before someone found it there – plus Louise might be annoyed that her book was ruined. Not that she would have any right to be annoyed.

Then Ida heard voices on the stairs, the first girls already coming back from early supper. She was standing next to the room April and Diane shared, though it now stood empty since both girls were in hospital. Ida tried the door – unlocked – and darted inside before anyone could see her.

It felt strange being in April and Diane's room like this. It looked much the same as the room Ida shared with Louise, except it had pictures on the walls: an image of Duran Duran, torn from a magazine, and the film poster for *The Outsiders*. Each of the beds had a piece of card Blu-Tacked above the headboard. One read, *April is the cruellest month*, in beautiful calligraphy with a watercolour picture of a clump of lilacs beneath it, and the other read, *Prais'd be Diana's fair and harmless light*, illustrated with a picture of a sun. Presumably each some kind of in-joke, Ida thought.

Recollecting herself, she took the things out from under her jumper and pushed them under one of the beds. Then she listened at the door and, since all was quiet, quickly made her escape.

She hadn't been back in her own room long before she heard voices outside and then the door opened without anyone knocking. Ida was taken aback to see Miss Christie and two policemen – the improbably handsome one and a considerably less handsome one, who looked particularly squat and anaemic beside his tall, dark colleague – with Louise trailing moodily behind them.

'Ida,' Miss Christie said. 'These officers are going to search your room. It won't take long.'

'Don't you need a warrant for this?' Louise said from behind them.

'No,' the handsome policeman said.

'And if I had poisoned someone, would I really hide the evidence in my own room? You should be looking in communal bins. That would make more sense.'

'That's enough from you, Columbo,' the less handsome policeman said. 'Pipe down.'

They rifled through drawers ('Yes, that's my underwear,' Louise said. 'Do you really need to inspect my knickers?' And Miss Christie said, 'Thank you, Louise, that will do'), searched under both beds and in both wardrobes. From one of the wardrobes, the less handsome policeman produced a biscuit tin.

'Sarge,' he said, handing the tin to his colleague.

Ida frowned. In her rush to get rid of the things from the attic, she'd forgotten about the wardrobes.

'What's this, then?' the handsome sergeant said to Louise, though he was already prising the lid off. He held up the two little plastic bags of seed pods, one set long and green, the others flat and translucent, as silvery and delicate as silk.

Honesty, Ida thought. Lunaria. It had grown in her grandparents' garden too.

'It appears to be some seeds,' Louise said.

'It's my tin,' Ida said.

'Oh, yes,' the officer said nastily. 'I'm sure it is.' He replaced the bags in the tin and said, in a significant tone, 'We'll take this for testing.'

'What are you going to test for?' Louise said. 'Compatibility with clay soils? Suitability for a herbaceous border?'

He gave her another of his looks.

Meanwhile, the short officer pulled back the cover on Louise's bed and lifted the pillow. He picked up the book beneath it gingerly, between his thumb and forefinger, as if it might be contaminated.

'What's this?' he said.

'I think,' Louise said, 'it might be a book.'

'That's enough, Louise,' Miss Christie said.

The police officer was still inspecting the book, a wary expression on his face. On the cover there was a picture of a girl in a white nightdress levitating off her bed.

'It's a novel called *Legion*,' Louise said patiently. 'By the author of *The Exorcist*.'

'Have you seen *The Exorcist*?' the policeman said.

'I haven't, unfortunately,' Louise said. 'It's quite hard to get hold of.'

'Do you have a particular interest in satanism?'

Louise frowned. 'Not especially.'

'Your reading matter suggests a concern with demonic possession.'

'I read a lot of things,' Louise said.

'What kind of things?' he said. 'Violent things?'

'She doesn't read violent things,' Ida said, before Louise could answer, since Louise seemed determined not to help herself in any way. 'Her favourite novel is *Anne of Green Gables*.'

Everyone seemed surprised by this, not least Louise. She gave Ida an annoyed look as if to say, *We will discuss this later.*

The officer threw the book back down on the bed. He said to Louise, 'We'll need to speak to you again in due course.'

The handsome sergeant, still holding the biscuit tin, said, 'And we'll be taking this.'

'Yes, you said.'

Then they were heading for the door. Miss Christie said, 'Ida, Louise, you'll have missed supper. Mrs Stoker should still be in the kitchens. Tell her I've asked that you be served sandwiches.'

'Thanks,' Ida said, and Louise nodded.

Miss Christie followed the policemen to the door. The constable had already opened it when the handsome sergeant happened to glance up at the ceiling.

'What's that?' he said, gesturing towards the trapdoor.

Ida looked at Louise and saw her expression falter.

'It's an attic,' Miss Christie said. 'The girls don't go up there. It's out of bounds.'

He had already walked over to it and was now pulling it open. The rope ladder fell down. 'Right,' the sergeant said, ignoring Miss Christie. 'Up you go, Armstrong.'

The other man seemed about to protest, but then sighed and began wobbling his way up the ladder. He couldn't have done it with less dignity if he'd been trying, Ida thought. Once his torso was wedged out of sight, they heard the *click* of his torch.

'Couple of books,' he said. 'Nothing else . . . Wait, there's something in the corner.' Excitement in his voice now. His legs scrabbled and then disappeared through the trapdoor, and they heard a creak as he crawled across the floor.

Ida glanced at Louise again. Her face gave nothing away.

'I've got something!' the constable called. Then, with less enthusiasm, 'Wait, it's only some old Epsom salts.'

The handsome sergeant was clearly trying to think of a crime that could be committed with Epsom salts. He called, 'Take them. We'll test them.' He looked at Louise. 'To see if they actually *are* Epsom salts.'

Louise rolled her eyes.

The other police officer began his clumsy descent down the rope ladder, clutching the packet of Epsom salts. When he was safely back on the floor, he handed it to the sergeant, who opened it and sniffed it suspiciously.

'That's all for now,' he said to Louise. And they made for the door, followed by Miss Christie, who said, 'Go and get your sandwiches, girls.'

Once they'd gone, Louise did a slow exhale and sat down on her bed.

'They were actually Epsom salts, right?' Ida said.

'Yeah.' There was a long silence, then Louise said, her voice deceptively casual, 'What happened to the other things up there?'

'I moved them,' Ida said.

Louise was now staring at her as if she'd never seen her before in her life. She said, 'You didn't need to do that.' Then, grudgingly, 'Thanks.'

'You're welcome,' Ida said.

Louise was still looking at her. She opened her mouth as if she were about to say something else, but then closed it again. After a few more moments, she said, 'Out of interest, where did you put them?'

'In April and Diane's room,' Ida said.

'You put them in April and Diane's room?'

'Yeah. Under April's bed.'

'You've . . . *framed* April?' Louise said.

'I haven't framed her,' Ida said, annoyed. 'I was in a hurry. I happened to be passing their room.'

Louise was grinning. 'I didn't know you had it in you. Clever of you to put it in April's room too, since she's hospitalized and can't defend herself.'

'Stop it,' Ida said. 'Anyway, you shouldn't have had that book in the first place. You need to get rid of it properly now. Burn it, or something?'

'*Burn* it? What, on this lovely open fire in our room?' She gestured towards an imaginary hearth.

'Or, I don't know, bury it somewhere in the school grounds.'

Louise was still grinning, but she said, 'Fine, yeah. OK. I'll get rid of it. It's a load of nonsense anyway.'

'And don't tell me where or how. I don't want to be involved any further.'

'OK.'

A pause, then Ida said, 'What did they ask you?'

'Nothing very complicated,' Louise said. 'Did I poison those girls? No. Am I sure I didn't poison those girls? Yes. What did I poison them with? Nothing, because I didn't fucking poison them. Since they only had some stupid rumours to go on, rather than any actual evidence, their questions tailed off pretty quickly.'

'Why have they taken the water canteens?' Ida said.

'Presumably because that's where I put the poison,' Louise said. 'Fucking idiots.'

'Those were laburnum seed pods in the tin,' Ida said. 'The long green ones.'

Louise frowned at the sudden change in direction. 'Is that right?'

There was a long silence.

Louise said, 'Why are you looking like that?'

'No reason,' Ida said. 'It's just . . . laburnum's poisonous.'

'Ida, for God's sake. You must know I haven't poisoned anyone, with laburnum or anything else.'

'I do know that,' Ida said. 'But the police will be able to identify the seeds. Then what if they test the sick girls for laburnum poisoning?'

'Well, obviously they won't find anything.'

'They might,' Ida said.

Louise shook her head. 'They won't, you idiot. I never touched your precious tin. I never even knew you had it. Like I said, I haven't actually poisoned anyone.'

'I know you haven't,' Ida said. 'But the thing is, I have.'

Fax from Dr James Halliwell to Dr George Fisher
Monday, 29th October 1984, 7 p.m.

Dear George,

In addition to the 7 in hospital, there are now 13 other girls at the school displaying neurological symptoms, mostly involving myoclonic jerks. Lehman's moved on from his epilepsy hypothesis & is now convinced the girls all have the same, as yet unidentified, virus. Wonder if Rhys will let me LP the lot of them to prove him wrong. Probably not, though it would speed things along nicely.

Apart from Diane, no further deterioration in the girls in hospital: 3 out of 6 still having seizures, despite anticonvulsants, which is quite interesting in itself, isn't it? The other 3 haven't had another seizure since being admitted.

All girls with seizures are currently on a ward together, except for Diane, whose condition is serious enough to warrant a private room. Conditions at the hospital haven't improved in your absence, by the way. Obviously would be more prudent to keep affected girls apart, but there aren't enough beds free. As it is, they're in a makeshift ward hastily assembled in the exam room off the nurses' station. It's like the bloody Crimean War.

Have insisted on at least examining them separately. Since

exam room is now ward, I've been allocated new exam room that used to be nurses' kitchen & is now mostly used for storage of bric-a-brac. Someone has thoughtfully put exam table in it, which just about fits, but there isn't room for a chair, let alone a desk. There's so little space that any observer (mother or nurse) has to be awkwardly pressed up against the wall while I squeeze myself in front of the girl to examine her. Water pipes run down the wall too, so there are constant clunks & gurgles while I'm trying to hear what patient is saying.

Apart from Diane, the other girls with symptoms appear well in themselves. Ictal duration is longer than 3 minutes in most cases, and sometimes seizures have occurred during a clinical exam or even during an EEG (what are the odds?). I wish you could see one of the fits for yourself: you'd be intrigued by the movements of the girls' limbs, which are arrhythmic, asynchronous and violent.

'I don't think there's any organic disease here,' I said to Lehman.

'Are you saying they're faking it?' Lehman said, belligerent.

'No.' The man has an unsophisticated mind.

Lehman then wanted to know what you thought. Told him I had no idea.

He said, 'I thought you two were friends.'

'We are,' I said. Friends who never see or speak to each other. 'But he's a busy man. Hard to get hold of.'

Lehman said, 'I don't think he's that busy.'

Inevitably, it's already been in local paper – article yesterday headlined 'Frightening Mystery Illness Hits Girls' School' – but I don't think it's been picked up by nationals yet. It will be, no doubt. Need to move quickly with diagnosis – the more papers stir the situation up, the harder it's going to be to untangle.

Then there's still the problem of Diane. Unlike the others, she's getting worse by the day, by the hour. Should soon see if the amantadine makes a difference. If it doesn't, not sure what to try next. Blast of dexamethasone? That will delay, not cure, but it might buy us some time. Why are we so limited on antivirals? Seems amazing to me sometimes that at this late juncture of 20th century, this brave new world, we're still at the total mercy of any mystery virus on any given day.

J

3

THEY HAD AGREED TO suspend further discussion until they'd picked up their sandwiches from the kitchen, since Louise had declared this was not a conversation to have on an empty stomach. Mrs Stoker seemed suspicious of their claim that Miss Christie had sent them, but she eventually conceded and gave them each a cheese sandwich, an apple and a KitKat.

'Easily the best meal I've ever had here,' Louise remarked, once they were back in their room eating their sandwiches. She paused, about to take another bite. 'Just to be clear, you haven't put anything in this, have you?'

'It's not funny,' Ida said.

'No, I suppose it isn't. You started this whole thing.' She almost looked impressed, Ida thought, which was worrying. 'All along, it was you.'

'It wasn't, actually,' Ida said. 'I told you, not all of it. I didn't do any-thing to Diane, or to any of the others. I swear I didn't. It was only April.'

'Just the one poisoning victim, then. Hardly worth mentioning.'

'I only meant to make her feel a bit queasy. Maybe make her throw up. I only ground up a few seeds. Barely enough to do anything.'

'It seems to have done enough.'

'I know. I didn't mean for the rest of it to happen. The . . . twitching.'

'And the fits,' Louise said.

'All right, I know.'

Louise was silent for a while, eating her sandwich thoughtfully. 'OK,' she said at last. 'Go on, then. Why did you do it? I don't like April, but I don't see what you had against her. You can't go round poisoning people just because they're annoying.'

'Well, it was . . .' Ida broke off, awkward. 'Look, you have to remember that you'd said you were going to force me to leave. And I can't leave. I have to stay here. So I thought I'd better make sure you couldn't force me to go.' Finally, she made herself look at Louise.

This was enough to make Louise pause in her eating. 'It was meant to be *me*?' she said, scandalized. 'You were trying to poison *me*?'

'I wasn't,' Ida said quickly. 'That's not it. I *was* going for April. It was a bit more complicated, that's all.'

'I'll do my best to follow,' Louise said dryly. 'Labyrinthine as your mind is proving to be.'

Reluctantly, Ida confessed. 'The thing is, I was going to tell everyone you did it,' she said. The stages of her plan would have seemed laughable to her now, if only the consequences hadn't been so serious. 'I thought April would feel unwell, and then I was going to tell Miss Christie that you'd boasted to me about poisoning her, and maybe even that I'd seen you put the seeds in her drink. And I thought all that together would be enough for Miss Christie to finally expel you, and I wouldn't have to worry about you trying to get rid of me anymore.' When Louise didn't speak, she rushed on, 'I thought you might even go along with it, because you were so keen to leave the school anyway.'

'Yes, *leave*,' Louise said. 'Not go to prison.'

'I possibly hadn't fully thought it through,' Ida said.

'So one of the water canteens was poisoned after all?' Louise said.

'No,' Ida said. 'I didn't put anything in the water. I put it in her tea at breakfast. Or rather, I put it in my own tea and then I bumped into her and swapped our cups over. Water wouldn't have disguised the flavour enough.'

Louise's eyebrows had gone up. 'And then the drill happened right afterwards.'

'Yes.'

'What made you change your mind about blaming me?'

'Well, things got out of hand. In the basement.' She looked at Louise earnestly. 'I don't want to get you expelled anymore. To be honest,' she added, risking her deepest confession of all, 'I'd rather you stayed.'

'How touching,' Louise said.

'You have to understand,' Ida said, 'I knew what you were capable of. You pushed April out of a window. You broke her arm!'

'Oh, that,' Louise said. 'It was a ground-floor window.'

'What?'

'It was a ground-floor window,' Louise repeated patiently. 'She just happened to land awkwardly, broke her wrist, the silly idiot. Anyway, you know how rumours work in schools. Suddenly I'm pretty much a murderer.'

'Why didn't you tell me it was the ground floor?' Ida said. 'I was terrified of you!'

Louise looked at her like she was a halfwit. 'Yes, I know. I wanted you to be.'

'Louise,' Ida said sternly. 'That wasn't very nice.'

Louise held her gaze coolly until Ida remembered what they'd previously been discussing and said, 'OK, all right. *All right.*'

'I'm still confused,' Louise said after a moment. 'How could you have made the others sick too?'

'I don't think I could have. I don't think I did.' And, seeing Louise's expression: 'Louise, I swear, I didn't do anything to the rest of them.'

'The doctors must have tested for poison, right?' Louise said, taking another bite of her sandwich. Ida was surprised she still had an appetite, given their topic of conversation; she had put her own sandwich aside. 'Or they must have at least considered it? Presumably there was nothing to suggest the girls had been given poison.'

'I told you, I only used a few seeds,' Ida said.

'So why hasn't April recovered? Shouldn't it all be out of her system by now?'

'Yes. I don't think she even drank all the tea,' Ida said. 'And she *did* recover. Only then she got worse again.'

'You could have killed her,' Louise said. A pause. 'I think you might be a psychopath, Ida.'

Ida considered it. 'I might be, yes. Except I do feel pretty bad about it, so maybe that means I'm not a full psychopath.' Half-orphan, she thought. Half-psychopath. She said, 'I'm going to tell Miss Christie. And she can tell the doctors. And . . . and the police. I should have done it sooner, only I was so sure it couldn't have been the laburnum. But now they're going to find out anyway.'

She got up, but as she went towards the door, Louise put out her hand. 'Wait.'

Ida paused where she was.

Louise said, 'They can't prove anything.'

'I'm still going to tell them,' Ida said. 'I've been going mad keeping this secret.'

'I think you should wait,' Louise said. 'You'll ruin everything for yourself. And for what? For slipping a few seeds to April Stephens?'

'You just said I could have killed her.'

'Well, you didn't kill her, did you? And you said you didn't have anything to do with the rest of it. So what's the point in confessing now?'

'I might feel better,' Ida said. Now she had finally confessed, the panic she had been trying to keep under control for the past month seemed to have burst its banks. She felt light-headed, as if she could hardly breathe.

'No you won't,' Louise said. 'You'll be expelled, and maybe arrested, and you'll either end up in borstal or back home with your mother, and everyone else here will still be just as sick as they were before.'

'I thought you wanted me to go,' Ida said.

'That was ages ago,' Louise said. 'Before I discovered you were interesting. Do try to keep up.' She had finished her sandwich and moved on to her KitKat. She nodded her head in the direction of Ida's half-eaten meal. 'Are you going to finish that? If not, pass it over here. It's such a novelty to be eating something that doesn't taste of rotten fish.'

Ida was hardly listening now. She had a strange feeling in her body, a kind of rising agitation that made it difficult to keep still. It was as though thousands of tiny creatures were crawling about underneath her skin.

Then something extraordinary happened: her right shoulder jerked and her right arm thrust forward, without her having any control over the movement.

Her eyes met Louise's.

Louise had gone still and was staring at her. 'Did you do that deliberately?'

Ida shook her head. Her arm jerked again.

'Oh no,' Ida said softly.

Dear George,

Day off today. Visited laundrette first thing. While I waited by machines, youth sidled up & offered me what I believe was heroin; suggests I was looking even more haggard & disreputable than usual. Told him I didn't need it, could get it at work for free. This interested him. Went home, paced my rooms. Thought about ringing my mother. Instead found myself sitting down & picking up my pen (the fountain pen you gave me; not sure if anyone's told you, but you give dreadful presents).

Yesterday, Rhys sent me to the school. The plan was, he said, for me to provide reassurance, while also conducting my own discreet investigations. 'Getting the lay of the land,' as he put it. Think he may be in conspiracy with Lehman.

Asked if I could at least examine the girls while I was there. Told him I strongly suspect conversion disorder. Rhys said no. He said I have to let Environmental Health do their job first, & Lehman needs to be in agreement too. Bloody Lehman!

Took me nearly 40 minutes to drive over from Eastbourne on terrifyingly narrow lanes, & when I finally did arrive, school looked like something out of gothic novel. Not surprising pupils are behaving strangely. Is there no budget for building repairs? Surprised there haven't been more casualties from falling masonry, never mind mystery viruses or environmental toxins.

Was given a brief tour by rather formidable headmistress, Miss Christie. She seemed suspicious of me, & even asked me how old I was at one point. Was relieved to be able to say I'd already crested thirty & could see it receding rapidly behind me. Managed not to mention I was just barely a consultant. Police also on site conducting interviews with pupils & staff; my presence clearly resented by surly police constable stationed in reception (should introduce him to Lehman, they'd get on well).

Reunited with my new friend the MOEH when Miss Christie took me into staff room. I greeted him enthusiastically. He didn't seem especially pleased to see me. (Apparently he & Lehman had rather uncomfortable interview after my initial encounter with him, which for some reason Lehman blames me for.) Name is Stevenson.

Miss Christie retreated to make a phone call. She seemed keen to get away from Stevenson, probably unsettled by his haunting air.

Was just asking Stevenson how his investigation was going when door opened again & another man came in. He looked somehow bulky & sleek at the same time, made me think of a rotund otter fresh from river.

He greeted Stevenson, ignored me, & told Stevenson they needed to arrange an official meeting so he (otter man) could brief Stevenson.

This did not go down well with Stevenson. Unedifying tussle followed over which of them was supposed to brief the other. Otter man, it transpired, was acting COEH (I've spent a while trying to work this out; EH must be 'Environmental Health', O is probably 'officer', but what is the C for?), & claimed therefore that it fell to him to brief the MOEH.

Stevenson argued that since the MOEH was appointed by the health authority, his role was to liaise with the COEH, not to report directly to him.

This went on for quite some time.

'Maybe you can just brief each other,' I suggested at one point. Both gave me quelling look.

Things finally took a turn when otter/COEH man said he could see Stevenson was determined to be as obstructive as ever, & that he would be taking this up with the DMO. This seemed to please Stevenson. 'Please do take it up with him.' Pause for dramatic effect. 'He's in the room with us right now.'

Otter man glanced doubtfully at me. I was feeling equally doubtful. Was it possible I could have been appointed DMO without actually noticing it? I do have a tendency to zone out in meetings. Then Stevenson announced, with great satisfaction, that he himself was District Medical Officer.

Otter man queried, with ill grace, whether the same person could be MOEH and DMO simultaneously. Stevenson insisted that he could, and was, and therefore he outranked the COEH. The COEH/otter man continued to deny this.

By this point, I wasn't feeling very confident about the state of the investigation, & all the abbreviations had given me a headache.

Stevenson departed, leaving me and the otter man alone together.

I asked him if the Environmental Health team had made any progress. He said it was still early stages, that they needed to rule out obvious things first, like lead poisoning. I told him it wasn't lead poisoning. He wanted to know how I could be sure. He went into his spiel about how these were old buildings, poorly maintained, etc.

I said they'd have had to have had a massive dose to produce these symptoms. He said maybe they have. I said unless they'd eaten an entire lead pipe each within the last week, I'd be very surprised.

Then he said they'd test for other heavy metals too. Mercury, arsenic.

Waste of time & money, I was thinking.

'And thallium, of course,' he added.

'Thallium?' I said.

He gave potted history of thallium in UK, despite me reassuring him I knew what thallium was.

'Like in the Agatha Christie novel,' he concluded. '*The White Horse.*'

Told him I hadn't read that one, & he said it was very good. Quite the twist, apparently.

I asked him how he thought these girls could have been exposed to enough thallium to poison them. Was genuinely curious about his theory. He suggested perhaps someone had been careless with an old batch of rat poison. Or it could be in the water, he said. Told me the water authority were looking into it.

Oh, well, if the water authority are on the case, I thought, but did not say.

Then he started on about pesticides. To divert him, I asked

if they'd have to close the site. He said he thought they would, unless I could cure them very quickly.

Told him I'd do my best.

Then he suddenly exclaimed, '*The Pale Horse*!' and slapped his forehead, nearly giving me a heart attack. 'It's *The Pale Horse*, not *The White Horse*. Do read it.'

Miss Christie returned & led me to her office to have an interview. Her main question for me was, having examined the girls in hospital, could they be putting it on? Felt I could at least answer this question confidently. Told her I was certain they were not putting it on.

She invited me to stay for lunch. Thinking of dismal fare in hospital canteen, I took her up on offer. This proved a mistake. For one thing, the food was very disturbing, & for another, I ended up sitting next to the bad-tempered police constable I'd met in reception. Miss Christie melted away as soon as she had us seated, & so for some time it was just the two of us, eating our dismal fish pie side by side.

Eventually, constable remarked that there was something funny about the fish pie. It had an odd taste.

'Maybe it has thallium in it,' I said amusingly.

Misjudgement. He looked round at me. 'What did you say?'

Retreated rapidly, but he was not willing to let it drop. Wanted to know why I knew so much about thallium. Told him I'd read about it in *The Pale Horse*, by Agatha Christie.

He continued to stare at me suspiciously. Could see he was now wondering if I was mysterious thallium poisoner responsible for all this trouble. He'd put down his fork & made no move to pick it up again.

In effort to clear my name, I said it had been Environmental Health who'd mentioned thallium first. He got even more interested in this, though I tried to convince him it was just a passing fancy. Told him I was certain these girls hadn't been poisoned. He remained unpersuaded, and started going on about undetectable poisons. Next thing I knew, we were on the Soviets, Georgi Markov & the poisoned umbrella.

Told him that even if a poison itself was undetectable, results would not be. Pointed out that despite florid symptoms, girls were not systemically unwell. None of them dying. (Thought it best not to mention first girl, whose case is more concerning.)

I'd abandoned my own attempts to eat the fish pie now. It tasted dreadful. If anything, a bit of thallium might have improved it.

Asked constable, since he seemed so certain it was poison, whether police had any suspects.

He said he couldn't disclose that to me. Then: 'But yes, actually. One.'

I hope he didn't mean me.

Back at the hospital, I went to check on other patients, and after that went back to see the first girl, Diane. Evening by then. The mother had gone home to get some fresh clothes, so for once she was alone. No need for nurse to watch her now; she's developed spasticity & is almost completely bed-bound. I found her awake, but not aware. She was staring at the ceiling, blinking occasionally, but otherwise entirely motionless. I spoke her name, & asked a couple of questions, but she didn't make any acknowledgement. She still isn't responding to amantadine. Not yet, anyway. Time to try the steroids? Broached it with

Lehman yesterday, but he isn't sure either. Rhys suggested we hold off a few more days.

Spent the next hour sitting by her bed, trying to think, until Rhys came in and said, 'James, go *home*.'

Keep thinking I just need to CT her, but already know what it'll show, & I still won't know the cause.

Will probably go into work later this afternoon, just to see how she is. Already tried ringing Lehman for an update 'Leave me alone,' was his response. Said something rude about considering my day off a day of respite for him too.

Might be better to wait until this evening to visit, when Lehman's gone home. I can fax you this letter while I'm there.

Hand cramping. Your stupid pen has stiff nib. No innuendo intended. Sorry. Very tired. George, I can't seem to sleep without you. When I said I'd never live with you, I was being ridiculous. Besides, I could have just told people I was your unfeasibly handsome cousin. This is typical of me: I have all my good ideas too late.

J

4

IDA WAS QUICKLY BECOMING familiar with what it was like to feel her body betray her. Mostly the jerks happened in her right arm, but occasionally her left arm went too, and once or twice one of her legs became involved. It was a deeply unsettling experience. Sometimes one of her limbs would jerk with no warning at all, as if she were possessed; but at other times she felt a sense of escalating tension, agitation bubbling just below her skin, that grew and grew until it became unbearable, at which point a sudden jerk resolved it. It was exhausting, trying to hold her arms and legs still all the time, and the harder she tried to suppress the jerks, the more violent and frequent they seemed to become. The cold weather didn't help either, making her limbs feel stiffer. They'd all copied Victoria now the temperature had dropped further, with most girls wearing at least two jumpers at a time.

'What's happening to me?' Ida said to Louise in despair, having dropped a pile of books in the middle of Yard as her arm went again.

'Not sure,' Louise said, stooping to pick them up for her. 'It's quite interesting.'

'I can't even write properly half the time. I can't keep up in lessons.'

'Well, at least you're not missing much there,' Louise said.

'And what if Miss Christie sends me home?' Miss Christie had tried to call Ida's mother the previous day, but thankfully she had been out at the time. Ida couldn't predict how her mother might react; she seemed to have washed her hands of Ida completely, so it was possible she would evince no interest at all in her daughter's strange new malady. At the very least, she would assume Ida was faking it.

'She hasn't sent the others home,' Louise said. 'And on the plus side,' she added, glancing around quickly to make sure there was no one within earshot, 'at least you're in the clear now. You'd hardly have poisoned yourself, would you?'

'I suppose not,' Ida said.

'Although it would be a very good misdirect,' Louise went on thoughtfully, 'to have a go at offing April, and then pretend to be a victim yourself.'

'I didn't try to "off" her!' Ida said. Rather hurt, she added, 'And I'm not pretending.'

'Well, excuse me,' Louise said, 'for overestimating your criminal ambition. You did try to frame me for murder.'

'It wasn't for murder!'

'So anyway,' Louise went on, 'if you're really not pretending, then the plot thickens further.' She made to hand Ida's books back, but, seeing Ida's arm twitch again, thought better of it and tucked them under her own arm instead. With the air of Poirot pondering a particularly fascinating case, she said, 'So if you're not putting this on, and you haven't actually done anything to anyone except for April, the question remains . . .' She left a dramatic pause.

Ida waited patiently.

Louise said, '*Who has?*'

THE NEXT DAY, IDA was driven to the hospital by Miss Christie, along with three girls in Lower School who had also recently developed symptoms: in the case of one, a persistent tremor in her right arm, and in the case of the other two, intermittently jerking limbs like Ida's. Miss Christie directed the girl with the tremor to sit in the front passenger seat, perhaps deciding she would be the least distracting of the four during the drive. Ida and the other two squeezed into the back. The winding and potholed roads did nothing to help with their jerking limbs, and the more one of them flailed, the more the limbs of the other two seemed to jerk in response, so that it must have seemed to Miss Christie, glancing in the rear-view mirror, as if they were recreating Michael Jackson's 'Thriller' on the back seat.

'Did yours start suddenly?' one of the girls next to Ida asked her as they approached the outskirts of Eastbourne.

'Yeah.'

'Mine too. It started in Maths. At first I thought it was just because I was so stressed about quadratic equations, but then it kept starting and stopping again throughout the rest of the day. Do you think we've been poisoned?'

'No,' Ida said, trying to keep her voice calm. These younger girls seemed eager to defer to her, which she found disquieting.

The girl on her other side said, looking anxiously at Ida, 'You know some of the others are saying we're putting it on? But I really can't stop doing it.' Her arm had started up again while she was speaking and she sounded close to tears.

'I know,' said Ida. 'No one thinks you're pretending.'

'They *do*. Barbara Bridges told everyone—'

'Barbara Bridges can fuck off,' Ida said, quietly so Miss Christie couldn't hear.

The other two giggled nervously at this. The girl with the tremor, who sat in the front, craned her neck, trying to hear what they were saying.

'It'll be all right,' Ida told them all – although in her experience, when she considered it, things did not usually turn out all right.

AT THE HOSPITAL, THEY were directed to the neurology department on the third floor, and then to a small waiting area in the main corridor. The girls sat side by side on a row of chairs, twitching and jerking intermittently, with Miss Christie at the end. At least they didn't look so out of place in a neurology department, Ida thought, an environment in which everyone's body seemed to be letting them down. But she hated hospitals; they made her remember those long months when she'd thought her mother was dying.

A nurse appeared, and took each girl in turn into a nearby bay to take some blood. This procedure required two nurses in the end: one to hold the arm still, while the other wielded the needle.

Then there was more waiting.

Ida knew that Angela and the other girls who'd been admitted must be on a ward nearby, and wondered if she might go and see them. Sophie had made her promise to try to get some news of them while she was at the hospital.

'Miss Christie?' Ida tried after a moment. 'Please may I visit Angela while we're here?'

'I'm afraid not,' Miss Christie said. 'We can't have you wandering the hospital willy-nilly, and anyway, the girls on the ward are supposed to avoid any excitement. It could set them back.'

Ida had never before considered herself to be a dangerously exciting person, but she didn't dare argue with Miss Christie.

Finally, a young doctor appeared. He looked tired, Ida thought. She wondered if he was worn out by all these girls and their strange maladies.

She noticed his nose: it was slightly pushed off centre, as though it had been broken long ago. That sort of thing didn't matter on a man, she thought; it just made him look interesting. It would matter on a girl.

'I'm Dr Halliwell,' he said. 'Right, who's first?'

There was a brief silence, and then, since they didn't all seem to be rushing at once, Ida said, 'I'll go.'

'Splendid,' the doctor said, giving her a tired smile.

He led her round a corner and through a door into what appeared to be some kind of meeting room. As he held the door open and stood back to let her enter, Ida noticed that he seemed to be observing her gait rather intently. She felt suddenly self-conscious. She was almost certain that she was walking normally, and at the very least her leg was behaving itself.

There was another doctor in the room, sitting on a chair in the corner and wearing a truculent expression. He was a few years older than Dr Halliwell, with fair hair and a ruddy face.

'This is my colleague, Dr Lehman,' Dr Halliwell said. 'He'll be sitting in.'

Dr Lehman made what sounded to Ida like a scornful noise.

'Sorry we're in a conference room,' Dr Halliwell added. 'The exam room has a dodgy pipe. It's the hot-water pipe, so we're afraid it might burst and leave us all lightly poached. Right. Can I start by just getting you to walk heel to toe, Ida?' He demonstrated what he meant, walking an invisible line.

Feeling still more self-conscious, Ida copied him.

'OK,' he said, after a few moments. 'Please take a seat.' He perched on the edge of the desk, facing her. 'Could you describe the twitches you're experiencing?'

'They're mostly in my right arm,' Ida said. 'Occasionally it happens in my left too. And sometimes one of my legs jerks.'

'Has the jerking leg ever caused you to fall over?'

'No.'

He turned towards his colleague. 'Interesting, isn't it, Lehman? The body compensates.' To Ida, he said, 'Do the jerks seem to have any particular pattern in when they happen? For instance, do they happen when you're sitting still, or when you're lying in bed, or when you're in the middle of moving about or doing something?'

'I don't think there's any pattern,' Ida said. 'They seem to happen at any time, sometimes when I'm moving about and sometimes when I'm still. I can't seem to predict them at all.'

Dr Halliwell looked at his colleague again. 'Multifocal, with distribution varied and inconsistent. Doesn't it seem unlikely to you that the origin could be brainstem, spinal and cortical?'

'Doesn't prove anything,' the other doctor said.

Dr Halliwell got a penlight out of his pocket. He checked Ida's eyes with the light, and then made her follow the movement of his finger with her gaze, and to look quickly between his two raised fingers. Next he got her to reach out and touch his finger, then to touch her nose with her own finger. He made her carry out this manoeuvre repeatedly. Ida managed all of this without difficulty, and felt rather pleased with herself when he said, 'Good.'

'Please could you extend your right arm for me?' Dr Halliwell asked her.

Ida did so. Gently, Dr Halliwell touched her outstretched fingertips with his own. Ida's arm jerked violently in response.

The doctor nodded.

Ida's arm continued to jerk, and she tried to hold it still with her other arm. But Dr Halliwell said, 'Don't try to keep it still. But I would like you to give something else a go. On the arm that's jerking, please could you tap your thumb and forefinger together? OK, good. Yes, like that. Can you repeat that five times, please? Really focus on getting the action right. OK, and now copy the pattern of my tapping.'

Ida followed his instructions as best she could. After about a minute, as if by magic, the jerking in her arm stopped. It was like someone had switched off a piece of faulty machinery.

She stared at Dr Halliwell. 'How did you do that?'

He looked thoughtful, but gave her no direct answer. He said, 'And do you feel well in yourself, apart from the jerks?'

Ida said she did.

'OK.' He nodded and was silent for a moment longer.

The other doctor said, 'We should do an EEG as well.'

'There's no need,' Dr Halliwell said.

Ida wasn't sure what an EEG was, but she didn't think she fancied one.

'Rhys will back me up,' the other doctor said.

'Oh, come on,' Dr Halliwell said. 'He won't sign off on the CT scan that we *actually need*, but you think he's going to encourage you to do as many pointless EEGs as you like?'

'Maybe he trusts my judgement,' the other doctor said.

'Well, that's hardly very likely,' Dr Halliwell said tersely.

They seemed to have forgotten Ida was there.

'But what's wrong with me?' she said, since she got the impression her appointment was about to end without her receiving any useful information at all.

Dr Halliwell looked back at her and seemed to recollect himself. 'We're not certain yet,' he said, in a gentler tone. And then, seeing Ida's dismay, he added, 'But I think you're going to be all right.'

You *think* I am? Ida thought.

Dr Lehman appeared similarly unimpressed by Dr Halliwell's comment, because he made another of his scornful noises.

'Are you all right, Dr Lehman?' Dr Halliwell said. 'Can I perhaps get you a tissue?'

'But have we been poisoned?' Ida blurted out.

Dr Halliwell frowned. 'I think that's exceptionally unlikely.'

'What about with something like laburnum?' Ida said, because in for a penny . . .

His frown intensified. 'Laburnum? What makes you say that?'

'It's just a rumour that was going round,' Ida said.

'Well, I can set your mind at rest there, at least,' Dr Halliwell said. 'This isn't laburnum poisoning.'

'Are you sure?'

'I'm certain.'

Ida hesitated. 'But hypothetically,' she said, 'could you harm someone with laburnum seeds?'

'*Hypothetically*, how many seeds are we talking about?'

Dr Lehman cleared his throat, but Dr Halliwell ignored him.

'Four,' Ida said promptly. Then she amended this to, 'Around four. Three to four. Just to pluck a hypothetical number out of thin air.'

'Well, no,' Dr Halliwell said. 'Four laburnum seeds aren't going to do much to anyone.'

'Even if someone's already unwell?' Ida almost whispered.

Dr Halliwell was still frowning. 'Laburnum contains an alkaloid called cytisine. That's the element that's harmful. But the total amount of cytisine in four seeds would be very low. At worst, it might give you an upset stomach.' He was staring rather hard at Ida. 'You know, for a hypothetical scenario, some of these details seem very specific.'

'Well, you know rumours,' Ida said. 'They get more detailed as they get passed on, take on a life of their own and so on.'

The doctor shook his head. 'I think you'd have to give someone about twenty laburnum seeds to do them serious harm.'

'Twenty!' Ida said, hugely relieved. 'Well, no one's going to be slipping anyone *twenty* laburnum seeds! How would you even disguise the flavour?'

'OK,' Dr Halliwell said slowly, still looking puzzled. 'Well, if you have no further questions about flora, I'd better get on with the next exam.'

He took Ida back to the waiting area.

As the next girl with jerking limbs got to her feet to be examined, her body suddenly went rigid. Dr Halliwell seemed to have very fast reflexes, and he shot forward to catch her as she toppled over. He laid her down on the floor and Ida watched in fascinated horror as the girl began to jerk and thrash violently.

Dr Halliwell kept his hand under her head, palm up, to cushion it against the floor.

The girl's eyes were squeezed shut as her arms and legs continued to thrash.

'Shall I get a nurse to help?' Miss Christie said. Her voice was steady, but Ida saw that she'd turned pale.

'No, we're all right,' Dr Halliwell said. 'What's her name?'

'Kylie.'

'Kylie,' Dr Halliwell repeated, raising his voice a little as he addressed the girl on the floor. 'You're having a seizure, but you're going to be fine. It's all right.'

He looked at Ida and then nodded at her wrist. 'Is that a Casio watch? With a timer?'

'Yes.'

'Could you start the timer now, please?'

Perplexed, Ida did as she was instructed. They waited in silence as Kylie thrashed and jerked on the ground, Dr Halliwell crouching beside her with his hand under her head as Ida timed the whole thing.

It was just over three minutes before Kylie's thrashing began to lessen, and then her body gradually stilled. Her eyes remained tightly closed, her breaths coming rapidly.

'Kylie, can you hear me?' Dr Halliwell said. He removed his hand gently from under her head and lifted her wrist to check her pulse.

'How long was that?' he asked Ida.

'Three minutes and eight seconds,' Ida said, looking at her watch.

He nodded. 'Could you restart the timer now, please?'

Ida did so.

'Why isn't she waking up?' one of the other girls said tremulously.

'She will,' the doctor said. 'You can talk to her, if you like.'

The other girls seemed overcome with stage fright at the prospect, but after a moment, the girl with the tremor in her arm burst out, 'Kylie! Kiss, marry, kill: Prince, Mark Thatcher . . . and Mr Langfield from school.'

The doctor minutely raised his eyebrow at this. Miss Christie, to Ida's surprise, said nothing. She was still staring down at Kylie.

Dr Halliwell took out his penlight and gently pried open one of Kylie's eyelids. He shone the torch in her eye and then clicked it off again. Kylie's eyelid closed tightly again as soon as he let go. Then Dr Halliwell took one of her hands and raised it above her face. The arm was limp. He let it drop, and her hand fell to one side, resting next to her head.

'What are you doing?' Ida said, fascinated.

'Testing her guarding response,' he said. 'Did you notice how her hand fell so as to avoid hitting her face? That's useful information for me. It's suggestive of a non-epileptic seizure. How long has the timer been going for now?'

'Two minutes,' Ida said. She was quite enjoying her role, and wondered if she could be a doctor herself. It probably wasn't too late to switch to science A-levels; she doubted the school would care much either way. 'Is she all right?' she asked Dr Halliwell.

'Yes, she will be.'

Since this was confirmed, Ida felt it wouldn't be too insensitive to ask, 'Do you have to be very clever to be a doctor?'

Dr Halliwell gave her a brief grin. 'God, no.' Then, catching Miss Christie's eye, he immediately sobered. 'She'll come round in a moment,' he said.

This proved correct. Moments later, Kylie's eyes began to flutter open. She seemed groggy and disorientated.

Miss Christie knelt next to her and gently helped her sit up. 'You're all right, Kylie,' she said. 'You're in the hospital. You had a funny turn, but you're quite all right now.'

Dr Halliwell crouched in front of her. 'Do you remember anything about the seizure, Kylie?'

Her tongue came out and licked her lips nervously. She swallowed. 'I remember starting to get up and then it was like the world suddenly tilted.'

'And while you were on the floor, do you remember anything then?'

She looked uncertain. 'I think I heard your voices. And I think I heard Sarah saying something about kissing Mark Thatcher.'

Dr Halliwell nodded, thoughtful again. To Ida, he said, 'If you're interested, that suggests involvement of both cerebral hemispheres and no loss of consciousness.' To Kylie, he said, 'And how do you feel now?'

'All right,' Kylie said.

'Any headache?'

'No.'

'Do you think you can get up, if your teacher helps you?'

Kylie nodded, and Miss Christie helped her to her feet. She swayed as she stood, but was steadied by Miss Christie's supporting arm around her.

'I think we'll get you to the meeting room for your exam now, if that's all right,' Dr Halliwell said. 'Perhaps you could stay with her for the examination, Miss Christie?' he added. Then to Kylie again, 'I'll get a nurse to find you a carton of juice from somewhere, too. Sort out that blood sugar.'

The three of them moved away at a slow pace, Kylie still leaning on Miss Christie, and Ida and the remaining two girls were left alone in the waiting area.

They sat quietly for a few moments.

'Will that happen to us too?' the girl with the tremor said.

'No,' Ida said, wearily accepting her role as wise old owl. 'And look, she's fine, anyway. We all saw that she's fine.'

'My grandpa got a tremor in his arm like mine,' the girl said. 'It got worse and worse, and then he started falling over and forgetting things, and then he died. It took ages and it was awful.'

'You're not going to die,' Ida said.

There was a silence. After a moment, Ida made herself reach out and pat the girl's knee reassuringly. Then, feeling her duty was discharged, she allowed her thoughts to drift.

'Shall we play "I spy" to pass the time?' the second Lower School girl said.

Ida surveyed the bleak, near-empty corridor without enthusiasm. 'I don't think there's much to spy here.'

'Perhaps we could recite our favourite poems to each other?' the second girl said hopefully.

254

'Perhaps,' Ida said, horrified. Then, in a flash of inspiration: 'But I really need the loo. If Miss Christie comes back, please could you tell her I've gone to find the toilet?'

'Lavatory,' the girl said automatically, but Ida was already almost out of earshot, heading down the corridor, round the corner and out of sight.

She didn't especially need the toilet, and it occurred to her now that while Miss Christie was out of the way and Ida herself had a plausible excuse for wandering, she might be able to find the ward where Angela and the others were. She could say a quick hello and probably still be back before Miss Christie returned.

She went past the nurses' station, past a ward which seemed to be full of elderly men, and after that there was one more room. Ida cautiously stuck her head round the door.

The room had only a single occupant, a young girl lying in bed with her eyes closed. Ida took in her appearance briefly: thin and pale, an oxygen mask on her face, a tube running from a bag of clear liquid and disappearing beneath the bandage over her hand. Coloured wires came out from the neck of her gown and connected to a monitor on a trolley by the bed.

A woman – the girl's mother, Ida assumed – was slumped in a chair beside the bed. She looked up when Ida appeared. Then, taking in Ida's uniform, she said, 'Hello. Are you a friend of Diane's?'

Ida hadn't recognized the girl in the bed until then.

'Yes,' she said, because it seemed impossible to say anything else. 'I'm in her year.'

On the bed, the girl who didn't look like Diane made a low noise in the back of her throat. Her eyes stayed shut, but one of her hands opened and closed, and then seemed to stick in a half-open position, raking feebly at the bedclothes. Her mother took the hand gently in her own, kissed it, and laid it back down again. Diane's fingers stayed fixed in the same position, rigid as a claw.

'How is she?' Ida said, uselessly.

Diane's mother gave her a look of such fathomless despair that Ida would never be able to forget it. 'As you see,' she said.

Ida couldn't think what else to say, but she was saved from making any reply in the end because Diane made an awful retching noise and her torso convulsed. Her eyes came open, wide and straining; it made Ida think unaccountably of a terrified horse. Then Diane was vomiting into her mask and there was a wheezing and gargling sound.

Diane's mother was already on her feet, pulling Diane's oxygen mask off and rolling her body on to its side. 'Get a nurse!' she shouted.

Ida ran. The nurses had heard Diane's mother shouting before Ida reached the station, and a nurse was already coming out from behind the desk as Ida rushed up.

'Diane,' Ida said, out of breath. 'I think she's choking.'

The nurse ran towards Diane's room, and Ida followed more slowly. She stood in the doorway again. The nurse had pushed the end of a long plastic tube into Diane's mouth. Ida saw that Diane's lips had a blueish tinge now. There was the noise of suction and slurping. Diane's mother stood to one side, her hands held very tightly together.

A few moments later, the nurse reached out to turn a knob on the tank on the wall, and the noise stopped. She pulled the tube carefully out of Diane's throat and then stepped back.

'Another choking episode, but she's OK now,' she said to Diane's mother. 'I'll go and get her a fresh oxygen mask, and I'll send the doctor in to check her over.'

Diane's mother nodded tightly. She smoothed Diane's hair back from her pale forehead and leaned in to kiss her. Diane's lips were returning to their normal colour. Her eyes were closed again. 'It's all right, my darling,' her mother said, almost too softly for anyone else to hear. 'You're all right now. Mummy's here.' Then she glanced up and saw Ida, still standing in the doorway as if transfixed.

'Thanks for your help,' she said.

Ida only nodded. She knew she needed to leave, but it felt strangely difficult to move. She was afraid for a moment that she might fall down and have a fit like the others, but then there was a steadying hand on her shoulder.

'Let's leave Diane and her mother in peace now,' Miss Christie said. And to Diane's mother: 'I'll be back to see you tomorrow, Joanne.'

Mrs Fulbrook nodded, eyes still on her daughter.

Miss Christie and Ida walked back to the waiting area in silence. Ida assumed Miss Christie was gearing up to give her a huge telling-off, but she only said, just before they rounded the corner to the waiting area, 'I think it would be better if you didn't mention this to anyone at school, Ida.'

'OK,' Ida said. Keeping things to herself was something she was very good at. She asked, 'Will she be all right?'

She hoped Miss Christie would offer some reassurance, however unconvincing, but she said, without any of her usual briskness, 'I really don't know.'

5

'BUSINESS AS USUAL,' MISS Christie reminded the staff during their briefings each morning. They now began each day with a staff meeting in the school hall, during which Miss Christie and the heads of year would share updates on the affected girls and bulletins from the doctors and Environmental Health team. Miss Christie began and ended each of these briefings with the reminder that lessons were to continue as normal, that it behoved them all to maintain normality and routine for their remaining pupils.

'We can and must continue. We will not close,' she said, in response to Trudy's question about whether they could really go on as they were.

Some parents had already come to take their daughters away, and now about three-quarters of the school body remained. In addition to the girls in hospital, there were now fifteen girls at school displaying jerks and twitches, ranging from Lower School to Sixth Form.

Eleanor admired Miss Christie's courage. She suspected that Miss Christie feared, as Eleanor did herself, that if the school closed now, it would never reopen.

Beyond the gates, journalists had been massing all week. The story had hit the national papers now.

'Reminds me of the siege of Mytilene,' Vera said, sounding as if she'd been there personally.

'Suetonius,' Eleanor said, to please her.

'That old windbag,' Vera said. 'Say what you like about Livy, at least he was succinct.'

The police presence kept the journalists at bay for the most part, but every now and then a more enterprising reporter managed to inveigle their way on to the site. Editors had realized quickly that it made more sense to send female reporters into the school, since they blended in better among the female teaching staff. Miss Christie had reminded all the girls in assembly not to talk to the press, and to alert a teacher should they notice a stranger on the school site, but their girls were not known for their ability or willingness to follow instructions. Besides, the excitement was too much for them.

'Some of them are bound to talk to the reporters,' Eleanor remarked to Vera. 'They won't be able to resist.'

'I'm more worried about the English department,' Vera said. 'I think Trudy and Linda might quite fancy seeing their names in print. And what about that beau of yours? Isn't he a reporter?'

'He's not my beau,' Eleanor said.

'Not anymore,' Vera said. 'But you'd expect him to be sniffing around now, wouldn't you? Trying to get a quote.'

'Yes,' Eleanor said. 'You would.'

She had already received three brief messages from Anthony this week asking her to ring him or write back. The most recent missive – which had arrived with this morning's post – had both irritated and disturbed her:

Dear Eleanor,

Please let me tell you in person how sorry I am, just one more time. I was weak and stupid. You didn't deserve any of it. Let me try to make it up to you?

A.

It seemed astonishing to her now, and humiliating, that she had ever believed a word he said. But she supposed she had wanted to believe him – that was the difference back then. She crumpled the paper up and dropped it into the bin next to the pigeonholes. Then she fished it out again and put it in her pocket, having been struck by the awful idea of someone else coming across it.

And speaking of men who lied, here was Matthew coming in to check his pigeonhole. He blushed when he saw her. Eleanor had mostly managed to avoid being alone with him in the week since the open day, pretending not to notice the slightly desperate looks he telegraphed in her direction.

'Eleanor,' he said.

'Hello,' she said, her hand still in her pocket, curled around Anthony's crumpled message.

'Look, I wanted to say I'm sorry,' Matthew said, after the briefest hesitation. She couldn't seem to move for men apologizing to her. 'And to say I'm going to hand in my notice,' he added. 'I've got the letter written. Here –' eagerly, he pulled it from his pocket and held it out to her – 'I'm going to give it to Miss Christie now.'

These men and their letters, Eleanor thought. She said, not taking it, 'I don't think that's necessary.'

'Of course it is,' he said. 'I won't ask you to cover for me. It's kind of you not to have told Miss Christie already. This way at least I can resign instead of being sacked. Thank you for that.'

'What will you do?' Eleanor said. 'Try the same again at another school?'

'No,' he said. Then, with an attempt at levity, 'I don't think I could pull it off a second time.'

'You didn't pull it off the first time,' she reminded him.

He smiled at her, rather sadly. 'I'd like to tell you the whole story. If you'd be willing to hear it. Once I've left, perhaps. I'd rather do it once I've left, and then you really won't have to see me again. I'll stay until the end of term, so as not to leave Miss Christie in the lurch. Do you think I ought to?'

'Yes, I do,' she said. Against her better judgement, she added, 'Does the whole story cast you in a better light than the bit of it I already know?'

His face fell. 'Well, no, actually. The whole story is quite a bit worse.' He was watching her. 'But I'd like to tell you all the same. If you'll let me.'

'You might as well tell me now,' she said.

'I don't think I can. The thing is, Eleanor . . .' He stopped. 'Once, not all that long ago, I did something awful. That's the part I need to tell you about. I did something that can't ever be undone. However much I wish it. Because if it weren't for that, I might feel able to ask you . . .' But he stopped again.

Eleanor waited, frowning.

But when he next spoke, it was only to say, 'I'll be gone at the end of term. And then after that perhaps we can . . . perhaps I can tell you all of it.'

The door banged, and there was Linda. Eleanor and Matthew both jumped, and to her intense irritation and dismay, Eleanor felt her face reddening.

'I hope I'm not interrupting anything!' Linda said merrily. Blasted Linda!

'Not unless you find the collection of post in any way illicit,' Eleanor said, with more asperity than was usual for her.

She felt Matthew's eyes on her, and then he said, 'I must go. I have a meeting with Miss Christie before lessons start.'

When the door had closed behind him, Linda said, 'He was in rather a hurry, wasn't he? Do you think he's good-looking, Eleanor? I didn't at first, but now I think perhaps he is, in a sort of delicate, dying-poet way, like Keats. I think in fact,' she concluded, 'I might have fallen in love with him. Trudy thinks she might have too. So that leaves us in something of a quandary. Especially if you love him too.' She looked at Eleanor rather challengingly.

'No, I don't,' Eleanor said. 'He's up for grabs. Right, I have to go and get ready for my Lower School lesson. They're doing presentations on sheep farming in New Zealand.'

'What a life,' Linda said, without any apparent cynicism.

AFTER HER SHEEP-FARMING LESSON, Eleanor had a free period, which was just as well, as she needed a pause to recover from the presentations she'd just witnessed. She was crossing Yard, which was empty for once, when someone abruptly emerged from the shadows of the wall and said, 'Eleanor!'

And there, to her consternation, was Anthony – unaccountably wearing a suit and carrying a clipboard.

'I pretended to be with Environmental Health,' he told her, coming closer and touching her elbow. 'People will let you in anywhere if you have a clipboard.' He sounded pleased with himself, as if he actually expected Eleanor to congratulate him.

She said, 'You shouldn't be here.'

'And yet,' he said, 'here I am.'

He drew her closer to the wall, where they were partially concealed from sight.

She said, 'Anthony, you need to leave. You're trespassing.'

'How else was I supposed to speak to you?' he said. 'You haven't replied to my letters.'

Letters? Eleanor thought. At best, they were notes. She said, 'You must know I'm not going to say anything to you.'

'I miss you,' he said, determinedly.

'Anthony, don't be silly. No, you don't.'

'Tell me what's going on,' he said. 'Is there anyone who might have wanted to harm these girls? Eleanor,' he went on more urgently, 'you know something isn't right here. You *know* it. And the public wouldn't have had a whisper of any of this if I hadn't broken the story. Now all the others are on the case too.'

She stared at him and didn't speak. It was cold, and although she was wearing her thickest cardigan, she had no coat. Her teeth were beginning to chatter, but he didn't notice.

'I'm just trying to uncover the truth,' he said. 'That's what we do. We shine a light into the dark places.'

'You make it sound very grand.'

'It *is* grand,' he said. 'Look, I know you don't have much respect left for me, but at least respect my work. I haven't cared about much in my life, but I care about this. I'm trying to do my job, and do it well. People need to know what's going on here. And the police and doctors won't tell them. Help me, Eleanor. You cared enough about truth once.'

What a contemptible thing to say to her. But she supposed she had, once. Perhaps that was a habit he'd cured her of. She thought of Matthew.

Anthony was still looking at her. Presumably he had intended to stir her with his speech, but she didn't feel stirred; she felt annoyed, and she felt tired.

'Please just go,' she said. 'Everyone will think I helped you get in. They'll think I've spoken to you.'

'You are speaking to me.'

'You know what I mean.'

'I'll anonymize you,' he said. 'Of course. No one will know it's you.' She saw him gather himself for a final attempt. 'I want the same thing as you, Eleanor. To help these girls.'

'We have different ideas about what that means,' she said. 'You need to go now, or I'll go and tell the police and Miss Christie you're here.'

She started to walk away from him, but he took her arm. 'Just wait, please.'

She shook him off. 'Go away, Anthony.'

'Is everything all right here?' It was Matthew, striding towards them.

Heaven help us, Eleanor thought. She was in no mood for chivalry.

'Everything's fine,' she said. 'This is a journalist who's managed to find his way on to the site. But he's just agreed to leave.'

'Anthony Marshall,' Anthony said. He was actually holding out his hand.

Matthew didn't take it. 'Can you find your way out?' he said. 'I can show you.'

Eleanor watched the two men eyeing each other.

Anthony said, conversationally, 'We used to be engaged, Eleanor and I.'

The brute.

Matthew's eyes widened.

Eleanor said, 'That was a long time ago now.'

'Not so very long,' Anthony said.

'Long enough.'

'All the more reason,' Matthew said, recovering himself, 'for you to leave when she asks you to.'

'Or what?' Anthony said.

Good God, Eleanor thought. Were they actually going to have a duel?

She said, 'Matthew, perhaps you could go and alert the policeman in reception.'

'Oh, never mind,' Anthony said. 'I'm going. But think about what I said, Eleanor. You have my phone number.'

He started to walk away from them, back across Yard towards the door to the main building, still clutching his ridiculous clipboard.

'We ought to tell Miss Christie anyway,' Eleanor said to Matthew, as they watched him disappear.

'Eleanor, was he really your fiancé?' Matthew said.

She sighed. 'Yes, he was.'

'He doesn't seem . . .' Matthew began. Then, 'It's obvious he didn't deserve you.'

Eleanor laughed, in spite of herself. 'I dare say he didn't.' She hesitated, then said, 'I think I told you before that he left me. That wasn't quite the truth. In fact, I left him. But only after I discovered he was already married, and didn't seem to have any intention of leaving his wife. Not that I'd have wanted him to. I have no idea what he was doing with me in the first place. He must have known I'd find out eventually.' The humiliation hadn't lessened much with time. Finally, she dared to meet Matthew's eye. He was looking at her with understanding.

'I expect he loved you,' he said. 'Even if he turned out to be an idiot.'

'Oh, I very much doubt that,' Eleanor said, more embarrassed still.

'I don't find it so implausible,' Matthew said. 'That somebody could love you.'

She looked away again.

After a moment, he said, 'I've handed in my letter.'

Eleanor seized with relief upon the change of subject. 'What did Miss Christie say?'

'She wasn't very pleased, because now she has to recruit again. But she has more time now, at least. More time than before.'

'What did you give as your reason?'

'I said it was for personal reasons.'

Eleanor gave a small smile. 'I'm sure that went down well.'

'It did not,' Matthew said, with a glimmer of humour. 'But it means I'll be gone at the end of term. I thought I might move to Brighton. Somewhere not too far away. And I wondered if we might, perhaps, be able to stay in touch. If you wanted to.'

'All right,' Eleanor said. Perhaps she did want to.

She might have said more, but the door to the main building opened again and suddenly the police sergeant and constable were coming towards them. They were moving, it seemed to Eleanor, with an unusual sense of purpose. She assumed at first they were coming over to ask about Anthony. She was so certain this was the case that there was a few moments' lag before she was able to process what the sergeant was actually saying.

Which was this: 'Matthew Langfield, you are under arrest on suspicion of administering a poison or noxious thing thereby endangering life or inflicting grievous bodily harm, contrary to Section 23 of the Offences against the Person Act, 1861.'

The sergeant had grasped Matthew's arm now, and turned him round to handcuff him.

'What?' Matthew said. 'I haven't done anything. What are you talking about?'

The sergeant snapped the handcuffs closed. He said, 'You do not have to say anything if you do not wish to do so, but anything you do say may be used against you in a court of law.'

'Surely there's been a mistake,' Eleanor said.

'Please,' Matthew said. 'Please, I haven't done anything.'

'The sick girls have tested positive for thallium,' the constable said. 'A poisonous substance.'

'Poison?' Eleanor said. 'That's impossible.'

'Unfortunately not,' the sergeant said, though he didn't seem too downcast about it. 'And we found rat poison in Mr Langfield's room. The old kind: the kind that contains thallium.'

Eleanor looked at Matthew in horror.

Matthew said, 'It's not mine. Really it isn't.'

The sergeant snorted at this. 'I'm sure Mary Ann Cotton said the same about her arsenic teapot.'

'But it's true,' Matthew said. 'We found it in a box above the stage when we were putting a play on. Eleanor, you remember?'

And suddenly she did. 'Yes,' she said eagerly. 'We put it to one side to dispose of, and then I had to rush off to see a sick student.' She'd forgotten all about it until now.

'So how did it end up in your room, then?' the constable said to Matthew.

'I didn't know how I ought to get rid of it,' Matthew said. 'I didn't want to just throw it into one of the bins where a girl might find it. I thought I ought to dispose of it safely. So I took it to my room for safekeeping, and then forgot about it.'

'Very convenient,' the constable said.

'It's true!' Matthew protested.

'This is silly,' Eleanor said, trying to sound reasonable. 'You can't seriously suspect Mr Langfield. We didn't even find the rat poison until the girls were already unwell. And besides, why would he want to harm any of the girls here?'

'I think there's a lot you don't know about your Mr Langfield,' the sergeant said. 'If you did, you might be less eager to cover for him.'

'I'm not covering for him,' Eleanor said, irritated. 'I'm simply pointing out how unlikely it is that he's poisoned anyone. You don't have sufficient grounds to arrest him.'

'It's funny that the poisonings started immediately after he arrived here,' the sergeant said. 'Would you call that a coincidence?'

'Yes, I would,' Eleanor said.

'I might have done too,' he said. 'But then we started looking into the backgrounds of some of the teachers here. Just as a precaution, you understand. And things became quite . . . interesting.' He paused. 'I dare say you don't know where your Mr Langfield was before he came here.'

Eleanor glanced at Matthew, who would no longer meet her eye. His shoulders had slumped.

'London?' she hazarded.

'No,' the sergeant said. 'Try again.'

'Please don't,' Matthew said softly.

'He was in prison,' the sergeant announced with satisfaction.

Eleanor felt herself go cold. 'No,' she said. 'You've made a mistake.' She looked back at Matthew, and finally now he met her eye.

He said, 'Eleanor, it's not how it sounds.'

'Oh, sorry,' the sergeant said. 'My mistake. Were you just on *holiday* in HMP Norwich, then? For almost a year? You must have got quite the tan.'

What an unpleasant man he was, Eleanor thought.

Matthew's face was ashen. He was still looking at Eleanor. 'I wanted to tell you,' he said.

'Yes,' she said. 'I've heard that before.'

'So you see,' the sergeant said, 'we have a number of poisonings, which begin shortly after a convicted criminal arrives here posing as a teacher. Then we get our lab tests back, which show the victims have been poisoned with thallium. Next, we find a batch of this very same poison, a banned substance, hidden in this man's room. One might be forgiven for feeling somewhat suspicious.'

'I didn't do anything to those girls,' Matthew said, but his voice was dull.

'Come on,' the sergeant said, taking his arm. 'Let's go.'

Matthew gave Eleanor a final, despairing look as he was led away.

Fax from Dr James Halliwell to Dr George Fisher
Friday, 2nd November 1984, 8 p.m.

Dear George,

No improvement in Diane's condition.

Meanwhile, we've got a new mess on our hands. Police have swept in before Environmental Health could, & have had their own toxicologists spot-test urine of several affected girls. They're now claiming to have detected thallium in girls' urine, & have made an arrest. A male teacher. Apparently the idiot had a stash of rat poison in his room. Which admittedly is a bit dubious, but perhaps he is particularly afraid of rodents.

Naturally, if it were thallium, we'd have known about it before now.

Tried to reason with police sergeant at the school this morning. Didn't find him very warmly disposed towards me (especially after I'd told him how wrong he was). He argued that tests don't lie, & wasn't very receptive when I tried to explain high false-positive rate of colorimetric method.

I told him they needed to test again using atomic absorption spectroscopy. Had been discussing it with COEH (the otter man; still haven't worked out what the C stands for, by the way), and he agreed with me.

Also pointed out that the girls don't have any gastrointestinal symptoms.

Sergeant said that one girl did – the 2nd girl to be taken ill, the one who vomited in the basement. Annoyingly, he had a point. Then he pressed his advantage by arguing that the girls also have neurological symptoms present in thallium poisoning. I feared he had been reading (& misunderstanding) some papers on subject.

Tried telling him those symptoms overlapped with lots of other conditions, but it seemed impossible to convince him it wasn't thallium. I even suggested the hospital could arrange the AAS testing on police's behalf. (Looking forward to seeing Rhys's face when I tell him.)

Reported whole thing back to COEH afterwards, & he said Environmental Health could also do the test if police continue to refuse, but that he'd rather it came out of police budget than theirs – so we'll just have to see who blinks first.

Found Lehman as soon as I got back to hospital. He informed me, when I'd finished updating him, that thallium poisoning isn't absolutely impossible. I said of course it was. Wondered if he was pretending to believe in thallium theory just to annoy me. It is the sort of thing I might do to him.

Considered ringing up police sergeant to warn him Lehman agreed with him, in case that finally made him see sense, but instead went to find Rhys.

Could see he was trying to be soothing. He said either police or Environmental Health would do the 24-hour urine test before long, & then we could all move on. Said in meantime I should just focus on my own job.

Asked him how I could focus on my own job when he wouldn't even let me make a diagnosis. We had to wait, he said. 'But we all know what this is,' I said. 'It's blindingly obvious.'

'By all means, request a consult with psychiatry, then,' Rhys said. 'But you also need to *prove* we've ruled everything else out.'

J

Dear George,

Spurred on by yesterday's conversation with Rhys, decided to try out interesting idea I'd got from old *BMJ* paper. Arranged another EEG on one of the girls on ward with suspected non-epileptic seizures.

'What, another pointless EEG?' Lehman said sarcastically.

Not so pointless this time, as you will see, George.

The mother came with us to recording room, & we made small talk as technician – it was Jim, which was good, because he's relaxed sort – applied electrodes & connected leads to amplifier & recording device.

Told girl & mother I was going to inject her with medication that would induce seizure. Reassured them it was quite safe etc. The mother seemed anxious. Explained this would give us best possible chance of getting useful info from EEG recording.

Helped Jim to tilt chair back, checked girl was comfortable & then told Jim to start recording while I prepared injection.

Injected her – 'Just a small scratch' – & then we all waited.

Couple of minutes passed. Was beginning to worry she wouldn't have seizure at all & EEG would be useless. But next moment she suddenly stiffened, & then her limbs began to jerk.

I moved closer to chair to ensure she didn't roll off. Mother was on her other side. Machine whirred & the pens scratched away.

Seizure lasted 3 minutes this time, & then jerking gradually decreased. After another minute, she lay still, eyes closed.

Asked if she could hear me, & she nodded. She opened her eyes slowly & I helped her sit up. Told her that she'd done well, that this would give us some really useful info.

Saw Lehman later on. His face was not a picture of delight. He roared, 'Did you inject one of my patients with *saline*?'

Conceded that I had, but added, in mitigation, that he should come & look at EEG recording.

He shouted that he 'didn't care about the bloody EEG' (what a strange thing for a neurologist to say) & then something about ethics.

Pointed out I didn't actually lie to patient or her mother, & he said, with unpleasant sarcasm, that he was sure Rhys would be incredibly relieved & grateful to hear that.

Finally persuaded him to come & look at EEG, which conveyed exactly what you will have already guessed: very little evidence of atypical activity, & none at all in run-up to the seizure. Just a bit of spiking during seizure itself.

Lehman seized on the small spiking, of course.

I pointed out she was thrashing about all over the place – her violent movements would have generated some artefacts. But even then, not to extent we'd expect in typical seizure.

Above all, as I reminded Lehman, I induced the seizure through suggestion. You can't just *suggest* someone into having a tonic-clonic seizure.

Lehman looked at me, & then admitted with gritted teeth that I might possibly be right.

I told him it's obvious what this is, & he said, smugly, that George Fisher said a neurologist should never use words like 'obvious' or 'obviously'. I told him George Fisher probably wasn't referring to neurologists in general, but to him specifically.

He asked if I really thought, after everything we'd seen, that they'd made the whole thing up.

Give me patience.

No, I told him. That was not what I was suggesting. We've both examined the girls, we've seen their symptoms. We've also seen plenty of malingerers in our careers. It's clear that these girls really believe themselves to be ill. They're frightened, & embarrassed.

I added to Lehman that I thought the diagnosis would need to be handled carefully for this precise reason: we don't want the girls to think we're accusing them of lying. Found myself actually wishing I had a psychiatrist on hand to back me up. Desperate times indeed.

Lehman was silent for a while, then reiterated that he was telling Rhys about my unethical conduct.

With that threat delivered, we tacitly agreed a truce, & moved on to talking about Diane. Both of us agree it's time to introduce a nasogastric tube. I asked him to let me speak to her mother again first.

He offered to do it, but I said I'd rather do it myself.

'Oh, right,' he said nastily. 'Because you've got such a way with the ladies.'

(What on earth does *that* mean??)

Anyway, sought out Diane's mother & told her as gently as I could. Introduced tube myself rather than getting nurse to do it, since I was there anyway. Horrible thing to have to do to a 17-yr-old.

J

6

Since Matthew's arrest, interest in the case had reached a frenzied pitch. The crowd of journalists outside the school gates had doubled in size, and his arrest was reported in the nationals on Saturday morning. Eleanor hoped Matthew hadn't seen any of the papers. The headlines were lurid. She wondered how he was.

Mid-morning, she cracked and went to see Miss Christie to ask how much she knew.

'The police have released him,' Miss Christie said. 'At least for the time being. He's at a boarding house in South Haven, lying low. I've sent Miss Morton over with his things. Of course, he can't come back here, whether or not they decide to bring charges.' She met Eleanor's eye. 'Sorry. I know he was your friend.'

'I didn't know him very well, as it turned out,' Eleanor said. Then she thought to add, 'Did *you* know he'd been in prison?'

'Of course not,' Miss Christie said. 'We're desperate, but we're not that desperate. I tend to just assume prospective staff members aren't hardened criminals unless they do something to convince me otherwise. For instance, commit a murder right in front of me.'

'My God,' Eleanor said, turning white. 'It wasn't murder, was it? He wasn't in prison for murder.'

'Don't be silly,' Miss Christie said. 'If you must know, he forged a will. Got eleven months in HMP Norwich for his pains. That's as much as the police have told me, though I dare say the papers will get hold of more before long. I know,' she said, noting Eleanor's expression. 'Quite enterprising of him, really. You'd hardly think he had it in him.'

IT TOOK THE PAPERS a day to unearth the details, but on Sunday morning most featured an account of Matthew's conviction. Matthew Langfield, then aged thirty-two, of Park Road, Norwich, had been sentenced at Norwich Crown Court in February 1982 to eleven months in prison for the forging of his mother's will. The forgery had divided the estate, worth only £7,000, equally between Matthew and his brother.

Eleanor pored over the papers at breakfast with Vera.

'What on earth was he thinking?' she said.

'I dare say he wasn't,' Vera said. 'That's usually the trouble.'

It did seem a rather pathetic crime to Eleanor, all things considered. And presumably had it not been for this, the police would never have looked at him as a suspected poisoner. What a bloody mess, she thought.

The girls, of course, were in a delirium over it.

'Just *think*! A poisoner among us, all this time!' Eleanor heard one Third Year say to another on their way out of the dining hall.

'I *knew* he had hidden depths,' the other replied. 'Didn't I tell you? God, I really fancy him now.'

SHE HADN'T EXPECTED TO hear from Matthew after his arrest, but at lunchtime on Tuesday she found a letter in her pigeonhole, and knew immediately it was from him. She took the letter back to her room to read in private. She could almost hear his voice again as she read it.

278

Dear Eleanor,

I hope you will forgive my writing you this letter. I won't try to get your forgiveness beyond that. I'm writing this from South Haven – the address is at the top, but I won't expect a letter back from you.

You already knew I'd lied about being a teacher before I came here. Now you know what else I was concealing. I said before that I'd tell you, once I'd left the school. I think I would have done, although of course there's no way of knowing now.

I would like to tell you a little bit about how I came to be in prison. You'll know the outline already from the newspapers, and you may not wish to know anything further. You may have decided to throw away this letter without reading it. But if you would like an explanation, I feel the least I can do now is provide you with one.

I think I've always been a dishonest person, at least in some ways. I knew from an early age that I didn't please my mother, though I will say in my defence that she was not easily pleased. My older brother managed her better, but I could never learn. I think I developed the habit of lying once I started school, but it may have been before then. I would boast about my achievements to her in the hope of impressing her – my popularity, my test marks, my sporting prowess – pitiful, of course, and all entirely implausible. I was not popular, I was not a sportsman by any means and I was not particularly clever. But perhaps I'm going too far back; I don't want to take up too much of your time. So: please take my word for it that I formed the habit of dishonesty at a young age.

As I told you, I went to university – I read history at the University of East Anglia, so I wasn't a total fraud in every sense – and then got a job working for a stationery company in Norwich. I was one of their salesmen – though as you might imagine, I wasn't particularly good at it. But things were all right. I had a little flat of my own, and I had a few friends, and I visited my parents at the weekends. My father died when I was twenty-eight, and that made things more difficult with my mother. My father was a very mild man, and I didn't realize until he was gone how much he had mitigated some of my mother's more difficult traits. It's ridiculous at almost thirty to be frightened of your mother, but I was. She still greatly preferred my brother, and lost no opportunity in reminding me of it, though he didn't visit her often, unlike me. (I can hear myself now, the resentment creeping back in, as if I'm still a child, as if I had no say in my own life.)

I'll try to abbreviate now, try to limit myself to only the essential information. The trouble is, I'm not certain what the essential information is. The plain facts you will know already. I was convicted of forging my mother's will, and sentenced to eleven months in prison, of which I served seven.

So: what can I add to the plain facts? There's no explanation that makes much sense, even to me. My mother became ill when I was thirty-one. I helped to nurse her towards the end. In the final week of her life, I found a copy of her will in the house, in her writing desk. I was looking for stamps. Or perhaps I wasn't, perhaps I was really looking for the will; I can hardly say now. She'd been holding it over my head for long enough: 'Your brother will get nothing. He never comes to see me.' This was only the most recent permutation. She'd been threatening me and my brother with her will for years, ever since our father died. One of us cut out one week, the other the next week, and on it went. We didn't pay much attention. I should say here that there wasn't much money. Very little, in fact. I'm not sure if that's a mitigating factor at all. Perhaps it isn't.

Anyway, I'm delaying now, because here we come to my crime. I found the will that day – just a two-page document, typed up and signed by her, with my aunt and a lady from across the street as witnesses. She had left everything to my brother. It was dated several years before, so all the time she'd been taunting us with the purported contents, she already knew everything would go to him. But it was the second page that upset me. It was an update to the original will, leaving five hundred pounds to the Labour Party, and the rest, as before, to my brother. It was signed again by two witnesses: the same woman from across the street and another neighbour. The date of this second page was only two weeks ago. There seemed to me something so deliberate in the cruelty of this gesture, reinforcing my own exclusion so recently and so intentionally, that for a few moments I found I could hardly breathe.

I put the will in my bag, and later, back in my flat, I got out my old typewriter and created a new page to replace the existing second page. In my version, I specified that my mother's estate would be split equally between me and my brother. I forged my mother's signature at the bottom, and then the signatures of the two witnesses. Then I took the new version of the will back to her house and replaced it in her writing drawer. She was bed-bound by then, and hardly aware, so it seemed unlikely she'd check the will again before dying, and she didn't. She died a few days later. I was with her. I wept for her.

It seems monstrous to recount it like this. As I said above, and as you will see from the newspapers, there wasn't much money:

just a few thousand each for me and my brother. I didn't really need the money. I don't think I even wanted it, not particularly. What I did want was to have mattered. I felt like I was correcting an injustice, and equally saving myself from the humiliation of it becoming known my mother had left me nothing. I think those were my reasons. But I'm not sure if I'm explaining it clearly, or even with complete truthfulness. It is so difficult to know.

Of course, I was caught. I was hardly a criminal mastermind in the first place, and I'd acted impulsively, emotionally, rather than with any intelligent planning. My brother was suspicious. He took the new document to one of the witnesses, who of course denied ever having seen it before. Everything unravelled quickly after that. I never tried to deny it, once I was arrested. What would have been the point?

This is the part where I ought to express my remorse. I would like to. And yet – I don't know how truthful that would be, either. I look back in embarrassment at my own stupidity, my own godlike sense that I could influence events in that way. I feel a certain amount of shame for my poor character, but I don't think that's a new shame; I've always known myself to be a feeble sort of person. I caused some pain to my brother, I suppose, but I don't think he really suffered much. He seemed cheerful enough when I was sentenced, anyway. My mother was already dead, and in any case I don't think she was capable of experiencing pain from any of my actions towards her. So I feel regret, I think, but perhaps not the remorse I ought to. I want you to know that. I don't want you to think my character is any better than it is.

After the collapse of one's life, what is there left to do? I came out of prison and tried to manage. I went to London for a while. I got a job in a restaurant. I was living in a flat-share, and one of my flatmates was a young teacher. That was how I heard about the job at St Anne's. He didn't want it, of course. Too short notice, too parochial, and dreadful pay. But I thought, If they're this desperate, might they not take me without being too particular about references? Might I not start again in this way?

I don't think of myself as an impulsive person, despite all the evidence of this letter, of my life. It was an extraordinary decision to try to pass myself off as a teacher. And as you know, I've never been much good at carrying things off. You realized almost immediately, of course.

Eleanor, there is one thing in particular that I'd like to say to you. I don't know if you believe what the police have said, but please believe me when I say that I haven't hurt anyone. I would never have tried to hurt those girls. Believe me to be bad, but not in that way.

I've already gone on for too long, and you may have stopped reading pages ago. I said at the start that I wanted to explain myself, but I'm not sure I've even managed to do that. Please accept the attempt, at least.

Despite everything, despite how I repaid you, I would like you to know how grateful I have been for your friendship. You were kind to me, and I didn't expect it. Your friendship mattered very much to me. I'm sorry I didn't deserve it.

Yours,
Matthew

After she'd finished reading, Eleanor sat for a long time with the letter in her hands. How much of it was true? No way of knowing, of course. Matthew had hardly established a reputation for truthfulness, and he had said himself that he was in the habit of dishonesty. Her head was a muddle. She wanted to talk to someone about it all, but she couldn't imagine confiding in Vera. No, in the end she found there was only one person she wanted to speak to, and that was out of the question. It was a shock to discover she missed him. Just when she thought she couldn't get any more absurd.

Fax from Dr James Halliwell to Dr George Fisher
Tuesday, 6th November 1984, 7 p.m.

Dear George,

Results of 24-hour urine test are in, after Environmental Health & police finally concluded their stand-off. (Environmental Health blinked first, which I suppose was inevitable, given the police were quite happy with original result.)

You won't be surprised to hear nobody has been poisoned with thallium.

Somewhat unbelievably, even then the COEH & I had to have argument about it with police sergeant. Some of the girls, it turns out, did have low levels of thallium in urine. Levels of $0.2\ \mu g/l$, $0.3\ \mu g/l$ & $0.4\ \mu g/l$ in one case.

COEH & I tried to explain that far from being a smoking gun, these levels are normal, safe, & indicative of (mild) background exposure. COEH told sergeant the girls could have got it from eating vegetables that have taken up thallium from soil. Or from contaminated fish. He added that if we were looking at $10\ \mu g/l$, then he might start to worry.

Trouble is, police sergeant doesn't really seem to understand degrees. He is not man of nuance.

In attempt to reassure him, told him that if we tested his urine, we'd probably find low levels of thallium in that too. He blanched. Not sure if it was because he was worried he'd been poisoned as well, or because he thought I was some kind of urinary pervert.

He said their toxicologists are going to examine strands of the girls' hair under a microscope.

'Well, there you go,' I said. Patted his shoulder kindly. 'That will set your mind at rest. Maybe they can do a strand of yours at the same time.'

I glanced at COEH & he rolled his eyes.

George, I can't believe how much time I've had to spend over past few days talking about thallium.

Asked sergeant when they were planning to announce that the teacher they've arrested is in the clear, but he told me he wasn't in the clear yet, & anyway, there was still the fact of his lying about criminal past.

Police absolutely determined to waste as much of everyone's time as possible.

Meanwhile, we've got a meeting at hospital tomorrow with various bigwigs to discuss 'developing situation' at school. Perhaps we'll finally see some progress.

Referral made to psychiatry, and Rhys and I had a consult with a Dr Tillard – know him? Has a beard that makes him look a bit like the Yorkshire Ripper. Possibly he was going for a young Freud instead, but the beard is too patchy for that. Someone should tell him.

He seemed indecently eager to get his hands on the girls – wanted them transferred fully over to the care of psychiatry immediately. Probably already imagining the paper he'll write in a year or so.

I told him we'd have to share for now, as we needed a
little more time with the girls, and he practically accused us
of hoarding all the interesting cases for ourselves. (Absolutely
true, but it's not our fault he picked the wrong specialism.)

'Conversion disorder isn't your bloody remit,' he said.

'Charcot was a neurologist,' Rhys said, unexpectedly. 'And
so was Freud.'

J

Dear George,

Meeting convened at 9 a.m. sharp yesterday.

There were 4 doctors present: Rhys, Lehman & I from
the hospital, & then also Stevenson as MOEH. Had hoped
we medical men would have upper hand due to our greater
numbers. I was wrong.

Other two attendees were local MP (Eric Harris, Lib Dem –
did you vote for him? I didn't), & then, staggering under
weight of his own importance, chair of the regional health
authority, Mark Baker. Apparently he is a 'captain of industry'.
Commented to Rhys on way to meeting that this is ridiculous
phrase; wondered aloud whether we should start referring to
ourselves as captains of medicine, colonels of healthcare etc.
Rhys replied that I am more of a lance corporal of being a thorn
in his sodding side.

Sullen-looking girl arrived with Baker to take the minutes.
Her first day on the job, apparently. As you will see from the
attached, she adopted a rather literal approach to minute-taking.

Lehman & I met with Dr Tillard & his colleagues in
psychiatry first thing this morning. Likely that later today we'll
be able to share diagnosis with affected girls & their parents.

I asked Lehman if he wanted to make a bet on how long it would be before someone mentioned Salem. He looked at me like he'd never seen me before, & then said, 'You know, this all might be a bloody joke to you, Halliwell, but it's not a joke for these girls. Do you care about that at all?'

So, George, I have now received a lesson in decency from Lehman. I should probably go and kill myself.

J

DATE OF MEETING: Wednesday, 7th November 1984, 9 a.m.

LOCATION: Eastbourne General Hospital, Board Room A

MEETING CALLED BY: Mark Baker, Chair of Regional Health Authority

MEETING CHAIR: Mark Baker

NOTE TAKER: Miss Janice Hopper

ATTENDEES:

MR MARK BAKER, Chair of Regional Health Authority

MR ERIC HARRIS, MP for South Haven and Crede

DR RHYS WILLIAMS, Head of Neurology, Eastbourne General Hospital

DR GILBERT LEHMAN, consultant neurologist, Eastbourne General Hospital

DR JAMES HALLIWELL, consultant neurologist, Eastbourne General Hospital

DR CHRISTOPHER STEVENSON, District Medical Officer for Eastbourne

DR CHRISTOPHER STEVENSON, Medical Officer for Environmental Health, East Sussex

MISS JANICE HOPPER, secretary to Mark Baker

Minutes

ITEM: Ejection of League of Friends from board room

DISCUSSION: Dr Rhys Williams informs League of Friends he has
  booked Board Room A for meeting. League of Friends informs Dr
  Williams they have booked Board Room A for coffee morning. Dr
  Williams offers League of Friends Board Room B. League of Friends
  depart with coffee urn and cake trolley.

ITEM: Mr Mark Baker calls meeting to order

DISCUSSION: Mr Baker reminds attendees of purpose of meeting: to
  agree plan of action for sharing diagnosis re. sick girls at St Anne's
  school. Meeting attendees introduce themselves. Mr Eric Harris, MP
  expresses confusion over dual role of Dr Christopher Stevenson.
  States that it appears from agenda as if there are two men, both named
  Dr Christopher Stevenson, attending same meeting. Dr Stevenson
  explains it is not uncommon for roles of DMO and MOEH to be
  held by same person. Mr Harris, MP suggests this is absurd situation
  and conflict of interest. Dr Stevenson explains it is due to insufficient
  budget. Dr James Halliwell suggests Mr Harris, MP should write to his
  MP about it. Dr Williams instructs Dr Halliwell not to be facetious.

ITEM: Possibility of environmental toxins on site

DISCUSSION: Mr Baker asks Dr Stevenson to confirm Environmental

Health team have uncovered no evidence of environmental toxins or pollutants on school site. Dr Stevenson confirms. Mr Baker asks him to confirm nothing to worry about on school site. Dr Stevenson states there is plenty to worry about on school site. Mr Baker queries. Dr Stevenson confirms no evidence of toxins or pollutants – though separately to this, site is 'death trap' requiring extensive repairs. Mr Baker states this is separate issue and should be set aside.

ITEM: Re-ejection of League of Friends from Board Room A

DISCUSSION: League of Friends return to Board Room A. Inform meeting attendees that Board Room B is in use by matron and sisters. Matron and sisters unwilling to share room. Dr Williams suggests Friends share their unhygienic carrot cake with sisters as inducement. Friends depart again, but request their displeasure minuted.

ITEM: Possibility of deliberate poisoning

DISCUSSION: Mr Harris, MP states police still concerned by possibility of deliberate poisoning with thallium. Dr Williams states subsequent tests have ruled this out. Dr Williams also states that if girls had ingested enough thallium to cause motor symptoms, they would have progressed to neuropathy and shown gastrointestinal symptoms from the start. Adds that hair shafts have been checked: no black or brown formations at the root. None of additional symptoms associated with thallium poisoning present. Dr Halliwell requests it be minuted that thallium theory is deranged.

ITEM: Clinical diagnosis

DISCUSSION: Mr Baker requests that doctors share their clinical findings. Dr Williams invites Dr Halliwell to speak. Dr Halliwell states that he, Dr Williams and Dr Lehman are now confident in a diagnosis of conversion disorder.

ITEM: Definition of conversion disorder

DISCUSSION: Mr Baker suggests 'conversion disorder' is ridiculous term, sounding like crisis of religion. Dr Williams confirms it has nothing to do with religion. Dr Williams invites Dr Halliwell to speak. Dr Halliwell invites Dr Williams to speak. Dr Williams re-invites Dr Halliwell to speak. Dr Halliwell speaks, stating that conversion disorder used to be known as hysteria, but this now considered unhelpful term. Mr Baker queries whether girls are actually ill at all or are faking. Dr Halliwell states that they are ill. Mr Baker queries whether they are neurotics. Dr Halliwell states that their symptoms are real, but that there is no underlying organic cause for their illness. Mr Baker suggests this is 'a load of Freudian bollocks'.

ITEM: Further clarification of conversion disorder

DISCUSSION: Dr Halliwell states that conversion disorder results from problem with how brain sends and receives messages to and from body. Real physical symptoms are produced without organic cause behind them. He adds that this kind of functional disorder more common than most people realize. Mr Baker queries. Dr Halliwell states that blushing is common example of real physical symptom with psychological cause. Mr Baker states that he does not blush. Dr Halliwell enquires as to whether he gets butterflies in stomach when nervous. Mr Baker states this is impertinent question. Dr Williams states that good news is girls have treatable condition. Dr Lehman clarifies that it is actually quite hard to treat. Dr Halliwell thanks Dr Lehman for his helpful and timely contribution. Dr Williams requests Dr Halliwell avoid use of sarcasm during formal meeting. Dr Williams adds that referral to psychiatry has already been made; psychiatry dept will determine treatment protocol.

ITEM: Condition of original patient

DISCUSSION: Mr Baker asks about condition of first girl admitted to hospital. Requests clarification that she has a different illness. Dr Williams confirms that this girl has virus, as yet unidentified. Dr Lehman states they are treating her with antivirals but still waiting to see improvement. Dr Halliwell adds that they believe this girl's illness triggered outbreak of conversion disorder. He states that, unconsciously, other girls began to mimic some of her symptoms.

ITEM: Sensitivities re. diagnosis

DISCUSSION: Dr Stevenson suggests conversion disorder could be inflammatory diagnosis, requiring careful management. Mr Baker states this especially case with press 'right up our arses'. Mr Harris, MP asks doctors Halliwell, Williams and Lehman what will happen if they are wrong: what if they diagnose conversion disorder but it turns out girls have something else, 'a real illness'? Mr Harris, MP suggests that if some girls die, this will be 'akin to manslaughter'. Dr Halliwell states that technically it would be akin to clinical negligence, not manslaughter. Dr Williams issues warning to Dr Halliwell.

ITEM: Evidence for diagnosis of conversion disorder

DISCUSSION: Mr Baker asks for confirmation of conversion disorder diagnosis 'beyond shadow of doubt'. Dr Williams states that evidence points overwhelmingly to pseudo-seizures. Asks Dr Halliwell to talk meeting attendees through the evidence. Dr Halliwell lists features out of keeping with typical seizures, including: longer duration of seizures; closed eyes; thrashing movements; intact guarding response; intact reflexes; shallow breathing patterns; failure of anticonvulsants to maintain control of the seizures after initial response. Dr Halliwell concludes that in addition, EEGs are 'pretty much normal'. Mr Baker queries use of phrase 'pretty much'. Dr Lehman states that the EEGs may be interpreted as showing some abnormalities. Dr Halliwell states that this would only be case if EEGs are being interpreted by an imbecile.

Dr Williams states that a couple of EEGs do show what could be considered mild epileptiform changes, but this not uncommon in healthy individuals. Clarifies that more dramatic spiking would be expected in cases of epileptic seizures. States that he agrees with Dr Halliwell that EEGs support diagnosis of conversion disorder.

Mr Baker asks Dr Lehman how confident he is of diagnosis of conversion disorder. Dr Lehman says, after hesitation, very confident. Mr Baker asks him to give percentage. Dr Halliwell expresses enthusiasm that Mr Baker has put on captain of industry hat. Dr Lehman states that he is 85% confident. Mr Baker expresses alarm at 15% possibility clinical diagnosis is wrong. Dr Lehman amends to 90% confident. Dr Halliwell takes Lord's name in vain.

ITEM: Treatment, and timeline for sharing diagnosis

DISCUSSION: Dr Williams suggests it would be detrimental to delay diagnosis any longer. Suggests that the longer the girls' symptoms persist, the more habitual they will become to girls' brains, and therefore harder to treat. Dr Halliwell states that media coverage may also feed and exacerbate symptoms. Mr Harris, MP asks what treatment is. Dr Halliwell states physiotherapy and psychological interventions to be determined by psychiatry dept. Mr Baker asks why there is no psychiatrist present at meeting. Dr Williams suggests room was getting a little crowded.

Mr Baker asks Dr Stevenson for his view on diagnosis. Dr Stevenson states that he is convinced by diagnosis of conversion disorder, and agrees that it needs to be made public sooner rather than later in order to contain outbreak. Mr Harris, MP suggests Environmental Health need to share their report first, for community reassurance. Dr Stevenson states report is complete. Mr Baker suggests conference held in two days to share diagnosis with wider community. Mr Harris, MP suggests school itself would be best venue for this. Mr Baker agrees.

CONCLUSIONS: Mr Baker will set events in motion to arrange press conference. His secretary will be in touch by COB Thursday.

MEETING CONCLUDED at 9.55 a.m.

7

FRIDAY MORNING, THOUGH ELEANOR was finding it difficult to keep track of the days now normal routines had gone out of the window.

Chairs had been set up in close rows throughout the draughty school hall for the meeting. It was a crush to get everyone in, since some parents were in attendance, as well as all the pupils who remained at the school, the staff body and a number of journalists (contained, as far as possible, in the back rows; Eleanor had already spotted Anthony among them, and had been conscious of him trying to catch her eye). The governors were there too, sitting in the front row.

Eleanor herself sat with the other teachers on the chairs placed along either side of the hall. Vera was beside her, wearing an expression of exaggerated forbearance. As they waited for the meeting to begin, Eleanor swept her eyes over the girls in the hall. She could spot plenty of jerks and tics when she watched for them, though she'd developed a trained eye for these things – they all had. She hoped that when it came to the parents and journalists, some of the twitching would be too subtle to be noticed amidst the normal restless movements of schoolgirls. Once you did notice it, it was very unsettling. As she watched, Rosie Buckley in First Year jerked her shoulder violently forward: once, twice, three times. Further away, across the hall, a hand shot into the air, though she couldn't see which girl it belonged to. It went down, then up again, then down. That one was hard to miss, Eleanor thought.

Sitting on the stage were four men, three of them in suits and one in what looked to be the uniform of a high-ranking police officer. Their arrangement in a row on stage like this made it look, Eleanor thought, rather like they were about to launch into a recorder recital. Among them she recognized Dr Halliwell, the young doctor she'd met at the hospital while she was visiting Diane. He looked uncomfortable in his suit, uncomfortable on the stage – just generally uncomfortable. Next to him was an older man with dark hair and a beard, who, she thought, bore a slightly unfortunate resemblance to the Yorkshire Ripper. Next was a cadaverous, unhappy-looking man with thinning grey hair. Finally, at the end, was the police officer, who appeared particularly large and robust next to the slender, mournful man beside him.

The noise in the hall fell to a low buzz as Miss Christie walked up on stage, and then to silence as she began to speak.

'Thank you, everyone, for attending this meeting at such short notice,' she began.

There was a sudden disturbance to Eleanor's left. Louise Adler had burst in late through the side door, trailed, as she usually was, by Ida Campbell. Heads turned in the direction of the noise. Miss Christie glanced down at them from the stage, eyebrows slightly raised.

Eleanor felt she'd better issue a rebuke. 'Louise, Ida, you're late,' she said in an undertone.

'Sorry, miss,' Louise whispered, not looking particularly abashed.

Miss Christie began to speak again, telling them that this meeting had been convened by the health authority to share an important update.

'We missed breakfast and didn't hear the announcement,' Ida whispered to Eleanor, more apologetic.

'Still made it in time to see Spandau Ballet, though,' Louise said, nodding in the direction of the four men on stage.

Vera snorted, but Eleanor tried to keep her voice stern as she said, 'You'll have to sit with us. There are no other seats left.'

Louise and Ida obediently took the two free chairs near Eleanor. Ida's arm began to jerk as she sat down, and Eleanor saw Louise lean against her, keeping the arm still.

Miss Christie had left the stage now, and the thin, unhappy grey-haired man got to his feet. He introduced himself, in a rather reedy voice, as Dr Christopher Stevenson, the district medical officer and also, simultaneously, the medical officer for Environmental Health. He made it sound like it was all very trying for him, Eleanor thought. He introduced the other men on stage lugubriously, as if he were about to deliver their eulogies.

'Here we have two of the doctors looking after the girls in hospital, consultant neurologist Dr James Halliwell and consultant psychiatrist Dr John Tillard.' Dr Tillard was the man with the dark beard. There was a stir in the room at the mention of a psychiatrist, a few confused murmurs throughout the hall. 'Finally, this is Dominic Horner, the chief constable. I hope today will be a chance to provide some clarity and reassurance,' Dr Stevenson concluded, sounding gloomy at the prospect.

'I feel reassured already,' Louise murmured.

'That'll do, Louise,' Eleanor said.

'As you all know, this has been a most challenging time,' Dr Stevenson said. 'There have been a number of girls over the past weeks who have developed a range of motor symptoms, including tics and jerking limbs. Some of these girls have progressed to seizures and have been admitted to hospital. We understand that it's been a very worrying time for everyone involved, and there has been much speculation and anxiety as to the cause of the girls' illness. We are now able to share further details with you about the girls' condition. But first, I'd like to invite the chief constable to speak.'

Dr Stevenson sat down, and the chief constable stood up. He said, in a deep, strong voice, 'I can now reassure you all that at this time we have no evidence of any crime having taken place –' he seemed rather grudging about this, Eleanor thought – 'though we are of course continuing our investigations.'

A journalist's hand went up immediately.

'If you could save your questions for now, please,' Dr Stevenson said. 'We've allowed ample time for questions at the end.'

Eleanor thought that Dr Halliwell seemed rather irritated by the chief constable's contribution. He was leaning in to whisper something to Dr Stevenson, who shook his head in response.

The chief constable sat down, and Dr Stevenson took over again. 'From an Environmental Health perspective, we've investigated the site thoroughly – *very* thoroughly – and found no evidence of toxins or contaminants that could have led to the girls' symptoms. We're confident that the site is safe.'

Eleanor heard a few mutters at this. She was getting the impression that the audience, while not actively hostile, was also not quite on the side of the men on stage.

Dr Stevenson said in his unhappy way, 'Now I'll hand over to the doctors to discuss the girls' diagnosis. Dr Halliwell?'

Dr Halliwell stood. He put his hands in his pockets, and then took them out again. Then he said, sounding rehearsed, 'This has been a complex case, and we've explored every avenue in our diagnosis and treatment of the girls affected. We've ruled out disease or infection as the cause of their symptoms, and are now confident that they're suffering from a condition known as conversion disorder. That is to say, their symptoms have a psychological basis.'

A ripple went through the room at these words, which Dr Halliwell was either oblivious to or had decided to ignore.

He went on, 'There's one exception to the diagnosis of conversion disorder, and that's the first girl who developed symptoms. We believe she has a viral infection. It's likely that her initial symptoms were the catalyst for the outbreak of conversion disorder among the others. She will remain under the care of neurology, while the other girls will be predominantly treated by the psychiatry team. I'll hand over to Dr Tillard now, who will outline the nature of conversion disorder in more detail.'

Dr Halliwell sat down again, looking rather relieved to have got his part over with, Eleanor thought.

The man with the beard stood. He smoothed his jacket down before beginning, and then didn't seem to know what to do with his hands. After a moment, he clasped them awkwardly in front of him. Then he said, in a rather pedantic voice, 'Conversion disorder is a complex condition which goes to the heart of the relationship between mind and body, one of the central tenets of psychiatry. It can be challenging to grasp the nature of somatoform disorders. In fact, to truly understand the roots of what we now know as conversion disorder, it might be helpful to cast our minds back to Paul Briquet in nineteenth-century Paris—'

A sharp clearing of the throat from Dr Halliwell, who clearly did not feel it would be helpful for those gathered in the school hall to cast their minds back to Paul Briquet in nineteenth-century Paris.

Dr Tillard seemed to recollect himself. He shifted his weight between his feet and said, 'In cases of conversion disorder, physical symptoms are produced without any underlying organic cause. We don't yet fully understand the process behind it, but one theory is that subconscious or repressed psychological stress is being "converted" into physical symptoms, which is how the disorder gets its name. When there are several linked cases of conversion disorder, we tend to refer instead to "mass hysteria", or, to use the more modern term, "mass sociogenic illness". In these cases, there is a strong degree of psychological contagion at work. An outbreak is more likely to happen in a closed environment, like a boarding school, and adolescent girls seem to be the most susceptible group. But the process is an unconscious one. We must emphasize that these girls are not producing their symptoms deliberately. Our plan now is to commence psychological treatment and physiotherapy, which will help to restore the girls to themselves.' He sat down to signal he'd finished.

All the key information having been delivered, Dr Stevenson said, 'All right, I think we might as well move on to questions now.' As chair, he fielded the questions.

Eleanor had felt that the atmosphere was just about contained until now; there was a certain tension within the hall, but it had been kept in check while the doctors were speaking. However, the feeling in the room seemed to shift quickly once the questions began.

The first was from a man near the front, who Eleanor assumed was a parent. He stood up and said, 'How can someone's *mind* cause them to fall down and have a fit when there's nothing actually wrong with them? It all sounds rather far-fetched to me.'

There were a few murmurs of agreement at this.

Before anyone on stage could reply, another man got to his feet and said, 'My daughter can no longer walk because her legs jerk so much. You cannot seriously be telling us that all this is just in her head?'

Now Eleanor recognized him as Mary Maxwell's father. His voice shook a little as he spoke, though whether from anger or distress she couldn't tell.

It was Dr Tillard who answered him. 'I know it's a challenging diagnosis to accept. The relationship between the mind and body is still not well understood—'

This, Eleanor saw quickly, was not quite the right thing to say. Dr Tillard seemed to realize it too, because he paused fractionally, which gave Mary's father the chance to cut in again.

'If it's not well understood,' Mr Maxwell said, 'then why are you so confident in diagnosing hysteria?'

The first man, still standing, added, 'It hasn't even been two weeks since the girls were admitted to hospital and you've already decided it's all psychological. That seems awfully quick to me. Can you seriously tell us you've ruled everything else out? Absolutely everything?'

Dr Halliwell said carefully, 'We've run a range of tests and we're confident there's no underlying organic cause for the girls' symptoms. We've also looked at the nature of the seizures themselves. The girls' seizures don't have any typical features of epileptic seizures, and the EEGs don't show the abnormal electrical activity in their brains that we'd expect. When it comes to their constellation of symptoms, there's no area of the brain which, if attacked or damaged, could account for all of it. We are completely confident that their symptoms are caused by psychological processes; nothing else can adequately explain their nature and range.'

Some of the audience seemed convinced by this, but the man who'd asked the first question said, 'Nothing else you're willing to consider, at any rate.'

'Are there any questions from anyone else?' Dr Stevenson said pointedly. All the journalists in the back rows had their hands up, and Dr Stevenson seemed to decide they might be a better bet than the distrustful parents.

'Yes, the lady at the back,' he said.

A female journalist stood and said, 'This is a question for the chief constable. The man you've arrested – the teacher – is he still suspected of any crime?'

The chief constable said, 'He has not been charged.'

'But is he suspected of any crime? He already has a criminal record, doesn't he? You said your investigations are ongoing.'

The chief constable sighed. Sounding regretful, he said, 'He is no longer suspected of any involvement in this case.'

Eleanor exhaled softly. Vera murmured, 'There you go. Cleared. For what it's worth, which probably isn't much by this point.'

'Why did you arrest him, then?' the woman said.

'I'm not at liberty to comment further.'

'Next question,' Dr Stevenson said. 'Yes, the man in the blue jacket.'

Anthony. Eleanor glanced at him as he stood, and then quickly looked away again. He said, 'This is a question for Environmental Health. How certain can you really be about ruling out environmental toxins? There are fields adjacent to the school which have been sprayed with organophosphates, and the strong winds round here would easily blow the residue across the school site. The girls could be inhaling dangerous pesticides all day long.'

There were anxious noises throughout the audience at this.

Dr Stevenson said, 'We've tested the site extensively for evidence of contamination, and found none. Blood tests on the girls have also been clear.'

This seemed to placate most people, but Anthony said, 'Well, you would say that, wouldn't you? The government would hardly want people finding out these young girls were poisoned by toxic pesticides that are currently being used all over the country. Imagine the scandal, and the compensation claims.'

'They haven't been poisoned,' Dr Halliwell broke in. 'There's no evidence of poisoning.'

'And your explanation makes more sense, does it?' Anthony said. 'Conversion disorder? Hysteria? What a load of rubbish. We're not in Victorian times anymore, are we? Is it possible you're using this diagnosis to cover up something else?'

Dr Halliwell stared at him, frowning. He was visibly irritated, but Eleanor could see he was in a difficult position. The more you tried to deny a cover-up, the more everyone became convinced that you had something to cover up. After a moment, he said, 'The clinical picture speaks for itself. And it isn't saying anything about pesticides.'

'It seems to me that you've settled on the most convenient diagnosis,' Anthony said.

'There's nothing convenient about conversion disorder,' Dr Tillard said tersely.

Another journalist: 'The girl you said really *is* ill — what's wrong with her?'

Dr Halliwell seemed to hesitate before answering. 'We're not certain yet.'

'You can't diagnose her? And yet you seem very confident about diagnosing the others. How can you be so sure about some, but so unsure about another?'

'Her condition is complex,' Dr Halliwell said. 'And I also need to respect her medical confidentiality.'

'You're not respecting the medical confidentiality of the other girls,' the journalist said.

'That's unavoidable,' Dr Stevenson said, taking over. 'We've agreed that the situation is serious enough to warrant sharing some information about their condition. It's in the best interests of everyone involved, including the girls themselves.'

Another journalist: 'Since you've found there's nothing really wrong with them, is it possible the girls are faking the whole thing?'

This drew the ire of some of the parents. 'How could they fake this?' one father said loudly. 'And *why* would they?'

'There's no suggestion that the girls are faking anything,' Dr Tillard said. 'It's important to understand that their symptoms are absolutely real, and they're outside the girls' conscious control.'

'Sounds ridiculous,' Eleanor heard someone mutter. It did sound a bit ridiculous, she thought. That was the problem.

The next question came from a mother. She stood and said tremulously, 'I still don't understand. These girls are having fits and falling down. Their arms and legs are jerking. Yet you say it's all in their heads. So if they're not faking it, are they mad?'

Dr Tillard said, 'No, they're not mad.'

'You mentioned that these symptoms might be caused by some kind of psychological stress? What did you mean by that?'

'As I said, we don't know precisely what causes conversion disorder,' Dr Tillard said. 'But one theory is that it's caused by the sufferer subconsciously finding some emotion or experience too difficult to face and therefore "converting" it into physical symptoms instead.'

'A difficult experience?' Mary Maxwell's father shot to his feet again. 'Difficult emotions? My daughter's never been unhappy or stressed in her life. Nothing is asked of her. Nothing's expected of her. She's happy and *normal*. So why her and not others? Why just girls and none of the teachers?'

'Are you saying these girls have experienced something they can't bear to face?' a journalist called.

There now seemed to have been a collective decision to ignore Dr Stevenson's role as chair. The meeting was unravelling.

'Has something been done to our children?' a parent said loudly.

'What about that teacher who was arrested?' another called out. 'Did he have anything to do with it?'

Oh God, Eleanor thought. They seemed to her to be teetering on the edge of mayhem.

'As I said before,' the chief constable said, raising his voice to be heard over the overlapping voices in the audience, 'we are confident at this time that no crime has taken place.'

'Then what have these girls experienced that was so horrifying it's caused them to have fits?' a journalist called.

'I wasn't suggesting there was any one particular experience that led to these symptoms,' Dr Tillard was trying to explain, though nobody seemed to be listening to him. 'In practice, it doesn't really work like that—'

'It's probably the case that there are several different factors that may have led to the outbreak,' Dr Halliwell said, raising his voice to be heard. 'And in reality, we may never be able to identify them all.'

'You don't seem to know much at all!' someone said.

'What are you not telling us?' Anthony called out.

Amidst the sound of audience members shouting more and more fevered questions, Dr Stevenson was attempting to draw the meeting to a close.

'We're out of time,' he said. 'Any further questions can be directed towards the relevant authorities. I'm sure you'll all wish to join me in thanking our panel—'

It seemed that the majority did not.

Eventually, the meeting concluded when Miss Christie returned to the stage. She had more natural authority, Eleanor thought, than the four men combined.

'Please rest assured,' she told the audience, 'that our utmost priority is keeping our girls safe. We believe the situation is under control. If that changes, you will of course be informed immediately. In the meantime, let's trust the doctors, who know more about the situation than we do.'

That seemed a slightly ominous note to end on, Eleanor thought, given that apparently half the audience already believed there was a conspiracy to conceal the truth, while the other half believed the doctors were as much in the dark as everybody else. Nonetheless, under Miss Christie's steady gaze, the audience allowed itself to be dismissed.

ELEANOR WALKED OUT AFTERWARDS with Vera.

'Well, that was a fiasco,' Vera said.

'I know,' Eleanor said. She was unsettled, especially by the questions about Matthew.

'Conversion disorder,' Vera said musingly. 'It does sound rather Victorian, doesn't it?'

'Perhaps we should have given the girls more to do,' Eleanor said. 'More to occupy them.'

'I'm not sure there's any suggestion that their illness was caused by boredom,' Vera said. 'Though goodness knows this place has sometimes made me feel twitchy enough myself.'

'Do you think the doctors have got it right?'

'Oh, I imagine so. Still, it's rather a humiliating outcome for our girls. No wonder the parents don't like it.'

'And yet we ought to see it as a relief,' Eleanor said. 'Isn't it a relief? They're going to be all right.'

'They're going to be objects of fascination for months, if not years. Whatever the doctors say, there'll be plenty of people who will assume they're lunatics, or neurotics, or that they were putting it on the whole time. It might have been better if they *had* been poisoned with pesticides. Have you heard from Matthew at all?'

'Why would I have?' Eleanor said, startled at the change of subject and finding herself unaccountably defensive.

Vera glanced at her. 'I thought you two were rather thick, that's all.'

'He wrote me a letter,' Eleanor conceded.

'Ah.'

'He wanted to say sorry.'

'Did he now?'

'And to . . . explain a bit, I suppose.'

'I see,' Vera said. 'It was rather an odd thing to do, forging his mother's will. Still, I dare say we all do odd things from time to time.'

'It was a crime,' Eleanor said firmly. 'He committed a crime.'

'Did I say he hadn't?'

They'd paused at the steps of the dining hall. Vera concluded the conversation by saying, 'Well. At least we can enjoy our fish pie this evening free from the fear that we're being poisoned by the kitchen staff.'

'I think "enjoy" is putting it a bit strongly,' Eleanor said as they went up together, and Vera laughed.

IF THE HEALTH AUTHORITY had hoped that the meeting would calm down the media furore, the headlines the next day were enough to disabuse anyone of this idea.

'Oh Lord,' Vera said as they sat in the staff common room after breakfast with several of that day's newspapers on the coffee table in front of them. 'They've really gone to town.'

Eleanor was staring at one headline which proclaimed, 'Doctors Blame "Stress" for Mass Outbreak of Twitching and Fits at Boarding School'.

'I suppose they were always going to make a lot of it,' she said.

From the papers they'd looked at so far, most of the coverage seemed to present the diagnosis of conversion disorder in the most sensationalist terms possible, with enthusiastic speculation about the possible causes of the girls' illness (stress? Repression? Abuse of some unspecified kind?). More worryingly still, there were also a few articles which treated the doctors' claims with scepticism, either suggesting they were panicking and relying on guesswork, or even that there was a conspiracy afoot. Eleanor noted that Anthony's local paper was pursuing this angle aggressively, with Anthony's name in the byline of an article headlined, 'Girls' Mass Sickness Prompts Fears of Cover-Up'. The article itself suggested pesticide poisoning as one theory, and deliberate poisoning as another. *Doctors remain puzzled by the girls' symptoms*, Anthony had written, which Eleanor thought was a bit rich: the doctors hadn't seemed puzzled to her. Most of the articles mentioned Matthew's arrest again, so it didn't seem likely this would blow over for him any time soon.

'Have you seen the *Gazette*?' Trudy said eagerly, arriving with Linda in a flurry of excitement and depositing herself on the sofa opposite them. 'It says there are suspicions of a conspiracy.'

'We've seen,' Vera said.

'Do you think they were telling the truth yesterday?' Linda said, sitting down beside Trudy. 'At the meeting? We think they were hiding something.'

'Don't let the girls hear you saying that,' Vera said. 'If they really think they're being poisoned, I dare say even more of them will go off the deep end.'

'Surely you can't think yourself ill,' Trudy said.

'Evidence would suggest otherwise.'

'What are the girls saying?' Eleanor said. 'Does anyone know?'

'I took prep last night,' Linda said. 'It's a mixture. Some of them still think the sick girls are doing it for attention. Some of them think the doctors are right. And some of them think we're not being told the whole truth.'

And I'm sure you encouraged them in that, Eleanor thought. Vera was right: this was the last thing they needed.

'I don't know why everyone is so determined to complicate things,' Vera said. 'We were given a perfectly adequate explanation. Why make such strenuous efforts to look for a less adequate one?'

'Pesticides are dangerous to humans,' Linda said. 'We all know that, even if the government won't admit it. Of course they won't. Imagine what a problem that would be for them.'

'And we're downhill from the fields,' Trudy said. 'So even if you don't think the pesticides travelled here in the air, they still could have run down here in the groundwater. They could easily have got into the water supply.'

'The water authority tested the water,' Eleanor pointed out, 'and said it was safe.'

'Well, why weren't they at the meeting yesterday?'

Eleanor shrugged. 'I imagine they were represented by Environmental Health.'

'The other thing is,' Linda said, leaning closer to them and lowering her voice, 'that apparently the police found laburnum seed pods in Louise Adler's room.'

Vera frowned. 'Forgive me, but I fail to see the significance of that.'

'Laburnum's poisonous,' Trudy said. 'If you swallow some, you can start twitching, and eventually go into a coma and *die*.'

'Oh, what nonsense,' Vera said. 'Louise Adler hasn't poisoned anyone. The doctors were quite clear that no one's been poisoned.'

'And of course there's still the mystery of Matthew—' Linda began.

'Matthew had nothing to do with it,' Eleanor said, so sharply that Linda and Trudy seemed startled. Then, maddeningly, she saw them exchange a knowing look.

'Don't blame yourself, Eleanor,' Linda said. 'He had us all fooled, not just you.'

'Can you believe he was a criminal all along?' Trudy said. 'Honestly, I wish we'd known sooner. It makes him so much more interesting.'

Vera rolled her eyes at this.

'Everyone's saying we'll have to close,' Trudy went on. 'Do you think that's true?'

Eleanor's spirits sank further. She hoped Vera might offer some reassurance; she was usually quick to dismiss the dramatic predictions of the English department.

But Vera said, 'Oh, probably. The writing's on the wall. Has been for years, really. I imagine this recent debacle will be the final straw.'

'Miss Christie will do everything she can to keep us going,' Eleanor said, trying to remain hopeful.

Vera said, 'She needs to learn when to admit defeat. Someone should tell her the game's up.' She took a final swig of coffee. 'And then hand her a whisky and a revolver.'

George, you may have seen today's newspaper coverage, &
inferred that the meeting at the school did not go well. Would
go so far as to say that rather than fulfilling stated mission from
health authority – *to clarify & reassure* – we seem to have done
exact opposite. We have muddled & worried. Perplexed &
unsettled.

I'd told Rhys I was well prepared, but this turned out to be
incorrect. Dr Tillard & I made up a calamitous comic pairing.
I hadn't considered how the audience might react, didn't foresee
the pitfalls. I'm like Icarus (i.e. a fucking idiot). Tillard & I
drove back to the hospital together afterwards. He seemed even
more shell-shocked than me. I told him not to blame himself.
He said he didn't, he blamed me. Apparently we should have
brought him in sooner, before the situation got so out of hand.
Take it up with the police & Environmental Health, I told him.
And Lehman.

'Now this is a bloody mess,' he said. 'It's impossible to treat
conversion disorder if no one believes the bloody diagnosis.'

'So what happens to the girls, then?' I said.

'They stay ill,' he said.

Went to see Diane when I got back to the hospital. Her

mother with her as usual. Diane seemed to be asleep. Face very pale. Had brief superstitious image of her already dead: could see her laid out cold & motionless on post-mortem table.

Asked the mother how she had been today. Mother said she thought she was getting worse. She reminded me I'd said she'd get better with the new medicine. (What I'd actually said was I hoped she would.)

Sat down by the bed & said her name. No response. Asked mother how long she'd been like this. Mother said since the morning. Said she'd only slept lightly past few days, always twitching & making noises. God knows she needs the rest, her mother said.

Checked her breathing & pulse, & then her pupils (normal). Tapped her cheek gently with my finger & spoke her name again. No response. Took out pen & lifted her hand, applying pressure to nail bed with tip of pen. After few seconds her eyes opened & she jerked her hand away from me. No coma, then.

The mother said that half the time she doesn't seem to know where she is. I told her, uselessly, that she is very unwell. The mother asked again what's wrong with her, & once again I couldn't tell her. Mother asked if she's going to die. Couldn't reply to that either, though this time I thought I did know the answer; but that was worse than not knowing.

J

Dear George,

Had unpleasant run-in with Rhys this morning. He said he'd
spoken to you on phone. (So heartening to know you'll answer
phone to Rhys at drop of hat.)

He said he'd called to ask if I'd been as infuriating to work
with when you were head of department! & apparently *you said
yes*!

Thanks very much, George.

Rhys said he wanted to get some pointers on how to deal
with me. Dare say he mentioned recent misunderstanding
over CT scan. He can't seem to stop mentioning it. He said he
wanted to ask you how you avoided actually killing me. Said
he didn't particularly want to fire me, since I'm actually 'quite
a decent neurologist' when not being 'a total pain in the arse'
(both direct quotes). Then he added that he also didn't have
anyone to replace me with.

I pointed out that technically only Health Secretary can
fire me, which didn't soothe him. We did end up agreeing it's
exceptionally difficult to get rid of a doctor, however infuriating
they may be.

So, the CT scan. Ignore whatever Rhys said: I didn't

actually lie to radiology. May have implied Rhys had signed off on it, but didn't explicitly say he had. And better to beg forgiveness than ask permission, etc.

'You haven't bloody begged forgiveness!' Rhys bellowed at me.

Anyway, scan revealed what I expected: extensive cortical atrophy.

Lehman & I looked at it together in the doctors' lounge.

'Shit,' Lehman said, with his usual penetrating insight.

George, I really need to speak to you. I don't know what to do. I'm going to call you again this evening, around 9. Please pick up the phone, if only as former colleague who might be able to advise on the case of a dying girl.

J

Fax from Dr James Halliwell to Dr George Fisher
Tuesday, 13th November 1984, 8 a.m.

Dear George,

Thank you!

Following our somewhat terse phone conversation yest., I've started her on inosine pranobex. You were characteristically fatalistic, but I feel more hopeful.

I could sense you weren't in the mood for idle chit-chat, but perhaps we'll get chance to catch up properly soon.

Thanks, again.

J

Fax from Dr James Halliwell to Dr George Fisher
Thursday, 15th November 1984, 5 p.m.

Dear George,

She seemed more lucid this morning. When I came into the room, she gave a small smile & raised her hand slightly as if in greeting. Seemed to be trying to say something, but neither I nor her mother could work out what it was. Mother asked me if she'd turn corner now. Said I hoped so. Didn't tell her we couldn't reverse cortical atrophy that's already occurred; seemed too cruel in that moment.

I'm beginning to feel rather worn by events of past weeks. Still don't seem to be sleeping much. I think I can hear what you'd say to me if I told you I've badly let Diane down: you'd tell me to stop being self-indulgent, that we are doctors, not gods, we do our best & beyond that, let the chips fall where they may. Still, though. As well as Diane, there's the worsening situation at the school. I know I've made an absolute mess of it. Now it's like a runaway train: too late to stop it gathering speed.

J

8

So after everything that had happened, it was all just in their heads?

A few days had passed since the meeting, but the uproar had not died down. The affected girls were not only perplexed by their diagnosis, they were offended.

'How can we be doing *this* to ourselves?' Ida heard Kylie in Lower School saying on the way to breakfast. 'I fell down and had a fit! The doctor saw for himself.'

'They don't think you're doing it to yourself,' Kylie's friend said consolingly. 'They just think you're mad as hatters.'

Kylie started to cry. 'It's something else,' she said. 'I know it's something else. We've been infected with something. Or poisoned by Mr Langfield, or by someone else.'

Ida's own arm jerked in sympathy as she passed them. She found Sophie and Victoria in the queue and hoped for distraction, but all they wanted to talk about was the diagnosis, which continued to fascinate them.

'The doctor said it might be caused by someone being stressed or unhappy,' Sophie said, as they sat down with their trays. 'So maybe all the girls who are ill have got some kind of secret sorrow.'

'Do you have a secret sorrow, Ida?' Victoria said.

'No,' Ida said. Her arm jerked convulsively as she raised her spoon, and she splashed milk all over the table.

'I don't think Angie does either,' Sophie said, reaching out with her napkin to mop it up. 'Not that I can think of, anyway. Though she was very stressed about the play, I suppose.'

'And Jean Thomas's parents are getting divorced,' Victoria said eagerly. 'So maybe that's why she started having fits. And Deborah Willis is in love with her cousin, so maybe that's why her legs have gone mad, because that's incest, unless you're in Jane Austen.'

'And April is probably stressed about Diane being so ill,' Sophie said.

'And also about having such dreadful frizzy hair,' Victoria added. To Ida, she said, 'She tried to straighten it with the iron from Home Ec last year, and burned a whole section off. She was even more horrible after that.'

'So it does all make sense,' Sophie said. 'Except for you, Ida. If you really don't have a secret sorrow.'

'I thought some of the others must be faking at first,' Victoria said. 'Not Diane, but definitely Jean, and perhaps Mary Maxwell. But not after you got it too, Ida. I know you wouldn't fake it, though it does look very strange.'

Ida knew only too well how convincingly someone could fake an illness. It seemed a peculiar irony that her mother had faked an illness that looked real, while Ida herself was afflicted with a real illness that looked fake.

And nothing about the outbreak made any sense.

'How is it possible that there's nothing wrong with me?' she said to Louise later, as they were getting ready for bed. Louise had shoved cardboard into all the gaps around the window, but the room was still very cold, and they wore their jumpers and dressing gowns to bed now. They both had chilblains.

'I wouldn't exactly say there's nothing wrong with you,' Louise said, watching Ida struggle to brush her teeth between arm jerks.

'And can this kind of thing really be caused by *stress*?' Ida went on, mouth full of toothpaste. 'I don't even feel stressed. Or no more than usual, anyway. I've been much more stressed than this before.'

Louise was thoughtful for a few moments. She said, 'No, I don't understand it either. But everyone here is stuck, one way or another. It might be this place, or it might be because we're girls, or it might be because we're short of ideas, or short of options. We're not given many of those. No wonder we're all going loopy.'

'*You're* not,' Ida said. 'And you hate this place more than anyone else. So why have I got it and not you?'

'No idea,' Louise said blithely. 'Perhaps you're just more susceptible to the influence of others.'

'And what's wrong with Diane?' Ida said. 'They said she had a virus. But what virus? Why won't they tell us?' She thought again of Diane lying in her hospital bed, her hand rigid as a claw, that terrible gargling sound.

Louise said, 'I can only assume they don't know.'

Fax from Dr James Halliwell to Dr George Fisher
Friday, 16th November 1984, 8 p.m.

Dear George,

Diane seemed worse again today, despite recent hopes. She was agitated & confused, jerking & making awful, distressed sounds; in the end it took a nurse & her mother to hold her still while I sedated her. Mother was weeping throughout. Felt shaken myself.

At the school, 3 more girls have developed motor tics – brings our grand total up to 24 (excluding Diane). Still plenty of people claiming it's pesticide poisoning. Eric Harris, local MP, held meeting at town hall in South Haven to calm local community. You may not be surprised to hear, George, that he did not succeed in calming the local community.

J

Dear George,

When I checked on Diane this morning, she was awake &
seemed a little brighter. Responded to my voice when I spoke
to her, & gave a nod when I asked if she could hear me. I found
this very encouraging, but did notice she seemed to be looking
past me rather than directly at me. Asked her mother about
this, & she said Diane doesn't look at her much now, but does
respond to her voice. I got the ophthalmoscope out & had a
look in her eye. Optic discs look pale. I think she's losing her
sight.

Increased dose of inosine pranobex.

J

Fax from Dr James Halliwell to Dr George Fisher
Monday, 19th November 1984, 9.15 a.m.

Dear George,

She died during the night. Her mother was with her, & so was I. Rhys paged me. Met Lehman in doctors' lounge first thing this morning, both of us very upset.

17 years old, George. It wasn't a good death. She was blind and howling like a wounded animal at the end.

[Unsigned]

Fax from Dr James Halliwell to Dr George Fisher
Monday, 19th November 1984, 8 p.m.

George,

Thank you for your call to Rhys. Obviously they'll be taking brain tissue at the autopsy. Give me some credit. I may be upset, but I haven't taken leave of my senses. PM happening right now. Pathologist is Barnett; haven't come across him before. Should be able to get results from histopathology as soon as they're in.

And no, I don't need any time off. It was very awkward when Rhys asked me. Please ring him back & reassure him I'm not having nervous breakdown, will you? I was very tired when I wrote you that last note.

J

9

'Have you heard?' Louise said, sliding into the seat next to Ida. It was History, the second lesson of the day, but Ida hadn't seen Louise since before breakfast. Since then, the terrible news about Diane had spread. They had not been informed by their teachers yet, but word had a way of travelling in school, sprinting out ahead of official announcements.

'I heard,' Ida said. She felt nauseated by the news, and it was difficult to think straight in the febrile atmosphere of the school. Many of the other girls, especially those with symptoms, were in a state of rapidly escalating panic, certain that more deaths would follow Diane's. One of the Lower School girls with jerking arms had vomited during breakfast and then fallen down in a faint, or perhaps a fit, and had been carried out by the teachers on duty. No one had seen her since.

'I can't believe it,' Louise said quietly.

'I know,' Ida said, though she could just about believe it. She thought she was probably one of the few people who had known how unwell Diane really was.

'But you have something different,' Louise said, and it wasn't clear to Ida which of them she was trying to reassure.

'So everyone keeps saying.' Ida didn't feel like she was going to die, but her sense of connection to her own body was so frayed now, she no longer trusted something so unreliable as a feeling.

'You're going to be fine,' Louise said.

'Hopefully.' Ida's arm jerked, as if to underscore her uncertainty. She added, 'But if not, you can have my Walkman. Don't let my sister get her hands on it.'

'That's not funny,' Louise said.

Ida was touched. She wondered for a brief moment if Louise might actually like her, then dismissed the idea as insane. Still, she hadn't forgotten Louise saying she was interesting after Ida revealed her poison plot. It seemed that all it took to finally win Louise over was an attempt to frame her for an offence against the person.

Miss Fox from the English department – Loopy Linda, as the girls called her behind her back – was covering their lesson today, in the continued absence of Mr Langfield. She was sitting at the teacher's desk reading a book of Tennyson's poetry, tears streaming silently down her face. She hadn't even acknowledged Louise's entrance, despite how late Louise had come in.

Usually when anything remotely out of the ordinary happened, it produced a carnival atmosphere among the girls, inducing a giddiness as they glimpsed possibilities beyond the usual monotony. Not today. Most girls were subdued, leaning their heads together to whisper or pass notes, perhaps predicting who would die next. Several were crying. No one was even pretending to work.

The atmosphere was not helped by Miss Fox herself, who kept interrupting them to read out the most poignant passages from *In Memoriam*.

'Listen to this, girls,' she said tremulously now.

> '*O life as futile, then, as frail!*
> *O for thy voice to soothe and bless!*
> *What hope of answer, or redress?*
> *Behind, behind the veil.*'

She began to weep again.

'It's a bloody shame about Diane,' Louise said. Her face looked hard, but Ida thought she could see a glimpse of Louise's distress beneath.

'Bloody shame' seemed a mild way of putting it. Ida wondered if April knew yet that her best friend was dead, if the girls in hospital had already been informed, or if they were being kept in the dark for fear of frightening them.

Before she could say anything else to Louise, there was a single sharp ring of the school bell. Miss Fox closed her Tennyson. She said, 'All right, girls. That's the signal. You can leave your things here. Miss Christie is calling everyone to a special assembly. She'll explain. Go to the school hall quietly now, and take your usual seats.'

One of the most unsettling things of all, Ida thought later, was the silence. The school was usually a noisy place. The girls here seemed, for the most part, constitutionally incapable of silence, even when under strict instructions. Even at the most sombre or formal occasions, there would be a background hum of whispers, giggles, scuffed feet, and the occasional half-subdued shriek as someone was pushed or poked in the ribs.

But today not a single girl spoke as they took their seats. Miss Christie was already standing before her lectern on the stage. Given the news of Diane's death, the twitches and jerks among the student body seemed even more ominous than they had previously.

'Thank you for coming, girls,' Miss Christie said. 'I'm afraid I have some tragic news to share with you.'

She must realize, Ida thought, that they already knew. In any case, she didn't waste any time; Miss Christie wasn't someone who talked for the sake of talking.

She said, without further preamble, 'As you know, Diane Fulbrook, our Head Girl, has been very unwell for some time, and has been in hospital. I'm very sorry to tell you that she died last night. Her mother was with her.' Her voice seemed to falter very slightly at this last sentence. She left a pause, and then went on, 'This is, of course, devastating news for Diane's family, for her friends, and for our whole school community. As her doctors have made clear, Diane had an illness different from that of the other girls. No one else is considered to be at any risk. While we are all terribly saddened, there is no reason to be alarmed. We'll be holding a memorial service for Diane in due course, so we can honour and remember her together.'

Some girls were crying now, and being comforted by their friends.

Miss Christie said, 'In a moment, you'll go to your form rooms instead of period three, where your form teachers will talk to you. It goes without saying, of course, that you must avoid discussing this awful tragedy with anyone outside the school community. We owe Diane's family whatever privacy we can give them. It's the least we can do for them now.' She glanced down at the lectern, seemed to take a steadying breath, then looked up at the girls again. 'Now we'll have a short reading from the Book of Wisdom, from the Apocrypha. Then I will dismiss you.'

In her clear, calm voice, she began to read: '"But the souls of the righteous are in the hand of God, and there shall no torment touch them. In the sight of the unwise they seemed to die: and their departure is taken for misery, and their going from us to be utter destruction: but they are in peace. For though they be punished in the sight of men, yet is their hope full of immortality."'

Ida tried to let the old words comfort her, though it had been many years since she had believed in God. When she looked up, she saw that several of the teachers had tears on their faces.

But the next moment the reading was over, and they were standing up to file out again. Ida felt a sudden desolation. Though the rational part of her knew Diane's death had nothing to do with her, she felt somehow responsible. The fact was that she felt guilty all the time, and she hadn't realized it until now. Perhaps she had buried it. Despite what she had done to April, she knew that this feeling had been with her long before she arrived at the school. What she was actually guilty of hardly seemed to matter anymore.

IN IDA'S FORM GROUP, the other girls were terrified.

'How do they know no one else is in danger?' Nanda Kapoor said. 'They don't know that. The doctors said themselves that they didn't know what was wrong with Diane.'

'And the doctors don't even know what's wrong with the rest of us,' a girl called Clare Whiteley said. She had a tic that made her jerk her head violently to one side. 'We're not *pretending*. And now look – Diane's dead!'

'Nobody ever suggested you're pretending,' Miss Vincent, their form teacher, said. She was supposed to be in charge of reassuring them, but Ida thought she seemed quite frightened herself.

'Diane started twitching, then having fits, and then she died,' Clare Whiteley said, head going. 'Lots of us have started twitching, and some girls are having fits. How do we know we're not going to die too?'

Miss Vincent did her best to calm them. 'As Miss Christie said, we know Diane had a different illness. A virus of some kind.'

'But they don't know what it was!' Nanda said. 'And viruses are contagious, aren't they?'

Miss Vincent seemed stumped by this. She taught sewing, not science, and couldn't be expected to field questions like this.

They were sent back to their lessons for the rest of the day, but the atmosphere was strange and unsettled, and even less work than usual was done. By lunchtime Miss Christie had managed to contact most parents to share the news of Diane's death, and some girls had also sneaked away to the pay phone to ring their parents. By the early afternoon, several cars had pulled up to remove girls from the school. Parents were no longer content to remain calm, now it seemed the illness might be deadly. By the evening, about thirty more girls had been taken home.

'I suppose the rest of us will just have to take our chances,' Sophie said, as she and Ida walked to supper. Louise had said she didn't want to be around all the weeping and gnashing of teeth at supper, and had somehow managed to extract another cheese sandwich from Mrs Stoker under false pretences. She'd offered to get one for Ida too, but Ida had declined. Although she seemed to have developed some kind of mental disorder that meant she missed Louise's company whenever they were apart, she didn't mind going to supper without her this evening. She wanted to hear whether Sophie or Victoria had more information on the girls in hospital, and they were generally too nervous around Louise to speak normally. Louise seemed to enjoy this, and made no effort to put them at their ease.

This evening it was casserole (meat unidentified). Ida and Sophie found Victoria already sitting at the end of one of the long tables. She announced as they joined her, 'I've heard from Angela again! She sent me a postcard to say she isn't dead. Or at least, she wasn't on Saturday when she sent it. That would have been before Diane died, though. It only arrived today.'

'So what else did she say?' Sophie said.

Victoria produced the postcard.

Hi Victoria,

I'm not dead. My arm's still possessed, so I'm dictating this postcard to a nice lady from the League of Friends. Haven't had any more proper fits, though. Food here is even worse than school. Write back immediately – I'm so bored I might die. Sorry, not actually die. Please can you cross that part out? I don't want her worrying. Oh, you're still writing. All right. Send me a Wagon Wheel if you can, V. Or I suppose a Curly Wurly might fit into an envelope better.

Love from Angela

'You see?' Sophie said, when she'd finished reading. 'She sounds exactly the same as ever. Thank goodness.'

'Though she might have taken a turn since then,' Victoria said.

'She won't have.'

'She might have. And it doesn't make any sense,' Victoria went on, 'that Diane had an illness bad enough to kill her, but all the others are just imagining it. Everyone got ill around the same time. It must be the same thing.'

'Well, even if it is, it's obviously a much milder version,' Sophie said.

'That only means they haven't got worse yet.'

Ida tried to sound measured and calm as she said, 'The doctors were clear about it before, weren't they? They said the rest of us are going to be fine.'

'Doctors?' Victoria said. 'What do they know?'

Fax from Dr James Halliwell to Dr George Fisher
Friday, 23rd November 1984, 10 a.m.

Dear George,

Christ, I've made such a mess of it all. I feel sure she wouldn't have died if you'd still been here.

Media circus hasn't calmed down. If we hadn't lost control of the situation already, we certainly have now. Lost it very thoroughly. Or never had it to begin with.

I wish you'd come. I miss you, but you already know that. I'm sorry I was such a coward before. Obviously I've had plenty of time to think about it.

J

IN THE DAYS SINCE she'd heard the news of Diane's death, Eleanor had found herself weeping at unexpected times, even when she was not thinking about Diane. She'd be in the middle of a lesson, or marking books, or making herself a hot drink before bed, and suddenly the tears would be coming again, streaming down her face and dripping on to her clothes.

Diane's funeral would be held the following week, a small family affair. The school's own memorial service would take place in few days' time. The papers had reported on the death, of course. 'Girl at Centre of School Contagion Dies' was one headline Eleanor had seen. It had done nothing to calm the public hysteria around the girls' condition.

She'd seen Diane's parents once since her death, when they drove over to the school to collect their daughter's things. It was Eleanor who took them to Diane's room. She didn't weep then, and neither did Diane's mother, perhaps by that point too exhausted to cry any more. It was Diane's father who disturbed Eleanor the most. He looked hollowed out. His skin seemed almost grey. He hadn't really believed she could die, Eleanor thought, even right at the end. He'd avoided her hospital bed, remained at work. He had been in London when she died.

'I'm sorry,' Eleanor told them, uselessly, as Mrs Fulbrook began to gather up Diane's things, and Mr Fulbrook leaned against the doorframe, not speaking. 'I'm so sorry.'

April was still in hospital and her side of the room, like Diane's, hadn't been touched since she was admitted. Now the state of the small room, still scattered with signs of life and activity, but missing both its occupants, struck Eleanor as eerie. It made her think of the *Mary Celeste*.

She watched as Diane's mother placed her daughter's clothes gently in the suitcase, followed by her books, her hairbrush, her face cream, her few bits of make-up, the trinkets on her bedside table. Finally, with infinite care, she removed the watercolour picture Blu-Tacked above Diane's bed – lilacs, with a line from the Sir Walter Raleigh poem about Diana written above – and laid that on top, before zipping the suitcase closed.

'The doctors still can't tell us why she died,' Mr Fulbrook said, rousing himself suddenly, as if there might have been some kind of mistake, as if Diane might be revealed to have lived after all. 'The post-mortem . . .' He gestured vaguely.

'As I understand it,' Eleanor said gently, 'they hope to know more soon.'

'How are the girls?' Diane's mother asked. 'Her friends.' She held the suitcase in her hand; when her husband stepped forward to take it, she merely tightened her grip.

'Extremely distressed,' Eleanor said. 'Diane was a lovely girl. Very well liked.'

This didn't do much to sum her up, she knew. She took in the sight of the room again: April's side still vivid with occupation, Diane's stripped bare.

And she thought, stupidly, Diane will never join the police now.

*

ELEANOR HAD NO LESSONS on Friday afternoon, so she caught the public bus into South Haven. She had told no one but Miss Christie where she was going. Miss Christie had been less than delighted.

'It's an awkward enough business for us, without you continuing to fraternize with him,' she said.

'Fraternize?' Eleanor said, amused in spite of herself.

'We can't be seen to be maintaining ties with him,' Miss Christie said. 'He's a convicted criminal.'

Whom you hired, Eleanor thought, but did not say. Instead, she said, 'Yes. But he served his time for the crime he did commit. He isn't guilty of any others.'

'He's dishonest,' Miss Christie said.

Eleanor wondered if she had a predilection for liars. It certainly seemed so. She said, 'He did lie to us all. I can't defend him there.'

'Well, at the very least, make sure no one finds out where you're going,' Miss Christie said.

Eleanor wondered if Miss Christie expected her to wear some kind of disguise. It was impossible to leave the school without attracting notice, in any case. The bus stop was a hundred yards down the road from the school gates, and to get to it Eleanor had to walk past the crowd of reporters. They began to shout questions at her as soon as they saw her coming out of the main entrance, and continued with increasing enthusiasm as she approached them down the drive. Eleanor tried not to show any reaction. The police constable was there, as he often was, keeping the crowd off school property, but as soon as Eleanor stepped out of the gates she would be without any protection. She began to think this had been a terrible idea.

She kept her eyes ahead, but her heart was beating fast as she passed through the gates. Then she was surrounded. There was a flash of cameras and Eleanor closed her eyes, feeling the crush of bodies closing around her.

'Gentlemen, show some fucking restraint,' the constable shouted. Was he going to wade in and help her? It didn't seem like it. Eleanor thought she was going to have to fight her way out of the throng on her own, and began to panic. There was so much noise, and so many people pressing in around her. She felt she might just sit down in the midst of them all and start weeping, vanishing beneath the mass of reporters as if the flood waters were closing over her head.

Then suddenly Anthony was there, his arm going round her shoulders, shielding her from the others and pushing his way out of the crowd, bringing her with him.

'Leave her alone,' he was saying. 'She's a friend of mine.' Then, 'I told you, Derek, fuck *off*.' When they'd put a little distance between themselves and the crowd of journalists and photographers, he said to Eleanor, 'Where on earth are you going?'

'South Haven,' she said faintly. 'I'm going to catch the bus.'

'Can't somebody drive you? This is no time to be getting the bus. Look at that rabble.'

Eleanor didn't answer.

'My car's just up there,' he said, pointing to the line of cars parked along the verge by the school gates. 'I'll drive you myself.'

'No, thank you,' she said. They'd reached the bus stop and Eleanor glanced at the timetable. There was a bus due in ten minutes. This whole plan seemed ridiculous to her now. Why had she decided today was a good day for an excursion? Except that she had to get out. Except that she had to see Matthew. She hadn't rung him up to tell him she was coming. He might not even be there.

Anthony said, 'Please, Eleanor. Let me drive you. It's the least I can do after everything.'

'It's kind of you,' she said, distractedly; she wasn't thinking of him anymore. 'But I'd rather catch the bus.'

'I'll wait with you, then,' he said. 'Stop that lot approaching you again.'

'All right.' She supposed his wife could hardly object to this, and he was keeping the other reporters away.

'So, how are you?' Anthony said after a silence.

Eleanor laughed, surprising herself. For a few awful seconds she was afraid the tears would start again, but thankfully the unsteady moment passed.

'Sorry,' Anthony said. 'Stupid question.'

She shrugged.

'Must be awful at school at the moment,' he said.

'Anthony,' Eleanor said, 'I'm not going to give you a quote.'

He smiled at her. 'Don't worry, we're off the record.'

'How are your daughters?'

This seemed to throw him off balance. 'They're fine. Growing up. You know.'

She didn't know. How could she? 'The youngest must have only been a baby when we—'

'Yes,' he said.

'What were you thinking?' Eleanor said. She found she was genuinely curious.

He scratched his chin, rueful. All of his moods, his affects, were still familiar to her. He said, 'I couldn't really tell you. I liked you. I didn't intend for it to go as far as it did.'

'But you were the one pushing it along. It can hardly have come as a complete surprise to you, how far it went.' After a moment, she added, in fresh disbelief, 'You proposed to me!'

'Things were difficult at home,' he said. 'I suppose I got carried away.'

Eleanor began to laugh again. Once she'd started, it was hard to stop. The tears had begun now, like her insides had turned to water, but at least she could pass them off as tears of laughter. He was looking at her like she was mad anyway. What did it matter?

'I will never understand men,' she said, wiping her eyes. She'd spotted the bus rounding the corner now, a little early, a gesture of mercy from the heavens.

Anthony said, 'They're not all like me.'

THE BUS DEPOSITED HER twenty minutes later in the centre of South Haven, and it was a ten-minute walk to Matthew's boarding house from there.

She rang the doorbell and waited on the steps until a woman about her own age answered. Eleanor introduced herself and asked if Matthew was in. She was grateful in this moment for her own dowdy, depressingly respectable appearance. No landlady would be likely to raise an eyebrow.

'Top of the stairs, first door on the left,' the woman said, without evincing much interest.

Eleanor proceeded. Outside Matthew's door, she would have liked to have taken a few moments to gather herself, but she could still feel the eyes of the landlady on her from the bottom of the stairs. So she simply raised her hand and knocked.

He seemed astonished to see her. Astonished, and then – immediately, gratifyingly – delighted. 'Eleanor! Come in, come in.'

She stepped in, once again regretting her decision to come. Strange impulses were generally best resisted. She said, vaguely, 'I just thought I'd see how you are.'

The room was sparsely furnished: a single bed, a chest of drawers, a desk and chair in front of the window, a small wardrobe. The floor was carpeted in a dark brown that had faded in places. The bed was neatly made, and there was no sign of any of Matthew's things except for a glimpse of his suitcase beneath the bed.

'Please, sit down,' he said. The only chair was the one by the desk, so she sat in that and he perched on the edge of the bed.

'Your room's very tidy,' she said, ridiculously.

'Yes, I've learned to be tidy,' he said.

Where? Eleanor thought. In prison?

There was a silence.

He said, 'It's good of you to come.'

'It was no trouble,' Eleanor said.

He was quiet again, and so was she. Eventually, he said, 'Such awful news about Diane. I'm so sorry.'

'Yes,' she said. 'Devastating.' She couldn't think of much else to add. 'Everyone's very upset. Of course.' Her voice wavered. She swallowed, got herself under control, and risked a glance at him. He was looking at her with understanding.

'Very hard for you,' he said. 'You knew her well.'

'I should have done more,' Eleanor said, realizing as she said it how deeply felt her guilt was.

'What more could you have done?'

'We could all see she was ill, even at the start of term. I should have made more of a fuss, insisted it was taken seriously.' Why hadn't she? She wondered how far back it was that she'd lost faith in her ability to influence events, either in her own life or in the lives of others. How long

340

had she been schooling herself in passivity, and was it too late to unlearn it? To Matthew, she said, without self-pity, 'I often wish I could have been a different sort of person. A more forceful person.'

He didn't speak at first, and she thought she'd embarrassed him. Then he said carefully, 'I know about weakness. I have it. You don't.'

She looked down at her hands in her lap. After a moment, she said, 'We still don't know what was wrong with her. But there's been a post-mortem, so perhaps we'll find out soon enough.'

'Eleanor,' he said. 'Did you read my letter?'

She made herself look at him. 'Yes.'

'Thank you,' he said. And then: 'I want to say how sorry I am.'

'You don't need—'

'I do. I am. I'm sorry I lied to you.'

'Well,' Eleanor said, and then realized she had nothing to follow her 'well' with. After everything that had happened, she couldn't muster much outrage for his lie.

'I have a lot of regrets from the past few years,' Matthew said. 'From my whole life, really. But I am glad I met you.' When Eleanor didn't speak, he went on, 'What I want to say is that I like your company. I like it very much.'

She exhaled slowly. Yes, she liked his company too. Despite his well-established dishonesty, he also had a strange sincerity about him which touched her. He'd always seemed an innocent to her, and seemed that way still.

'Would you consider coming with me?' he said. 'To London, or Brighton, or wherever you like, really. We could get married. If you wanted to, of course.' Hurriedly, he added, 'I know I'm not handsome, or clever, and I've been to prison. I don't have much to offer. All I can promise is that I'd enjoy talking to you every single day, even if we just said the same things to each other over and over again. Even if we didn't say anything at all.'

'Matthew, you know I don't have any money,' she said gently.

'Neither do I. I'll get another job, though – in a pub, or a shop, or as a gardener. An estate agent, even. There must be something I can do.' He looked at her earnestly. 'I've never wanted to be rich, Eleanor. I really haven't. It was just the . . . *unfairness* I couldn't stand. I acted like a stupid child. It isn't a mistake I'll make twice.'

She watched him, wary.

He said, 'I like you more than anyone else I've ever met. That's all. You're kind, but you're also wry.'

Wry? Eleanor thought. She wondered if anyone else in history had ever been proposed to for being wry.

'And even if you don't want to be married to me,' Matthew added, 'I'll always be your friend. We could write to each other. If you'd like to.'

'I would,' Eleanor said. 'As for the rest, I don't know.' The school might stay open, or it might not. When she tried to picture the future, it was a blank. She said to Matthew, 'I'll think about it.' He looked grateful for that, at least.

It seemed impossible to her, the idea of leaving St Anne's. Perhaps whoever came into possession of the house many years from now would find her still there, transfixed. Maybe she would have been transformed into a tree in College Garden, her roots tunnelling deep into the earth. She thought it would take a stronger nature than Matthew's to wrench her free.

Fax from Dr James Halliwell to Dr George Fisher
Monday, 26th November 1984, 7 p.m.

Dear George,

You are, as ever, a man of surprises. I couldn't believe it when you loomed up suddenly outside my office door. Thought I might be hallucinating at first. Why do humans cry? No neurologist or psychiatrist has been able to explain that to everyone's satisfaction. Anyway, you were very nice about it, bundling me back into the office before anyone could see.

Thank you for everything you said. I've taken it to heart. And I was glad to have you look at the biopsy results. Don't know if you were just pretending to be unsurprised, which would be typical of you, or if you really had worked it out already – but there we are. Horrible luck for poor Diane. Horrible luck all round.

Had emergency summit with Rhys, Lehman, Stevenson & Tillard after you left. Stevenson is liaising with Mark Baker. I think we're ready now. I'll ring you up afterwards to let you know how it goes.

J

MEETINGS AND ASSEMBLIES. THERE seemed to be a never-ending supply of them now, Eleanor thought, and they always brought bad news.

On Wednesday, the health authority held another briefing in the school hall. The audience was made up of the teachers, the girls, the governors, and any parents who wanted to be there. And reporters: the usual suspects.

'What fresh hell,' Vera murmured to Eleanor as they took their seats.

On stage with Miss Christie, who had stood up to welcome them all, were three doctors. There was the thin, sad-looking man from the health authority; then seated alongside him the young Dr Halliwell; and next to him the psychiatrist with the dark beard.

'He should cut his hair shorter,' Vera said. 'Or at least shave his beard off. It makes him look like the Yorkshire Ripper.'

Eleanor was growing concerned that Vera was going to deliver this kind of running commentary throughout the entire meeting, like a one-woman Greek chorus; her whisper was more of a stage whisper, and Eleanor could feel other people's eyes on them every time Vera spoke. She tried to discourage Vera by giving a nod instead of replying, but this only prompted Vera to say, in her carrying whisper, 'Was that a deliberate nod, Eleanor, or has the twitch got you as well?'

Miss Christie left the stage, and the man from the health authority got to his feet. 'It's good of you all to join us again,' he said, having reintroduced himself as Dr Stevenson. 'We're now able to shed further light on the diagnosis of Diane Fulbrook, who tragically passed away ten days ago. Our deepest condolences are with her family.' He was the right sort of man to deliver condolences, Eleanor thought. He belonged in a Thomas Hardy novel: he seemed to have a deep appreciation of the futility of all human life, the general drama of pain. 'Now I'll hand over to Dr Halliwell,' he said, 'to deliver a statement on behalf of the medical team who were treating Diane.' He sat down again.

Dr Halliwell stood. He was holding a sheet of paper – rather nervously, Eleanor thought. He began to read out his statement.

'With permission from Diane's parents, I'm here to speak to you about her illness.' He paused and glanced up at the audience. He seemed to take a breath, to be steadying himself. He said, 'After her death, a post-mortem was performed, which included a biopsy of Diane's brain. The biopsy showed that Diane was suffering from a progressive neurological disorder called subacute sclerosing panencephalitis, or SSPE.'

Eleanor tried to understand the words, but it was a foreign language to her – an illness she had never heard of.

Dr Halliwell said, 'The first thing I'd like to make clear is that this condition is not contagious. It is not transmissible from person to person. There is no risk that any of the other girls could have caught it from Diane. It's a rare, long-term complication of the measles virus.'

Measles? Eleanor thought. After all this, had Diane died of the measles? It seemed so unlikely, although Eleanor knew the damage measles could do. She'd had it herself when she was young and had recovered, but like everyone else of her generation it was easy for her to call to mind the measles casualties of her childhood: the brother of her friend in primary school who was left blind from the infection; the toddler of her mother's cousin, who had died from it. Diane's year group would have been among the first to have had the vaccine available to them as children, though many would not have had it.

'Diane caught measles when she was a baby,' Dr Halliwell said, 'though we're told her symptoms at the time were mild and she appeared to make a full recovery. However, in cases of SSPE, the infection then lies dormant for many years before it reactivates and begins to attack the central nervous system. This disease is always fatal. There is no cure, only prevention in the form of the measles vaccination. Once the course of SSPE has started, there is nothing that can be done except try to ease the symptoms as they progress. This is an exceptionally tragic case. Diane was doubly unlucky, both to have caught measles as a baby, before she was old enough for the vaccine, and then for the infection to have developed into SSPE. But just to reiterate again, this awful condition is not contagious. It's a rare reaction to an infection from many years before.'

Dr Halliwell paused in his statement to let the audience absorb this information. His voice had grown more confident as he went on. Now he said, 'With regard to the other girls with symptoms, we could see from the start that the presentation of their illness was markedly different from Diane's. Their symptoms resembled hers only at the most superficial level, and whereas tests on Diane suggested an organic infection from the start, there was no evidence of this in any of the other girls. This was what first led us to suspect a diagnosis of conversion disorder, which was subsequently confirmed by further testing. For instance, the lack of abnormal electrical activity shown on EEGs during the other girls' seizures.'

He straightened his back and met the eyes of the audience as he said, 'Diane's diagnosis provides some clarity on the origin of the outbreak of conversion disorder among the other girls. Her illness, which was marked and frightening in its presentation, was witnessed at close quarters by the other girls, who unconsciously began to express their own versions of Diane's symptoms. This is not an uncommon trajectory: outbreaks of conversion disorder often have as their catalyst a case of genuine illness. But one of the interesting things about conversion disorder is that the symptoms seem to be based not on real biology but on the brain's *understanding* of biology, which is often incorrect or incomplete. For instance, in seizures caused by conversion disorder, the sufferer tends to have their eyes closed throughout, because this is what their brain believes happens during a seizure. But in fact, in epileptic seizures, the eyes generally remain open. The same applies to many of the other symptoms generated by conversion disorder, such as the longer duration of the seizures, and the distribution of jerks and twitches throughout the body, which, if caused by organic disease, would involve too many different areas of the brain to make biological sense.'

He paused again here. 'I would like to reiterate that none of the doctors treating the girls are in any doubt about their diagnosis.' Very firmly, he added, 'Wild theories about environmental toxins or poisoning have only served to exacerbate the severity of the symptoms. I'll pass over to my colleague Dr Tillard now, who will clarify the treatment protocol for the affected girls.'

Dr Halliwell sat down again, and the psychiatrist stood and outlined the course of physiotherapy and weekly psychiatry appointments the affected girls would receive.

'I'm confident,' Dr Tillard concluded, 'that these girls will make a full recovery, in time. The prognosis for mass sociogenic illness is actually better than it is for an isolated case of conversion disorder. Counterintuitively, since a number of girls are affected, recovery is likely to be more straightforward than if only one girl were affected. That's probably because environmental factors play a greater role in a mass outbreak than in an isolated case – by which I primarily mean the influence of other people. And there are also the patient's beliefs about themselves and the world around them. This is a treatable condition, and in some cases the symptoms even resolve on their own.'

There were questions at the end, but they seemed to Eleanor to be of a markedly less hostile nature than at the previous meeting. The audience overall, in fact, was somewhat subdued. Now that a clear explanation had been offered for Diane's illness, one element of the mystery had been removed. With this gone, people appeared more willing to accept the possibility of a psychological cause to account for the symptoms of the others. One case of a rare, provable, non-contagious neurological condition and then, separate to that, a mass poisoning of unknown cause, or a different mystery virus that mimicked the symptoms of the original neurological condition, was too much of a coincidence for most people. So they did what people usually do: looked for the neatest explanation. Conversion disorder had been too messy before, too difficult to grasp. Now, following Diane's diagnosis, it had become the explanation that offered the fewest loose ends.

'Is that it, then?' Eleanor said to Vera as they joined the crowd leaving the hall.

'Who knows?' Vera said. 'It could be. Most things in life don't have a satisfactory resolution. They simply fizzle out.'

Rather depressing, Eleanor thought.

They joined the other teachers and girls who'd been disgorged from the hall into Yard, blinking in the daylight. In this slightly dazed, transitional state, they did not notice that Nigel Land, chair of the governors, was approaching them until it was too late for escape.

'How are you ladies?' he said. 'A terrible time indeed. Still, I hope we can consider matters under control now, especially if the newspapers leave us alone. Hopefully they'll turn their attention back to those blasted miners.'

'It has been dreadful,' Eleanor said. 'A terrible mess. And poor, poor Diane.' She was surprised to find she was able to keep her voice steady. Perhaps she'd used all her tears up.

'Most unfortunate for the school,' Nigel Land said. 'And all this fuss because a few silly girls lost their heads.'

This irritated Eleanor. It didn't seem to her to have been primarily the girls who'd lost their heads. 'Well,' she said, 'if there hadn't been so much talk about poison, if the police hadn't made an unnecessary arrest, and if the papers hadn't got everyone so worked up, I'm sure things wouldn't have got so out of hand. I don't think most of the adults involved behaved any more sensibly than our girls.'

Nigel Land smiled indulgently at her. 'You're loyal to your pupils. It's admirable.'

'Not loyal,' Eleanor said. 'Factual.'

'But you could hardly imagine this kind of nonsense happening among a group of boys!' he said.

'I can imagine it very easily,' Eleanor said. She paused, and then went on, impelled by the sort of unexpected impulse she'd fallen prey to recently: 'In fact, if you looked at every muddle throughout history, I think you'd find the vast majority had as their root cause a group of boys, or rather *men*, being ridiculous.'

Vera snorted. The conversation grew a little awkward after that. Nigel Land cleared his throat several times and said he must catch Miss Christie before he set off back to South Haven.

'Well, I enjoyed that,' Vera said, when he'd gone. 'Eleanor, you were *almost* rude.'

'I don't know what came over me,' Eleanor said. It had been such a strange few months.

'It's a promising start,' Vera said. 'With a little more practice, I think you might one day actually manage to offend somebody!'

12

WHEN THEY DROVE OUT through the school gates in Miss Christie's car, Ida saw that the crowd of reporters had thinned.

'Looks like our moment's ending,' she said to Angela, who was sitting next to her in the back of the car, along with the Lower School girl with the tremor. Deborah Willis, of the dancing legs, was in the front passenger seat next to Miss Christie.

Angela had been released from hospital two days before, and now Miss Christie was taking the first group of girls for their outpatient appointments with Dr Halliwell at the hospital. Before long, they'd all be handed over to the care of Dr Tillard and his team. *Thrown to the wolves*, as Angela put it, dramatically.

'And just think,' she had said to Ida and the others at breakfast, 'all along we weren't ill at all, we were just mad!'

Ida frowned. 'I don't think they said we were mad.'

'Then why do we have to see a psychiatrist?' Angela said, which admittedly was a good point.

'At least you get to see the handsome neurologist first,' Sophie said encouragingly.

'Do you think he's handsome?' Angela said. 'His nose is quite wonky. He should really get someone to fix it.' She paused. 'He has nice eyes, though. Long lashes, for a man. I shall gaze into them to distract myself from his nose.'

'Even if you're mad,' Victoria said, 'at least you're not dead, like poor Diane.' They all grew sombre at this.

'Has anyone seen April yet?' Ida said.

The others shook their heads. Most of the girls who'd been in hospital had been discharged now, but April didn't seem to have come back to school.

'Maybe she's too upset about Diane,' Angela said.

'Miss Christie said we can plant a tree for Diane in the gardens,' Victoria said.

'Why?' Sophie said. 'Did she really like trees?'

'I don't know. I think it's just something you do.'

'What she liked was liquorice,' Angela said. 'And her Levi's, and Duran Duran. But I suppose we can't plant any of those.' Ida saw that tears had come into her eyes. 'And I think she was probably the only person in the history of the school who actually enjoyed lacrosse. Now she won't be able to do any of the things she liked ever again.'

BUT NOW, SITTING NEXT to Ida in the back of the car, it appeared that Angela's usual high spirits had returned. She hadn't had a seizure for several days, and her jerks seemed to be under control too. She was more interested in discussing the crimping iron she would be getting for Christmas and whether Ida thought she could pull off a beret than she was in dwelling on their illness.

'We should take this opportunity to practise our grown-up conversation on Miss Christie,' she whispered to Ida as they reached the outskirts of Eastbourne. 'Shall I start? Miss Christie,' she ventured, raising her voice, 'do you mind me asking how you vote?'

'I do mind, Angela,' Miss Christie replied tersely.

The Lower School girl in the back with them was less cheerful. Her arm had been trembling for most of the journey, and now she said forlornly, 'What if it's like this forever? What if it never stops?'

'It will stop,' Ida said.

'You don't know that. Nobody will ever want to marry me if I'm like this.'

Ida remembered one of the things Dr Halliwell had got her to do when he examined her. She said, sounding more confident than she felt, 'The doctor taught me a special way to make it stop for a bit. You have to tap your thumb against your forefinger. Yeah, like that. Try to do it ten times in a row. Now copy me.'

The girl looked at her in amazement. 'You're right. It's stopped.'

'I don't think it's a cure,' Ida said. 'But it might help a bit.'

'So you can just do that every time you meet a man you might want to marry,' Angela said. 'And then excuse yourself to go to the toilet whenever the shaking starts up again.'

'*Lavatory*, Angela,' Miss Christie said from the front.

AT THE HOSPITAL, IDA was the first to be shown into the exam room to see Dr Halliwell, who greeted her and her Casio watch like old friends.

He examined her briefly, and then said, 'Good. Now I'd like to try a few new exercises with you, if that's OK.'

He asked her how she felt when a jerk was about to come on, and Ida told him about the sense of growing agitation she sometimes experienced. Then he taught her some distraction techniques for when she felt that tension, like trying to say the alphabet backwards. If the jerk had already started, or if it started anyway, he told her to try doing the same movement consciously, even exaggerating it if she could.

For a while, they practised together. There was plenty of opportunity, since Ida's arm had become especially jerky as soon as she entered the exam room. Ida didn't have much success in holding the jerks off, but the second set of exercises went better: every time her arm flailed involuntarily, she would focus all her attention on converting the movement into an even more dramatic up-and-down motion, like she was trying to do a one-armed Mexican wave. By the time she'd been waving her arm about for a while, she noticed that she could bring the motion to a complete stop when she wanted to, having regained control of her limb – at least temporarily. It seemed more effective than the tapping, though they practised that again too.

'Will I be doing this kind of thing with the psychiatrist as well?' she asked Dr Halliwell.

'I don't know,' Dr Halliwell said. 'I'm sure he'll have some useful suggestions of his own. It won't hurt for you to keep up these exercises as well, though. I've written them all down for you. It's always worth trying to turn the involuntary action into a voluntary action if you can. And you might be able to achieve the same effect with smaller voluntary actions over time.'

'How does it work?' Ida said.

'I'm not exactly sure,' Dr Halliwell admitted. 'It was just something a colleague suggested to me, from something he'd read. Quite a new idea, in fact. One theory is that it overrides whatever unconscious message your brain's sending. Or maybe it just distracts your brain long enough for you to regain control.' He smiled at her, though he looked as tired as ever. 'Sometimes things just work without us really knowing why. The truth is, so much of medicine is just about throwing things at the wall and seeing what sticks.'

Ida was intrigued by this. 'But you all look like you know what you're doing,' she said.

'Trust me,' Dr Halliwell said, 'a lot of the time, we really don't.'

It seemed to Ida that anyone could have a go at being a doctor, then. Perhaps even her. She looked into his nice eyes above his broken nose. 'Do *you* think we're all mad?' she asked him.

He was thoughtful for a few moments. 'Dr Tillard, the psychiatrist, said something interesting to me the other day. He said that we tend to think of mass hysteria as something that comes from within – the result of some particular weakness or damage within its sufferers. But it's perhaps better understood as a social disorder, something created by external circumstances, a shared set of anxieties or preoccupations, in a closed environment with nowhere else to go.' When Ida didn't immediately reply, he added, 'So, no. I don't think you're mad. I think your brain can be a bit unpredictable, but only in the way that all our brains can be.'

'OK,' Ida said, wondering how heartened she should be by this. After a moment, she thought to ask, 'Does it happen to girls more than to boys?'

'It seems to. We don't know why that is, either.'

'Maybe girls' brains are different,' Ida suggested.

'Maybe. Or maybe we place more limits on girls, and that has something to do with it.' He hesitated. 'This is going to sound ridiculous, but it might be helpful if you try to view these jerks as annoying rather than frightening. I know that's easier said than done. But there's every likelihood your symptoms will disappear completely in due course, especially once all the fuss has died down. That's often how these things go.'

'But even if they do stop, might they come back again one day?' Ida said. 'Might it all start up again?' Now she knew she could lose control of her body like this, she was afraid the possibility would hang over her forever.

Dr Halliwell regarded her carefully. 'The honest answer is, I don't know. Probably not, but I can't say for certain. Our bodies are not reliable.

No more than our minds. I suppose most people don't encounter that fact as stunningly as you have. Though plenty do. There are so many ways your body and brain can go wrong.'

'That doesn't make me feel any better,' Ida said.

Dr Halliwell shrugged, but he was smiling at her, a little sadly. 'Well. That's doctors for you.'

Dear George,

I'll ring you again tomorrow when you're off, but a quick update for now.

A week on & no new cases at the school. Headmistress informs me that some of the parents who'd removed their daughters have now returned them again. You'll have seen that newspaper coverage is petering out. School term ends in 10 days. That will help too.

I've continued the girls' treatment with the exercises we discussed – I've got one more week, then after that it's over to psychiatry. Perhaps Dr Tillard will be able to help them after all: he seems rather more enlightened than I expected, and hasn't so far suggested pumping them full of tranquillizers. It is possible – just *possible* – that I am sometimes too quick to judgement. (Maybe one day I'll discover Lehman is actually a brilliant neurologist.)

I've been thinking more about how we treat conversion disorder – or how we fail to treat it, I should say. Should we really be so willing to cede everything to psychiatry? Might be an area for further study. Those exercises you suggested, for instance. They work. I think they could work even better. And here's an idea: let's say that the symptoms in conversion disorder are produced by our brain's complex predictive processes, causing it to generate symptoms based on expectation rather than reality. If so, might we not assume we all experience this kind of predictive messaging all the time, even when healthy, and conversion disorder is just the brain's sudden failure to suppress it?

We might do something on it together, perhaps. One day.

J

13

THE PENULTIMATE WEEK OF term. Although Ida was dreading going home, she could at least console herself with the fact that it would only be for four weeks, after which time she could return to the safety of school. The sporadic jerking of her arms, and occasionally her legs, hadn't improved much so far, despite Dr Halliwell's exercises, and she didn't feel very enthused by the fact that she had left the island as a pariah, and would be returning as a pariah with strangely jerking limbs.

She was already looking forward to coming back in January, to hearing Sophie's, Angela's and Victoria's excited accounts of their Christmas holidays, and to seeing which troubling books Louise had brought back with her. It was a shock to discover that, despite everything, she was happy.

Most of the affected girls were back in lessons now, and nobody took much notice of their twitches and jerks. Miss Christie had told them all very sternly in assembly that they must react as little as possible to the symptoms, and while usually this would have only ensured louder shrieks every time someone twitched, even the girls of St Anne's hit their boredom threshold eventually. They'd all been taught to offer calm reassurance and beyond that to intervene as little as possible if someone had a seizure, though the seizures were rare now.

Besides, someone had started a rumour that Cindy Riley had given the groundsman a handjob in the works shed, so that was keeping them all occupied for the time being.

Angela hadn't had another seizure since coming back to school, and neither had Jean Thomas. Martha Taylor only had a tic in her shoulder occasionally. Mary Maxwell was still recovering at home, and so were a couple of the girls in Lower School, but Susan had come back the previous day.

April was back too, and seemed to be on the mend. At least, she hadn't had any more fits, though she was still twitching sometimes; but even so, Ida thought, she didn't look well. She mostly went around on her own. Ida felt sorry for her, which was an unfamiliar feeling; she rarely felt sorry for anyone, she realized. There was probably something wrong with her.

She asked Louise if she thought there was, and Louise looked at her incredulously for a few moments and then said, 'Well, yes, Ida. You poisoned someone. Of course there's something wrong with you.'

Fair enough, Ida thought. They were killing time before supper, sitting opposite each other on their beds and bouncing a tennis ball back and forth between them like prisoners in Colditz. Ida said, 'You know what you told me, about Diane being your friend in First Year.'

'What about it?' Louise said.

Ida bounced the ball to her. 'It must have been sad when the friendship ended.'

'I appear to have survived the experience,' Louise said, catching the ball one-handed.

'Were you . . . different when you were younger?' Ida said, pushing her luck.

'Wasn't everyone?' Louise said. Ida thought she wasn't going to add anything else, but after a moment she said, 'I was shyer, maybe. Or perhaps I just minded about things more than I do now.'

'What was Diane like?'

Louise looked at her. 'Why are you asking?'

'Just curious.'

Louise sighed. 'Well, she was similar to how I was. A bit awkward. Maybe that's why we got on so well. But then she got the chance to be somebody else, and she took it. You can hardly blame her.'

Ida was silent for a moment. 'I'm sorry,' she said.

'Don't be hackneyed,' Louise said.

The supper bell went.

As they crossed Yard, Ida matched Louise's stride. She was still trying to picture what Louise might have been like in Lower School: quiet, watchful. Tall for her age. Awkward. Ida wondered what might have happened if she had met Louise when they were both eleven, if they might have been friends.

They joined the queue. It was Wednesday: some kind of awful corned-beef hash awaited them. Ida could see April a few places in front of them, queuing on her own, her gaze fixed ahead. She asked Louise, 'Is there anything we can do to help April, do you think?'

'I suppose you could try to avoid poisoning her again for a few weeks,' Louise said.

Ida glanced around, horrified, but everyone else in the queue was absorbed in their own conversations and no one seemed to have heard them over the din of chatter and cutlery on plates. She said, 'She looks so unhappy.'

'Her best friend died,' Louise said. 'There's not much we can do about that.'

'I'm going to speak to her,' Ida said.

'Don't,' Louise said. 'You won't make it better. You might make it worse.'

'Someone ought to speak to her,' Ida said. She was turning over a new leaf, becoming a nicer person. 'No one's speaking to her.'

'That's because no one knows what to say, and she'd probably bite their head off anyway. You're not her friend,' Louise said. 'You just feel guilty. With good reason, obviously. But still. Leave it alone, Ida.'

Ida ignored her. She squeezed past a group of Second Years ('Hey!' one of them said half-heartedly), and touched April's arm.

April turned. 'What?'

'I just wanted to say I'm sorry,' Ida said. April would never know, of course, how much she was apologizing for. 'I'm so sorry about Diane. If there's anything I can do . . .'

There was a slight delay as April frowned and her eyes seemed to refocus on Ida. The next moment, Ida recoiled. The anger in April's expression frightened her.

'Fuck you,' April said, in a low, bitter voice. '*Fuck you*. Everything was fine until you arrived.'

'Come on. There's no need for that,' Louise said mildly, appearing alongside them.

April's gaze shifted to her. 'You don't care at all, do you? In fact, you're probably pleased. You hated Diane.'

Louise frowned. 'I do care. I didn't hate her, actually.'

April stared at them both for a few moments longer. Then abruptly she said, turning to Ida, 'You think I don't know what you did, but I do.'

Ida felt her whole body flinch. 'I didn't,' she said automatically.

A strange, savage delight had come into April's expression now. 'You thought you'd got away with it.'

Ida took a step back, out of the queue, and bumped into a girl going past behind her, knocking her tray. There was a violent crash as the girl's plate fell to the floor and shattered loudly, corned-beef hash and peas flying everywhere. As always, a few moments of smashed-plate silence descended on the hall.

April said into the silence, her voice clear and carrying, 'Here's something interesting about Ida Campbell, everyone. Back in Scotland, she helped her mother pretend to have cancer. They deceived everyone they knew. Everyone thought she was dying, but all along there was nothing wrong with her. I've got *all* the details, so come and see me if you want to know more. Perhaps I'll write an article for the school magazine. It was an evil thing to do. Ida's sick. She's a liar. She's dangerous.'

Ida felt the eyes of every single girl in the hall rest on her. 'It's not true,' she said, but she already knew it was no good. Her face was giving her away. Her arm had started to jerk, more and more wildly. Her entire body had flushed with heat. It was the sort of thing she could probably have brazened out, if only she'd had a bit of warning, a bit of time to prepare. As it was, her body betrayed her. Her face betrayed her. Across the hall, she caught Sophie's eye. Sophie was staring at her, open-mouthed, appalled.

'Ida,' she heard Louise say, but Ida was already walking out.

Louise caught up with her at the bottom of the steps.

'Ida, wait.'

'Leave me alone,' Ida said, shaking Louise's hand off her arm.

'I didn't tell her, I swear,' Louise said. 'It wasn't me.'

Ida said, 'It doesn't matter. I deserved it.'

'But I didn't. I never would have.'

Ida shook her head. She walked away.

CROSSING YARD AFTER HER escape from supper, Ida suddenly rediscovered her fictional passion for the piano. She went to reception to extract the key to the music practice room from Miss Morton.

'You want to practise again?' Miss Morton said, looking up from her magazine. 'You already practised on open day.'

The woman had an excellent memory, Ida thought. She said, 'I think you're supposed to practise more than once. I think that's sort of the point.'

'Can you even play with your arm like that?' She nodded her head at Ida's arm, which had disobligingly jerked again a moment before.

'I'll manage,' Ida said.

Miss Morton frowned at her for a few seconds, but then seemed to lose interest and gestured in the direction of the key cupboard. 'It's open,' she said. 'Help yourself.' She returned to her magazine.

Ida stayed in the practice room for a long time. She really did lift the piano lid and play a few notes for good measure. It would be nice, she thought, to know how to play properly, so she could lose herself in the music. But there was to be no losing herself. She had come all the way down south to shake off her old self, and yet here she still was, and now everybody knew.

She was still pacing the room long after bedtime, determined not to return to her room until Louise was asleep. It wasn't as though Miss Morton would come looking for the key, given her blasé attitude to security. Ida half wondered, as it grew later and later, if Louise might come to find her; it would be fairly obvious to her where Ida would be. But more time passed and Louise didn't appear, and Ida was relieved – and disappointed.

When she did finally slip back into her room after midnight, she was careful to be as quiet as possible. She could hear from the steady sound of her breathing that Louise was asleep. Ida got into bed still wearing her clothes and lay with her eyes open for a long time, looking at the darkness.

THE NEXT MORNING SHE got up while it was still dark and went quietly out of the room, managing not to wake Louise. She was reminded of Sophie's suggestion when she first arrived at the school – it seemed like years ago now – that she could avoid Louise indefinitely simply by keeping different hours from her. The memory amused her, while also making her sad.

The school was quiet in the darkness of the early morning. It had just gone six. Ida met no one. She hadn't eaten since lunch the previous day, and now she found she was ravenous. Perhaps she could stop by the kitchens and steal some food, she thought, as she went towards the main buildings, if Mrs Stoker wasn't already in there setting up for breakfast. She could eat it in the music practice room and then work out what to do next.

Only there was no next, not really. The truth was, she might as well leave today. There was little point in staying here now they all knew exactly the same thing as the people back home. It defeated the purpose of being here. So much for reinvention.

Fuck them, she thought. Fuck them all.

*

AND SO SHE MISSED the scene at breakfast, only hearing about it later.

The *Today* programme was playing as usual over the speakers when it was suddenly interrupted by a moment of silence, then the noise of static. Around the room, girls glanced up from their cereal. A technical fault, the speakers in the hall finally giving up the ghost. Or Miss Christie about to use the old tannoy system to make an announcement.

But then came the clipped voice of a male broadcaster: 'We are interrupting our normal programming for an emergency broadcast on behalf of Her Majesty's Government.'

Around the hall, girls looked at each other, puzzled, anxious. Some looked towards the teachers' table, but the teachers appeared just as confused.

And the words the broadcaster said next were so horrifying that Sophie would tell Ida later that she simply couldn't take in the meaning at first. It was like hearing a sentence in Russian.

The man's voice said, 'We have received warning of a nuclear attack against our country. The current attack level is critical, meaning an attack is likely to be imminent.'

There was a sharp intake of breath throughout the room as the meaning penetrated. A few girls started sobbing. The *Bulletin of the Atomic Scientists* had this year set the hand on the doomsday clock at three minutes to midnight, the closest to mutually assured destruction that it had been since 1953. They all knew this; Miss Christie had delivered an assembly on it. And of course they'd all seen *Threads*. But they still hadn't really believed this could happen.

'We ask you to remain calm,' the voice continued, inexorably, 'and to stay indoors. If you have a fallout room prepared, take shelter there now. When the immediate danger has passed, the sirens will sound a steady note. The "all clear" message will also be given on this wavelength. We shall bring you further information as soon as possible. Stay tuned to this wavelength. Other communications may be severely disrupted. To repeat, take shelter now. An attack is imminent.'

A brief silence after the broadcast ended and then came the eerie rise and fall of an air-raid siren, emanating from the speakers, its whine filling the room.

Miss Alston was on her feet at the teachers' table. Over the noise of the siren, she said, her voice admirably steady, 'Girls, while we work out what's going on here, you'd better go straight to your house bunkers. Stay calm, please. I can only assume this is a practice.'

Nobody stayed calm. Here it was, the destroyer of worlds. There would be the blinding flash, the terrible wall of heat, nothing left at the centre except shadows on the ground. Then the firestorm rushing outwards and beyond that the violent shockwaves, all hurtling out from the centre to level anything still standing. For anyone who survived that, the air itself would turn to poison and kill them slowly. They had been taught a little about Hiroshima, about Nagasaki. Not enough. They hadn't been taught much of anything. Many of the horrors of their own century had passed them by. Still, perhaps they had got the gist.

Pandemonium in the hall. Screams and the scraping of benches being pushed back, and then a mass of people jostling and rushing to get to the door. At the bottom of the steps, the crowd splintered as girls sprinted in different directions towards their houses, followed more slowly by their teachers, many of them expecting, any moment, the world to turn white.

Out of the speakers in the dining hall, the siren continued to wail to the empty room.

*

367

IDA HAD CONSIDERED JOINING the others in the bunker, but decided against it. Instead, she went back to her room. She thought perhaps she could use the time to pack up her things.

But she found when it came to it that she couldn't get up the energy to pack. She lay on her bed and thought about everything that had happened over the past term. She wondered if her mother would be pleased to see her when she came home. If Charlotte would be.

Louise was standing in the doorway.

'You should be in the bunker,' Ida said after a moment. 'Fallout will get you if the explosion doesn't.'

'I'll take my chances,' Louise said. She went to sit on her own bed. Ida could feel that Louise was watching her, but she refused to look back.

'How did you do it?' Louise said.

Briefly, Ida closed her eyes. 'Do what?'

Louise said thoughtfully, 'Miss Christie's at the hospital this morning, meeting with the doctors again. It's on the bulletin board. So her office is empty. I don't know if it would have been locked. If it was, you could have got the key from the reception desk easily enough, if you managed to lure Miss Morton away for a few minutes.'

Ida said, 'Didn't need to lure her away. She let me go into the key cupboard myself.'

'And operating the tannoy's easy,' Louise said. 'But what about the siren and the message?'

'Taped it off the radio ages ago,' Ida said. 'Before I even came to the school. It was part of a programme on nuclear war that Miss Christie told me to listen to. I just turned on the tannoy and played it back.'

There was a silence and then, unexpectedly, Louise began to laugh: a brief, shocked sound. She recovered herself quickly. 'So all quite straightforward, really.'

'Very straightforward.'

Louise said, 'They'll work it out. And then they'll expel you.'

'I know. It doesn't matter now.'

'You know, people here won't care about what your mother did as much as you think,' Louise said. 'We've had so many scandals. They come and go. You could have toughed it out.'

'I don't want to tough it out,' Ida said. 'I'm tired of toughing things out. I just want to be left alone.'

'I didn't tell them,' Louise said.

Ida sighed. This again. 'I didn't tell anybody else.'

'I know that. But *I* didn't tell anyone else either.'

'It doesn't matter now.'

'Stop saying that. It does matter. Stop being so . . . You're like Macbeth at the end of the play. "Tomorrow and tomorrow and tomorrow." There are still things that matter.'

'You never seemed to think so.'

'Well, don't listen to me. I've been here too long.'

Ida didn't reply. After a moment, Louise lay back on her own bed. She said, 'How long, do you think, before they realize it isn't real?'

'Probably not long. An hour? Or less, if Miss Christie gets back sooner than that.'

Louise put her hands behind her head. 'Then I suppose,' she said, 'we might as well enjoy the peace while we can.'

15

J UST WHEN THINGS WERE finally calming down, Eleanor thought, this fiasco with the fake nuclear attack. They were so close to the end of term, as well: so nearly home and dry.

There had been a flood of parental complaints, of course. Worse still, they'd made it back into the local paper. 'Nuclear Hoax: Fresh Scandal at Embattled School', the headline ran. One of Anthony's better efforts, Eleanor thought.

Two days after the incident, the governors summoned Miss Christie to an emergency meeting. There was no hope now, Carol told Eleanor afterwards, of getting sufficient numbers for next year. There was a strong feeling among the governors that the long-awaited tipping point had been reached.

'It's over, I'm afraid,' Carol said, drinking tea in Eleanor's room. 'We already had barely anyone on the list to start next September. Then there was the outbreak, the newspaper coverage, Matthew Langfield's arrest and poor Diane's death. It's just possible Miss Christie might still have got things back on track if it weren't for this incident with the nuclear drill. She's a remarkable woman. But this was the final straw. No, I'm afraid you're finished.'

'Will we make it to the end of this year?' Eleanor said.

'Probably,' Carol said. 'We're still discussing it. But certainly not beyond that, I'm afraid. In confidence, Eleanor, the school's absolutely drowning in unpaid bills. I don't think any of us had realized how bad things had got. The school hasn't even had a proper bursar since 1976, for God's sake. Perhaps, with a more proactive chair, we might have addressed the situation sooner. Though honestly, I'm not sure how. This isn't the kind of school that was ever going to survive in the modern world. Most parents want more for their daughters now. As they should. And they can get them a better education for free just down the road.'

The end of St Anne's, Eleanor thought. Now it was finally upon her, she felt nothing but a cold sense of unreality.

'Look, would you consider moving to Brighton?' Carol said. 'I can keep an ear out for openings there. You're still young,' she added bracingly. 'It's a good time to start again.'

'Thank you,' Eleanor said, trying to sound braced.

And in some ways perhaps she would discover it was a relief that the event she'd dreaded for years was finally happening. Aristotle had said that fear was pain arising from the anticipation of evil. If the fear was all in the anticipation, perhaps the event itself would prove bearable after all. And she'd been stuck for so long, she thought. Perhaps, if she was truly honest, she'd been stuck ever since her father had died. What was Newton's first law? An object at rest would remain at rest until an external force acted upon it. It was a pity she had never learned to exert any force of her own.

She'd spoken to Matthew several times on the phone since her visit to him in South Haven. Nothing was resolved between them, and yet she found herself thinking about him more and more. Was she going to marry him? Really, she had no idea. It seemed possible. She suspected that in some obscure way it might be a capitulation of a kind, though she couldn't articulate it any more precisely than that. Nonetheless, she could think of worse capitulations. What were we all looking for in the end except a bulwark against the darkness?

So: a new job in a new place. A fresh start at nearly forty. It was beginning to seem tentatively possible to her, which was extraordinary in itself. She tried to picture herself walking out into this brave new world, battered but perhaps a little hopeful, her father's old watch keeping time on her wrist.

16

L OUISE CAME BACK INTO their room.

'So I've finally done it,' she said.

'Oh, good,' Ida said. 'Done what?'

Louise said, 'I've been expelled.'

It was Monday evening. They'd reached a tentative rapprochement over the past couple of days, but Louise had told Ida she was going to the library, not to get herself fucking expelled.

Ida had been lying on her bed but now she sat up quickly. 'What? Why?'

Louise sat down on her own bed. She was infuriatingly casual. She studied her nails for a moment, then said, 'I've just been to see Miss Christie. Confessed everything about the nuclear attack. I was even able to tell her how I did it.' She smiled. 'I thought it was impossible for me to get expelled, but it turns out even Miss Christie has her limits. I suppose it's been a challenging term for her. Her patience, it appears, is somewhat frayed.'

Ida said, 'Louise, no.' She couldn't imagine why Louise had done this. But then she had never been able to predict Louise's behaviour.

Louise waved her hand. When she spoke again, her tone was airy. 'It's what I wanted, isn't it? My parents are coming to get me tomorrow. They're not best pleased, by the sound of it. So close to the end of term, too. You'd think I'd be allowed to stay a few more days. Miss Christie said she was shocked by what I did. She'd thought me many things, she said, but she'd never thought of me as cruel.' She looked at Ida. 'I suppose she didn't know me very well.'

Ida was on her feet. 'I'm going to tell her it was me.'

Louise had stood up at the same time, blocking her way to the door. 'No. It's better this way. You need to stay. You always wanted to stay. Do your exams, turn eighteen, work out what to do next. Keep away from your mother.'

'No,' Ida said. 'You're doing this out of guilt. And you don't have to.'

Louise laughed incredulously at this. 'Guilt? If you mean about telling people your secret, I don't feel guilty. I told you: it wasn't me. Who would I even have told? I don't *talk* to anyone except you.'

'I already said, I don't even blame you,' Ida said. 'But just admit you did it. There's no other explanation—' Then she stopped. She thought, Oh, *fucking* hell, Charlotte.

SHE FOUND APRIL IN the house common room and took her by the arm.

'Get off me!' April said, viciously trying to shake her off.

Ida held on. 'Did my sister write you a letter?' she said.

'I don't know,' April said. She had stopped struggling and wore an expression of satisfaction. 'Somebody did. Who can say who it was from? It wasn't signed, and I can only assume there are a lot of people who hate you.'

'It was my sister,' Ida said. 'Nobody else would have known your name.' Fucking Charlotte, she thought again. But then, hadn't Ida abandoned her? Admittedly, Charlotte had never seemed to like Ida much, but Ida was all she had. And still Ida had left. No wonder Charlotte was furious.

She looked at April and considered telling her that Charlotte was crazy, that she was in a mental institution, that Charlotte was prone to dangerous obsessions and April should be worried that Charlotte now knew her name and address. Then she thought, No. She would not try to scare April. It seemed like she and April were even now.

Instead, she said, 'I'm still sorry about Diane.'

And she saw April's face change, but she walked away before April could reply.

BACK IN THEIR ROOM, she said to Louise, 'I'm sorry.'

Louise shrugged. 'Doesn't matter.'

'I'll go to Miss Christie and tell her the truth,' Ida said again.

'No,' Louise said. Her voice was gentler now. 'You need this school. I don't. It's your chance to get yourself free.'

'What about your chance?'

'I always planned to find other means.'

'You can't leave,' Ida said.

'I can. Am.' She smiled at Ida, sardonic, almost fond. 'I owe you, really, for getting me out. You accomplished in less than a term what I've spent five years trying to do.' She paused. 'It's funny, you know. You seemed so reserved when you first arrived. I didn't expect you to be such a disruptive influence.'

'I suppose I have hidden depths,' Ida said sadly.

17

With only a few days until the end of term, Eleanor had begun her packing. She was to spend the first week of the holidays in Switzerland with her friend Margot, some kind of last-minute arrangement Margot had secured through a colleague. Eleanor was looking forward to seeing the snow on the mountains.

Lessons had wound down, and there was a sense of relief throughout the school. They would all be returning after Christmas, hopefully to enjoy a less eventful term than the previous one. And the school would be waiting to receive them.

In a surprise turn of events, St Anne's was to carry on after all. A double reprieve: not only would they make it to the end of the current school year, but they had been granted one more year after that. Diane's parents had made a donation in their daughter's name, stipulating that it be used to keep the school open long enough for all of Diane's year group, now in Lower Sixth, to finish their schooling.

The gesture moved Eleanor. It seemed to her one of uncomplicated grace.

She herself would not be here to see the end. She would stay for the rest of the year, and then she would be moving to Brighton, hopefully having secured a job by then in a local school. Carol was already on the lookout for her.

'But why now?' Vera said. 'You might as well stay on for another year until we close, surely.'

'I can't,' Eleanor said. How to explain it? She was terrified of going, which meant she had to go as soon as she could, otherwise it would become impossible. If she stayed until she was forced to leave, she thought she might fall apart completely. She had already stayed far too long.

'I shall be sorry to see you go,' Vera said, rather unexpectedly. 'I've liked sharing the double set with you.'

Eleanor was surprised; Vera had never given much indication of this.

Then Vera ruined it by adding, 'You're very unobtrusive. I dare say I'll be landed with someone much more *noticeable*, now.' She was silent, brooding for a few moments, before saying, 'You know, I think it's always a mistake for a clever woman to get married.'

'I don't know if I'll get married,' Eleanor said. She didn't add that she didn't consider herself to be particularly clever.

'When clever girls are young, they think the only battle that needs to be waged is women's education,' Vera said. 'But there's another one: housework.'

'Oh, come on now.'

'You can be as well educated as you like, but get married and you'll still end up wasting all your time washing his underwear rather than reading Demosthenes. And of course it would never occur to him to wash yours.'

Why would Demosthenes have any responsibility for her underwear? Eleanor thought confusedly. She said, 'I think men are more modern about these things nowadays.'

'They might believe they are. Some, anyway. But even the most modern man will let you down in this arena. I'm sorry not to be more congratulatory,' Vera concluded. 'But I've never believed marriage is a happy ending for women.'

Eleanor was beginning to feel rather bleak. She said, 'What will you do?'

'Oh, me? Well, I'll stay on until the end, obviously. And then I'll either retire or get another job. I dare say girls are much the same everywhere. I'll probably hardly notice the difference.'

ELEANOR FOUND MISS CHRISTIE in her office the following morning.

'I've come to tell you that I'm leaving at the end of the year,' Eleanor said. 'I'll give you my notice in writing, of course.'

Miss Christie didn't seem to take this in for a few moments, so that Eleanor had to repeat herself, feeling foolish.

Finally, Miss Christie nodded. 'So even you're abandoning me, Eleanor,' she said. It wasn't like her to show self-pity.

'I'm sorry,' Eleanor said. 'It seemed only fair to tell you as early as possible.'

'But why not wait another year?' Miss Christie said, echoing Vera, as Eleanor had expected she would. 'Surely you might as well.'

'It's the right time for me to go,' Eleanor said.

'But where will you go?'

'I'm going to try for a job in Brighton. There are a few being advertised already for next year. Comprehensives.'

'A comprehensive?' Miss Christie said. 'After here? You won't survive.' Accusingly, she added, 'You're very mild-mannered, Eleanor.'

'I know,' Eleanor said humbly. 'But still. I'm going to give it a try.'

'Matthew will be in Brighton, I assume.'

It wasn't really a question, but Eleanor nodded. 'Yes.'

'Following a man, of all things. I would never have expected it of you.'

'I think he might be following me.'

There was a silence. Miss Christie rubbed her hand across her face. When she spoke again, she sounded very weary. 'I did my best,' she said. 'I kept it going for a long time. Far longer than anyone else would have managed.'

'You did a wonderful job,' Eleanor said gently. 'You've been very resourceful.' And, with only a little awkwardness, she put her arm round the other woman's shoulders as Miss Christie began to weep.

IDA AND LOUISE WERE in their room together for the last time. Louise had finished packing a while ago. Now the moment of her leaving was so close, neither seemed to know what to say to the other.

'It'll be strange without you,' Ida ventured at last.

'Not very strange,' Louise said. 'You'll still have Sophie and those other idiots.' Seeing Ida's frown, she amended, '*Nice* idiots. But idiots nonetheless.'

'I'm disgraced now,' Ida said. 'They might not want to be friends with me.'

'You'll live it down if you want to,' Louise said. 'Give it a term or so. And it's Sixth Form, not First Year. You'll be all right.' She glanced out of the window, down at the school drive below. 'My father's here,' she remarked.

Ida went to stand beside her at the window. A dark green car had pulled through the school gates. It had come to a stop halfway up the drive rather than parking in front of the school's entrance, as if unwilling to risk an encounter with anyone.

'By the way,' Louise said, 'I've left you my books. I've already read them all loads of times. And you could do with reading them. It'll be educational for you. They're all up there.' She gestured towards the trapdoor.

Great, Ida thought. A ceiling full of disturbing books. 'Thanks,' she said.

'My address is at the front of one of them,' Louise said. 'You can write to me if you want. Don't ring – you'll only have to speak to my parents or one of my awful brothers.'

Ida nodded. 'I'll write.'

Louise stood watching her for a few moments. At last, she said, 'Didn't think I'd meet someone like you. Not here, anyway.'

'Me neither,' Ida said. She hadn't known there was anyone like Louise. And perhaps she had been a stranger to herself too, before coming here: it seemed to her that a new Ida had emerged in Louise's presence, as if in response to some unseen stimulus only Louise could provide.

Louise slung her bag over her shoulder and picked up her suitcase. 'Well, so long, Ida,' she said. 'It's been pretty fucking formative.'

This made Ida laugh, and Louise smiled. Then she strode to the door and was gone.

Ida went and stood by the window, looking down at the main driveway. It was a few minutes before the small figure of Louise emerged and walked down the steps, bag on her shoulder and suitcase in hand. She began to walk away down the drive towards the waiting car. Her father did not get out to greet her. Ida put her palm against the window as she watched Louise stash her things in the boot, though Louise wasn't looking up at her. Even if she had been, she wouldn't be able to see into any of the windows, not with the sun bright outside and so little light in the rooms within.

Ida kept her eyes on Louise as she opened the passenger door. At the last moment, Louise paused and turned, looking straight up at Ida's window. She raised her hand in a final salute. Ida kept her own hand on the windowpane. She watched as Louise got into the car.

Then the car set off, grew smaller still, passed through the gates and disappeared.

Dear George,

All right, yes. I concede, I'll join you in London. You have until my notice is up to find us somewhere half-decent to live. Lehman's going to take over the lease on my flat, which is a shame for the neighbours.

I never liked the sea air much anyway.

J

EPILOGUE

September 1985

IDA DIDN'T BOTHER CLOSING her book when she heard the voices outside the door. She lay where she was on her bed and waited.

'She's got a bit of a . . . reputation,' she could hear Sophie saying.

'What reputation?' another voice said.

'Oh, well, that's quite a long story,' Sophie said.

There was a brief knock at the door then, and Ida said, 'Come in.'

The door opened and Sophie appeared. 'Ida? This is Katy.'

Another girl stepped into the room behind her. She looked nervous and had a large holdall in one hand.

Ida looked at the new girl. 'Hi,' she said.

'I've got to rush off,' Sophie said. 'I've got a rehearsal.' To the new girl, she said, 'Miss Clarke, in Classics, is in charge of the play this year. She's getting us to do *Titus Andronicus*. It's dead good. Our friend Angie gets both her hands cut off. And her tongue. I think Miss Clarke wants us to go out with a bang. See you at supper, Ida. Don't forget to be there early. Chips. Meet in the usual place.' And she hurried out.

Ida and the new girl were left alone.

'You've come at an interesting time,' Ida said. 'This is our last year. You must know we're closing?'

'Yes.' Katy seemed transfixed by the image on the cover of Ida's book. 'Is that . . . pornography?'

'It is not,' Ida said, eyes returning to her book. 'Why have you come?'

'To meet some girls my own age,' Katy said, with just the slightest hesitation. 'I've been learning at home until now.'

Ida glanced up again. 'You have?' she said. 'Why?'

'My parents thought it was a good idea at the time –' a defiant tilt of her chin – 'but now they've had to go abroad for a while. So I've come here. They won't want me looking at pornography.'

'You'll have to try your best not to look at any, then. This, incidentally, is a novel by J. G. Ballard. Surely there was a better option than here?'

'Not one they could afford.'

'Fair enough.'

'What happened to your last room-mate?' Katy said. 'Sophie said there was an incident.'

'There was,' Ida said. 'Actually, there were several incidents.'

'I know about the girls last year . . . The fits. The twitching.'

'Yes, we had ourselves quite the time.' Ida sat up, grew brisk. 'Well, that's your bed, obviously. That's your chest of drawers, your wardrobe. Don't go in the ceiling – that's my space.'

'The ceiling?'

'Look lively,' Ida said. 'I'll show you round before supper.'

On their way out, they encountered April Stephens on the stairs. April looked the new girl up and down.

'So you've really come,' she said. 'I heard they put you in with Ida. Bad luck.'

Katy nodded, glancing nervously between them.

384

'She's a psycho,' April said, conversationally. 'Even worse than the last psycho we had.'

'Louise won't be very pleased to hear that,' Ida said.

'There are a lot of rumours about Ida,' April said to Katy. 'Most of them are true.'

'Shut up, April, or I'll push you out of the window,' Ida said, walking on. Over her shoulder, she added, 'And it won't be the fucking ground floor.'

Katy hurried to keep up with her. She looked like she might cry. 'Is everyone horrible here?' she said as they went out through the door.

'Not quite everyone,' Ida said, dropping the door on April, who was following behind them.

As they approached the alleyway that led to Yard, a tile cracked and slid off the roof to their right. Ida grabbed Katy's arm and pulled her out of the way. The tile smashed by their feet and Katy gave a small shriek.

'Keep your wits about you,' Ida said. 'The school's on its last legs.'

'They're going to pull down some of the buildings once we've gone,' April said, catching them up. At the entrance of the alleyway, she said to Ida, 'So, final reviews next week.'

'That's right,' Ida said. They went into the darkness of the passage. Trailing her hand along the old, damp stone, Ida said to Katy, 'We're about to be discharged by our psychiatrist. Apparently we're not hysterical anymore.'

'Same deal as usual with Dr Tillard?' April said.

'Let's raise it,' Ida said. 'Fiver for whoever manages to stay in there the longest.'

They re-emerged into the late afternoon sunshine and began to cross Yard.

'I won last time,' Ida told Katy, who was looking perplexed. 'Started telling him about my absent father. He couldn't get enough of it. I'm going to talk about my mum's boyfriend this time.'

'Well, I've been researching Freud,' April said, falling into step beside her. 'And I have a lot of questions.'

Ida said, 'All right, then. Sounds like we're on.'

ACKNOWLEDGEMENTS

Thank you to my agent, Caroline Hardman, a titan of shrewdness, tenacity and straight-talking. (This does make her sound a bit scary, which she is not. She is very nice.) I also owe huge thanks to the whole brilliant team at riverrun. In particular, my editors, Jon Riley and Jasmine Palmer, have been wise and generous in the help they've given me; the novel is unquestionably stronger for their guidance. The dynamic duo of Elizabeth Masters and Ana McLaughlin bring such enthusiasm and humour to book publicity that they make it feel fun (are they tricking me somehow?). Penelope Price is an exceptional copy-editor, and I think I have become emotionally dependent on her to the extent that I would now be too afraid to publish a book she hasn't looked at.

Thank you to the doctors who lent me their expertise while I was writing this book. My dad was invaluable in sharing his experiences as an anaesthetist in the eighties (doctors back then all seem to have been a bit slapdash, to be honest) and being a medical sounding board. I'm not sure I could have written this book without him. In addition, a generous neurologist shared her insights from a long career, and answered my questions with quite saintly patience – thank you so much, A! My brother – who admittedly was tricked into helping me – was very useful in suggesting SSPE as a condition that would fit my narrative purposes. He will never read this. Tim, it was me who made the hole in your ceiling that you got blamed for. Any anachronisms or medical errors in the book come from me, not from the doctors, the reader may be reassured to know.

Many books and papers were helpful to me in writing this book, but I'm particularly indebted to Suzanne O'Sullivan's work on functional neurological disorders and mass psychogenic illness. Her book *The Sleeping Beauties* (Picador, 2021) contains a fascinating account of the 2011 outbreak in Le Roy, New York. More recently, Dan Taberski's 2024 podcast *Hysterical,* from Wondery, provides a thoughtful and interesting introduction to the subject of mass psychogenic illness, and also covers the Le Roy outbreak. Both of these are excellent starting points for anyone wishing to learn more.

Ysenda Maxtone Graham's book *Terms and Conditions: Life in Girls' Boarding Schools 1939–1979* shares some extraordinary insights into boarding-school life in the postwar period. It offers a somewhat bleak picture of girls' education and opportunities during this period, but it is also very funny. I am constantly recommending it to people. Thank you, as well, to my brilliant colleagues in the various English departments I've worked in over the years. Rarely have I seen so much creativity and hilarity concentrated in one place. Sorry I made the English teachers in this book insane.

The play that the girls perform in the novel is made up, but it was inspired by a story a colleague once told me about a school production he'd seen of Anthony Shaffer's *Whodunnit* (1977), in which the students accidentally skipped out an important chunk of the script and therefore baffled the audience. I haven't seen or read *Whodunnit,* since it felt both more interesting and more practical to use my own fictionalized play; but that anecdote did plant the seed for what would eventually become the play scene in this book.

I adapted the broadcast played during the hoax nuclear attack from the script prepared by the Wartime Broadcasting Service during the Cold War, to be read out in the event of a nuclear attack. The original script was released by the National Archives in 2008; it is a fascinating and terrifying read.

Thank you so much to my early readers: my mum and dad, who are always my first readers (because we are codependent), and Chris. Thank you to Gerard Lee and Charlotte 'quick to anger' Bennett, who offered very perceptive comments on the early draft; they disagreed with each other on the faxes, which was brave of Gerard. Huge thanks to Sarah Butler, a writer I admire and also a trusted friend, whose thoughtful comments led to some late, useful rewriting.

Helen Komor was my Louise, though nicer (I guess . . . ?); thank you for everything.

Chris, like me, lived with this book for a long time. It was not a great housemate and never did the washing up. Sorry from both of us, Chris.

Thank you, last of all, to Iris: the funniest person I know.